AETHER AND ASH

REIGNS OF TELMORIA

FABINS

OLIVERHEBERBOOKS

Cover design by Dar Albert at Wicked Smart Designs

Sword Chapter Illustration by Chú Ti, @uncl.ti.flash

Published by Oliver-Heber Books

0 9 8 7 6 5 4 3 2 1

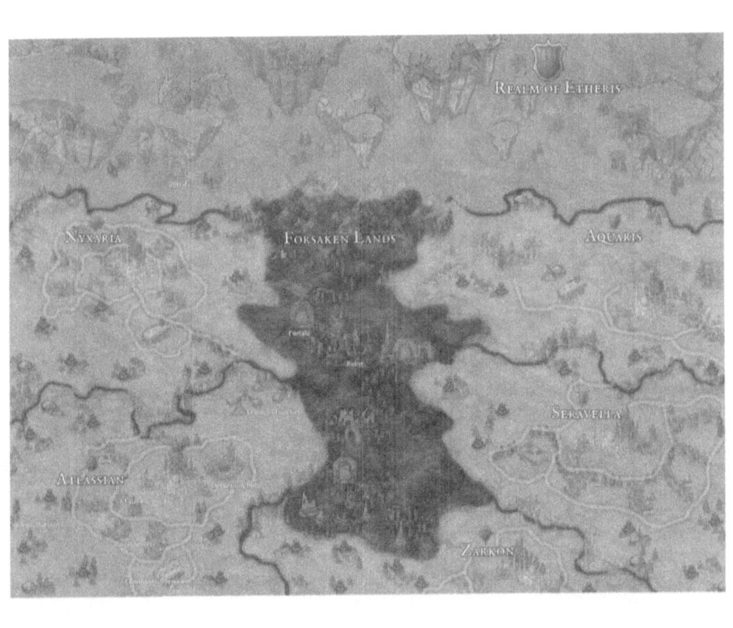

Realm of Etheris
Forsaken Lands
Nyxaria
Aquaris
Seravella
Atlassian
Zarkon

PROLOGUE

Somewhere in the Silence.

Before the first Bond was ever forged, before Aether was named, there was the Breach. It did not open with fire or thunder. There was no scream in the wind, no tear in the Celestia. Just silence. A silence so absolute, the birds forgot their songs. The trees held their breath. And the world waited, unknowing, as something ancient slipped through.

They called it the First Ripple. A moment when time twisted on itself and the Veil between Realms thinned. And from that place beyond, where light did not reach and names had no weight, came whispers. Not words, but impressions. Hungers. Promises. A touch on the spine when no one is near. A shape in the fog that vanishes when you look too hard. Some were beasts. Some were worse. But they came, in silence or storm, and for a time, nothing held.

Until, at great cost, the wounds were sealed. Contained. And forgotten. A wound healed.

But wounds, if not watched, reopen. A missed rhythm. A shadow where light should fall. A shape that doesn't vanish when you blink. They've been waiting. Watching. And when the first threads have begun to pull loose, it has already begun to wake.

CHAPTER I
MIRABELLE

Soap suds clung to my fingers like regret, the pool below shivering with each weary plunge. My reflection wavered back at me—red hair limp with steam, eyes dulled by repetition, and not a hint of the girl who once believed she was meant for more.

Seven years. Thirteen escape attempts. Most dissolved into fragile plans by night and unraveled by dawn. And still I stood, elbow-deep in linens, as if this pit were my altar and scrubbing its sanctified ritual.

A wet tunic slapped against my face before the thought had fully formed. *Lovely.*

I drew a slow breath and peeled it away, the fabric weeping suds down my sleeve. Above, a boy barely past ten beamed like a court jester nailing his finest joke. Behind him lounged an older sibling, arms crossed, amusement flickering in his eye, the true culprit by the look of it.

I held the tunic between two fingers. "Just what I was missing."

The younger one hesitated, uncertain whether to laugh or flee. In the end, he dropped a crooked bundle of cloth at my feet and scurried off, his brother's chuckle trailing behind.

In this place, remorse was a luxury, and courtesies were as scarce as freedom. Among commoners, dignity is something you bartered away with age. I sighed and dunked the tunic under, watching it swirl like it was trying to escape. Eventually, I wrung the last of the laundry, fingers pruned and knuckles raw and climbed out of the pit. My skin was damp and itchy from the soap mix, and I smelled like steeped herbs and wet stone.

I grabbed the two wooden bowls we kept tucked behind the laundry hall. We'd had them for years, edges worn smooth by use. Mine had a chip on the rim; Amara's bore a scorch mark shaped vaguely like a fish, which she insisted was proof she should never be allowed near open flame again.

The queue for noon meals stretched long. All queues were miserable, but noon held a special brutality. Tempers ran high, stomachs hollow, elbows sharper than normal. I took my place in the slow shuffle forward, shoulders hunched against the casual jostling. Midday commoners snapped over scraps, muttering complaints just loudly enough to be heard.

Amara handled them with a grace I couldn't fathom. A smile here, a quip there, and suddenly people made space for her, gave her extra portions, or just liked her. That sort of magic didn't come naturally to me. I didn't charm. I endured.

By the time I reached the front, my feet throbbed. I accepted my bowl without a word: gloopy klea-root mash, a few pale slivers of roasted tuber, and miracle of miracles, a scrap of meat that smelled like it might've once walked on legs. Amara would've groaned at the kleaf soup, said it felt like swallowing a slug, but I liked it. It was hot. That was enough.

Balancing both bowls carefully, I slipped away from the crowd and headed back toward our shared corner near the Dorm arch. She'd probably be back soon, fresh off her cleaning shift, grumbling about stone floors and sloshed buckets.

I sat cross-legged, the warmth of the bowl seeping into my palms. A thin sheen of sweat clung to the back of my neck, and I could feel it gathering in places I didn't need it. I shifted with a quiet sigh. My thighs—thick, heavy—rubbed together with sweat slicking between. It was the kind of sensation that always made me want to jump into cold water.

Still my thoughts drifted as I sat, legs folded, bowl warm in my hands. Aether ruled our Realm—Telmoria. Five Clans. Fire for our Atlassian. Shadows, Lightning, Blood, Illusion for the other Clans. It whispered in bloodlines and billowed from sigils. Everyone had Aether in some shape or shimmer, except us. The ones without it scrubbed linens, mopped floors, carried crates.

Majors—those born with Aether—lived with soft beds beneath them, warm meals before them, and servants at their beck and call. In return, they tossed scraps our way: rations every few months, bolts of cloth and linen, the occasional pair of boots. Fire and iron and rules that bent only for bloodlines. Power was written into their bones, and some Royals carried it so thick it shimmered beneath their skin. Elders even more so. I didn't care. Not really. Not unless their good moods happened to come with second helpings.

I used to dream of Aquaris. It was the only Clan less tangled in bloodline politics, or at least less vocal about it. Outsiders weren't welcome, but they were tolerated. That was enough. For a while. Then last year, a new Heir took the throne. Young. Ruthless. His first decree? Ban all commoners from entering their borders. No petitions or appeals. Joke's on him—I'd stopped uttering hope long before he slammed the gates shut.

By then, I'd just begun to piece together the shattered edges of my life, when Amara stormed in and claimed me like a half-drowned stray she refused to let go of. I started hoping again because she hoped. Because she carved a space for me in a world that didn't have any.

I was taken by the Royals after the raid. After the screamings. They called it mercy, as if mercy came wearing a nametag and handed out Dorm assignments. I was barely twelve. Ash-footed. Mute. They fed me, clothed me, gave me a number and a job. Then tucked me away like a ledger they'd finished balancing.

And I learned quickly: forgotten was safer. The other children didn't like the red hair and my sharp canines. Or maybe it was the fact I didn't cry when they whispered about fire and bad blood or pulled the blankets off my cot. Maybe it was the way I always stole them back.

Once, they shoved me into a barrel of wash water and sealed the lid. I kicked until the stars came, until I heard my mother's voice again. But that was just my own voice, screaming underwater.

Then this girl showed up, all elbows and attitude, a few years later.

"You're scowling at your soup," she said one day, sliding into the seat across from me.

"It looked at me first," I told her. She blinked. Then snorted.

And just like that, we were friends. She was the only one who never asked about my parents. And I was the only one who never asked about her limp. We didn't need to. We just...knew.

❧

A DRAMATIC SIGH cut through the air, followed by the thud of someone collapsing into the grass beside me like the weight of the world had just pinned her down.

"Stars, I'm dying," Amara groaned.

I passed her the scorched bowl, still warm in my hands. She took it without hesitation, already poking at the greens with a kind of tired malice.

She shoved a bite into her mouth, chewed, then tilted her head toward me. "Is it just me, or does it feel like every part of me is sweating today?"

"Definitely not just you." I grimaced, tugging at the front of my dress where it clung stubbornly to my breasts. I tried blowing down the neckline, as if that might lessen the hot, sticky mess.

I nodded toward the tree line. "Let's jump off the forest cliff into the lake?"

Amara grinned. "Already planned on it. Was going to drag you there even if yours was a no."

I rolled my eyes and kept eating.

"Did you hear?" she asked between bites. "Tomorrow's events are near the main arena."

I made a noncommittal noise and tore a strip of meat from my portion. She leaned in with a knowing smirk. "Rumor is, the Young Sovereign might actually be there."

"I have better things to do," I said, mouth full.

"Oh, come on," she nudged me. "Let's go together. You know what they say, shared thirst builds character."

I snorted. "I'm already drowning in character, thanks."

"Well, if we stay here, we'll have to pick up all the duties of those who go to the arena," she added, "So."

She had a point. And unfortunately, she knew it. Before I could craft a reply, she pivoted. "And guess what else?"

"Hmm?"

"Jasper's been asking about you again."

I dropped my spoon back into the bowl with a dull clink. "I'm far too exhausted to entertain this conversation."

Amara grinned into her vegetables. "Suit yourself. But if you're not interested in a little royal treatment, I'm always here to—"

"Don't you finish that sentence, Amara." The smile tugged at my lips anyway.

When the bowls were empty and the breeze had cooled, we slipped away from the crowd and walked the narrow trail that led toward the cliffs, past the kitchen halls and drying lines, the tall trees growing wilder the farther we wandered.

Celestia hung in their usual olive-green dusk, cloud mists curling like sleeping beasts overhead. Ancient trees loomed along the palace grounds, their gold-veined trunks glowing softly in the shade. The blossoms pulsed with slow breaths, like the trees themselves were thinking. Watching. Breathing.

It was beautiful, but in that way a sleeping animal is beautiful —right before it opens its eyes.

The cliffs gave way to a spread of open air, and below, the lagoon gleamed like a shard of star had fallen into the forest and stayed. Deep, cold blue water stretched in a perfect oval, untouched, hidden by the trees above and the cliffs around.

From here, our Clan stretched in layers of green and stone, fire towers and gilded rooftops rising like points on a broken crown. Beyond them, the shimmer of old wardlight flickered faintly across the horizon—the edge of Atlassian.

Sometimes I wondered what it looked like from the outside. If anyone ever tried to look in.

I'm hearing things again...*damn this.*

Whispers. Always at the edge of sound. Vague, like something half-remembered: *getting...not yet...feed...*

I closed my eyes and took a deep breath.

I was sleep-deprived. Which wasn't a lie. The whispers had started a few weeks ago. Always in moments like this—when the air was too still, the trees too quiet. I ignored them, same as always. Sleep, eat, scrub, survive. It worked well enough.

We reached the edge of the drop and kicked off our boots. The stone was warm underfoot, the lagoon below cool and calling. I pulled off the top layer of my dress, folding it over a root.

Amara did the same, tossing hers down with far less care. She grinned at me, wide and bright and wild.

"For old times?"

I returned the smile, though it felt a little softer. "For old times."

And we jumped. The cold hit like a thousand tiny needles—shocking and sharp and perfect. We squealed, screamed, laughed like the girls we used to be, before chores and trials and raids and rules. Before we learned to keep our heads down and our hearts quiet.

For a moment, the world was nothing but blue and breath and freedom. And for a moment, it was enough.

CHAPTER 2
MIRABELLE

I f it didn't cost us actual nickels to buy replacement strings for this bow, I would've given Amara five morris per arrow just to watch her waste the last two. Both had skittered harmlessly off a rock and vanished into a patch of thorns we were definitely not retrieving them from.

"Two morris and a half, straight into the weeds," I muttered, crouched near the underbrush.

She rolled her eyes and shoved the bow into my hands. "Oh, go on, then. Prove your great destiny as Huntress."

I stood, drew, and aimed without ceremony. The string creaked under tension, my fingers sore where the linen grip had rubbed raw last week. One breath. Then I loosed.

The arrow hissed through the dusk and struck with a muted *thwack.*

The brush rustled violently, then stilled. Amara's head tilted.

"You didn't—" she started.

"I did," I said, already moving.

We found the creature draped across a broken root, its feathers iridescent in the dimming light. Long-tailed, fire-eyed, with shimmerplume crests trailing down its spine. Its breathing was slow but steady, the arrow still nestled in its flank—blunted and laced with sleeproot resin. Enough to knock it out for a while. Just a nap.

"Oh stars," Amara whispered. "That's a dusk-binder."

"Looks like someone's getting a warm supper."

She turned to me, wide-eyed. "Bella, that pelt alone—Majors will pay for it like it bleeds Aether."

It wasn't just rare. It was *unheard of* this close to the commons. Normally dusk-binders roamed highland cliffs and lunar groves. But here it was. And still breathing.

We didn't waste time. I knelt by the wing and gently lifted the side to find the underfeathers—delicate, opalescent slivers tucked against the creature's skin like starlight woven into down. Amara held the cloth as I plucked them, careful and swift. We'd done this before—once. If you were quick and quiet, the dusk-binder wouldn't even notice what was missing when it woke.

"Three," I said, easing the wing down again.

"Four," she corrected, grinning. "That one by the shoulder. Look."

She was right. I added the fourth, tucking it in with the others. That many would fetch more than a few nickels. We stepped back. I took the arrow from its flank, wiping the resin tip against the grass before slipping it into the pouch.

We didn't wait. Just backed into the brush and watched as it blinked awake, slow and dazed, then stretched its wings with a shimmer that lit the twilight. It lifted into the air like a wisp of dream and vanished through the trees.

"This'll fetch more than just bread and root paste," Amara said, her enthusiasm palpable, fingers nimble even in the half-light. "We could get something real. Searfruit maybe. Or those pickled plum slices with spiced salt."

"And firebean stew," I added. "The kind that burns your lips and makes you feel rich while sweating like a mule."

Her grin flashed. "And paints for me. Reds and whites, not just charcoal."

I raised a brow. "Think we'll save it this time?"

She gave a short laugh through her nose, her eyes still on the shimmering feathers. "Save it? Bella, please. That's a word for people who don't get their boots stolen while they sleep. Let's just be reckless and overfed for once."

"We're practically nobles already."

We stood and rushed toward the market quarter, boots crunching soft leaves beneath us. The Major stalls would still be open, gold lamps burning, sharp-eyed traders already halfway through their nightly haggle rounds.

The cloth was full now—each feather nestled like a secret, glowing faintly in the dusk. It wasn't a fortune. But it was enough. Enough to feel, just for a breath, like the Realm owed us something sweet.

Little joys like these didn't come often. But when they did, we held them tight.

⊰⊱

THE PATH to the arena shimmered with that strange twilight glow —neither full morning nor night's retreat, only a muted haze that turned stone to silver and dust to light. We moved with the swell of the crowd, drawn toward the amphitheater's looming gates like flotsam carried on tide.

The stone underfoot shifted here, lighter and smoother than what we were used to. Polished walls arched overhead, trimmed in copper veins that glowed faintly with residual Aether. These halls were built for the ones who carried power in their bones. Every tile, every panel of stone and ironwood, was reinforced to withstand the unpredictable flare of Aether—mostly fire, here in Atlassian. But I'd heard stories: of walls designed to absorb storms, of windows sealed against sound that could shatter bone.

Ahead of us, the main atrium opened into a garden split by stone paths and glinting pools. At its center, children played under the watchful gaze of robed instructors. Their laughter echoed off the walls like chimes.

One boy cupped flame in his palms and tossed it like a ball to the girl beside him, who caught it and rolled it along her arms like ribbon. Another conjured sparks that danced in patterns between his fingers, bursting like stars when he clapped.

Ashroot powder bins were tucked discreetly into the stone recesses nearby—ornate containers shaped like flowering vines. Emergency measures, supposedly. Instant flame suppressants if things ever went out of control. But I doubted they were ever needed here.

This was magic with training. Aether with supervision. Power that never had to be questioned.

"I wonder what it's like," Amara murmured, "to know the world was built to suit you. To keep your tantrums from burning down the halls."

"To play with fire and never get burned?" I said.

She gave a half-laugh. "Exactly."

We walked a little slower then, watching the pebbles hover around a little girl who looked barely five. She wasn't even paying attention. Humming under her breath, bored. The pebbles bobbed around her like lazy stars.

"She's got better control than half the Majors I've cleaned up after," I muttered.

"She probably *is* a Major," Amara said. "Or better—a Royal. Look at her cuffs, those are silk. Castle-spun."

I made a face. "So, what—Royals playing in the garden now? Don't they usually stay inside the upper rings?" I asked.

"They do," she said. "Unless it's one of *his* orders."

I didn't have to ask who she meant. Damien Azarios. The Heir. Since his formal induction last year, he'd taken on more of the Sovereign's mantle—issuing commands, presiding over ceremonies, speaking for the Crown without wearing it.

Not that anyone had taken it off Alaric's head.

"He gives me a headache," I said. "Too polished. Too...still."

Amara snorted. "And Sovereign Alaric *doesn't?*"

"I've never seen the man smile."

"Maybe his face can't bend that way."

I shook my head, but not in disagreement. "What an awful soul."

"To be fair," she murmured, "it was the Heir who made sure the palace sent more provisions and pressured the Majors to open their reserves."

"That was him?"

"Guess even a cold Heir can feel hunger if he tries hard enough."

We passed beneath a low arch carved with runes I couldn't read, into a corridor that gleamed like a sunken temple. Majors stood above the flow of bodies, their flame-sewn robes catching what little light the Celestia offered. And below them, pressed shoulder to shoulder, commoners craned for glimpses between gaps in linen and wool. The scent of ember-root clung to the breeze—sharp, smoky, and slightly sweet.

Then came a sudden sound. A sharp crack—like thunder with its breath held. Heads turned. Even the Majors paused.

But all I could hear was faint whispers that made no sense to me.

I tensed. "I don't like that."

Amara's hand found my sleeve. "Are you hearing those whispers again?" she murmured. "Something is buried Bella. Something they don't speak of. And last night...you felt it, didn't you?"

She didn't wait for confirmation. She already knew.

The crowd began to surge up the steps into the watching gallery, drawn forward with that quiet urgency only uncertainty could summon. Amara held fast to my hand and pulled me with her.

"This better be worth it," I muttered, heart thudding in my throat. I didn't know it then, but that sound would be the first fracture in the world as I knew it—the ripple before the fall.

THE ARENA CAME ALIVE. Murmurs swelling into a low roar as the Royals began to arrive. They entered the high box one by one, slipping behind carved balustrades with the kind of grace that could only be inherited. Silvers and crimsons shimmered in their robes.

Our attention shifted by instinct to the figure standing at the end of the stairs, still speaking with one of the guards. Whatever he said earned him a sharp nod.

Then he turned and began to climb. The Heir who'd built a reputation on choosing Atlassian first, always first. He ascended the stairs, no rush or fanfare. Just enough to shift every gaze in the arena—like gravity had quietly decided it belonged to him now.

He was tall, absurdly so. Too refined to be anything but royal, from the symmetry of his features to the way he stood. His hair was artfully disheveled, like he'd run a hand through it and forgotten to care. Faint stubble dusted his tanned jaw and cheek, a shadow of something untamed beneath all the polish—

Beside me, Amara let out a low breath, not quite a whistle. "Alright," she muttered, "I take back every complaint."

I didn't have to ask which ones. "Skipping laundry," she added, "was clearly divine intervention." A smile tugged at my lips before I could stop it—partly at her lame joke, mostly at her overblown enthusiasm.

Whispers stirred.

"What's Young Sovereign doing here?"

"Too minor a gathering..."

"Unless this Selection..."

Our eyes shifted as the arena gates opened. One by one, the competitors emerged. Some bore sigils, others colors of noble houses. But one woman came cloaked in plain cloth, face unreadable, her step too calm. She wore no mark at all. The murmurs returned.

"This isn't a game?" Amara asked herself too loudly.

She was right. A cloaked woman behind us leaned forward. "It's a trial," she murmured. "For the Sovereign's Guard. Only five will be chosen to swear the Oath."

"And the rest?" I asked before I could stop myself.

The woman met my gaze. "They either bleed...or vanish."

CHAPTER 3
MIRABELLE

The ground trembled beneath our feet like something waking. A pulse from the deep places of the ground.

From the center of the arena, the sand began to writhe. Black tendrils pushed through the surface, slick yet smokey, coiling things that moved with too much purpose to be mere shadow. They twisted skyward, glistening like oil, alive with a wrongness I felt in my bones.

The crowd gasped as one. A few competitors stumbled back. One hurled a torrent of flame, but it was swallowed whole, the fire evaporated on contact, like breath on glass. Another cried out and struck with flamed lightning. The tendrils drank it in, crackling for a heartbeat before dimming into nothing.

Then one lashed out. It wrapped around a young man's leg with a serpent's speed and flung him upward, so fast, so high, his scream never even formed. He hit the ground like a marionette with its strings cut, limbs twisted at impossible angles. Screams rippled through the stands.

My fingers found Amara's arm, and I clutched her without thinking. "What are those?"

Her eyes didn't leave the arena. She didn't even blink. "Dread-claw, deadliest of our Tameables," she murmured. "I've read and heard about him." *Oh, even I have.*

Another fighter—young, fast, tried to run. The shadows caught him mid-stride and dragged him down. Not swallowed. Not hidden. Shredded.

I heard someone retch behind us. The crowd had come expecting Aether. They got terror. "What kind of trial is this?" Amara whispered in horror.

Now the tendrils were everywhere, writhing like a nest of serpents let loose in a cage. Screams rose from the fighters and the stands alike. Two Majors fought side by side, back-to-back—one with a glimmering ash shield, the other launching blasts of flames. But all were losing. Still, I could see three or four of the Majors stood within the chaos, bloodied, scorched, barely breathing, but somehow still alive.

Something was building beneath my skin again, low and sharp and hot, like a flicker of lightning trapped under bone.

The Dreadclaw lunged again, this time not toward a fighter, but toward the perimeter. The stands. Panic rippled through the crowd. They shoved, shouted. And then it turned. No, it *stopped.*

The tendrils froze, half-lashed midair. One hovered directly above a boy shielding his sister. Another hovered inches from the arena's glowing barrier, where the protective wards shimmered uncertainly, flickering like a dying flame. With a sound like a thunderclap torn sideways, the Dreadclaw slammed into the outer barrier and shattered it.

Wards screamed as they broke. The light webbing the edge of the arena exploded in shards of gold and silver, vanishing into smoke.

Then came the silence. A breath. A blink.

Screams tore through the stands. Bodies surged like a tide, commoners tripping over benches, clambering over each other in blind panic. The scent of scorched leather and fear hit all at once.

Somewhere behind me, someone was sobbing. Somewhere else, someone shouted orders no one listened to.

The Majors didn't move. Neither did the Royals. Their golden box towered above the carnage, untouched. The Heir stood at its edge, arms crossed, head tilted. Watching everything as if this were nothing more than a passing storm.

And the Dreadclaw came through the ruins like it owned Atlassian.

"Amara," I choked. "Run. Now."

We turned, forcing our way through the panicked swarm. Commoners screamed, some fell, others shoved us without looking back. The scent of scorched cloth and raw fear soaked the air.

Amara's fingers dug into mine. "Why is no one stopping it?!"

"They're *watching*," I spat, my voice shaking. And they were. As if waiting for a cue that never came. As if they'd rather lose a dozen commoners than act without royal permission.

My fury spiked sharp enough to push back the fear. Amara yanked my hand. We ran. Feet pounding over sand that shifted like it wanted to hold us back. But it wasn't fast enough. I glanced over my shoulder, and terror crept through me like ice.

It was subtle. No flashing eyes or pointed claws. Just a soft redirection, like a hunter adjusting its step when the prey strays off course. The tendrils skimmed the ground with deliberate grace, curling slightly. But I knew.

I knew.

It was coming for *me*. And it was moving like it knew exactly where I'd run, how far I'd get, where I'd stumble. It didn't need to rush. It had the patience of a nightmare that had waited centuries to be unshackled.

My lungs clamped shut. My vision tunneled.

"It's coming after me," I choked.

"What?" Amara shouted, still pulling me.

I shouted. "It's *me* it wants!"

She pulled harder. "Don't be ridiculous, just run with me."

We ran until our lungs burned, ducking behind a shattered column near the south arch. Commoners still flooded past, faces wild, screams unending, limbs flailing in every direction. For a breath, we were hidden.

Until we weren't. A tendril came out of nowhere, arcing overhead and crashing into the pillar beside me. The stone exploded. I hit the ground hard, pain tearing up my spine. My ears rang.

"Amara!" I gasped.

She turned, just a second too late. That beast struck. It didn't kill her. It didn't even *try*. It just whipped one monstrous limb into her chest and sent her flying like a kicked sack of grain. I screamed and bolted after her, but I froze a moment later.

I couldn't go to her. Not with the creature still searching for me. If I stayed, I'd lead it right to her. So I ran, changed my direction. And something inside me *broke*.

I turned, chest heaving, rage lashing inside me like a storm barely contained. The Royal Box towered above the carnage like nothing beneath it could touch them.

I ran toward it. My legs moved on fury alone. I tore across the courtyard and hurled myself up the marble steps, steps carved for reverence, not rebellion. Not today.

I reached the base of the platform, breath ripping out of me, and stopped just short of the polished steps. My fists trembled and my body burned. My voice came out hoarse and ragged and loud enough to crack.

"Get your damn beast under control, you flame-blooded coward." I didn't care if the Royals gasped, or the guards bristled. I didn't care.

My words cracked against the hush like a whip. "If something happens to her, I swear I'll become your death—"

The beast's claws wrapped around my ribs and yanked me from the ground. Claws like iron bands closed around my torso, lifting me effortlessly from the stone. My vision blurred. Just one last glimpse, of *the Heir*.

Still calm. A single brow raised. And the faintest—faintest, curve of his lips. The sky spun. My scream never made it out. Only the silence did.

CHAPTER 4
DAMIEN

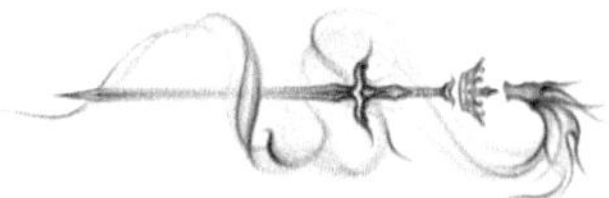

The ascent to the Sovereign's wing was steep and spiraling, carved through the uppermost corridors of the Atlassian Palace where light dared not linger. Up here, silence had a different quality—sharp-edged and listening.

The two guards flanking the final arch shifted as I approached. One stiffened a fraction too late. Noted.

The council chamber was built for intimidation, cold marble veined with black obsidian, high windows that filtered dawn into something gray and sterile. At its center stood the man who'd ruled since long before I'd learned to walk, let alone wield power.

Alaric Azarios. Sovereign of Clan Atlassian. My father.

He didn't look up, but I felt the weight of his attention settle on me the moment I entered. Nothing about his posture moved, yet everything tightened.

"Damien," he said at last, voice low and worn like iron pulled from a forge. "Report?"

I stepped forward, clasping my hands behind my back. "The four Majors who survived the trial have been relocated to the Argent Estate. Under quiet guard, as instructed."

He said nothing. So, I continued. "Cassian Arlith—speed affinity, excellent reflexes. Rhevas Krell—volatile but shows rare signs of elemental blending. Alden Varro—sharp mind, battlefield intuition, but his family's allegiances are, murky."

I paused, then added, "Lyria Farrow. Controls fire by sheer will. No glyphwork, just raw will bending flames to her command like it's an extension of her pulse."

That earned a flick of his gaze. "And their condition?"

"Recovering. Lyria's injuries are extensive. The others will be ready soon."

He nodded once, a clipped gesture. "We will need them sooner than that. Our Sages are seeing more breaches forming like cracks beneath the wards. The Elders argue, as they always do, but time no longer favors us."

"I am aware," I said. "And the artifact recovered from the southern ruins?"

He drummed one finger against the armrest of the obsidian throne. "The Elders say the seal is fraying. Each relocation risks fracturing the Crown's bind. And we still don't understand how deep that connection runs."

It had been recovered to aid us, but no one knew if it would rise to our call or turn on us when the time came.

I didn't look away. "Then stop moving it."

He did look at me now. Measuring. "You speak as though you weren't raised by men who built empires on gambles."

"We're gambling with something we don't understand."

"That's the only kind of bet worth placing."

The silence between us thickened. Finally, I broke it. "We'll need more candidates outside the noble lines. I want a full detachment trained under the Legion's secondary protocols."

His eyes narrowed slightly. "You'd build a shadow force?"

I held his gaze. "I'd build survivors. Hunters. What we need now isn't loyalty—it's instinct."

A pause. "You'll oversee it personally."

"I already am."

He studied me again. Longer this time. "Was the Dreadclaw incident—contained?"

"Contained," I replied.

He studied me. "It broke formation. That's not normal behavior."

I nodded once. "It wasn't a breach. It was a hesitation. I wanted to observe, not just *what* he would do, but *why*. He shifted his focus and that intrigued me." I paused, "But I had control, and I wouldn't have let it harm the commoners."

His jaw tensed, but he didn't argue. After a breath, he said, "Make sure the Throne Council doesn't catch wind of any of this. If the Elders suspect we're training outside bloodlines *for Royal Legion—*"

"They already suspect. Let them. It keeps their focus on rumor instead of fact."

He gave the ghost of a nod. I inclined my head, turned, and stepped back into the shadowed corridors, each footfall swallowed by stone. The kind of silence that kept secrets.

For now.

⬧

THE HALLS beyond the Arena had fallen quiet since the carnage. The stench of scorched sigil-dust still hung faintly in the air. I made my way toward the chamber where that girl had been taken. *Mirabelle.*

She'd been stabilized by the healers stationed beneath the Arena tier, far enough from the others that her presence wouldn't draw questions. The Dreadclaw hadn't mauled her, it had hesitated. And that was a problem.

She'd cursed me, hissed like a feral thing with cracked lips and blood on her brow, moments before she lost consciousness. A commoner girl with enough fury to spit in the face of a Royal Heir.

When I'd left the arena, I'd turned to Rowane, the only man in this palace who didn't flinch at my silences. "Find her," I'd said. "Name. History. Everything."

His smirk had been infuriatingly knowing. "Since when does our Heir chase after half-mad girls from the laundry pits?"

I hadn't answered. He hadn't expected me to.

Now, as I walked, I forced my mind to the real threats—the fractures in our wards, the Untameables slipping through, the weight of a kingdom balanced on a blade's edge. Control was the only currency that mattered. That was why my alliances were precise, my pleasures efficient.

I've long accepted that my life will never be tranquil. But what I do demand is control.

Which is why I shouldn't think twice about dealing with a wild girl with no discipline and nothing to lose. I had no time for petty theatrics, especially not now, with the weight of half the Clan's emergencies settling on my shoulders.

She should be compensated for her injury. Quietly escorted out.

The door to the arena's healing chamber opened without sound. Mirabelle was seated on the cot, color having returned to her cheeks, though a bandage still wrapped her upper arm. Her friend sat beside her, vigilant, wary.

And then she looked at me. Big green eyes. Bloody stars, *too green.*

How had I missed that before? Maybe I'd just been too distracted by her mouth hurling insults.

My rehearsed speech dissolved. I cursed inwardly. "Are you well?" I asked, voice lower than intended.

She blinked, clearly caught off guard. Then a small flicker of blush beneath her skin. I cursed myself again for not looking away in time.

"I'm fine. I mean—" She cleared her throat. "I apologize. For what I said earlier."

Her friend leaned forward, arms crossed tightly. "She really thought you were going to let that creature kill us." Still gathering all her nerve to stand guard beside her friend.

I looked back into those green eyes. No longer fierce. Still holding pride like a shield, but the anger had gone out of her.

"You weren't entirely wrong," I said. "But your delivery could use work."

A slight dip of her chin. Grace where I'd expected defiance. I should have left it there. Walked away and returned to the thousand matters that actually required my attention.

But instead—

"Stay."

Her brows lifted. "Pardon?"

"With the new Majors."

"My Liege—"

"Damien," I corrected, sharper than I meant.

Her friend choked—on a laugh or a protest, I did not care.

Mirabelle kept her gaze steady. "Thank you. But I believe I have overstayed already. I should go."

She was offering me an exit. A graceful one, and I should have taken it.

"Come to the palace in two days," I said, leaving no room for debate. "There is a matter I would like to discuss. I will send my carriage."

She hesitated. "What matter, if I may ask?" Her friend was practically vibrating with unspoken commentary.

I kept my voice neutral. "A matter requiring insight from those who survived the trial."

Not entirely a lie.

She nodded slowly, still puzzled. "Very well, then. Again, apologies and—"

I turned before she could finish. The door clicked shut behind me, sealing her out. I exhaled slowly. Out of all the disasters waiting for me—why had I just created another?

⚜

I DRAGGED the first parchment across the desk, quill scratching dismissively. My signature bled through the vellum as I shoved it aside. Another. And another.

Supply requisition for the eastern barracks—approved.
Complaint from Elder Nyssa about training noise—dismissed.
Request for additional healers in the lower wards—

My quill hovered. The ink pooled, a dark stain spreading like a wound.

I knew this dance. The way my fingers moved faster with each document, as if speed could outrun the inevitable. The way my shoulders tightened when only one report remained.

Rowane's.

I exhaled sharply, rolling the tension from my neck. Outside, the wind rattled the balcony doors, a restless echo of my own unease.

Life as a child in Atlassian taught me early, trust is a currency far too costly. You never know the price until it's already claimed something you weren't ready—or willing—to lose. I learned that lesson the hard way. And like most painful truths, I overcompensated beforehand. Hardened. Built walls. Now, there are only a handful I trust, and even they are measured against memory.

That overcompensation shows up in every damn form. Like now. I couldn't delegate the trials, couldn't walk away from training without tracking every breath drawn beneath the sigil barriers. And I especially couldn't afford to be absent while the new Majors were sparring with our Tameables.

The last report sat untouched, its edges too crisp, its wax seal unbroken.

No point avoiding it. I cracked the seal with more force than necessary.

Discipline notes, history, Dorm origin, parental status. Orphaned at twelve. Raised in work Dormitories. Scar above her left brow from an accident with a shard-press. Of course it was.

Then I did a double-take. Age: nineteen.

I exhaled sharply and pinched the bridge of my nose. *Nineteen.* Barely a woman. I tossed the parchment into the drawer with more force than necessary and closed it with a quiet click. Enough— *what a pointless distraction.*

But even as I leaned back, my thoughts looped treacherously. I had to know more. To dissect whatever had lodged itself in my mind before it became a distraction. Knowing more would pacify this unwarranted curiosity. And while I was at it, I could ensure the new additions from yesterday's trials were properly managed.

A ruler does not, and should not, turn a blind eye to matters that require his hand; he addresses them before they become problems. After all, getting two kills with one stone is nothing new to me.

The door creaked open.

Fiora—the eldest of the three intimate Thralls, entered, the soft clink of her anklet the only sound in the room.

"My Liege," she said gently, "shall I prepare your bath? You've had a long day."

"No." My tone wasn't harsh, it never was with her. Not after all these years of flawless service, nor how precisely she respected every unspoken boundary.

She moved closer, hands folded. "You've not eaten since morning. Should I—"

"That won't be necessary, Fiora." I glanced up and met her eyes. "That will be all."

She hesitated. A flicker of something passed across her gaze, worry, perhaps, but she inclined her head and crossed to the side table with practiced ease. A tumbler of warm water, steeped with whatever herbal concoction she insisted helped sleep. A folded cloth. The vial for my forearm. The things I hadn't asked for, but she knew I required, after all these years.

And then she pulled the chamber door gently shut behind her.

When the room fell still again, I stood and turned to the far window. The view of the moonlit Atlassian always set me at peace.

I should've turned back to the next pile of reports. Instead, my fingers found the drawer. The parchment was still warm from my grip. The girl's file was ruthlessly mundane until you read between the lines. My gaze snagged on the sketch beside her vitals. That frown. Not the blank deference of servants, but unfiltered, like a blade left bare in its sheath.

Outside, a gust rattled the balcony doors. Somewhere below, the girl was likely sorting linens with that irritating frown she wore like armor. A commoner well-acquainted with daily labor.

She would be useful. Grounded. A perfect example of familiarity with only base tasks. I'd see that clearly once she was in the field. See her as she was. See her fade.

I stood there far too long, watching the wind stir the lanterns outside the range, until Celestia grew darker than my excuses.

CHAPTER 5
MIRABELLE

The carriage rumbled to a stop, its wheels scraping against the uneven stones as we approached the grand gates of Argent Estate. I hadn't expected much, just an overblown version of what I had already seen in the royal quarters. Velvet drapes, bored nobles, and enough marble to pave the moon.

I stepped out, my feet landing on the cold, polished stone. And, of course, Jasper stood waiting, his posture like a regal statue, one hand resting on the pommel of his sword—really unnecessarily if you asked me, and his eyes flicked over me with the same calculating look he'd had before.

"Ah, Mirabelle," he intoned, his voice thick with condescension. "I trust your journey was without trouble?"

"It was tolerable," I said.

He took a step closer. "Now that you have arrived, we may begin in earnest. I could arrange for your quarters to be moved closer to mine. It would be more convenient. You would be near, and I could ensure you want for nothing."

I met his words with a raised brow. "And you believe I would simply take up residence at your side? As in your...Thrall?" I let out a short, derisive laugh.

For a brief moment, his smile faltered, just a flicker. "Thralls are born, Mira. But what I'm offering...is a choice. It's not just about claiming you."

I let a slow, unimpressed smile lift the corner of my mouth. "I think I'll pass on that, thank you. I didn't claw my way out of acid and fire to become anyone's *arrangement*'"

The coldness in his gaze flickered again before he rolled his shoulders and let out a laugh, lighter than I expected.

"Still sharp. I like that." He tilted his head, and the shift was almost imperceptible. His posture eased, and his tone softened, just slightly. "Though you'd be surprised how many think that arrangement would be a promotion."

"Oh, I'd believe it," I said dryly. "I just happen to have a wildly inconvenient sense of self-worth."

That earned a real laugh.

"Very well," he said with a shrug. "I will wait till you change your mind then. Now follow me to the Heir's study."

⟶◇⟵

THE STUDY DOOR was already ajar, firelight spilling across carved stone and polished obsidian tiles. The scent of spiced parchment and burnt cedar hung in the air, subtle but unmistakable—the signature of a space meant for thinking.

Damien sat behind his desk, pen in hand, as composed as ever. But I wasn't the only one in the chamber.

A woman—a Thrall, stood close, *too close*. Tall, with hair like silver thread cascading over her back, skin pale and smooth as ivory where faint green veins shimmered just beneath the surface. Her fingers trailed the edge of Damien's desk, not touching him, not quite. But near enough that the message was clear: she belonged.

Amara had once explained about this system to me in the blunt way only she could: Thralls are what Royals keep when they want someone obedient, beautiful, and bound. I hadn't understood it.

Not until I saw one this close, poised like sculpture, owned without chains.

She looked like she was sculpted to be adored. Poised. Serene. What I did know, without question, in that moment, was that I did not like the way she leaned toward *him.*

As if you have any right to feel something over someone carved from power and privilege.

But that rang hollow too. Because lineage—all of it, the banners, the titles—was never truly earned. It was luck dressed up as legacy. They were born to it, wrapped in it before they could speak, as if that alone made them more. But it didn't. And if it didn't mean they were better, then it shouldn't mean I was less. So, no—that wasn't the problem. I know I wasn't foolish enough to romanticize proximity.

Damien's attention was fixed solely on the parchment in his hands. Then his eyes lifted, cool and clear, deep blue that struck like steel through fog, and found mine.

I blushed instinctively and cursed myself for it. Because of course, he had to look like that—rugged yet impossibly composed. But his eyes were the real problem: a deep, magnetic blue, the kind that made you forget why you'd been mad in the first place.

I hadn't had time for soft feelings, not between the wash lines and the steam. The Majors who came down to the laundry always expected me to swoon at their boots. And when someone did approach me nicely, I barely had the energy to flirt back. No one ever lit that spark.

So now, out in the Realm for barely a breath, I find myself flushing at the sight of one inconveniently attractive man, blushing like a tavern maid in spring who'd never seen a man in uniform before. *Pull yourself together, Mirabelle.*

The Thrall stepped back immediately. Lowering her gaze without needing to be told. "My Liege," she murmured, then swept from the room in a glide of silver silk and subtle perfume.

Only once the door shut behind her did Damien speak. "You will be expected at the training range tomorrow." When he spoke, his lips parted just enough to reveal a flash of sharp canines, just...too perfect. Unnerving in a way that sent heat curling under my skin. There was something feral in it. Beautiful, but coiled tight. Dangerous.

I blinked. "Join them? For what, exactly?"

His reply was casual. "To oversee and manage. We need someone who understands structure, and tension."

My mouth parted, a small breath escaping. "You want me, a laundress, to direct Majors?"

"Because you are not *just* a laundress," Damien said, eyes still on the parchment in front of him, as if that settled the matter.

I blinked. "That's not a real answer."

He looked up then, slow and deliberate, like he wasn't used to being spoken to like that.

Realizing the edge in my voice, I faltered. "I mean...my Liege?" The title felt awkward, sudden on my tongue. Like trying to patch a tear in silk after it had already unraveled.

He set the parchment down with a soft tap, his gaze never leaving mine now. "You have been flagged in multiple internal logs," he said, voice even. "Six separate incidents where you stepped into conflict before it escalated—between commoners, guards, and more than one Major."

I stiffened. "I didn't—"

He leaned back slightly. "You rerouted supply crates during the ration delay so no Dorm went hungry two nights in a row. You have improvised chain-of-command in emergencies, coordinated triage when the infirmary was overrun."

He stood then.

"That's not leadership," I muttered.

"No," he said, crossing slowly toward me. "That is survival."

I didn't know what to say. So, I said nothing.

"You are not well-liked," he added, as if discussing weather. "But you are obeyed when it matters."

I crossed my arms, but it didn't help. My first instinct was anger—tight and bristling. They'd been keeping records. Pulling pieces of our lives from ledgers and logs, like everything we did could be reduced to inventory. It felt cold. Invasive.

But the anger flickered. And then a quieter thought crept in—he'd noticed things no one else had. The small, invisible choices. The ones made when I thought no one was watching. The ones I hadn't thought mattered. Because no one had ever acted like they did.

Not even me.

My throat ached, like I'd swallowed a lump too large and too old. I'd never expected anyone to care enough to name it. Let alone call it strength.

Then, with a tilt of his head, he added, "You will organize their training, their supplies, their needs. I trust you will manage."

Before I could recover, he took another step forward and said, "And call me Damien."

My mouth opened. Closed. "My Liege, I—"

That was as far as I got. He reached out gently and tilted my chin upward with the lightest pressure of his fingers against my jaw, just enough to guide my eyes to his.

"Damien," he said again, softer now. Just a breath above a whisper. I forgot how to breathe.

The heat that rose inside me wasn't from embarrassment or fear. A kind of pressure that curled low in my belly and made it hard to breathe evenly.

He didn't move his hand right away. And I didn't step back.

I wet my lips without thinking, pulse stumbling once, and cleared my throat to chase the tremor in my voice.

"Right," I said softly, "Damien."

His hand fell away at last. But the space between us felt warmer. I looked away, trying to catch the rhythm of thought again, but it scattered like leaves before a storm.

Still, the thoughts of yesterday's madness flashed in my mind. The way I'd leapt out of my common nature, into the line of fire like a scorned myth-beast. All because of Amara. And curse me, I'd do it again in a blink. And I should be grateful to this Heir for not making an example out of me.

"I'll come tomorrow," I said, "If only to see whether you've truly lost your senses." I added, since I couldn't help it.

This time, the corner of his mouth lifted, restrained but real. "We will see."

I moved to leave, but his voice caught me again.

"Mirabelle. Be here early."

I paused. "Why?"

A beat. "We will find a reason."

He turned from me before I could respond. Walked back toward the firelight desk, toward the growing weight of everything waiting for him. And I left before I did something just as mad as him.

Like agreeing to take all the responsibilities. Or worse, smile like an idiot and ask if he preferred silver or gold for his *next* Thrall's gown.

CHAPTER 6

MIRABELLE

I wasn't sure what I'd expected when he told me to arrive early the next morning. A sealed scroll, perhaps. A whispered directive behind some arched hallway. Maybe even another half-glance from those ridiculous blue eyes that seemed to see and unsee me in the same breath.

What I did not expect was to be handed a pair of reinforced gloves and told I'd be learning *how not to die.*

"You'll need to know how to duck, roll, and scream—though preferably not all at once," said Elder Haldric, dropping a fire-retardant cloak across my arms like he was feeding a furnace.

The material was coarse, heavy with salt and singed wool. It smelled like something that had survived past fires and their lessons.

"Majors are unpredictable," he continued, tightening the clasp at my collar. "You'll want to stay out of their way. Mostly."

I hadn't said a word, but somehow already felt like I'd said too much. We stood near the edge of the courtyard—a wide, stone-carved arena where even the shadows looked scorched. Flames danced along the far walls from spiraled Aether conduits. They hissed and coiled in place, as if waiting for a command that hadn't yet come.

Ophira arrived a few breaths later, her presence slicing through the space like drawn steel. She let her gaze sweep across the field —the old runes etched deep into the stone, the smoldering sigils, the Majors beginning to warm up across the arena floor.

Then her gaze found mine.

"You're not here to teach," she said. "You're here to understand what Aether looks like—up close."

"I thought I was assigned to logistics."

"You are," she said, like the word bored her. "And fire is logistics. So is injury and death." She turned before I could reply, her cloak trailing sharp edges in the air.

Behind me, the real trial began. A tall, brassy device was wheeled into place beside me—an old flame blower, repurposed from Royal childhood combat drills. I'd read about them once. Half weapon, half teacher. It rotated with a slow hum, releasing bursts of controlled fire in unpredictable arcs. Children of noble blood were taught to dodge by instinct before they learned to conjure defense.

Now it was my turn.

"Feet apart. Keep moving. Don't think too hard," Haldric muttered, tweaking the dials. Easy for him to say.

The flame-buster clicked to life with a hiss that was predatory. I barely had time to adjust the heavy cloak before the first stream of fire burst from the device's rotating mouth. It came fast, searing across the air like a whip of molten breath. I dove sideways, my shoulder hitting the dirt with a hard thud. Heat roared past my back, close enough to scorch the edge of my braid.

The second blast came low. I rolled—sloppy, instinctive—but it missed by inches.

Not elegant. But I wasn't ash yet. The fire-retardant cloak clung to my arms, heavy with heat. The salt-treated fabric smelled like sweat and smoke now. By the third volley, I was already trembling.

My boots skidded on scorched stone. I barely kept my footing as the flame arced again—

sharp and fast and too close. I threw myself to the side, landing hard on one knee. Pain flared. But I pushed up. Again.

Then a flicker of black started curling at the edge of my vision—I looked down. My left hand, lifted instinctively in front of my face, shimmered—black and silver. I blinked. It vanished.

Hallucination. It had to be. I was exhausted. Dehydrated. Losing sense.

Another flame screamed toward me, and I dropped just in time—cloak dragging across the dirt, elbow burning. I couldn't keep going. My legs had gone sluggish, my breath ragged and shallow, my body heat-slicked and shaking.

Then, a distant voice from across the courtyard: "That's enough."

I barely had the energy to lift my head. The flame-buster stuttered, then clicked off. Damien's fingers closed gently around my wrist as he peeled back the scorched fabric. He turned my arm inspecting the raw skin at my elbow. He looked up, then ran a knuckle just above the burn, confirming it wasn't severe.

"You'll survive," he said slowly. *Erm, thank you?*

I opened my mouth, but nothing came.

Across the arena, Haldric stood with arms crossed, a few Royals observing from the archways nearby—staring now. Damien rose smoothly, still between me and the others.

"I don't recall asking you to put her through this."

Haldric crossed his arms. "If she's meant to oversee Majors, she should at least know how not to die standing next to one."

Damien's jaw didn't move at first. "Putting her in the direct path of flame on her second morning is not what I call training," he said, measured. "If I'd wanted her broken, I would have ordered it."

Haldric raised an eyebrow but said nothing.

"She will oversee the Majors from a position where she can actually be useful," Damien continued. "I want reports and observations. Not scorched flesh."

His eyes flicked back to me then. "Rest this afternoon," he said simply. "I will be briefing the Majors on the Tameables. You are dismissed."

I gave a shallow nod, biting back the thanks. He had already turned away, cloak catching the air like the trailing edge of a storm. I looked down at my cloak, scorched and heavy, burned at the edges where the flames had kissed too close. I had tried to preserve it. It was, without exaggeration, the most expensive thing I'd ever worn. But there was no point pretending it would last another trial.

I didn't return to my chamber immediately. Something in my limbs still felt too taut, like a pulled wire refusing to snap. Instead, I moved toward the edge of the training yard where the lattice wrapped the courtyard wall, the ivy grown thick through the carved stonework. I leaned close, letting the leaf-veiled gaps cool my skin as I took a long, steady sip from my water flask.

Through the greenery, I could see the Majors forming a loose half-circle, more still than I'd ever seen them. Tension rolled through them like a shared current.

Beside them towered a creature that could have been carved from myth. *A Tameable.*

Its red hide shimmered like molten clay, horned and broad-backed, breathing in slow huffs that steamed the sand. Its eyes glowed—not with heat, but intelligence. Familiarity. And Damien's hand rested calmly on its shoulder. The creature did not snarl. It waited and obeyed, Tethered to him.

I watched them, these chosen ones, stand proud and unflinching as the creature snorted steam. I would never be that. Not with fire dancing in my veins or power trailing my footsteps.

The thought struck bitter. And then shame followed fast. I was being ungrateful.

I was here. Not back in the laundry pools, scrubbing blood from tunics with water so cold it numbed the bone. I was eating real food. Wearing boots that fit. Speaking to Royals who looked me in the eye.

I turned from the arena at last, the scent of scorched sand still clinging to my skin and walked toward the tower wing where my chambers waited—rooms lined with soft linens and quiet abundance.

The nickels they'd handed me yesterday were still tucked in my satchel. Enough to persuade a guard to deliver a small share of this new fortune, and food Amara actually liked. For now, that was enough.

⸻⟨⟩⸻

THE MAJORS' training yard was nestled in the crook of a wild hillside, shielded by flame-inscribed pylons and Aether seals so old they glowed faintly even in daylight.

Cassian, Rhevas, Lyria, and Alden.

They'd each survived the trial. I had met them briefly then—Cassian, all teeth and swagger, had winked like I was a barmaid who'd spilled ale on his boots. Lyria, lean and pale, kept her mouth shut but her flames flickering. Alden had the clumsy, eager look of someone who didn't know what to do with his own talent yet, while Rhevas stood apart from all of them, calculating and quiet, eyes flicking across every motion like he's seeing twenty moves ahead.

And now here they were again, half-lounging in the court like they hadn't nearly died days ago.

They weren't alone. A small cluster of Royals clad in deep crimson and silver-trimmed training tunics, moved among the Majors with the effortless ease of those born to power. Their voices carried in waves of laughter and teasing barbs.

Amara would've hated it here. Too many smug grins. But she would've liked that I was standing among them, boots scuffed and cloak clean, not as an intruder but as something more.

I shifted my satchel higher, biting back a grimace as the strap dragged against the tender skin beneath my sleeve, reminding me I wasn't quite healed yet.

"Hey, lady reporter…" One of the Royals handed me a parchment—a young woman with high cheekbones and effortless beauty. She handed over a leather wrap next, pens tucked beside tally sheets, notations scribbled in Haldric's sharp hand, and a neatly bundled stack of fresh parchment tied with a crimson ribbon.

"You're to observe the morning drills. Highlight weakness, recommend reinforcement exercises, assess viability of mixed-unit rotations," she recited quickly, clearly trying to remember the phrasing. "Oh, and if you see anything...odd, report it to Elder Ophira."

"If?" I asked.

She only shrugged. "Things have been odd lately."

I didn't argue. How could I? I could feel it, even hear it.

Instead, I tucked the notes beneath my arm and turned toward the training field, where a new set of pylons had been raised, fire glyphs already active, illusion glyphs flickering faintly beneath. Each pylon bore the Aether marks of every Telmorian Clan so that if—well, more like when—they turned on each other, they'd at least know what hit them.

Across the field, flame spiraled into the air like a whip, cracking against shadow. Lyria ducked, her own magic surging to life—flames coiling up from her boots to meet the illusionary fire unraveling from the pylon and eating it whole.

Cassian whistled. "Show-off."

"Says the one still bitter about being upstaged," Lyria shot back.

He ignored her, stepping forward as the next illusion flickered to life—this time, a beast made of shattered glass and fire. It lunged, all muscle and molten light.

Cassian grinned and lifted both hands.

The fire he conjured wasn't elegant. It was raw and bursting outward like it had waited all morning to be let loose. The glass illusion shattered in a cascade of sparks, Aether flickering in its wake.

"Subtle," Rhevas muttered.

"I don't do subtle," Cassian said, flexing his fingers with a cocky little flourish. "That's Alden's job."

I turned to where Alden stood, indeed doing nothing. His gaze flicked to mine, then away.

The Royals joined them one by one—their Aether flowed differently, less force and more finesse. One woman painted spirals of heat through the air with her fingers before releasing them toward a simulated phalanx of enemies—burning away illusion-shadows mid-charge.

It was beautiful. Deadly. And efficient.

The Majors, in contrast, were raw power. Impressive in isolation but sloppy in coordination. Rhevas cast fire over Alden's flank without a word, forcing him to duck. Lyria's flames lagged half a breath behind the command glyphs issued by the lead Royal, throwing off the illusion's timing.

I scribbled notes fast, parchment filling with missing elements:

—No coordinated fire lines

—Weak communication under duress

—Hesitation between transitions

—Strong offensive instincts, low cohesion

I cringed at my own audacity, judging the Crown's chosen like I was born with a scepter in hand. But I was doing it fair and square. Hopefully, the mighty Heir and his collection of Elders would understand that before deciding I was too mouthy to live.

Another simulation rose, this one faster, crueler. Multiple attackers with unnatural speed. One Royal woman fell behind, her Aether shield failing. Cassian was the only one who reacted fast enough, a whip of fire curling through her illusion attacker's chest before it landed a blow.

And then—poof. Nothing. The entire field blinked. Gone. The illusions vanished mid-motion, a blur of light dispersing like doused embers. The glyphs went dark. "Control your Aether," a Royal said flatly. "Or it will control you." Then he turned and walked off. I glanced down at my tally sheet and wrote *note to self: high stakes and lukewarm payoffs.*

Stars, who was I? Next, I'd be scribbling "*Aether burns, but duty scorches deeper*" or something equally lame.

I underlined it anyway. Twice. For effect.

CHAPTER 7
MIRABELLE

A short break was called, and the group scattered, breathless and steaming under the morning sun. I jotted down a final entry and closed the note.

"Fellow reporter," came a voice to my right.

I turned to see the Royal woman again—the one with the high cheekbones and perfectly balanced posture. She didn't smile, but her tone lacked edge. "We'll be running simulations against Zarkon's Aether next. You may want to note how the Majors respond to false movement. Most don't notice until it's too late."

"I'll watch," I said simply.

She gave a small nod and turned, joining her unit again. Her name escaped me—Selira? Sireen? Something with too many vowels. A few others stood nearby, one of the red-cloaked Royals kept circling the edges of the yard like he was judging all of us, including me.

The Majors were already back in formation, and still somehow managing to look like they hadn't trained a single coordinated day together in their lives.

I took my seat near the base of a low-boughed tree at the edge of the yard, the parchment stack balanced on my lap, ink already drying on my fingertips. From this angle, I could observe the formations clearly without getting singed—a happy middle ground between useful and flammable.

Further down the path, a row of cushioned benches sat in the shade of pergola with flowering vines. That was where the Royals had gathered. A full clutch of them—mostly women in their twenties, all polished and poised, light glancing off their lacquered braids and gold-trimmed sashes. Platters of fruits and meat circled among them, passed with the languid grace of those who'd never known hunger as anything more than a missed luncheon.

Their voices floated on the breeze—soft laughter, the occasional exaggerated gasp, a teasing jab that earned mock protests. I kept my gaze on the field or at least pretended to.

A shift in the air pulled my attention sideways. Lyria approached the pergola, she must've slipped away during the break and changed out of her scorched tunic into a crisp slate-gray dress. She hesitated at the edge of the group, brushing soot from her sleeve.

"Mind if I sit?" she asked.

One of the Royals glanced up and gave a shallow nod toward the open end of the bench.

Lyria sat, legs crossed. Silence hovered until someone finally spoke.

"So...when's your next brush with death?" one asked, popping a candied plum between her teeth.

Lyria shrugged. "Suppose that depends on who's casting the illusions."

That earned a few chuckles. The kind that didn't quite reach the eyes. Another Royal leaned forward, blonde and poised like she'd been born with diplomacy in her cradle. "You're lucky, you know. Direct training under the Heir isn't exactly common for Majors."

Lyria blinked. "We've barely spoken."

"Oh, please," a second woman chimed in. "You asked about his training schedule this morning. We all heard."

"It was a logistics question," Lyria said quickly, sitting straighter. "I'm just trying to keep up."

"Mm-hm," the first one said, exchanging a grin with the others. "Careful. It starts with pace and ends with pining."

"I'm not pining," Lyria snapped, cheeks coloring. Her hair had come undone in places, wisping around her flushed face. Poor thing. *I'd have snatched the seared meat from the platter and rolled straight off the bench.*

A third one, perched like a falcon on the bench arm, tilted her head. "Don't make it personal, dear. He's not exactly known for... *interest.*"

"Unless you're a Thrall, nowadays" someone muttered, eliciting a ripple of laughter.

The blonde one smirked. "Oh, he *knows* what he's doing. Stars, does he. But it's like being kissed by Aether—intense, *consuming.* But feelings? Never part of the trade."

"Believe me," said a brunette smoothing her sleeve with theatrical indifference, "we've all tested the waters. He doesn't even blink anymore."

"But," said the one with a mouthful of sugared fruit, "compensates elsewhere, if you know what I mean."

That earned a ripple of laughter—low, knowing. Lyria looked like she wanted to melt into the bench and vanish.

And I—well. I looked down, suddenly fascinated by the shape of my own boots. I didn't even know what I felt exactly, Embarrassment? Annoyance? Jealousy? I couldn't tell. Just that my stomach curled and my cheeks felt too warm.

"No offense," the blonde added lightly, "but if we're all playing pretend, we'd rather take the first turn. He's...not simple. And unlike some, we are actually eligible. He will be Bonded. Clan duty, Council decree, all of it."

"And let's be honest," another chimed in, "when that day comes, they're not pairing him with someone who can't recite their family tree back to the Founding."

"Nothing personal," said the last, sweet as poison. "Just—back of the line, love."

And here I was, trying to make sense of one glance in a hallway and the way his voice had softened for half a breath.

Lyria didn't reply. She didn't storm off either. She just sat very still, her lips slightly parted like she'd bitten off her retort and swallowed it whole.

I said nothing from under my tree. Watched the illusions rise again as if none of it mattered.

And maybe it didn't.

But I still underlined the final line in my notes—*Not all i(de)llusions are projected—some are cast over fruit bowls.*

Then I tucked the parchment away and stood. It was going to be a long afternoon.

THE FOLLOWING days blurred into rhythm. Routine, almost. The Majors drilled from morning till dusk—basic formations, elemental control, combat footwork—and I watched. I observed. At first, my notes were clumsy, half-filled with what I didn't understand. But soon, they sharpened. I began noticing patterns— how Rhevas's fire spells always surged slightly left or how Alden overcompensated in defense but faltered when pushed to attack. Before long, I was suggesting adjustments, assigning them to specific drills depending on what needed refining. No one questioned it. Not even the Royals.

One of them—Callen, all quick grins and dark eyes, had taken it upon himself to train me whenever there was a lull between drills. "You can't just hover around with those notes forever," he'd teased the first time, handing me a practice staff. "Your bones need to learn too."

So, I did. Defense techniques, mostly. Just enough to not die if cornered. Meanwhile, the Royals themselves had begun instructing the Majors—basic drills from their own training years, occasionally offering insights into the inner workings of the Royal Legion of Atlassian. It was simply *the Legion*, and the way they spoke of it made it clear that entering it was less a promotion and more a rite.

Soon, their training sessions would shift. The current instructors, mostly Crown-selected Royals, would hand over command to the Legion's head: Nathan Tavaryn. Apparently, a name that made seasoned soldiers stand straighter.

Damien had joined us after the lunch meals. One moment the Royals were sparring with Majors, the next they were standing a little straighter, nodding as he spoke. They played it casual like they always did. But I'd seen it often enough now to spot the shift—the way their eyes lingered whenever he came by to oversee drills with the Tameables.

I couldn't blame them if that attention was because of how delicious he looked. But I never quite saw what made the Heir their star. Or maybe it just hadn't sunk into me yet—the awe, the belief, whatever it was that made the others tilt subtly toward him like flowers toward the sun. I'd led a bitter enough life to know how little those pretty stories comforted when the world turned cruel.

By the time he turned to address us, we'd already gathered around him.

"Tomorrow, there will be a short trial, before Nathan takes over your training." he said, voice even. "Consider it a test of your foundation. Not your Aether. Just you."

My heart skipped. *Not* Aether. Could I?

I looked up at him. "And if someone without Aether wanted to try?"

Damien's gaze flicked to me. "This isn't a test you pass through willpower alone."

"But it's not a no," I mumbled quietly. He didn't respond. So, that wasn't a no. And frankly, I didn't care if the Heir thought it was unwise. I was still standing. I would be tomorrow too.

Damien paused, as if weighing the silence. Then, in that room-quiet hush, he spoke.

"Now," he said, voice smooth, "we will give your muscles a moment's mercy. Let's test the instincts of our new recruits—their decisions, intellect—without Aether this time."

All of us exchanged glances—eyes bright with anticipation.

He stepped forward, and a small wooden table rolled into view —pushed by a silent attendant. Set atop it were two carved stone busts, each nearly the size of a helmet, mounted on iron plates. Their faces were lifelike. Stoic, sculpted, marked with insignia.

One wore a hawk at his collar. The other had a wolf etched into his pauldrons. They looked like statues of old generals, captured mid-council. But their eyes glinted faintly, as if enchanted.

Damien stopped between them. "These two represent officers who held joint command during a failed flank maneuver," he said evenly. "One of them falsified orders costing an entire scouting party."

A quiet ripple moved through the group. "One of these two is the saboteur." He stepped back, letting the weight of that hang. "Here is what you need to know: One of them will always tell the truth. One will always lie—the saboteur."

He let that sink in. "You may ask one question, to only one of them, for a yes or no. Then you *must* find the saboteur. But this time—" he glanced over his shoulder "—you will state your intended question first. I will only allow you to proceed if the question can lead to the truth. If it can't, you return to your place."

He paused. "Cassian."

Cassian rolled his shoulders, gave a quick grin, and approached the table like he was picking who to spar with. "Let's keep it simple. Just ask anyone of them if he is guilty."

Damien folded his arms. "And?"

Cassian opened his mouth, closed it. "That'll catch one lying, right? Uh...If he will say yes...or maybe not. Both will say no to that, or—I don't know," he admitted at last.

"Lyria," Damien said, turning without expression.

Cassian exhaled and dragged a hand through his hair.

"Should've asked if they wanted to be the saboteur," he muttered on his way back.

She stepped forward, arms folded. "Then I'll ask each one if the other is the saboteur."

Damien didn't move. "And if one says yes?"

"Then I know one is lying?" Lyria's mouth thinned. "...Right." She gave a nod and backed off. Cassian muttered something about *bloody riddles.*

One by one, Majors stepped up. One tried, "Would you answer yes if I asked if you're not the saboteur?" All shot down. More questions and possible answers.

"Too indirect."

"Not isolating a variable."

"Still relies on uncertainty."

The Royals had begun murmuring among themselves. A few stepped up, testing out more direct questions at the statues— getting scattered yeses and nos in return. None of it led anywhere.

I stood still behind the Royals, watching the two stone faces like they might flinch.

So.

Only two.

One always lies—the saboteur.

The other always tells the truth.

The trap was simple: the truth lived in how the rules tangled when you added just one more layer.

If I asked a stone, "Are you the saboteur?" I'd still be stuck.

Because if I asked the truth-teller, he'd say "No" —because it's the truth.

But the saboteur, would also say "No." Because he's a bloody liar. That question gets me nowhere.

But then came a better one. Not about what they were, but about what they would say.

It forced the logic to bend in just one direction. I felt it click. I took a breath. Then lifted my hand. "Mind if I try?"

Heads turned. A few brows rose. One of the Royals muttered

something under his breath. Damien only studied me for a moment, then gave a small nod. "Let us hear it."

I faced the busts, their stone faces watching back with glinting eyes, too still to be lifeless.

I pointed to the Hawk. "If I asked the Wolf, 'Are you the saboteur?'... would he say yes?"

A pause. Then the Hawk's mouth moved. "No."

Now I just had to follow the logic. If the Hawk was the saboteur, the liar, then the Wolf was the truth-teller.

So, the truth: Wolf would answer "No, I'm not the saboteur."

But Hawk is a liar. So, he would lie about that answer—and say: "Yes, he would say yes."

But he didn't, did he? He said "No."

Which means the Hawk isn't the saboteur.

Now if you flip it.

If the Hawk is the truth-teller, and the Wolf is the saboteur—

Then the truth: Wolf would lie and say "No, I'm not the saboteur."

Hawk, being honest, would report that exactly as it is—so he'd still say: "No."

Either way, "No" only comes from the one who's not guilty.

I looked at Damien.

"It's the Wolf, isn't it?"

The base of the wolf bust pulsed once, then flared with a deep, unmistakable red.

A hush fell. Then—

Someone whistled. A sharp, startled exhale from one of the Royals.

Damien's gaze lingered on me. A faint smile curled at the corner of his mouth. "Well-reasoned," he said. There was an unmistakable approval in it.

And in that moment, I grinned. Big. Unapologetically.

Callen let out a whoop and, before I could stop him, lifted me clean off the ground like I weighed nothing at all.

"Put her down," came a clipped voice from Damien, his gaze locked on Callen.

He did—immediately—mumbling something that sounded like an apology, though the grin he wore said he wasn't sorry at all. A beat of silence, then murmurs swelled, surprised, amused, maybe a little impressed.

Now that...that felt good.

CHAPTER 8

MIRABELLE

The Emberlock Theatre was nothing like the polished royal amphitheaters with velvet banners and acrobats balancing on enchanted beams. This was stone, old and scarred. Carved into the belly of the outer cliffs, it had no roof, just a gaping Celestia overhead, hemmed by steep tiers of viewing balconies.

My hands were dry and shaking all at once. My heart drummed in my throat with a rhythm that didn't match the pulse of my body. I was split open—part fear, part hunger, part the sharp, dizzying thrill of doing something I'd never done in my life.

The survivors, if that was what they were calling themselves, had gathered in a loose semi-circle near the maze edge. There were five of us. Me, Cassian, Rhevas, Lyira and the boy with ash-colored hair who still hadn't spoken a word.

They had been bred for it, most of them. Aether flickered in the air around them like it was simply part of their breath. And then there was me. Unaethered and unarmed. I hadn't been invited to participate. But no one said I shouldn't compete. They just assumed I wouldn't. *And where is the fun in that?*

Cassian was grinning like he'd just returned from a successful hunt, both canines on full display. Aether gave them all fangs, but apparently not all of them could pull it off. Unlike a certain brooding noble whose scent made my knees untrustworthy.

"You didn't die...yet" he said to me, cheerfully impressed. "Didn't think you had it in you, Aetherless."

I blinked. "Me neither."

There was a beat of silence. Cassian laughed—thankfully, and elbowed Rhevas.

"She's got that half-dead confidence. Dangerous stuff."

Rhevas didn't so much as flinch. He stared at me for a second longer than I liked, then turned away, adjusting the bracer on his wrist. I stood there for a moment, trying to think of something else to say. Something...friendly. Normal.

"So," I offered. "Nice maze. Very stabby."

Cassian snorted into his hand. Lyria might've rolled his eyes. Ugh...*try to keep your mouth shut for a while, will you?*

I didn't dislike the presence of others. I just didn't understand what I was supposed to do with them. There was no clear choreography. Just eyes, and expectations, and pauses that were probably meant to be filled with...laughter? A compliment? Whatever it was, I never had the right pieces.

Cassian leaned back against the railing and gave me a slow once-over. "You're not really supposed to be here, are you?"

I shrugged. "No. But no one stopped me."

Probably should've stayed back and watched from the shaded edge like a sane commoner. Or at least like someone not actively nursing bruises from yesterday's fire gauntlet.

I looked around, something unspoken was always buzzing beneath the surface. Maybe it was the same rising rumors— outposts falling silent, scouts gone missing. Some blamed disease. Some blamed rebellion. But others spoke of Celestial Dissonance. The kind of rupture that cracked between two Realms every decade, when boundaries frayed and power tilted out of place. Atlassian was sharpening itself. It was obvious in the way they were training Majors now—with speed. With desperation.

The stands filled partially. Elders took their places beneath the high columns, murmuring in pairs with hands folded behind their backs. Royals sat in their terraces. Far fewer than for any formal event. To them, this was nothing more than an event to stir the Majors' blood before real trials began. A warm-up.

At the far edge of the pit, the floor shifted—the etched stones in a grid of copper-veined tiles pulsing faintly under the morning light. The maze looked simple, but it wasn't. Runes carved into the walls flickered with a slow pulse, reacting to the energy of those who entered. They called it the Ember Lock.

No one explained what that meant. We were expected to understand.

Damien crossed the ring. He walked past the others without pause. Cassian straightened. Others offered a shallow nod. When he stopped in front of me, I tensed automatically. Maybe because everyone else did too. Or maybe he'd decided that spilling a commoner's blood on the first day wasn't the most diplomatic way to start training for their new recruits.

Either way, I wasn't stepping out of this ring. He'd have to drag me back, boots scraping and pride howling, and even then—I'd make sure it was a scene no one forgot.

He said to all of us. "You will be handed your bowl once the first bell rings. No Aether. No shields. No resets." *As if I had anything to reset.*

His tone was calm. "Guard the bowl." He paused. "The floor reacts to pressure and intention. Watch the shifts. One step off rhythm, and it locks you out. If your bowl spills or shatters, you're out."

He was still speaking when his hand reached toward me. I flinched—barely, but he was already drawing my sleeve out of the way, inspecting the scrape at my elbow. His thumb turned my wrist just enough to get a clearer look. The pain had mostly numbed, but his touch still made me go oddly still.

He didn't stop talking. "The sequence changes every minute unless it's executed in order. Watch those ahead of you. It is simple

—learn fast or burn slower. Just make it through to the second bell." *Ah...as simple as tying a boot.*

His hands were holding mine, and all I could focus on was how infuriatingly handsome he looked up close. And his scent. Stars, his scent. Like musk and cedar and a darker trace. I was halfway convinced it was laced with some kind of narcotic. I couldn't really hear the instructions anymore. And my brain, apparently, had decided to abandon all higher function.

I knew he was saying something useful—something about not bleeding to death, probably—He pulled a length of cloth from his inner lining and wrapped my arm, securing it with the same mechanical ease as someone wrapping a sparring grip. He was *really* close now, towering without trying, his forearm brushing mine, all lean strength and heat, and I hated how it was currently melting my insides like butter in a forge.

I could sense a few glances flicking toward the binding, then toward Damien's hands.

Finishing, Damien gave a curt nod to the group. "Good luck." Then the others turned to go.

But I didn't move. I lingered a heartbeat too long, waiting for him to walk away like the rest. He didn't. His gaze stayed on me.

"Did you rest?" he asked quietly. "Eat?"

I blinked. "Yes. I mean—yes, I did." A beat of silence. Then I added—because apparently my brain had left the arena—"Did you?"

The corner of his mouth curved barely. "Yes, Mirabelle. I have eaten."

Then his voice shifted, leveled into command. "Get into position. The Majors will begin the trial on the second bell. Stay near the outer rim, and wave if you want out."

He turned slightly, like he meant to go, but then paused, eyes finding mine again, softer now. "We are all different," he said. "And knowing how to accept the difference does not make you weak."

I wanted to tell him this wasn't false bravery or a bid for attention. It was hunger, the quiet, aching kind. The kind born from spending a lifetime watching the world happen to others. I wasn't trying to prove I was strong. I just wanted to feel what it was like to belong to something I'd never been allowed to experience.

But I didn't say any of that. Instead, I nodded once. Then reached out and gently squeezed his arm in gratitude. His gaze flicked to my hand, then back to my face. He didn't pull away.

Then I turned and walked toward the maze, the hum of runes beneath the floor rising to meet me like a held breath.

⬥

THE FIRST BELL RANG, and the maze awoke.

Tiles beneath my boots pulsed with coppery light, reacting to each step like they could feel me. The bowl in my hands, nothing more than uneven clay and water, suddenly felt like the most fragile thing in the Realm. Every breath, every vibration, every wrong move threatened it.

Around me, the Majors began to move, all of them driven by the same silent urgency. I'd overheard whispers earlier: *The closer to the center you go, the safer it gets.*

I stepped forward. One foot. Paused. The tile beneath me hummed low and steady.

Another step. Same sound. I crouched low and pulled the bowl close to my chest. I didn't want to rush. That wasn't the point— not for someone like me. I stayed still, listening. Everyone else had already disappeared into the shifting paths, except for one brief glimpse of Rhevas moving across the center like he owned the maze.

And then the humming changed. Just a low gurgling sound from somewhere deep in the maze. It started as a distant trickle, almost like rain falling in a tunnel. Then the smell hit. Bitter and metallic and wrong, like acid and scorched herbs twisted together.

I looked to my left—and froze. A crack had opened in the stone tiles. From it, something green and shimmering was pouring upward, a slow, viscous liquid that steamed as it moved. It wasn't anything natural. It slithered across the tiles with almost deliberate intent, curving around corners, licking toward me.

But the moment the bottom of my clay bowl grazed the surface of that green sludge, it hissed violently. The base sizzled and began to melt. It's melting! *The bloody thing is melting?!*

Internal cursing gave way to panic. I bolted. My legs kicked into motion before my brain caught up. I ran as fast as I could, my arms clenched around the softening bowl, water sloshing dangerously close to the rim. The green liquid was rising faster now— filling the gaps between the tiles, spreading like a sentient flood with no patience for hesitation.

I darted toward the only safe tile I could see ahead—glowing faintly, untainted. But even that was shifting underfoot, its edge flaring with golden light.

Across the maze, Lyria came into view—charging straight toward me, bowl in hand, green tide rising around us. Her eyes locked on the ledge above my position. *She was so going to use me to escape it.*

I shifted sideways, bracing myself instinctively as Lyria barreled closer, not even bothering to shout a warning. Her boots slapped against the stone, bowl clutched high.

"Hold still!" she barked, already leaping.

I ducked without thinking, felt her foot scrape across my shoulder as she vaulted upward. Her fingers caught the edge of the wall ledge just in time. For a second, she hung there, bowl teetering, liquid inside trembling with every tiny sway of her arm.

I stumbled back, chest heaving. The tile under me was beginning to pulse faster, an offbeat rhythm like a skipped heartbeat. The green liquid reached my knees.

We were out of time.

Stone doors around the maze perimeter began flashing open wide slabs of stone sliding away for just a breath, then slamming shut. The exits—too far, too fast, too random.

I pressed myself to the wall, ignoring the sting in my thighs, the way my lungs burned. I watched.

Pulse. Pulse. Pause.

One of the doors—east—wasn't aligned with the others. Its rhythm was slower. Off-beat.

I shouted, breath ripping from my chest. "East door—two pulses, then it opens! Only once!"

She didn't look down. "You're lying! You just want me off your back!" *Is she serious?*

She dropped from the ledge anyway, boots splashing into the rising green. It was up to our hips now, thick as treacle, dragging at every step.

I turned toward the path, moving slowly, carefully, bowl pressed to my chest like a fragile life. My arms ached from clutching the half-melted bowl. I could feel the bottom softening further, my fingers sinking into the clay with every step.

The door pulsed.

Once.

Again.

Silence.

I counted, "Three, two—NOW!"

I lunged. Slid on slick stone. My elbow hit the floor. The bowl tilted wildly, water nearly spilling over the rim, but somehow, it held.

I stumbled through the door just as it started to shut behind me...Lyria screamed behind me. I turned, catching a glimpse of her —her hand outstretched, bowl cradled against her chest, green liquid swallowing her. She jumped. The bowl hit the water. The moment her bowl touched it, the base disintegrated in her grip. Water burst upward like a snapped pipe, drenching her front.

And the hiss that followed was haunting.

Silence pressed in like a wall. The only sound left was the trembling breath in my chest, and the faint creak of the ruined bowl still clutched—barely intact—in my hands.

The floor beneath my boots began to tremble again—only this

time, it wasn't the pulse of light or the hiss of flames. It was move-ment. Sideways.

I tensed instinctively, eyes snapping to the ground, half-convinced I was about to be sandwiched between collapsing tiles. My bowl was still clutched to my chest, wobbling like it shared my confusion.

The tile beneath my feet slid with an unnatural grace. I blinked, steadying myself as the entire platform glided along hidden tracks. Ahead of me, stone doors parted like theater curtains, revealing a narrow hallway bathed in flickering torchlight.

CHAPTER 9
MIRABELLE

That's it? No flames? No airborne blades or magical beast set loose for a second round? I'd been so mentally prepared to sprint through fire that now the absence of it felt suspicious.

The platform halted with a gentle jolt. The wall in front of me creaked open into what looked like a changing room carved from the rock itself—simple wooden stalls, stacked crates, hooks holding spare tunics and training breeches. Well, apparently I survived long enough to earn pants.

I moved inside, peeled off my soaked, acid-splattered outer layer, and snagged a clean tunic and loose-fitting trousers from one of the shelves. I was halfway through tying the cords when voices drifted in from beyond the far wall. The stone was thick, but not thick enough to hide the familiar cadence of Damien's voice.

"...I didn't bring you here to flatter your bloodlines," he said evenly.

A pause, then another voice—Cassian, I thought. "It's not about flattery, my Liege. We weren't trained for that kind of trial."

"...we all got blindsided," someone muttered.

Damien said. "It was meant to teach you perspective. You think Aether makes you untouchable. It doesn't."

I eased closer to the wall, careful not to bump the shelf behind me. The torchlight flickered through the narrow slats between the stones.

There was a pause, the kind that carries weight.

"I'm not blaming you," Damien continued, his voice as steady as I'd come to expect. "But recognizing arrogance matters. Especially now. That is why this section exists—to bruise your egos before Dissonance does it worse."

Another voice chimed in—Lyria, clipped and skeptical. "Perhaps a gentler warning would have spared us a few burns."

"It could have," Damien said mildly. "But none of you would have listened."

"There are battles ahead," he went on. "Dissonance does not wait for you to be ready. Clan borders will break. Tameables don't ask for fair fights. And the Hunts? They will expect you to track and defend regardless of your pedigree."

No one answered immediately.

Then a quieter voice, maybe the ash-haired boy who hadn't spoken much, asked, "So the Aether's not enough anymore?"

"It never was," Damien said, and for a second, I almost imagined the flicker of warmth beneath all that steel. "If a commoner with no Aether made it out while you didn't, take that for what it is. A lesson."

A short silence followed. Then Damien, with a faint edge of dry humor: "Good that she stepped in willingly. I trust your bruised egos will keep you from leering at her when she oversees the training."

That earned a quiet chuckle. I couldn't tell who.

I leaned back against the stone with the tunic half tucked, not really knowing how to feel. Not flattered, not quite. *Maybe a little.*

The conversation moved on—back to tactics and rune calibration and how Rhevas apparently broke his first bowl by blinking too hard.

I stepped out into the passage. My limbs ached from the day's endless charades, my jaw a little tight from the focus I'd forced through that entire ordeal. I wasn't ready for conversation, but Jasper was waiting.

He stood at the end of the corridor, his cloak was immaculate, boots polished. The moment he spotted me, his expression lit up.

"You really did well, Mira," he said, stepping forward with deliberate charm. "I must say, I'm rather proud."

Before I could respond—or duck—he swept me into a hug. A very full-bodied, very uninvited hug.

It caught me entirely off guard. My arms stiffened uselessly between us, and I gave what could only be described as a deeply uncomfortable pat to his shoulder, the kind one might offer a slightly over-affectionate relative. His grip lingered longer than it needed to, and when he finally released me, I took a subtle half-step back and offered him my driest thanks.

"Why are you here?" I asked, adjusting the collar of my tunic and trying not to grimace.

He smiled like I'd just flirted instead of flinched. "How could I not come find you?" he said, voice smooth as poured ink. "You've become the talk of the hall. Royals are whispering your name like you actually matter now."

My brow lifted, unimpressed. "Mm-hmm, and?"

He laughed softly, as if I'd said something adorable. "*I* noticed you first," he added, his tone lower now. "That counts for something." *I noticed you first—a historic moment, truly.*

I didn't respond to that comment. I rolled my eyes, just enough to dismiss him politely while making it clear I'd rather be anywhere else.

"Am I free to leave?" I asked, hoping this conversation had an endpoint.

"Not just yet," he said, turning toward a heavy wooden door along the inner corridor. "Ophira was here earlier. She said you're to join the others in the study chamber. I, of course, volunteered to pass the message along."

"How nice of you." I murmured.

He leaned in and pressed a quick kiss to my cheek, then opened the door before I had time to process his overfamiliarity or the sheer audacity. I stepped through, brushing past him without waiting for another word, and wiped my cheek on the way in.

Inside, the chamber had the warmth of brown stones. The far windows let in slanted gold light, pooling over scrolls and maps unfurled across a central table.

The Majors were already gathered, standing in a half-circle. Damien stood at the head, flanked by two Royals I didn't recognize. He spoke to them in low, measured tones.

As I entered, the room quieted slightly. Heads turned. Cassian offered a crooked grin and a lazy salute.

"The bowl doesn't break, and neither does she," he said.

Lyria, arms folded at the far end, gave a nod—not warm, but not sharp either. "Didn't think you'd make it," she said. "But you did. Fair enough."

Even the ash-haired boy glanced over and gave a small nod, acknowledging me in his quiet, unreadable way.

With that, the Majors filed out, boots echoing against stone, leaving only a few murmurs behind. Damien glanced in my direction, gave a small nod, and turned back to his conversation with the Royals.

Wait, that's all? Maybe there was meaning buried in it—there always was with him, but at that moment, I didn't care. I scanned the room. One seat left. His. Without breaking stride, I walked over and sat. If he wanted to pretend I didn't exist after proving them all wrong, he could do it while I occupied his chair.

And just like that, a hush fell over the entire room.

⊰•◦❖◦•⊱

I'D BE LYING if I said I wasn't bothered by the sudden attention pressing in on me from all corners of the room. But I wasn't focused on them. What I noticed was the way Damien stilled while leaning over the table. Whatever he was explaining to the Royals flanking him had stopped, the words cut clean.

Then he dismissed them with a quiet, "That will be all."

Even the Thralls who had been lingering at the corners, pretending to busy themselves near the drink tray, straightened at his voice and began to retreat.

Damien turned at last. Leaned back on the table's edge, arms folded, head cocked just enough to be intentional. His uniform fit too well and I hated how aware I suddenly was of all that strength beneath it.

Cool eyes locked on mine. "You always make this much noise just by sitting down?" he asked, voice calm.

I matched his tone with one just as dry. "Only when someone's being especially dismissive."

He gave a small hum that might've been approval or interest, then tilted his head toward the side of the room. "Fiora. Bring us two." His voice cut through just before the chamber doors could fully close behind them.

The Thrall from the other day—the one who'd been following him around the training range with an entire tray of command scrolls, appeared without needing a second call. She crossed the floor quietly and offered us the tray she carried. There were two tumblers. Identical. The drink inside looked promising enough— amber-gold, with a soft swirl that caught the light.

"I was wrapping things up," he said simply. "So, we could talk properly."

Internally, I cringed. As if he owed me any explanation. *Stars, I needed to get a grip.* He hadn't even looked at me properly until now —and here I was, acting like I'd been stood up at a private dinner.

I nodded, trying to keep my tone polite. "Kind of you to make the time."

A ghost of a smirk tugged at his lips. "Drop the formality, Mirabelle," he said, the syllables almost lazy. "It is a bit late for you to start playing court manners with me, don't you think?"

I shifted in my seat, cleared my throat, and reached for the drink like it was a lifeline. I took the one closest to me. The first sip hit wrong. I choked. It was bitter, probably expensive, and thoroughly awful. I swallowed it anyway.

"I need you to be more self-aware," he said after a beat. "You are going to be surrounded by Aether-wielders and half-bored Majors looking for something to test themselves on. I let you stay in the trial because I knew it was harmless. The rest won't be."

I lifted my tumbler, considering him over the rim. "Do you usually care this much for all commoners? Or are you just this generous with your concern in general?"

Since we were apparently tossing out decorum, I set the glass down with a soft clink and met his gaze head-on.

Then he asked, evenly, "Are you always this reckless with Royalty?"

"If they're rude," I said sweetly, "yes. I can be."

He shook his head slightly, trying hard not to smile. "That confidence will get you far or torn apart."

I leaned in. Just a little. Not enough to scandalize the room, but enough to test the charged space between us. "Which do you think is more likely?"

He mirrored the motion, close enough that I caught the heat of his breath, something clean with a faint trace of citrus, his piercing blue eyes locked onto mine for a beat. Then he leaned back, the drink now in his hand. *Oh.*

"You," he said, "are going to be a problem." He took a sip, paused, then pinched the bridge of his nose with a low sound of protest. "Fiora," he called.

The Thrall appeared almost instantly, sliding into the room like she'd been waiting just outside.

"Why does this taste like it went bad three weeks ago?" he asked, holding up the tumbler and frowning.

I blinked, looking at the tray to find the second tumbler still untouched. "Wait—that's mine." Oh. She made *me* that drink. On purpose, probably. This Fiora had been watching him like he strung up the stars himself. I internally rolled my eyes.

Fiora looked flustered. "Apologies, my Liege. Something must have—slipped. I'll replace it immediately."

I held up a hand, polite as could be. "That's all right. I can share Damien's. May I?"

His gaze flicked to me, a hint of darkness passing through it. Then he nodded, slow. "Yes. You may."

Fiora hesitated. "It's not...proper."

"It is fine, Fiora. You can return to your chamber." Damien said.

She gave a sharp nod and left the study, the door closing with a faint snick. I turned back to Damien and reached for his glass. He didn't speak immediately, just watched me taking sips from his tumbler. And this drink actually tasted good—*how unsurprising.*

"I meant what I said," he murmured. "About the trial."

I arched a brow, glass still in hand. "That I'm reckless?"

"That," he said, "and that you should prioritize your safety. You have already proven more than you needed to. I couldn't have made a better choice for someone to oversee them."

That turned my insides to a warm, ridiculous pile of goo. To hide it, I looked down at the tumbler and swirled what was left. "Well," I said, keeping my tone light, "I suppose I should start acting like I belong here, then."

"You do," he said quietly.

A beat of silence passed between us, not uncomfortable but full. Then he straightened and stepped forward, extending a hand toward me.

I hesitated for only a second before taking it. His fingers were warm, his grip confident but careful as he helped me to my feet. I told myself it didn't mean anything to him—just manners. But it lingered a heartbeat too long.

We walked a few quiet steps to a cushioned divan tucked along the study wall. He gestured for me to sit, and when I did, the tension in my legs finally gave way to something like relief.

"Rest here," he said. "You'll have a healer in a moment to fix that hand. Properly this time." The skin still ached faintly beneath the wrap he'd tied earlier.

I looked up at him. "You're not staying?"

"As much as I would love to spend the rest of my day basking in your insolence," he said dryly, "there are other matters to attend to."

He turned and walked off, his scent lingering even after the door clicked shut behind him.

CHAPTER 10
MIRABELLE

The sky above Emberlock had dipped into twilight, olive Celestia melting gold into its dusky greens, while the last light whispered goodbye over the weeping trees swaying at the edge of the training range. The field was empty now—Majors long gone, Tameables crated and carted.

I hadn't come to linger. I needed sleep, and I came here to grab my notes on my way back to my chambers.

Damien was still on the range. And despite every intention, I lingered. Maybe it was the way I'd let my well-crafted politeness slip around him today. Or maybe it was just the sight in front of me. Either way, I didn't move.

He stood alone near the archery stones, his cloak slung carelessly over a post like he'd forgotten it existed. Whatever shirt he'd worn beneath was unlaced halfway down, the dark fabric clinging to him in all the right places. Corded muscle under tanned skin, veins standing out like lines of intent, flexing with every casual movement.

He moved his hand in a slow, circular sweep, and the water obeyed—rising, as if it longed to be near him. It climbed upward in a glasslike spiral, elegant and impossibly smooth, each droplet catching the fading light like crystal.

Then came the shift. A flicker of Aether surged through him, subtle as breath. Heat followed.

And the water ignited. Not boiled. Not burned. It caught fire from within, flames blooming inside the spiral like a living thing. The helix unraveled in a burst of steam that twisted into the wind, catching moonlight as it dispersed like breath on frost.

One pulse of his hand—no louder than a whisper, and the vapor collapsed inward, condensing into a spear of ice, white and lethal. He spun it once in his palm, then hurled it forward. It struck the stone pylon with a thunderclap, shattering into mist and sending tremors through the range.

Before the silence could settle, he turned, arm raised. Fire bloomed. A wall of flame burst outward, towering above him, wide as wings unfurled. The air warped with heat.

Then with no warning, he cleaved it. A lance of ice shot through the heart of the inferno, slicing it clean down the middle. The two halves roared apart, hissing and vanishing into curls of smoke.

He just stood there, backlit by ruin, still as a storm between lightning strikes.

"You train alone?" I asked, my voice cutting softly through the cooling air. He didn't startle. Of course he didn't.

I didn't mean to speak. But the way he commanded the elements with such ease left me breathless in a way that made silence impossible.

"I prefer it," he said, turning just enough to glance at me. "Fewer distractions."

I stepped in fully, boots brushing over the singed earth. "Then I suppose I should apologize for being exactly that."

He looked at me properly this time. "Not all distractions are unwelcome."

I cleared my throat and focused a little too hard on straightening my sleeve to hide whatever I am feeling. His gaze lingered on me a beat longer than necessary before returning to the pylon he'd scorched.

He turned back toward the pylon, exhaled, and raised one palm. A flicker of Aether pulsed out. Fire and wind braided in a violent dance and then dissipated again.

"I was working on transition speed," he said, more to the air than to me. "The time it takes to switch from one element to another. If you can change fast enough, even Tameables hesitate."

I didn't know what to say to that. So, I watched instead, arms crossed as he summoned a wall of fire, cleaved it with a spear of ice, then shattered both with a current of wind sharp enough to slice bark off a tree. Every movement was balanced. Clean.

"Could I applaud?" I asked lightly. "Or would that throw off your perfect form?"

He didn't look at me—just flicked his fingers again, a shimmer of flame coiling briefly around his knuckles. "Depends," he said. "Are you impressed yet?"

I smirked. "Moderately."

That made him pause. He finally turned to face me, brow arched. "Moderately?" he echoed. "I will try to live with the shame."

"I wouldn't bother trying," I said. "I'm difficult to impress." *Liar. You're impressed by the way he even breathes.*

"Hmm," he murmured, stepping a little closer. "And yet, you stood there watching me for a good while before saying a word." My ears burned.

A faint smirk tugged at his mouth as he walked past me toward the weapons rack and retrieved a training staff, spinning it once before leaning on it lazily. He was still flushed from the exertion, sleeves rolled up. His collar was open at the throat, sweat slicking faint lines along his jaw, forearms taut beneath the twilight glow... *And stars, those forearms.*

"And what are you good at?" he asked like he already had a guess "You mentioned once that you weren't meant to be here."

I shouldn't have been looking at his mouth like that when he spoke. "I wasn't," I said, crossing to the bench. I kept my hands occupied, gathering my notes and tucking them into the satchel as if they deserved all my attention. "But I have skills. Bow and arrow, mostly. I'm good with aim."

"Where'd you learn?" He seemed genuinely curious.

"I taught myself. Whenever I could spare nickels, I bought an hour or two with mercenaries passing through the cities. Then I started entering small contests for nickels. Enough to buy better arrows. Eventually, I even paid for some dance lessons."

"Dance?" he echoed, faintly amused.

I shrugged. "Footwork is footwork. You'd be surprised how much it helps with dodging flying objects." Not the whole truth. The whole truth was, I paid to learn a skill that was purely beautiful. A luxury. A small, stolen piece of a life that wasn't mine.

"Seems like it paid off. You are quick." He leaned back against the pylon now, the staff resting against one shoulder. "And you don't flinch."

"Flinching costs nickels." I grinned. "You learn that early."

A flicker passed over his face. He didn't offer false sympathy, just said, "You made your own way in."

"And you?" I asked, before I could stop myself. "What's it like being raised in a Clan? In...Legion?"

He didn't answer immediately. His gaze lifted to the canopy of darkening green above, as though it might provide a cleaner version of memory. "Strict," he said finally. "Precise. Legacy matters. Aether matters. You don't question. You exceed."

"Sounds exhausting."

"It was." A pause.

We stood in quiet for a moment. I shifted slightly, the cloak he'd left earlier still lying where it had been. I hesitated, then picked it up and wrapped it around my shoulders.

He looked over again. "Are you stealing my cloak?" *Good question. Am I?*

"It was left behind," I said, seizing the first excuse that came to mind as I smoothed the front. "I'm simply giving it a better home."

"So you collect strays?" he asked.

The wind picked up. I tugged the cloak tighter. "Let's say...I have a soft spot for abandoned things."

A breath of amusement, and he pushed off the pylon and walked toward me. I steeled myself, half-expecting him to reclaim the cloak with some self-righteous Heir comment. Instead, he stopped close—too close, and reached out to brush lightly along the collar, fixing the fold I hadn't noticed I'd left crooked. His gaze dragged over me, then again, slower this time. His eyes had gone darker.

"I am not sure you realize what you are doing," he murmured, voice edged with warning. "But be careful, Mirabelle. You might end up with more than you bargained for." The words should've made me vary. Instead, they burned my core.

Then, as if the entire world hadn't just tilted sideways, he said, "Come on. It's late."

He tilted his head toward my chambers. I followed him without a word, heart still tangled somewhere in my throat, the weight of his cloak wrapped tight around my shoulders.

⊱━⬦━⊰

DAYS BLED INTO ONE ANOTHER, settling into a rhythm that felt both predictable and restless. Mornings began the same, waking early, dressing with practiced efficiency, and making my way to the training grounds. Some days, I observed the drills up close, noting the precision of their footwork, the way their power moved like an extension of their bodies. Other times, I watched from a distance, the heat of their Aether curling through the air as they honed their craft until Celestia's light began to bleed away.

And I began to understand more. I began to predict. I could predict certain movements before they happened, see the subtle shifts in stance that signaled an attack, the flicker of power just before it was unleashed. I recognized the way fire-wielders relied on bursts of speed, how those who fought shadows and illusions thrived in unpredictability, how defensive techniques could be just as devastating as offensive ones.

This so-called *reporting* had done more for me than for the warriors I was watching.

A smile crept in as I pictured the line scribbled at the bottom: *I accept bribes in fireproof boots, hot baths, or the proximity of non-catty Royal women.*

Not that I will actually write it. But I have written plenty of things in there, depending on my mood, how they've treated me that day, or how utterly exhausted I was. Sometimes I jot down observations. Other times? Thinly veiled complaints. A few lines I've written were sharp enough that I half-expected to be fired for this role.

Lately, I wasn't even sure if any of it mattered. I hadn't seen Damien in days—no presence, no passing shadow, not even a muttered correction through a proxy. For all I knew, he wasn't even reading my reports.

He had never given a single sign of it. Sometimes I wondered if these reports were just a waste of parchment, my time, and his coin. Not that I was complaining. Compared to the rest of my life, this was easily the most worthwhile use of my hours. So, who cared?

Now, where once Royals had commanded the Majors, the Elders and the Legion had taken over. If Damien appeared at all, he was a fleeting presence, there one moment, gone the next, like a phantom moving through the ranks. So, my reports, which once found their way directly into his hands, were now collected by an aide, passed along with vague assurances that he was too busy to meet with me.

Meetings. Gatherings. Visits to other Clans. Who knew what else?

It wasn't as though his absence affected my work, nor should it have mattered to me what he did beyond these walls. And yet, I found myself irritated, a slow-burning frustration I couldn't quite justify. It was absurd—wasn't it?

I let out a breath, shaking my head.

This was ridiculous. I wasn't some pining fool waiting for his attention—despite what that blonde one, Elise, claimed we'd all turn into. I had work to do. Work that might actually let me stand on my own feet one day. My world didn't revolve around things I couldn't have. And if I ever let myself believe that anyone—anyone but Amara—was sparing me more than a passing thought, I'd deserve the fool's crown.

Still, if he was so consumed by his duties, so ensnared in whatever intricate web of politics and power that kept him away—why did it feel like something had shifted between us before he disappeared?

⸺◈⸺

NEXT DAY, the noon sun hung heavy over the arena, casting long shadows on the ground as the Majors gathered. They were in their usual form, dressed in their tailored training garments.

I wasn't allowed close on days they had Tameables for training. My lack of Aether or any discernible skills apparently made it too dangerous. So, I stood from a distance, watching with a mixture of fascination and resentment as Damien and Nathan took command of the field. Damien returned without preamble, slipping back into the rhythm.

This Tameable, a monstrous creature the size of a small house, was locked in battle with the Majors. Its arms shimmered like dark purple, and its eyes burned with an ancient fury. The beast was an elemental force, controlled only by Damien's hand—Tethered to him. Tether was the bond between the Tamed Hunter and the Tameable, from what I know.

The Majors, although powerful in their own right, struggled under its massive weight and strength. I could see the strain on their faces as they tried to land a blow on the creature, but it swiped them away with ease, its tail smashing into the ground like a battering ram. Occasionally, Damien or Nathan would call out an instruction. The Majors would follow their orders without reluctance.

I found myself wondering why the training was so intense. Why push them to their limits in such a way? The Celestial Dissonance was coming, no doubt, but surely, this wasn't only about being prepared for battles between the Clans or Realms. There was something more to this. I could feel it deep in my bones.

"Impressive, isn't it?"

The voice came from beside me, and I turned to find Fiora standing there, her smile wide, but there was something cold about it.

"I see you've decided to just watch today," she said, her eyes flicking to the Majors, then back to me, appraising.

I met her smile with one of my own—small, even. "Well, when the lions are parading, the smart rabbits stay off the field."

Her lips curved into a smirk, though I could see the slight narrowing of her gaze as she took in my presence. Fiora had always been pleasant enough to me on the surface, but there was an undeniable edge to her demeanor. She was an observer.

For a moment, we both stood there, silently watching the sparring match, until she spoke again. Her tone was casual, but her words struck with the precision of an arrow.

"Curious," she said, voice light, but her gaze sharp. "You didn't seem like the cautious sort the last time I saw you near a lion."

My brow lifted slightly. "You'll have to be more specific."

"Oh, I think you remember." Her eyes flicked deliberately to my shoulder, "Why did you put on Young Sovereign's cloak?" Her voice was smooth, but the question held an undercurrent of something sharp. "You're supposed to respect him, young girl. And yet..." She trailed off, her gaze never leaving me.

The memory hit like an ember caught in the wind—days ago now, yet clearly fresher in her mind than mine. I felt my pulse quicken, irritation bubbling beneath the surface. How dare she question me like this? I resisted the urge to snap back immediately, but the words were already forming in my mind.

"Why, Fiora?" I asked, my voice low but controlled. "Were you spying on me? I didn't realize the Thralls took such an interest in *my* wardrobe choices."

Her smile didn't falter, but it became sharper. "Not just *a* Thrall, Mirabelle. His *intimate* Thrall."

The possessiveness in her voice lit a slow burn beneath my skin. Her words stung and I felt my hands curl into fists at my sides. But I said nothing. Who was I to him, anyway? Just someone pulled from the Commoners' Pool, assigned to observe a handful of Majors...and foolish enough to ache for him like every other woman in his orbit.

I was still trying to find my footing in a Realm that barely noticed I existed. He was a generous Heir—he'd treated me with unexpected kindness. I shouldn't risk it by snapping back at someone like Fiora. She was part of his world. And I have no right to be unreasonably jealous. So, I looked away, fixing my eyes on the sparring field, willing the moment to pass.

But Fiora wasn't finished. She stepped in closer, her voice lowering to a near whisper, a softness that didn't belong in her words. "It's one thing to be playful with someone like him but remember—he tolerates only a certain level of...*immaturity*."

My breath caught—though not from anger this time. *Immaturity*. Maybe because the word struck too close to the truth. Maybe she wasn't entirely wrong. Compared to Damien—his composure, his command, the weight of a Clan he wore like it was part of his skin—I probably did seem naïve. Unpolished. Fiora was bitter—spiteful, even—but that didn't mean she was wrong. Or that she didn't know him better than I ever could.

Hiding my emotions somehow, I managed to ask, "And you think I'm just a child, then? You think this just because I wore a cloak?"

I swallowed, biting back the words that threatened to spill out. I could practically hear them whizzing through the air. Her eyes glinted, satisfied with the reaction she had drawn from me. "You don't get it, do you?" she said, her words heavy with implication.

"I've seen more of him than you can imagine. I know more of him. And that means something."

I held her gaze, but this time I didn't reply. Some battles weren't worth the bruises. She stepped back, her smile widening. "Just remember," she said softly, almost like a warning. "Not everything is as innocent as you think."

With that, she turned and walked away, leaving me seething. I could still feel the sting of her words. Turning my attention back to the arena, I watched as the Majors continued to struggle against the Tameable, their movements faltering, their frustration evident. And I realized, perhaps too late, that Fiora was right about one thing—there was more at play here than I could understand.

CHAPTER II

DAMIEN

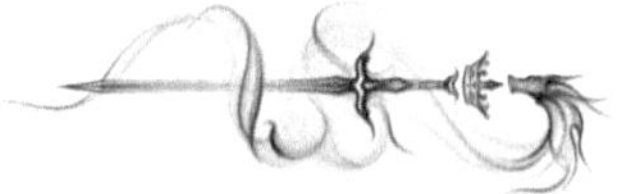

The weight of war loomed—not as a distant shadow, but as a presence pressing close, like breath on the back of the neck. The Untameables were breaking through the seals. Again. But it wasn't just the breaches that unsettled the Legion. It was what lay beneath them.

Whispers had begun to circulate, not the usual fearmongering or tavern gossip, but the kind that passed between clenched jaws and furrowed brows. There was talk of a cursed artifact buried deep within the Forsaken lands. Something old and wrong. A Crown, they said, with power enough to twist the boundaries of nature itself.

The seals closing the breaches had been restored, technically. After the Elders and Sages launched the Hunts and redrew the wards, the land had quieted a decade ago. For a time. But then it started again. Not just about the breaches, but about *why* they were happening. Some said this mysterious Crown wasn't just corrupt—it was alive in some way, whispering through the cracks it made in the world.

Across the Clans, the tension spread like hairline fractures in glass. There had been no direct confrontation, no monstrous assault. Just signs. A slow, cold certainty crawling up the spines of even the bravest. The Crown's influence, whatever it truly was, seemed to be seeping into the cracks.

As Heir, I'd seen war before. I'd sat at Council tables where alliances were stitched together with smiling lies. I'd watched them unravel just as quickly, torn apart by greed or fear. But this was different.

I stood at the edge of the war table in the Council Hall, torchlight dancing across stone walls and old banners. The room smelled of wax, steel, and unease. Nathan, head of the Legion, broke the silence first. Always direct. "Four Majors aren't enough. We need more wielders— elemental control, tactical instincts, those who don't break when the ground shifts beneath them."

Across the table, High Strategist Arlia nodded grimly. "The Forsaken Lands grow more volatile by the week. If even half the sightings are true, we're on the edge of a war we're not prepared for."

"We are pushing for more trials," I said. My voice didn't rise. "The next round of Majors is already being selected. We need every branch of elemental affinity, trained and tested. The trials will be harsher. Only the strongest move forward."

Haldric, the Elder known for his disdain of anything that couldn't be measured or explained, raised a brow. "And what of the rift sightings? The Sigil seals are failing. You can't train that away."

He wasn't wrong. The ancient wards that had once kept the Forsaken Lands at bay were thinning, revealing silhouettes of things that didn't belong in this Realm. Beasts that should only live in the stories.

The Crown's curse—if that's what it truly was—seemed to pulse with each breach. There were theories that it resonated with the seals themselves, loosening their hold. Not tearing them open with brute force.

I met Haldric's gaze. "If the Crown is behind the failures, then it's only a matter of time before the seals collapse entirely. I have already sent Sages to Nyxaria, and I went to Zarkon myself. They are searching—using every sliver of Aether and wisdom we have left. But the breach is closer to us than to them. They will take their time. We don't have that luxury."

My hand moved across the table's map, tracing the jagged border where the wards were weakest. "We will search beyond the usual pools for new Major recruits. The next phase of trials starts within days. I want candidates who can shape the elements—but more than that, who can hold *them*."

A long silence. Then murmurs. Agreement, mostly. Another pause. Then I added, "And we have already begun preparing the Hunt."

That drew their attention. The Hunt wasn't something taken lightly.

It was what made us stronger. It gave us Tameables—creatures drawn from Etheris, a Realm older than us, older than even the myths. It was Etheris that had seen us through the Celestial Dissonances, the old wars, the long winters of flame and famine. Without Tameables, the Legion would be half what it is. They were more than beasts—they were strength, legacy, survival.

But the Hunt was not without cost. A misstep in Etheris could mean weeks trapped in its warped time, or worse. If the Hunt failed this year, we wouldn't just lose our edge—we'd lose our footing entirely.

"I take it this won't be a symbolic Hunt," said one of the Elders, her voice dry, eyes sharp beneath silver brows.

"No," I said. "It will be the most vital one in decades. But that doesn't mean we will succeed. I've already sent for Izmer from Nyxaria—they seem to have more success than the rest of us."

Nathan leaned forward, his tone level but urgent. "Then we need to expand the roster. More Majors. More recruits. If half the Hunt falls, we need the other half ready to prepare for whatever is coming for us."

A murmur of agreement followed. A few grim nods.

"Only the strongest must be chosen," said a Sage beside me, steepling her fingers. "And discreetly. We can't have panic running through the Major camps."

Haldric folded his arms. "They'll sense it anyway. The recruits aren't fools. They know when the air changes."

"They do," I said. "Which is why we prepare the bunkers."

That drew a pause. "You mean...evacuation?" asked a younger Royal, barely past twenty. He looked to me, as if hoping for a denial.

"Preparation," I said instead. "If the breaches come closer, we don't risk civilians. Especially not the Pool or the lower wards."

"Quietly," Nathan echoed. "So we avoid another Caernfall."

That name still echoed in the stone halls, even years after it fell. A steady rhythm of tapping began as orders were penned, seals prepared.

"If the seals fail," I said, "we fall back to Phase Three protocols. We train. We expand. We don't spread alarm. We don't lie, either. Tell the Majors what they need to hear: the Hunt will decide the next leaders of their era. Because it will."

The Council nodded. One by one.

Nathan said. "We'll alert the Scribes. Get the maps updated. Etheris has changed. Even a few weeks can twist its paths."

Murmurs of agreement rippled through the chamber. One by one, the others began to depart, their footsteps echoing against stone as plans settled into motion.

Then I turned, moving toward my father—the Sovereign in name, but the burden now passed quietly to me. He had laid it at my feet without ceremony. And I had accepted it—not as duty, but as the marrow of my purpose.

***

BETWEEN ENDLESS MEETINGS, preparations for the Hunt, and the weight of trials that never seemed to end, I found myself grasping at stolen moments, glimpses of something that offered an escape, however fleeting.

Logic insisted she was too young, too inexperienced—a spark thrown into the heart of a battlefield, fragile against the storm I carried in my chest. I had no softness to give her. No future she could safely hold. And she deserved both—warmth, safety, a path untouched by blood and ruin. But no matter how many times I tried to reason myself out of it, that irrational pull remained.

I have no right to call it irrational. I'm the one who brought her here and I knew exactly what I was doing when I signed her name. I told myself it was logic and yes, on paper, she fit. But she wasn't the most suitable. Not by a stretch.

There were others who were trained for these duties. But I didn't choose them. Instead, I opened the door and pulled her into my world. So no, I don't get to blame the storm on fate. And maybe that's why the guilt tastes so bitter now, because I knew the risk. I know desire when I see it. And she—stars, she was clearly, intensely drawn to me. When she should've turned and run for the hills, she did the opposite.

And now, here we are, both of us standing in the fire I struck.

Even when my days blurred with exhaustion—negotiations in Zarkon, tense talks with the Sages of Nyxaria, standoffs with Elders and my own father—it found her. In passing glances. In her scribbled parchment reports, folded neatly by aides who didn't realize I still read them. Especially the parts she likely assumed I never would.

I hated that I hadn't called her out for turning reports into clever little games, into something light-hearted in the midst of blood and fire. Even with no time to eat or rest, I still read them. The little details never escaped her, and she adjusted the drills to patch every gap. She would make an excellent leader. And more than anything—I hated that I laughed at some of her jabs and doodles.

I told myself that it was mere curiosity or a passing fixation. But I knew better. It wasn't my Aether that held her attention. Not the cold reputation I'd earned from the wars I'd fought since I was a child, nor the tales of surviving them. She never looked at me like I was some unreachable myth. No poised praise, no careful charm —just her, maddeningly real. Insolent, at times. And reckless. And I, against my better judgment, found that I liked it. Perhaps too much. Perhaps in ways I did not care to examine, for she was young.

Now, I found her in her usual place—perched atop the watchtower, her gaze cast toward the distance where the Tameables roamed. Her hair caught the last light of dusk, wild strands lifting in the wind, strong like fire. A storm was brewing on the horizon, the Celestia tinged with deep hues of violet and indigo.

I approached her. "You want to be near the Tameables, I suppose?"

She turned, slowly. "Should I be flattered that you've started reading my thoughts, or concerned?" She had grown more comfortable around me since the trials, letting her words flow freely.

I let the silence stretch before replying, "Flattered."

She snorted. "Somehow, I doubt you care about my vanity."

"Then perhaps you should reconsider what you think you know of me."

She blinked, as if caught off guard or thinking about something I don't know about. But just as quickly, her smirk returned. "A mystery, are you? How tragic that I am entirely unimpressed."

My lips twitched. She turned back to the horizon, and I used the moment to step closer. Not enough to be invasive, not enough to cross the invisible boundary I set for her, and more for myself— but enough to catch the faint trace of her scent—an undertone that made my pulse tick off rhythm. I exhaled, slow, steady, fighting the instinct to move closer still.

"You don't fear them," I observed. "Most would."

She shrugged. "Fear is useful, but not when it controls you." A breeze lifted her hair, and she absently tucked a lock behind her ear. "Besides, fear alone doesn't make anything dangerous. You, for example, are terrifying, but I'm still here."

A strange, sharp pleasure curled in my chest at that. I wasn't sure if I wanted to warn her not to test the boundaries of that statement. Instead, I only murmured, "Foolish of you."

She huffed a small laugh, tilting her head. "Or wise," she countered. "Anyway, it hardly matters. I'm not allowed near Tameables even if I wanted to be, so my fearlessness is completely wasted."

Silence stretched between us, neither of us feeling the need to break it. It was a rare thing.

Then, out of nowhere, she spoke. "What is your dream?"

I frowned, caught off guard. "Dreams are for those who have the luxury to chase them."

She rolled her eyes. "Avoiding the question already? That's no fun."

I exhaled, shifting my weight. "I do not avoid things, Mirabelle. I discard what does not serve me."

She hummed as if she didn't quite believe me. "So tell me, then —what you *wish*, not what you do, or what is expected of you, but what you truly want?"

I hesitated. The answer should have been simple. "To protect and cherish Atlassian," I said, because it was the truth. It had always been the truth.

She studied me for a moment, then tilted her head. "Is that truly yours? Or just what you're expected to do?" She turned fully, leaning back against the wooden railing, arms crossed.

It was a question I had never been asked. I had grown up knowing what my life was meant for, what my father and Elders had prepared me for. The wish was theirs before it was mine, and in time, it had become mine as well. Hadn't it?

"It is expected of me," I admitted after a pause. "I grew up believing that one day, I would honor my family's legacy by protecting Atlassian by leading them well. And I am nearly there. So yes, it should be my wish."

"Should," she echoed, her lips curving slightly as she turned her gaze back to the horizon.

I exhaled and shifted my focus to her. "And what about you? I suppose your wish is superior."

She thought for a moment, then said, "To create something that outlives me. Maybe a story that will be whispered in places I'll never step foot in. Or perhaps a single act of kindness that shifts the course of someone's fate, unknown to me but infinite in its ripples. Whether small or great—it doesn't matter, as long as it's mine."

I watched her, intrigued. There was nothing grand or unreachable in her words. No hunger for conquest, no desire for glory. I let her words settle between us. She was young, and yet, perhaps she had already grasped something that I had never thought to question.

"You are strange," I murmured.

She grinned, the corner of her mouth curving with mischief. "And you're predictable, Damien."

The way her voice wrapped around my name made something inside me twist, dark and wanting. *Since when did I start reacting like this?*

She expected no reaction. But she got one. I moved, pushing past the voice in my head telling me to stop. The wind had already turned savage, carrying with it the sharp scent of rain, and the wooden platform beneath us gave a faint creak. The storm was rolling in faster, and the last thing I needed was her standing this close to the edge, distracted.

My arms braced on either side of her, hands gripping the railing behind her as I caged her in, to steady myself, but truly, to steady her. Mirabelle froze. She turned to fully face me, even from the raised ledge she stood on, she had to tilt her chin to meet my eyes. Her teasing smile faltered, her big green eyes widening even more. I watched it all, the hesitation, the sudden awareness of how close we were. I *should have* stepped back. But I didn't.

I felt her uneven breath. "What are you doing?"

Good question. I glanced down at her. "Making sure you don't fall." My voice was even somehow.

She scoffed, though her voice wasn't as sharp as she probably intended. "I'm not an idiot. I can stand on my own."

I knew. But I wasn't sure I wanted her to.

The first drops of rain broke through the Celestia, cold against the heat still lingering in my skin. Then the rain fell harder, drenching us both in a matter of seconds. Water dripped from her lashes, tracing a path down her cheek to the fullness of her lips. My throat bobbed, betraying the way my gaze lingered. Her bodice clung, outlining the delicate slope of her collarbone, the curve of her breasts, details I noticed before I could stop myself.

Her breath hitched. That sound snapped the restraint in me. I leaned in. Not enough to touch, but enough to taste her breath, faintly sweet and warm from the inside out. My restraint thinned like brittle thread. Every part of me screamed to stay, to hold on to just a fraction more of this moment.

Then the storm howled violently between the sails and made the wooden beams groan. The railing jolted under her grip, and she staggered, and before a thought could even form, I caught her. She fell against me with a soft thud, her hands splaying across my chest for balance—fingers clutching the fabric of my cloak. Her body, rain-slick and trembling, pressed into mine. Every curve met the sharp planes of me like we'd been carved for this moment. My arms closed around her, instinct and something far more dangerous guiding the motion.

She froze. So did I. Her cheek hovered near the base of my throat, and I could feel the faintest tremble in her exhale against my skin, and it took everything in me not to bury my face in her hair. Her fingers unconsciously curled tighter into the fabric at my chest. I felt the rapid thud of her heart, frantic against mine.

I held her a second too long. Then, jaw tight, I pulled away. My hands released her like they burned. Like her body hadn't just been pressed perfectly into mine, fitting far too well for my peace of mind.

I stepped back, my jaw still clenched. Hard. I could feel myself slipping into the dangerous territory of disbelief—because this wasn't me. This was not who I was. Not with anyone.

"You are not built for storms," I muttered. My voice came out lower, rougher than I intended. "You should go inside."

Mirabelle raised a brow, pretending to regain her composure. Her face was flushed, breath still ragged, water streaming in slow rivulets down her temple and catching on the curve of her cheek. "Afraid of a little rain?" she managed, voice light—but it wavered just enough to betray her.

And stars help me, I almost laughed—at the ridiculous, dangerous temptation she was. Standing there soaked and breathless, baring her teeth like she wasn't the one who'd nearly fallen apart just moments ago.

"Afraid you will catch a fever," I countered smoothly, taking a step back to give her space, "And you are not going anywhere looking like that."

"Then maybe I'll just sleep here." A part of me wanted to call her bluff, to leave her here until she realized the stubbornness of her own words. But the rain was relentless, and she was shivering slightly beneath the bravado. With a sigh, I shrugged off my cloak, the heavy fabric slick against my fingers, and wrapped it around her shoulders.

She glanced down at the heavy cloak draped over her shoulders, fingers brushing the fabric. Then, with a smirk that was far too reckless for her own good, she murmured, "Is this some secret pleasure of yours? Dressing women in your clothes..."

The words had barely left her mouth before realization dawned —her eyes widened, a flush creeping up her neck. She stiffened, then blurted out, "I–I didn't mean—I shouldn't have said that...I am..."

I let the silence stretch, watching as she fidgeted under my gaze. Then, slowly, my lips curved into something dark. "Haven't had the time to explore," voice low. I leaned just slightly closer, just enough for the space between us to feel heavier. "And no. Not women. Just you."

Her eyes widened for a fraction of a second before narrowing. This wild girl was going to unravel every last thread of my restraint.

"Come on," I said, turning away before she could turn what was left of my working brain into mush. "Let's get you inside before you catch your death."

And to my shock, she complied.

CHAPTER 12
DAMIEN

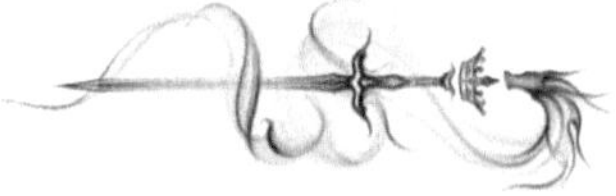

The war room was dim, lit only by the flickering of sconces and the pale gray spill of dawn through high windows. Rain lashed the stone walls outside, and thunder cracked distantly like a warning.

Nathan stood across from me at the long council table, his arms folded, jaw tight. "Three breaches this week alone," he said. "One in the northern pines, one along the eastern sealine, and the third—too close to the Emberlock stretch for comfort."

I nodded once.

"We have had no *direct* encounters yet," I said. "Just flares. The warnings only come through the Sages' Sight, not from our own scouts. We are preparing for this battle blind."

Nathan frowned. "You think it's the Crown?"

"I think we'd be fools not to suspect it." I stepped around the table, eyes narrowing on the map of the Realm spread across its surface.

Nathan gave a low grunt. "Izmir will arrive in two days."

"Good," I said. "We will need him."

He hesitated. "But what about Haldric?" Nathan went on, cautious. "He is skeptical. Says the patterns don't match. That we're rushing. And as the War Advisor to the Sovereign, he *has* the right to halt the Hunt if he sees a reason."

I didn't look away from the torn parchment. "And does he have one?"

"No. But he is close. He needs a reason to stay behind with the Sovereign. If we are riding out, someone needs to guard this side of the Realm. Preferably someone the other Elders won't question."

I braced my hands on the table, the lines of each territory etched into my mind. "Haldric follows his own logic and rarely bends. Right now, that logic says the Hunt matters more than staying back for the Clan." Nathan gave a short laugh, humorless. "Then we're already out of options."

"No," came a female voice from behind us. We turned. Irin stood just inside the threshold, backlit by torchlight, Haldric's daughter, all blonde waves and practiced poise. "You have one option left," she said. "Me."

Nathan straightened. "How long have you been standing there?"

"Long enough," she replied, unapologetic. "And before you ask, no—I don't feel guilty for listening—be honest. Would you have invited me in?"

"Irin," I said quietly, voice edged with warning.

She turned to me with feigned innocence. "What? You *need* him to stay, don't you? He listens to me."

"That doesn't mean you should involve yourself."

"Oh, but I already have," she said, brushing past Nathan to stand near the table. "You'll be leaving with the Hunt. My father will want to follow—unless someone gives him a reason not to."

I crossed my arms. "And what would that be? Flattery? Another political deflection?"

Her smile slipped, just a little. "A reminder of what's at stake. Of what we stand to lose if he abandons his post to chase theories in the field." She met my gaze head-on. "My father fears that if the Crown really is corrupting the seals, we're already too late. He doesn't say it aloud, but I know him. So I'll remind him why our Clan needs him here, not out there."

And although I knew she was the perfect solution—sharp, informed and persuasive—I wouldn't choose her. Not even if she were the last option left. My jaw tightened as a memory surfaced —a conversation that had turned sideways. A moment misread, or maybe willfully distorted. She'd wanted more than what was ever on offer. Dragged things toward promises I never made, toward rituals that meant more to her than they ever could to me. It was the kind of mistake you only make once.

Since then, I'd learned to keep things simple. Clean. Thralls had their place, and that place wasn't tangled in ambiguity. Irin had been the final lesson in that.

"I won't have you baiting your father with half-truths and charm," I said, voice cold now. "We walk a fine line already."

Her smirk faltered. "And what would you have me do? Sit and embroider? While the rest of you charge into the storm?"

"I need you not to meddle with this and do things I haven't asked for," I said, voice low and deliberate. "The situation is already twisted enough. I don't need more complications, especially ones I can see coming."

Silence settled for a beat, thick with something unspoken. Nathan watched us both, one brow raised, but wisely said nothing.

"I meant what I said," Irin murmured at last. "If you change your mind...you know where to find me." She turned and left, her perfume lingering in the air.

Nathan exhaled slowly. "You never did forgive her for *that*, did you?"

I didn't answer. Instead, I turned back to the map. Nathan's footsteps faded behind me, leaving only the wind curling through the stone arches. If Haldric agreed to stay, good. But if he didn't— then we'd proceed anyway. I wouldn't stall the Hunt for the sake of one man's doubts, no matter how seasoned. I'd find a way to make it count. One way or another.

My gaze drifted back out the window to the training field. The

Majors were finally adapting. Learning the rhythm of Tameables—how to anticipate, redirect and survive them. Even Cassian had stopped trying to outshout the fire-breather, but it wasn't enough. For every strike they landed, there was still a hesitation in their eyes. The kind that would get them killed beyond the walls. We needed sharper instincts. A kind of ruthlessness you couldn't train, only provoke.

I ran a hand down the back of my neck and closed my eyes for a breath.

They'd earned a break that afternoon, though I hadn't planned on staying. An old tradition—cake during Solstice drills. Sweet, spiced, and round as the moons. Some relic from an older time, when breaking bread together meant survival.

I would've passed, but the moment I said, "Make eight equal pieces with three cuts," eight pairs of brows furrowed in perfect synchrony.

They gathered around it like it was a second trial. Sketching cuts onto parchment, arguing angles. Rhevas theorized radial symmetry, another tried stacking slices. Cassian claimed he could do it if the knife were longer. The discussion went on for longer than I expected. It said something, I thought, about how easily brilliance could overcomplicate clarity.

Mirabelle lazily strolled over, like she was bored of the noise. Picked up the knife, made two quick cuts in cross, then a single horizontal slice through the stacked layers. Eight perfect pieces.

She plucked one free, lifted it to her lips, and took a slow, deliberate bite. And all the while, her gaze never left mine. Eyes bright with mischief and smugness. The little minx.

Then she turned on her heel and walked off and I hadn't seen her since.

❖

THE STORM'S breath still lingered in the stone corridors of Argent Estate. I'd come early, supposedly to review the reports and final training assessments before the Hunt—but we were both long past pretending that was the only reason.

I turned down the eastern wing, each step bringing me closer to her chambers. Voices drifted through the partially open door—muffled at first, then sharpening into clarity as I drew near.

"Come now, Mira. You act like I'm offering you chains," a man said, his tone too familiar, too smooth. *Jasper.*

"I'm *sincerely* not interested, Jasper." Her tone was cool. "You're wasting your time."

"Oh, I think you are interested," Jasper continued, clearly ignoring her, "just afraid to admit it. Don't pretend it wouldn't be easier—no more laundry and not even training bruises. Just silk sheets. My attention. All of it."

"Hmm, tempting. I get to be your pet *and* your furniture?" Her tone was bored. But he started to laugh, as if she'd made a joke.

It was the last sound I heard before I slammed the door fully open.

Jasper jolted where he stood. Mirabelle blinked up at me, startled—but not afraid. Before I could take another step, Jasper started to explain, "I think we—"

"You think far too much for someone who clearly doesn't know when to shut his mouth," I said, my voice like a blade unsheathed.

Jasper straightened. "My Liege—"

"Don't." The word snapped out, even as I clenched my fists, reminding myself that Heirs don't settle matters with fists. He shut his mouth.

"Damien." Mirabelle stepped in front of me the moment I moved toward him, her hand closing around my forearm, seeking my attention. "Trust me," she said softly, glancing up at me. "He is a little persistent. But certainly not smart enough to be dangerous." Her eyes flicked toward Jasper with cool disinterest. "I forgive him. Let it go, please."

I didn't move. The urge to throw Jasper straight through the nearest wall still simmered like hot coals in my blood. But I ground my teeth and turned my gaze back to Jasper. "If anyone—ever—

attempts to speak to her like that again," I said, voice low and level, "if I so much as catch a glance in her direction that I don't approve of, they will beg for the cells long before I am done with them."

Jasper's mouth twitched to say something. "Save your breath," I said coldly. "And get out of her sight."

Not brave enough to make eye contact, he mumbled a few words that may have been an apology and slunk out the door. I stood there for a long moment, jaw tight, hands still curled at my sides as I tried to breathe through the anger clawing at my ribs.

"That was...a bit excessive, don't you think?" she said, the corner of her mouth twitching upward, eyes gleaming with smile.

"Was it?" I asked, my voice still cold.

"You looked ready to murder him with your bare hands." She blinked, then laughed.

I shouldn't have looked at her when she did. Her cheek still flushed, mouth tilted in a smile that was all wrong for the aftermath of a confrontation. I took a step closer.

"Don't let anyone talk to you like that again," I said, low.

"I wasn't exactly letting him." Her tone softened. And then something shifted behind her expression. The teasing ebbed. Her eyes searched mine, just for a beat.

"Why do you care?" she asked.

I stared at her. Too long. The real answer rose—*because I'm worse for you than any of them. Because I haven't been able to rid myself of the urge to claim what was never mine to begin with.*

But I didn't say any of that. "You are under my protection. I don't take kindly to anyone who crosses that line. The entire Atlassian knows that, and it should stay that way."

Her eyes dimmed, just slightly. The flicker of disappointment, maybe. She had drawn out a side of me I barely recognized, the animal I barely restrained. It wasn't what she needed. If she thought she liked this part of me, she'd be wrong. And if I encouraged it, I'd be worse than every man I'd just threatened to bury.

So I didn't say another word. I stepped past her, picked up the parchments she'd left on the desk, and turned back toward the door. But at the threshold, I paused. Met her eyes when I said, "There is archery now, near the lower fields. You can train there if you want."

It took a breath—or two—for the words to land. A slow smile tugged at her lips, unsure at first, then blooming into a grin. Bright and entirely real. The sight of it cracked something low in my chest.

I turned away before it could splinter what lay buried in my depths.

CHAPTER 13
MIRABELLE

I was never one of those pampered children, not even when my parents were alive. No one ever tucked me in at night or told me tomorrow would be better. Even as a girl, I never dreamed of silks or sweets. All I wanted was a full belly and a quiet night where the three of us could sit together on the floor and eat without someone pretending they weren't hungry. That was happiness, to me.

I never asked for anything. Not because I didn't want things, but because I understood what wanting cost. Every nickel spent on me meant something else went missing. A thinner broth, a colder night, a quieter mother.

The only thing I ever truly bought for myself was a bow, my first real one. I must've been ten, maybe eleven, when a Duskbinder feather dropped near me in the woods. I wasn't even looking for it. Just out gathering firewood like always, hands raw from bark and cold. But there it was—dark as shadow, glimmering faintly in the light.

I traded it to a merchant and used the nickels to buy a bow and arrows. Not the carved branch and wild twine I'd fashioned in secret for years, but one with true tension and weight.

My father broke it across his knee when he found it.

Said I'd wasted nickels we didn't have on toys I had no right dreaming of. My mother tried to soften the blow, hands shaking as she held my face and whispered that she'd talk to him, that she'd explain, only to grow silent when I told her I'd earned the nickels myself. She looked at me like I'd broken something fragile and asked, quietly, never to do it again...reaching for something that wasn't meant for commoners like us.

And maybe I listened. Because even when I started earning here and there, odd work, errands for guards too lazy to do their own—I still never wasted. I reused everything. Every strip of hide, every feather I could re-bind. My arrows wore down to brittle splinters before I let myself replace them. I stretched each one until the flight warped and the heads cracked. Even then, I filed the edges to use them again.

Which was why now, standing before a polished rack of bows and arrows with strings tight, heads gleaming, and fletching sorted by weight and use, I felt almost...criminal. It sounds absurd, to feel shame for something most would see as mundane. But I couldn't breathe past the knot in my throat as I counted the different types. Different sizes, purposes. Wind resistance marked in delicate script. Everything perfectly placed.

All for me. Not something I'd asked for. Not something I'd even thought to want. Just...given. And it hadn't come from duty. That was what undid me most. It was a gift from someone who saw what I didn't say. Who had no obligation to think of me at all and still did. That kind of gesture...it split a part of me in me that not even my parents had touched. It pressed against some old wound that had never really scarred over. And somewhere in the middle of all that sharpened steel and tight-pressed strings, a thread in me quietly unraveled.

I stood there for a long moment, fingers hovering over the unfamiliar curve of polished wood. I drew the bow. The weight settled into my palm with startling familiarity, like muscle memory slotting into place. I selected one arrow, just the one that felt right.

My eyes drifted past the target boards lined up across the field, rings painted crisp in white and brown. To the side stood a post lined with carved heads—each smaller than the next. And at the very end, nestled just above the post, was one barely bigger than an apple—its wooden eye still faintly outlined in faded black.

That one.

I exhaled slowly, fingers adjusting around the bow's grip. Drew the string. One eye closed. The wind pulled faintly at my hair, steady but not unforgiving.

Then I loosed the arrow.

It sliced through the quiet, whistling through open air. It struck with a satisfying thunk—clean and exact, right through the painted eye of the smallest head. For a second, I just stared. Then, slowly—stupidly—a grin broke across my face. So maybe the skill wasn't in my imagination after all.

⚜

I WATCHED THE RECRUITS SPAR. The heat shimmered off the cracked ground, and the air was thick with the sound of clashing weapons, grunts of exertion, and barked instructions. My focus, however, was on two figures at the center of the field.

Alden, too rigid, and Lyria, too fluid for him to follow.

"Is that supposed to be a counterstrike?" I muttered.

Callan, beside me, gave a low chuckle. "Pretty sure that qualifies as attempted arson."

The midday light struck his golden hair. He wore no armor, only a fine tunic rolled up at the sleeves.

"You're not even sweating," I said, squinting at him.

"That's because I'm not the one training, dummy." He grinned. "Why would I suffer in the open heat when I can loiter beside the cleverest reporter on the field and pretend I'm offering strategic insights?"

I rolled my eyes. "You're offering commentary. There's a difference."

Callen gave a shrug. "Semantics. Either way, your friend Alden is going to get himself set on fire."

"He's not my friend," I muttered. "And yes. Probably."

From the opposite end of the sparring line, Nathan's voice rang out like a crack of thunder. "FOCUS!"

Half the recruits flinched. Cassian, on the other hand, wiped a sleeve across his brow and stage-whispered to no one in particular, "If the heat doesn't kill me, his voice will."

"Better his voice than Lyria's blade," said Rhevas dryly, never looking up from where he was adjusting his stance.

As I stepped forward, intent on pointing out to Alden that leading with your dominant shoulder was an invitation to get gutted, something shifted. Just a flicker at first—like a ripple in the air. My vision blurred, just slightly. Then came the pressure—low, at the back of my skull, like a hand pressing inward. The noise around me dipped, as if I'd sunk underwater. My limbs felt too distant from the rest of me.

I blinked. Then again.

Callen's voice was still there, but it was hazy now—soft-edged and far away.

"—Are you alright?"

I swallowed. "Fine." My voice came out too fast, too defensive.

I forced a breath in through my nose. My pulse quickened. I blinked hard, trying to steady myself, but the sensation only grew worse.

I am hearing them again. At first, it was nothing more than a faint murmur, like the rustling of leaves in the wind. But as the moments passed, the whispers grew louder, more insistent. They weren't words exactly—not in a language I could understand— but they carried meaning nonetheless.

They fight well, but they are predictable...Their strength will crumble...tide turns against them...

The voices weren't coming from the recruits. They were...elsewhere. My heart pounded as fragments of thought, alien and cold, wormed their way into my mind.

Few of us...more will come...the sigil...and will drown...ashes...price of theirs...

My knees buckled slightly, and I reached out to steady myself against the nearest post. My vision blurred, the scene before me fading in and out like a dream. The sounds of the training field— the clash of weapons, the distant shouts of the recruits—all faded into the background, replaced by the relentless whispers.

"Mirabelle—"

The voice was faint, distant, like a thread of light cutting through the darkness. I recognized it but couldn't focus. My head throbbed, and my body felt disconnected, as if I were floating somewhere far away.

Soon. They will see...will fall...regain...

"Mirabelle!" This time, the voice was louder, sharper, cutting through the haze. The tone was edged concern.

"Bella, look at me!" Another voice, steady and commanding, and it pulled me back just enough to realize I was falling. Strong hands caught me before I hit the ground, steadying me with a grip that was both firm and careful.

I tried to respond, but the words wouldn't come. The whispers were still there, faint but persistent, like a distant echo. The last thing I saw was Damien's face, his sharp features tight with worry, before the darkness closed in entirely.

⚔

My head felt like it was splitting apart. For a moment, I couldn't make out where I was. The soft mattress beneath me felt unfamiliar, and as my eyes fluttered open, I could hear voices, low, serious, and filled with tension.

"I saw it myself," came one voice, tight with alarm and barely concealed disdain. "The way those shadows rose from her hands. It comes from something corrupted. You shouldn't be keeping her this close to the castle. And certainly not to yourself."

I strained to focus, my breathing shallow as I tried to move, but my limbs felt heavy. The words of the first stranger sent dread down my spine, but another voice, equally cold, responded.

"If that's the case," the second voice said, its tone calm but laced with authority, "then she should be moved to somewhere she can be watched. With everything happening now—she could be a liability."

A deep, familiar voice cut through the tension, one I'd recognize anywhere. "Are you done?" Damien said, his tone harsh. "She's not going anywhere." he said. "And if any of you think you are going to lay a hand on her, you are welcome to try."

"Damien, you're letting this get personal," the first one...Elder, countered, his voice hardening. "We're blind to the danger she poses. It's not just a threat to you, it's a threat to all of us. You want to risk her being this close to the heart of the Clan?"

"There is nothing to risk," Damien said coldly. "If she somehow carries a Major bloodline, then we'd be fools to cage her. And if she doesn't—" he stepped forward, slow and deliberate, "—she's still mine to risk. I will oversee her myself."

His tone dropped into something darker. "Unless you're ready to challenge my command outright, I suggest you remember your place."

A few beats of silence. "She could be compromised," another Elder said more quietly. "Or worse—what if she's aiding *them*?"

"I know exactly what is at stake," he said, voice steady. "You don't need to concern yourselves with her. Attend the responsibilities that actually need your attention." He paused. "And this doesn't leave this chamber—understood?"

There was a tense silence, the kind that felt like a held breath before a storm.

"Damien—" the first Elder started again.

His tone dropped even lower, "Understood?"

There was a reluctant shuffle of feet, and I heard the Elders murmur something indistinct before their voices faded, their presence retreating. The door shut behind them with a solid thud.

I felt Damien's presence close to me, his voice softening but still edged with tension.

"They are gone," he said, as if reading my thoughts. "You can open your eyes."

I did. "Damien," I croaked.

He was beside me in a second, kneeling, his eyes scanning mine. "You should be resting."

"I'm fine," I lied, though my hands trembled where they gripped the blanket. "But I need to know...about the portals."

His expression hardened. "You don't."

"But I do." I sat up further despite the pull in my spine. "Before I collapsed, I heard something. Voices. Whispers about a sigil. About more coming through. This isn't the first time it's happened —but it's the first time I fell. I *need* to understand."

Damien's jaw ticked. He looked toward the door, then back to me. For a long moment, I thought he might deflect again. But finally, he asked. "You heard whispers?" he said, his voice measured but laced with intensity.

I nodded. "I don't know whose voices they were, but they were talking. About...more coming through."

"The portals," he began, "are in the Forsaken Lands—vast, desolate territories shared by us and the other four Clans of Telmoria." His gaze flicked to mine. "We go through these for Hunting Tameables."

"Are they the ones breaking through?"

He shook his head once. "Not the ones we brought through, but something else might be. We don't know yet."

He knew more. I could feel it in the slight delay between his words. But I didn't push. Not after what I'd just overheard. And still...he'd told me this. Even this much. And he didn't strike me as someone who trusted easily.

He hesitated again. Then, with a slow exhale, "If you hear them again. Or are not feeling well like today—you come to me. Immediately. Don't try to manage it on your own. And never hide it."

I nodded once, quietly. He studied my face for a breath longer, eyes searching. Then he straightened. "Rest," he said, voice firm but gentler now. "You will need your strength." He reached for the blanket and drew it up around me, just before exhaustion pulled me under.

<hr>

MY BODY ACHED, my limbs heavy with exhaustion, I had only fainted. Then why did it feel like I'd been dragged through something.

The sound of a door creaking made my eyes open. Damien stepped out of the bathing chamber, steam curling behind him like the remnants of a forgotten dream. His black hair was damp, clinging to his forehead before he pushed it back with a careless hand. Water droplets traced slow, glistening paths down the ridges of his shoulders. A thick velvety linen hung low on his waist, nothing more.

Heat rushed to my face. *Divine stars.*

I had never seen a naked body this close before—at least, not one like *this*. He was carved by war, honed by years of discipline. Broad chest, sculpted build that told stories I couldn't begin to guess.

It was entirely too much shoulder. Too much everything. I should look away. Instead, my traitorous eyes lingered. Then I forced them shut a heartbeat later, maybe a few heartbeats later. *Idiot.* The shame was immediate, what in the depths of the abyss was I doing?

Feign sleep, that was the only way out of a humiliating encounter. If he caught me staring, I would never recover from the mortification.

The room was silent save for the rustling of fabric from the wardrobe. I counted the seconds, waiting for the moment he would go out for his duties, waiting for the weight of his presence to dissipate so I could gather the shattered remains of my strength and escape.

"If the fading blush is any indication," came Damien's voice, low and amused, "you are not asleep."

Embarrassment bloomed like wildfire across my skin. Of course he'd waited until the silence was heavy enough to hurl a comment like that straight through it. I cracked one eye open, just enough to spot him standing near the edge of the bed, now dressed in loose, dark trousers that did absolutely nothing to make this situation easier.

"I—" My voice cracked. I cleared my throat and tried again. "You bathe too loudly. It was impossible to sleep."

His laugh was low, rich. It did things to me I really wished it wouldn't. I groaned, dragging a hand over my face. "I loathe you."

He shook his head, laughter still glimmering in his eyes. "So I have been told."

He sat beside me on the bed, the mattress dipping slightly under his weight. I kept my eyes half-lidded, watching the firelight flicker against his damp skin.

His hand reached up—unthinking, maybe, and brushed a loose strand of hair away from my face, tucking it behind my ear. "How do you feel?" he asked, his tone quieter now, stripped of amusement.

I tried to sit up, winced, and immediately gave up. "Like I got trampled by a dozen warhorses."

He reached out, adjusting the pillow behind me. "Then stop trying to sit up like you're invincible. Lie back and just rest a little longer."

For a moment, silence stretched between us. I found my gaze lingering on him, tracing the faint furrow in his brow, the tension in his shoulders that never seemed to fully ease.

Damien always carried himself with the unshaken confidence of a man who had never faltered, never broken. But now, in the dim glow of the room, freshly bathed and stripped of his armor, there was a quietness about him. Something almost...weary. He looked like someone who had been bearing weight long before anyone asked him to. But he'd grown up with the man he was meant to follow, so he should've had time to grow into that shadow.

I didn't plan to speak. But the words slipped out before I could catch them. "What's your bond with your father like?"

Damien didn't answer right away. His thumb dragged once over the curve of his palm, slow and distracted.

"A Sovereign, first and always," he said at last, like it was a phrase he'd said too many times before.

"That's not what I asked."

His lips curved—something too dry to be called a smile. "You're persistent."

"I've been told."

He leaned forward slightly, forearms resting against his knees, hands clasped loosely together. "He was…everything a Sovereign should be. Strong. Calculating. Steadfast." A pause. "He ensured I would be the same." There was something distant in the way he said it.

I hesitated before pressing further. "But was he your *father*?"

His gaze flicked to mine then, sharp and assessing. "He raised me," he said simply. "He trained me. He prepared me for the weight of the crown. For the duty that would always come first." A brief pause, then, quieter, "But no. Not in the way you mean."

I let the silence hold a beat longer before I asked, softer now, "Did you ever want him to be?"

That got him. For the first time, his expression faltered. It was only a flicker, barely there before it was smoothed over again, but I caught it.

He didn't answer. Maybe he couldn't. Either way, I didn't press.

"What about your mother?" I knew I was pushing. But this Damien—sitting beside me, stripped of duty and shadows, I hadn't seen him before. And I'd heard even less. Something in me wanted to hold onto it a little longer.

His jaw ticked. Just once. Then let out a quiet, humorless breath. "Strange, how easily you make me forget to hold back." His fingers smoothed a fold in the blanket, a gesture too gentle for the harshness in his voice. "Some things are better left untouched," Then he straightened, nodding once. "Get some more sleep, Mirabelle." Well...Ouch.

He turned before I could answer and walked out, closing the door behind him.

⬥

I BLINKED against the dim light filtering through the heavy curtains, my mind crystal clear as I came back to myself again. I pushed myself up slightly on my elbow and noticed a young woman standing at the far corner of the room, fiddling nervously with the hem of her apron.

She was small and timid, her brown eyes darting to me before quickly lowering again. Her pale silver hair was tied back in a loose braid, strands slipping free around her face.

"Who are you?" I asked cautiously, my voice still hoarse with sleep.

Her head snapped up, her cheeks turning pink. "I'm Nowa," she stammered, her voice barely above a whisper. "Young Sovereign asked me to attend to you when you woke."

I tensed. "Attend to me?" I repeated slowly, my gaze moved over her again, taking in the plain but elegant dress, the deferential way she held herself.

She nodded, her hands clutching at her apron. "Yes. I...I am one of his Thralls."

My stomach twisted unpleasantly, the word Thrall settling heavy in my chest. It shouldn't have surprised me—but the idea of another female, especially one so timid and compliant, being at his beck and call sent a jolt of something sharp through me, again.

She nodded quickly, her gaze flicking to me nervously. "I...I don't mean to intrude. Young Sovereign only asked me to make sure you were comfortable."

I shook my head, suppressing the sudden irritation bubbling up inside me. It wasn't her fault, after all. "It's fine," I murmured, brushing a hand through my hair. That's when I noticed the soft feel of the sheets beneath me, the rich scent of Damien surrounding me.

A horrible realization *hit me* for the first time. I was in *his* bed.

But then, a disquieting thought crossed my mind. How many of his Thralls had likely found themselves in the same situation? A wave of unease washed over me, and I suddenly felt uncomfortably exposed, as though diminished in some way. With a steadying breath, I pushed the thought away and rose to my feet, determined to restore a sense of composure.

Nowa cleared her throat softly, pulling me out of my thoughts. "The Young Sovereign left earlier. He's meeting with the Sovereign and the Elders."

"Oh." I tried to keep my voice steady. "So, he's not here?"

"No," she said quickly, shaking her head.

I shifted uncomfortably, it wasn't just the awkwardness of being in his bed or the timid presence of Nowa, it was everything. The unfamiliar estate, the too-close proximity to Damien, and the swirling emotions I couldn't quite pin down.

"Thank you, Nowa," I said, trying to keep my tone polite. "But I'm feeling much better now. I think I'll return to my chambers."

Her eyes widened slightly, but she nodded. "O-of course, miss. I'll let Young Sovereign know you're feeling well."

I forced a tight smile, "Thank you."

I didn't wait for her to say anything more. I made my way to the door.

CHAPTER 14
MIRABELLE

I made my way toward the old Dormitories, seeking solace in the familiar presence of Amara. She would know how to ground me, to pull me back from the storm and confusion raging in my mind or at least distract me long enough to breathe freely.

The dusk wrapped around me, illuminated only by the weak glow of a single lantern in my hand. Its trembling light cast shadows that danced just beyond the edges of my vision. The path wove through the training fields, the same path I had taken countless times. But as my steps carried me closer to the spot where I had collapsed just days ago, a chill crept over me.

And then, they returned again. Faint at first, a distant murmur that rose and fell like the rustling of leaves caught in an unfelt breeze. They were whispers, fractured thoughts sliding into my mind like shadows slipping through a crack in the door.

Each step I took felt hollow, the dirt crunching once, then unnervingly quiet. I realized I wasn't walking toward the Dormitories anymore, I veered down the side corridor toward a small clearing behind the training fields, the place where I'd collapsed before. *Why was I drawn here?* I couldn't say. But a pull was drwaing me forward, deeper into the hush.

The darkness *shifted* just ahead, between trees, like a curtain was drawn back a fraction of an inch. I froze, heart pounding, then I stepped forward. The air stilled, the world held its breath. My lantern light trembled across the grass.

Something moved in the dark. An absence of light, a horrible dent in the night. And I felt it keenly as though distant eyes were trained on me. A single drop of dread filled me.

One more step.

Leaves rustled. A shape or a ripple—no substance, just a suggestion of movement near the tree line. My hand went to my bow, fingers brushing wood.

I swallowed, hating how loud that sounded in my skull. The lantern's flame guttered but didn't go out. *Stay calm.*

My eyes darted to the tree line again. A breath of sound blew past my ear. Goosebumps prickled my arms. It felt *alive* back there, *watching* me. Just beyond the lantern's edge. Not coming forward, just movements lingering in front of me. I held my breath.

Then—the whispers again. *Difficult to learn...powers...Let them perceive...see...won't matter...Not yet...*

I forced myself to breathe. Forced my legs to move. Every nerve screamed. I didn't look back again. By the time I reached the Dorm door, the silence was louder than ever. My heart pounded in the hush. I fumbled with the latch, hands shaking so hard I thought I'd drop the lantern.

Just before I slipped inside, I glanced over my shoulder. Nothing but empty blackness, and the feeling that whatever watched me *grinned in the dark.*

I slammed the door shut.

"By the stars, Clara! I just scrubbed that floor spotless, and you're out here blessing it with your clumsiness!"

Peeking around the corner, I saw Amara standing in the middle of the hallway, hands on her hips, glaring at Clara, who was frozen mid-panic with an overturned bucket in hand. A puddle of soapy water spread across the stones at their feet, and Clara looked moments from tears.

"I–I didn't mean to—" Clara stammered.

"Didn't mean to?" Amara repeated, her voice lifting into an incredulous octave. "Didn't mean to? Oh, well, let me just call the mop faeries to come fix this, shall I? Oh, wait. *I'm* the mop faerie!"

She gestured wildly at the suds, her boots already soaked. "We were done for today, Clara. Done! The floor was spotless, I had already gone to lie down, *and now* we're mopping by lantern light because you thought the clean floor looked a bit parched?"

I couldn't help it, a laugh slipped out. Amara's head snapped toward me, her scowl dissolving at once.

"Bella!" she cried, arms thrown dramatically in the air. "You showed up just in time! Maybe you can save me from drowning in soap and sorrow. Clara, clean that up before I become the villain of the story!"

Clara nodded hurriedly, scrambling to retrieve the bucket and mop. Amara turned her full attention to me, her features lighting up as she crossed the room in a few quick strides and pulled me into a tight hug.

I let out a small laugh, the fear from earlier easing ever so slightly as I wrapped my arms around her. "You haven't changed one bit," I teased.

"Of course not," she said, stepping back to study me with a raised brow. "Someone around here has to keep things running smoothly." Her brows furrowed. "What's going on, Bella? You look like you've just seen a ghost—or a particularly nasty chore list."

Her tone was light, but her eyes betrayed her concern. For a moment, I considered telling her—about everything. But the thought of burdening her with something she couldn't possibly understand stopped me.

"I'm fine," I lied, forcing a smile. "Just...tired, that's all. Things have been a bit hectic lately."

Amara's eyes narrowed slightly, as though she didn't entirely believe me, but she didn't press. Instead, she folded her arms and tilted her head, studying me like she could see right through my words. "You sure? Because if you need to talk, you know I'm here. Always."

"I know," I said softly, reaching into my pocket and pulling out a small leather pouch. I placed it in her hands, and her eyes widened slightly as she felt the weight of it.

"What's this?" she asked, her voice quiet with surprise.

"Just a little something," I said, brushing off the gesture. "So you don't have to work yourself to the bone cleaning up others' messes. Take a break for once, Am."

Her eyes shimmered as she opened the pouch, the glint of nickels catching the light. She looked back at me, her lip quivering slightly before she threw her arms around me again, holding me tightly.

"You didn't have to do this," she whispered, her voice thick with emotion.

"I wanted to," I replied, my own voice softer now. "You deserve it."

She pulled back, wiping at her eyes with a laugh. "I'll be sobbing all over this freshly mopped floor and then blaming you for ruining it."

I laughed at her audacity. For a moment, the darkness I had felt earlier seemed like a distant memory. Amara flopped down on her narrow bed, arms flung wide. "You have no idea how dull this place is now," she said, staring up at the low wooden ceiling. "I've been reduced to arguing with Majors."

Kicking off my boots, I climbed onto the bed. It creaked as I lay down beside her, the mattress so thin we were practically touching the wood beneath. But it felt...safe. Like we were girls again, before everything became complicated.

She turned her head, curls spilling over her cheek, eyes still glinting with unshed tears and the threat of more mischief. "So," she said, dragging the word out with suspicion, "you gonna tell me why you look like someone just handed you both a crown and a knife?"

I hesitated. Her eyebrow arched. "Don't make me guess."

I groaned, covering my face with my arm. "Am I a moron?"

"That's a strong start," she muttered.

I peeked out from under my sleeve. "I mean it. Am I an idiot for reading something more into every little thing? Every kind gesture? Like, what if someone's just...being decent and I ruin it by thinking it means something?"

Amara turned on her side, propping her head on her hand. "Bella," she said sweetly, "you wouldn't know the difference between basic decency and romantic interest if it grabbed your face and kissed you."

I sputtered. "That is not true."

"It's adorable," she continued, like I hadn't spoken. "Sad. But adorable."

I gave her a look. "It's not Jasper."

"Oh, thank the stars," she said, placing a dramatic hand over her heart. "I was about to chuck that pouch straight back at you out of sheer disappointment."

I snorted. "He tried something, but no. Definitely not him."

Amara went still for a beat. "He tried what? Wait, wait...is it the Heir?"

I didn't answer. That was enough.

She sucked in a sharp breath, her voice dropping into something between horror and awe. "Mirabelle," she whispered. "You're doomed. I *knew* it, knew it from that first day."

"I didn't say anything happened."

"Yet," she sing-songed, eyes gleaming. "But the way you're clutching that pillow like it betrayed you in a past life? Yeah. It's not 'nothing.'"

I looked away, fingers twisting in the edge of the blanket. "It's not that I want anything from him. I just...I don't know what to do when someone's kind without reason. I can't tell if I'm reading too much into things or not enough."

Amara's expression softened, the humor in her gaze dimming into something warm. She scooted closer. "Hey. First of all, if he's being kind, that's on him. And second..." She sighed. "You're not the only one who needs to learn how to figure all this out. I've had a crush on someone who offered me a spoon."

I blinked. "A spoon?"

"A really nice spoon," she deadpanned. "Polished. Engraved." She laughed at herself. Despite everything, I also laughed with her.

"I think I'm emotionally illiterate," I admitted.

Amara gave an exaggerated shrug. "You'll survive," she said confidently, patting my shoulder. "And when you don't, I'll be right here offering terrible advice."

I smiled at her. I'd come here intending to spill and solve it all —every knot of confusion. But looking at Amara, seeing the way she tried to play advisor with all the grace of a panicked deer, it struck me that maybe she was just as clueless as I was.

So we shifted to something easier. Fiora, for one, being an insufferable pain. She got properly outraged on my behalf, muttering curses and plans, and from there, we spiraled into the usual mess of mundane things. Sore ankles. Vanishing bread from the kitchens. Whether the stars above Celestia really looked different when your heart was a little bruised.

Talking like we always did.

The room dimmed to the soft rhythm of her drifting into sleep, her hand still resting loosely on the pouch I had given her.

I watched her for a moment longer, a quiet fondness swelling in my chest. Then, silently, I slipped off the bed, pulling the blanket up to her shoulder as I stood. The floor creaked under my steps, but she didn't stir.

THE NIGHT AIR was cool against my skin as I made my way back to Argent Estate. The hallways were dim, save for the soft glow of light flickering from the far end. As I drew closer, I heard talking. Curious, I moved closer, my footsteps muffled by the stone floors. I peered into the room. Cassian, Lyria, Rhevas, and Alden were gathered around a large wooden table.

They didn't notice me at first, too engrossed in their discussion, but their expressions were tense, serious.

"What's going on here?" I asked, my voice breaking the quiet hum of their conversation.

Cassian looked up, a sharp glint in his eyes, but he smiled faintly upon seeing me. "Ah, Mirabelle. You're back." He gestured toward an empty seat, but I shook my head, not yet ready to sit.

Rhevas, always the more composed of the group, leaned back in his chair. "We just got back from a meeting with the Young Sovereign. The Elders and Royals were there too. They're preparing for something...big."

He hesitated, his gaze flicking to the others, as if weighing whether to share the details.

"Big?" I repeated, curiosity piqued.

Lyria spoke next, her voice low and careful. "They're planning to Hunt more Tameables. We'll be included in that Hunt. But they didn't say why. We only know that it's going to be dangerous." Her brows furrowed in frustration, as if the lack of information was gnawing at her.

Rhevas leaned forward, tapping his fingers absently on the table. "You know we've been hunting Tameables for decades? Whole Clan's been at it. And in all that time?" He gave a dry shake of his head. "Only two have been tamed in the last decade. Both by Young Liege."

He glanced around the table before adding, "Those two brought the number up to seven. That's all we have in the Hold, counting the old ones from the past century."

Lyria continued from there. "The odds rarely favor the tamers. These creatures are wild, unpredictable. If they sense danger, they won't hesitate to strike first."

I glanced at the map of Etheris—the land of Tameables, studying the marks and lines. "How many are you planning to hunt?"

Cassian snorted. "Better question—how many of us are coming back alive after cleaning up centuries of failed hunts?"

"And what about Young Sovereign? What does he say about it all?" I asked, my voice cautious.

Alden shook his head. "He's leading. But there's a coldness to him. It's as if he knows more than he's letting on." He sighed, sitting back. "None of us feel right about any of this. Why are we pushing Hunts? It's too soon."

I could see the unease in their eyes, the uncertainty that lingered even in the midst of their usual bravado. As if something far darker was on the horizon.

I swallowed, my stomach tightening. "And you four—are you ready for it? You know how dangerous this could be."

Lyria nodded gravely. "We don't have much of a choice, do we? We'll do what we must." Her tone was resolute, but I could hear the faint edge of fear beneath it. I looked at each of them in turn, feeling the gravity of their situation.

There was no turning back now for any of them. The stakes had been raised, and the road ahead was filled with more questions than answers. And as I turned to leave, my mind was filled with the echoes of their words, the weight of the unknown pressing in from every side.

CHAPTER 15
MIRABELLE

I had just begun to stir, the remnants of sleep still clinging to me when a sharp knock echoed through the door. The early morning light filtered through the heavy curtains, casting a muted glow across the room.

Before I could even move to answer, it swung open with a force that made me flinch. Damien stood in the doorway.

"Where were you?" His voice was cold, demanding, and utterly unyielding as though my whereabouts were of the utmost importance.

I sat up in bed, the shock of his sudden intrusion burning through me. "Wherever I please," I snapped, my words sharper than I intended. "I'm not your prisoner." Maybe I was overreacting. But if there were boundaries here, he'd never set them for me.

Damien's eyes darkened. "Don't test me, Mirabelle." His voice cut clean through the room. "You could barely stand when I left. And when I came back, the bed was empty."

I lifted my chin, forcing calm into my voice. "So what? I woke up, I felt well enough to stand, so I left." I met his gaze, refusing to flinch. "I didn't think you needed a report the moment I could walk again. Why would you even care?"

The restrained fury in his voice said enough. "I care because you disappeared without a word after collapsing in my arms. You don't get to vanish and play stubborn when I'm the one trying to make sure you don't drop dead somewhere."

His jaw clenched, his gaze fixed. "So no, you do not get to act like a brat and call it freedom. Not when I am the one dealing with the consequences."

I scoffed, shaking my head. "Did I ask you to bear the consequences?" My voice was low, the bitterness curling out before I could stop it. "And if you were that concerned," I bit out, "you wouldn't have left me with one of your—" I faltered, jaw tightening, "—mistresses."

"Nowa is not my *mistress*," he said, clipped and cold. "She's the quietest of them, the kindest. I asked her to sit with you because I trusted her not to overstep while I was handling what *you* don't yet know about."

I looked away, the anger still prickling at my skin, though I couldn't even trace where it began. I didn't know why I was this furious, or if I even had the right to be.

But damn him for expecting me to fall in line just because he'd shown me a fraction of warmth.

"What if I don't want to be looked after by your kindest Thrall. I don't want to sit on your bed—the one they warm." My eyes snapped back to his. "I am not blind, Damien. Or stupid. And I'm sure as hell not one of your Thralls." My voice cracked slightly, and I hated the sound of it. "So stop treating me like one."

Something in his expression shifted with realization. His gaze softened. "Come here," he said quietly.

"No." The word came out sharp. I shook my head, backing away a step. "Don't do that. Don't—whatever it is you're doing."

"I haven't touched any of them," he said. "Not since I met you."

I blinked. "Why?" I asked, almost a whisper. "Why would that even matter?" Still, it eased a weight in my chest I hadn't meant to feel.

His eyes didn't waver. "You know why."

I swallowed, hard. "Do I?" My voice came out quieter now.

"Because it feels like I'm meant to understand things you never say. You give me pieces, Damien, and I never know if they mean anything, or if I'm just confused—"

He crossed the space between us in a single breath, and before I could say another word, his hands were on my jaw, and his lips were on mine.

His lips were warm, soft, and devastatingly sure. My heart leapt against my ribs, and heat rushed up in me like wildfire. His mouth moved over mine like he was tasting something rare— coaxing, devastatingly gentle, yet threaded with a desperation that made my pulse stutter.

I'd never imagined it could feel like this.

My body reacted before thought could catch up, arching into him with a soft gasp as something low and unfamiliar curled deep in my core. A hunger for more. My knees buckled, but he caught me like he'd known I would fall. A quiet grunt escaped him as he pulled me in, one strong arm wrapping around my waist, lifting me effortlessly to meet him and I clutched at the front of his tunic, needing some anchor to hold onto.

His kiss deepened, and with each movement, it felt like he was taking something more from me. A quiet, involuntary sound slipped from my mouth—half shock, half need, and he swallowed it, answering with a low growl that vibrated through his chest and into mine. I didn't even know my body could feel like this. Warmth pooled between my thighs, aching, and I was dizzy with the need I didn't yet know how to name.

When he finally pulled away, we were both breathless, hearts pounding, eyes wide and full of something we hadn't said aloud. He gazed down at me with awe, as if he was seeing me for the first time, his expression both tender and full of admiration.

Then, gently, he leaned in again and pressed a soft kiss to the corner of my mouth. But when he started to pull back, I instinctively chased his lips, deepening the kiss before I could second-guess the impulse.

He smiled against my mouth, that maddening, knowing smile of his, and kissed me again. Slower this time, like he was memorizing the shape of my lips.

When he finally stopped, his lips lingering just an inch from mine, his breath still warm against my skin, he murmured, "Was that clear enough for you?" The edge of a smile tugging at his mouth.

I blinked, still trying to remember how air worked. My lips parted. "I—um..." I swallowed. "Yes. No. Maybe?"

He looked right into my soul while I just stared at him like my senses had been thoroughly kissed clean from my head. "I have never had anyone in my chambers for anything other than changing the linens or cleaning it."

I could feel my skin flush with embarrassment. I quickly turned my gaze away, suddenly feeling shy in a way I hadn't expected. Damien, however, didn't seem to mind my sudden discomfort. He reached up and tilted up my chin gently with his fingers, his eyes taking in my red face. "I am done pretending I don't see you, or want you, or feel like I am losing my mind every time you walk away." His words landed somewhere deep in my chest.

His thumb brushed my jaw, "Mine? That's too simple. You have settled under my skin and made yourself a home."

My breath caught. My voice came out smaller than I meant it to. "Are you mine as well?"

What was I saying? Who says that? Who asks that? Apparently, Mirabelle the Mortifying. But I didn't take it back. Couldn't, because somewhere beneath the horror of having actually said it...I meant it.

He looked at me then, really looked, and asked. "Do you want me to be?"

Something fluttered and twisted inside my chest. I gave a small nod, lips brushing his. "Yes. I'd like one of those...if you're offering."

His smile deepened. "Then you have me."

I thought he might laugh, maybe tease me for how ridiculous I sounded. But he looked at me like I'd just handed him the stars. My throat clogged, unsure if I was supposed to feel this safe. This claimed.

"You know," he murmured, brushing his thumb gently across my cheek again, "you hiss like a feral cat when cornered. But the rest of the time, you are just a wide-eyed kitten who hasn't realized her claws are sharp."

I narrowed my eyes, trying to summon a glare, but it lacked conviction. "Maybe stop cornering me, then."

He cocked his head, in that way that made him look unfairly good. "But then, what if I miss the hissing?"

I swatted his hand away. "If I am going to be with you, your intimate Thralls are gone. I'm not walking in to find one of them fluffing your pillows or cooing at you from the foot of the bed."

His brow arched, but he didn't even pause. "Fine."

I blinked. "Fine?"

He nodded. "Yes. Gone. All of them."

I stared at him suspiciously. "Just like that?"

"Just like that," he said, far too easily.

It threw me more than I cared to admit. "You can't agree that fast—it makes me sound unreasonable."

He laughed—low, warm, far too fond. "I owe you the right to be unreasonable," he murmured. "After dragging you into something you never chose."

"Hmm...yes, maybe you do," I hummed.

He reached for my hand, his touch steady and unhurried. "Let's take a walk."

"Where?" I asked, glancing up at him.

"You will see," he said.

With one hand, he picked up my cloak from where I'd left it folded across the chair and wordlessly draped it over my shoul-

ders. Then he turned toward the door, and without needing a tug
—I followed, my fingers still wrapped in his.

⚊⚊⚊⚊◄◊❖◊►⚊⚊⚊⚊

WE WALKED through a shadowed tunnel carved into the stone fort,
dim lights flickering along the path. The air was hushed, our footsteps echoing in the stillness.

"There is more at stake than what the Majors see," he said, his
fingers shifting slightly, skimming the soft skin at the bend of my
elbow before retreating. "The Elders and Royals have their own
agendas. The Majors fight battles, but the real war is being decided
elsewhere."

I swallowed hard, willing my voice to remain steady. "And
that is?"

"Etheris." He paused. Etheris was the land of Tameables. We
grew up hearing a lot about it.

He continued. "Nyxaria has captured more Tameables than we
have in recent decades. Their methods are unconventional, but
effective. Their Royal leading the Hunts will accompany us this
time."

I already knew of Nyxaria's reputation—their ruthlessness,
their ability to wield shadow like an extension of themselves. But
that wasn't what unsettled me most. It was Damien. The way he
was telling me this. The way his trust was growing, word by word.
Was this a test or something?

I hesitated. "And you? Do you agree with this?"

His gaze was sharp. "Atlassian's survival depends on what
happens next. So I support the decision."

Before I could press further, his hand wrapped around my
wrist as he guided me down a narrow hallway. We turned past one
of the unused east corridors, where dust curled in the lantern light
and the air felt cooler. His pace slowed as we reached a low
archway half-hidden by a crumbling tapestry.

"You trust me?" he asked without looking back. I nodded back.

He lifted the edge of the tapestry and revealed a passage carved into the stone—even more narrow, torchlit, and descending at a sharp angle. A tunnel. A hidden way.

"There are places here even most Royals don't walk," he replied. "This one's been kept sealed from the outside for a reason."

As we stepped into the hush of the tunnel, the stones seemed to absorb the sound of our footsteps. Cooler air met my skin, tinged with damp stone and a trace of the past.

I hesitated as he pushed the stone doors open, revealing a vast chamber bathed in an eerie blue light. Cages and pens lined the walls, but they weren't the crude prisons I had expected. Each enclosure was crafted with care, adorned with symbols that seemed to pulse faintly. And within them...creatures unlike anything I had ever seen.

"Aetherium Hold," Damien said, both of us looking into the chamber. "This is where we keep the Tameables after they have been captured." He paused, his gaze steady on mine, as if measuring my reaction. "I'm sure you have *seen* Dreadclaw." *Seen him? That was one way to put it.*

The creatures were massive, some with scales glistening like gemstones, others with fur that shimmered as if catching light from another Realm. Their eyes glowed faintly, and though they were restrained, their presence was overwhelming.

I froze in place, my breath catching in my throat. "They're..."

Damien held me closer. "They won't attack. Not after they have been captured. They are loyal to the one who tamed them."

I tore my gaze away from the creatures to look at him. "And you brought me here because...?"

He looked at me. "You need to understand the depth of what I am tangled in." His eyes flicked to the glowing enclosures. "And I figured this was the right place to start. You were always too curious not to wonder about them."

I swallowed hard as I took in the sight of the creatures before me. My gaze flicked nervously from one to the other. My boots echoed softly on the stone floor as I moved past the first set of enclosures, careful, slow.

One of the Tameables turned its head slightly— its eyes glowing with something ancient, something aware. I could feel Damien's gaze on my back as I moved. He was letting me explore this on my own terms.

I stopped in front of a pen veiled in soft, shifting shadow. Whatever was inside breathed in time with the light, steady and deep, as though it had long since made peace with being here. But as I drew closer, I felt a pull deep within me, a stir of emotions that hadn't been there before. And in that moment, some *thoughts* began to surface.

At first, the whispers were faint—mere fragments brushing the edges of my mind, like distant echoes on the wind. But as I neared one of them, the murmurs sharpened, gaining clarity with each step. This one's form was colossal yet ethereal, its fur a shifting, gray that seemed to ripple like storm clouds in twilight. The color undulated with the light, as though it were made from the very fabric of the Celestia itself. Its eyes, deep, molten pools—held an ancient, knowing gaze, unblinking as they locked with mine, drawing me in. Its long limbs moved fluidly, something rippling beneath the shimmering surface. Despite its immense size, there was a tranquility about it, an air of ageless wisdom, as though it had witnessed eons pass in silence.

I hesitated at first, unsure of what was happening, but then it happened again—the murmuring whispers, a language I couldn't comprehend, yet somehow understood. The feeling was like warmth. Not just warmth in the physical sense, but a warmth that came from deep within. A bond, almost, though it was not quite the same as what I understood from Atlassians.

The creature's thoughts filled my mind like an echo. *Safe...*It wasn't words, but the meaning rang clear. It wasn't angry, nor fearful—it was at peace, longing for connection. And somehow, I understood.

My hand reached out instinctively, trembling at the feel of the creature's thick fur. As my fingers brushed along its side, the warmth deepened, and the creature's massive body seemed to lean into my touch. I began to focus on my thoughts, trying to respond, unsure if I could, but knowing I had to try. The feeling was over-whelmingly gentle. We spoke without words, just a gentle exchange of emotion.

I sent back a thought—*I'm not afraid. I'm here to see.* And in response, the creature's body eased, its breathing slow and steady, and then, much to my surprise, it began to purr—a low, resonant sound that seemed to vibrate through my very bones. The purring was like music, and it made me laugh, a soft, uncontrollable giggle escaping from my lips as the warmth of it washed over me, filling me with a strange sense of joy.

For a moment, everything felt perfect. Everything felt right. The world around me seemed to fade, and I was caught in the beauty of this connection, this strange bond with a creature I didn't fully understand but still felt like something pure.

But then I became aware of Damien standing just behind me and I glanced over my shoulder. His expression was one I couldn't quite read at first—surprise, perhaps, mixed with something else, maybe awe. He was staring at me, his gaze was fixed, unblinking, as if he couldn't tear his eyes away from the scene unfolding before him.

I turned back to the creature, a smile still lingering on my face, my heart fluttering from the unexpected connection. As I took another step closer, a murmur from behind me broke the moment.

"You are not supposed to be able to do that," he said at last, voice low and uncertain.

I blinked. "Do what?"

He nodded toward the creature, its head now resting against the bars, pressed lazily to where my hand had been. "They don't behave like that. Especially not with someone who hasn't hunted them. Not with—" he caught himself.

"You can say it," I said, a bit dryly. "A commoner."

Damien's gaze flicked to mine at the word. "That's not why I stopped myself," he said. "You being a commoner has nothing to do with this." He looked back at the creature. "They don't behave that way with someone outside the Legion. You weren't trained for this, haven't been conditioned for the bond or the threshold rituals. Yet—" his gaze flicked to me— "it responded to you."

He took a step closer. "Most who try to approach without formal ties end up mauled —Whip-tail aside. They sense intent. You didn't assert dominance or Aether. Still, it leaned into you like it had known you all its life."

There was no judgment in his tone, just calculation, awe beneath control. "That doesn't happen. Not even with Tamers who have spent years building a bond."

He folded his arms, his voice quieter now. "So, no—I didn't mean *commoner*. And commoner is not an insult. I meant untrained. Unbound. You shouldn't be able to do this. But you did."

I stood there, hand still half-raised, fingers tingling from the warmth that lingered in the creature's fur. My mind fumbled somewhere between why is this happening and what in the stars am I supposed to say now.

He spoke with layered logic—centuries of protocol, weighty truths, and I stood stunned, wordless and wide-eyed. Definitely not like someone who belongs in this chamber.

I panicked. "I mean...it was fluffy."

Damien blinked once. Then he rubbed a hand over his mouth, smiling like he didn't know what to do with me. "I don't know if you're adorable, or maddening, or if I am just in awe of the entity that is you," he said.

I fluttered my lashes in mock offense. "Definitely the last one."

He makes it feel easy to just *be*. So maybe I didn't need to second-guess every breath I took near him. Maybe he wouldn't regret opening this door or treating me like I belonged on the other side of it.

We walked back the way we came, the soft echo of our steps swallowed again by the tunnel. When we reached the chamber's entrance, Damien paused, his hand brushing the carved edge of the stone as if sealing something away. A moment later, the door hissed shut with quiet finality—hidden once more behind time and silence.

"Don't tell anyone what just happened," he said without looking at me.

That caught me off guard. "Why?"

"The Elders are already interfering with everything," he said, voice certain. "After yesterday, and with the Hunt coming, I can't have them sniffing around you while I am not here."

I swallowed and gave a small nod. My pulse skipped, but I understood more than I could say.

He stepped closer, and though his tone dropped, it held the weight of steel. "Promise me you will keep this between us. Until I can figure out what it all means. Until I am back."

I nodded again, this time slower. "Alright. I won't say a word."

His shoulders eased on the exhale, somewhere between relief and resignation. Then, as if we hadn't just shared a secret that might unravel both of us, he extended a hand.

"Come on," he murmured. "Let's get out of here before someone realizes the chamber's been unsealed."

I slipped my fingers into his and walked back to my rooms.

DAMIEN

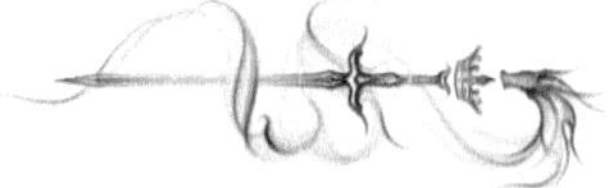

The preparation hall buzzed with motion, too much for the hour, and just enough for the weight of what was coming.

Long wooden tables groaned beneath crates of dried meat, bundles of herbs, coils of rope, and rolled up sleeping furs. Aether-treated tools lay arranged in precise lines, catching the firelight in soft glints—daggers, hooks, climbing picks, reinforced gloves. The scent of leather oil and woodsmoke hung in the air, undercut by a sharp trace of forge-ash.

Thralls, men and women, moved with quiet efficiency, slipping between the long benches with practiced grace. Some hammered final brackets into chests or added last-minute stitching to packs. Others carried bundles of firewood, wrapped oilcloths around food stores, or bent over makeshift tables filled with scrawled maps and wax-sealed directives.

Ophira was at the center of it, naturally, bent over a weapons rack, checking each blade and bolt like she meant to carry them into battle herself. She didn't look up as I approached, only muttered, "The latches on the eastern packs need checking. Again. I don't trust them to do it right."

"Then swap them," I said, rolling my shoulder as I surveyed the room. "Better to be sure now than test them mid-hunt."

She nodded once and moved on. I turned toward the main corridor, only to find Izmer leaning casually against a column near the archway, a satchel slung over one shoulder.

He pushed off the column when he saw me, his long coat shifting like smoke behind him. "Well, well. Look who's still pretending to sleep in a bed of diplomacy instead of the knife-strewn nest we both know this is."

"You are early," I greeted the hunter from Nyxaria, keeping my tone flat.

"I prefer punctuality. Besides, I thought you'd appreciate the joy of my company before everything turns to ash."

His smirk was familiar, but beneath the easy posture, he knew he wasn't here to play games.

"You brought your own gear?" I asked, eyeing the blade at his hip. The hilt gleamed with polished silverwork. Izmer followed my gaze, brushing his gloved fingers lightly across it. "I trust my Hunters less than I trust yours," he said easily. "And yours less than I trust the Elders. So yes. I brought my own."

I let out a dry breath. "That bad?"

"Please." His smile curled slow. "I've survived this long by assuming someone's always two steps from betrayal. It's worked well so far."

"That is one way to live," I muttered.

"It's the only way if you're planning to return from Etheris with your throat still intact."

We stood like that for a moment, the space between us filled with shared silence. Then, his tone changed. "So. Haldric's coming."

My jaw tightened. I didn't respond at first, just met his eyes. "None of our attempts to stop him worked," I said finally. And I wasn't about to involve Irin again.

He clicked his tongue, a sound of disapproval, but he didn't push. "Then it's tomorrow."

"First light."

He tilted his head, a more serious look settling in. "Don't let him get under your skin. Haldric might think he's leading this expedition, but we both know who everyone will look to when things go wrong."

"I am aware."

Izmer gave a soft grunt of approval and vanished down the corridor with the same ease he'd arrived, and I turned the other way, toward the deeper wing of the estate.

I found Rowane where I usually did—tucked between two stacks of scrolls. He looked up as I approached, then tilted his head toward the bench beside him without a word.

"I started looking into her," he said, not bothering to clarify. He didn't need to. Mirabelle.

"And?" I asked.

Rowane sighed, dragging a hand through his curls. "Records are thin. Conveniently so. Her town has one surviving census from seven years ago, and her family's listed as merchants. No mention of any relocations, no debts registered. She barely exists on paper."

He gave me a long look. "You still want me to keep going?"

I nodded once. "Quietly. She's already being watched. I don't want anyone catching wind of this, not until I understand what I'm protecting her from."

Rowane leaned back, studying me like he was deciding whether to say what was clearly burning behind his eyes. Then he said it anyway. "You know, I think this is the longest I've ever seen you talk about someone without looking like you want to kill them."

I glanced at him. "Do you want to be killed?"

He grinned. "There he is."

A beat passed. The room was quiet and comfortable, almost.

"She's softened something in you," he said at last, more thoughtful than teasing. "You used to be all motion and instinct. You calculate, decide, act with purpose. You don't usually linger on a terrace watching a woman train with a bow for half an hour like a smitten statue."

I didn't rise to the bait. "She needed a better grip."

"She needed you to stop looking like you were two seconds from offering to hold the damn bow for her."

I looked at the scrolls in front of him, then to him. "You finished?"

"For now." He sat back, smug.

I leaned a shoulder against the wall, folding my arms. "That smugness—does it work on that healer you keep pretending not to notice?"

Rowane blinked, caught off guard for a moment. "Who?"

I gave him a pointed look. "The one who always finds a reason to brush past you in the infirmary. Twice yesterday, and you didn't move either time."

He scoffed, too quick. "Coincidence."

"She nearly sat in your lap."

"That was *once*—"

"And you looked like you forgot how legs worked."

He pointed a warning finger at me, eyes narrowing. "You're deflecting."

"Am I?" I asked, deadpan. "Or are you just bad at dodging?"

He shook his head, muttering something under his breath about Heirs being insufferable, but he was grinning all the same.

He stood after a moment, stretching with a low groan.

"You should go see your father," he said. "Before he starts rewriting war plans in blood out of spite."

"I will go." I paused. "He is not in a good mood lately."

Rowane snorted. "Was he ever?"

I shook my head "No. But it's gotten worse lately."

"Maybe you will both finally get along through mutual brooding." Rowane said, patting my shoulder as he passed and vanished around the corridor.

FATHER'S STUDY was cloaked in shadows, the golden glow of the lanterns doing little to dispel the weight of its atmosphere. He sat at the head of a long table, his silver hair, sharp jawline, and piercing blue eyes as regal as the crown he wore during court.

My relationship with my father has always been formal, distant even. I grew up knowing he wasn't cruel, nor was he neglectful, but we never acted like we were related. My mother, the Empress of Atlassian, had died giving birth to me. Not immediately, her decline had been slow, drawn-out, as if the act of bringing me into this world had cracked something inside her that never healed. No one ever said it aloud, but there had always been a whisper of belief— that my birth had cost her more than her life.

A tragedy that seemed to hang between my father and me, unspoken but ever-present. From the moment I could walk on my own, I carried the weight of expectations pressed onto my shoulders without room for complaint.

I'd heard whispers from the Elders, though—how he'd once been a different person and deeply in love with my mother, his Eternis. It's hard to reconcile that image with the person I know now. Sometimes, I wonder if losing her broke something in him. Perhaps, in some ways, it broke something in both of us.

I stepped inside, my boots clicking against the marble floor. His gaze met mine. "Your Hunt departs tomorrow," he said without preamble, voice as smooth and cold as glass. "Are your units prepared?"

I stepped into the room, letting the door shut behind me. "They are."

He looked up at me then, blue eyes steady. "And are you?"

"I don't have the luxury of not being ready."

A beat passed. Something unreadable flickered across his expression, maybe a calculation of how little I'd give away.

"You'll be crossing into territory where alliances bend like reedgrass," he said. "Nyxaria will be watching. The Sages will be listening. Do not mistake the silence for peace."

"I don't."

I paused, then added, "The Majors didn't take the news well. About being deployed. They think it's too soon for them." I didn't blame them. Most had barely caught their breath since the last trial, and now they were being sent into Etheris with creatures that didn't belong in any natural order.

"They will be coming anyway," I said. "Everything's moving faster than we are ready for. Waiting won't slow it down."

He nodded once. "That's yours to command." No approval or disapproval. Just that ever-neutral tone, the way he handed me full responsibility without ceremony. But I knew what that meant. If I failed, I'd fall alone.

"Was it the Elders' council that insisted on sending more of their own to accompany us?" I kept my tone even. "Or was that your call as well?"

My father leaned back in his chair, fingers steepling. "The decision originated with the Elders. Haldric, Ophira, Velis and the rest were deemed essential oversight, given the weight of this Hunt. I agreed to it. It's only for a few days."

Only. I bit back a sound that wasn't quite a sardonic laugh. "So, we strip the capital of its council for the Hunt none of them are prepared to face," I said. "And leave the remaining Royals to manage what exactly?"

His eyes narrowed just slightly. "Your concern is noted. But I trust the remaining council can manage. The Hunt takes precedence."

"Haldric thinks he can command the field. That will be a problem."

"Then make it not one."

I held his gaze. There was no point in arguing. I didn't argue further. So I gave a short nod.

His eyes narrowed in thought before his tone shifted, becoming more pointed. "And what of the female? Mirabelle, isn't it?"

I stiffened, though I kept my composure. "She's been moved to a palace chamber," I answered calmly. "The Majors who live with her will be joining the Hunt, and it was necessary to ensure her safety in their absence."

His lips pressed into a thin line as he studied me. "Damien," he said, his voice weighted with an edge of warning. "Do not lose sight of what is important. That one is a distraction. Whatever this is, treat it as a passing indulgence, nothing more."

My jaw tightened, but I didn't respond immediately, waiting for him to continue.

"You know your future holds greater potential," he said, his tone taking on a note of certainty. "An eternal-alliance with a Clan, potentially Zarkon or Nyxaria, could solidify our standing in the Realm for Celestial Dissonance," my father continued, his voice steady and calculating. "Their Heiress would make a formidable Eternis for you. The ceremony would bind her to you, ensuring their loyalty, securing our future."

Zarkon—wielders of lightning and storm. An alliance with them would be invaluable and I'd agreed to the idea the last time it was raised in passing—out of strategic sense rather than personal interest. Back then, I didn't care much about my Bonding. I knew it would happen eventually, for the sake of the Clan.

A union that would tether me not just to a person, but to a duty, to a fate that was never mine to choose. Yet now, the very thought was suffocating. I masked my reaction. The memory of Mirabelle flared unbidden, and the idea of binding myself to another felt like a chain tightening around my throat.

That was also a reason why I had tasked Rowane with uncovering more—quietly, thoroughly. Her story had too many cracks, and if she wasn't what she claimed to be, I needed to know before anyone else did. Whatever I found, it would stay with me. For her sake as much as mine.

For now, let them overlook her, dismiss her as unimportant. The longer their attention strayed from her, the safer she would remain. I kept my voice steady. "I understand," I replied, concealing the discomfort that churned beneath the surface.

"Good," he said, his gaze steady with quiet approval. "You've always known where your duty lies, Damien. See that you don't forget it."

"I will take my leave," I said finally. "I need rest before tomorrow."

My father nodded, dismissing me with a wave of his hand. I turned and left the study. I could not afford distraction. Yet my foot led me to her chambers.

⸎

I'D MOVED her to a chamber closer to mine. I told her it was for convenience—closer to the infirmary, easier to keep an eye on her. But the truth was simpler, and far more selfish. Part of me feared that one day she'd wake up and see it all clearly, how reckless it was to give herself to me. But even if she did...there wouldn't be much she could do about it.

I stepped in without knocking. The door creaked softly, but she didn't notice, too absorbed in the task before her. She sat on the floor, hunched over a balance scale and a set of small metal weights. All of them were identical to the eye. But only one was heavier.

I stood at the doorway, silent, arms crossed, watching her.

A simple trial. One used to test recruits in logic and restraint. Most of the Legion could solve it in two weighings or fail miserably trying.

She was frowning, plotting, scribbling something across a half-creased parchment, then scratching it out again with a frustrated grunt. She twisted a strand of her hair so tightly around her finger I half expected it to snap. Then she released it, only to bite her bottom lip and mutter something under her breath before trying again. Her sleeves were rolled to the elbow, ink smudged along the side of her wrist.

She was breathtaking in the kind of way that crept up on you, even when she was like this. Absorbed in her thinking. She shifted again, huffing, leaning back on her palms like she'd just sparred a full round. The neckline of her tunic dipped just enough to reveal the soft curve of her breasts, the faint, flushed shadow resting in the space between.

The sight made my mouth go dry, not from desire alone, but from the brutal awareness of how easily she turned want into something far less manageable. She wasn't trying, and that made it worse. My every instinct screamed to go to her. To drag her up into my arms and finally taste what I'd denied myself since the first night she stood in that courtyard—full of defiance and trembling grace.

I shouldn't have found it as enticing as I did. But she wore her femininity like a second skin, effortless and unknowing. Was she crafted from everything I ever desired, or had I simply come to desire everything she is? I don't know.

But I didn't move. I couldn't, wouldn't, be the man who reached first and claimed what he wanted. Her first touch, her first trembling sigh, her first surrender—they were all mine to savor. And she deserved to feel them too. To trace the shape of each new sensation before the next one came like a tide. If I took too much too soon, she might not know where one feeling ended and another began. And I wanted her to devour every single one of them—every breath, every ache, every flicker of what I would give her, until she knew exactly what it meant to be wanted by me.

So, I stayed—leaning against the doorframe like a man bewitched, biting down on the need like a curse, and watched the most dangerously beautiful thing I'd ever seen try to solve a puzzle with ink-smudged fingers and absolutely no idea that she was undoing me.

There were eight identical-looking weights in front of her, one of them just slightly heavier. You were allowed only two weighings to find it. Most of the players failed on the first try. Some took longer just trying to figure out where to begin.

At first, those being tested consider just splitting the eight weights into two groups of four and weighing them. But that wouldn't work. Even splitting the weights into four groups wasn't enough to narrow it down.

I'd already watched her cross those options out with an annoyed scowl. Then, I saw it—that gleam in her eyes. And before I realized it, my own lips curved at her smile.

She had it. *Three, three, and two.*

She split the eight weights into three groups— three on one side, three on the other, and two left aside. Then she weighed the first two sets of threes. The right side dropped lower.

If they had balanced, it would've been easy. The odd one would be in the *pair* she'd set aside, and one final weighing would reveal which.

But since one side was heavier, she ignored the lighter group and the two extras. That left her with three suspects. She picked two from the heavy group and weighed them. Equal. Which meant the last one, the one she didn't weigh—was the heavy one.

She smirked at it, and tsked softly, "There you are, little shit."

I shook my head—half smiling, pushed off the doorway and stepped forward.

She startled. Just for a breath, but her entire body flinched. She scrambled back a step like she'd been caught trespassing.

That stopped me cold. A bitter, furious pulse surged through me at whatever twisted piece of her past had carved that reaction into her bones. She blinked up at me, then caught herself, cheeks flushing. "You really shouldn't sneak up on someone when they're solving the world's most important riddle."

I didn't smile. Not until she gave a small, crooked one of her own, and I let it ease the tightness in my chest.

I crossed the room and lowered myself onto the floor beside her. My leathers weren't made for it, and neither was I, but I sat anyway. Then reached for her wrist, slow, and pulled her toward me.

She let me. I settled her between my knees, her back resting lightly against my chest, my arms bracketing either side of her.

"Why did you flinch?" I asked softly.

There was a beat of silence, then, "I didn't."

I said nothing. She sighed, curling her legs under her. "It's nothing. I'm just mostly…aware. Of everyone. Their presence. Movement." A pause. "I don't react well when caught off guard."

Could be a deflection, but I didn't press. Her voice dipped quieter. "When are you leaving?"

"First light."

She nodded slowly. "Will it be dangerous?"

"Yes." She didn't ask more, just leaned slightly back into me like she hadn't meant to but forgot to stop herself.

My chin hovered near her hair, close enough to catch the scent of parchment and the cedar-musk bath brick she must've stolen from my bathing chamber. It was a distinct scent— sharper on me but softened somehow on her skin and I was starting to like it too much.

"I have arranged for a Thrall to assist you while I'm away," I said quietly. "She will see to anything you need. And Rowane will be staying behind. If you need help, he'll find you."

She didn't reply, but her fingers tightened slightly around my knees. Like she was grounding herself.

"Be good," I added, voice low, near her ear. "Stay low. Don't give anyone reason to look too closely right now."

"I'm always good," she murmured, but her voice was softer than usual. Then, a beat later, added, "Mostly."

I leaned in, my breath skimming the shell of her ear before I caught the delicate curve between my canines with just enough pressure to make her moan. The sound went straight to my groin, hot and insistent. I shifted her to my lap, turning her toward me, breaking contact before I lost the will to.

Her head tilted, just enough to glance at me from the corner of her eye. "I don't like the sound of you making arrangements, like you're planning to disappear."

"I am not." The words came out heavier than I intended. "But I need to know you are looked after."

She studied me for a long moment, then, with a slow exhale,

she reached up and curled her fingers into the front of my tunic, pulling me to her.

I leaned down, catching her chin between my fingers and pressing a kiss to her lips, slow, grounding, like I meant to tuck a promise into her skin. Then one more kiss on her brow.

"Sleep," I said, voice low. "Before I forget why I shouldn't take you to my chamber tonight."

Her fingers curled in my tunic, a silent pause like she might protest. But after a breath, she let go. I rose, stepped back and looked at her one last time. "Don't ever leave your door open to the hall again."

Then I left, before I gave myself another reason to stay.

CHAPTER 17

MIRABELLE

Sleep had been elusive. No matter how I twisted and turned, rest would not come. The new chamber in the palace was grand, adorned with silken drapes and polished stone floors, yet it felt anything but welcoming. An uneasiness had crept into the night, curling into the corners of my mind, clinging to me like a second skin.

By the time I finally succumbed to shallow sleep, the morning had already begun its slow ascent. I awoke groggy and later than usual, the remnants of restlessness still clinging to my limbs. Not that it mattered, there was little for me to do here.

Everyone I had worked alongside had already left for the Hunt, and with Damien gone, the palace felt even less like a place I belonged. If I were being honest, I doubted anyone here was particularly fond of my presence. Even the very walls seemed to regard me with disdain, their gilded embellishments cold and unwelcoming.

I exhaled sharply, brushing off the foolish thought. Staying here felt suffocating, and with nothing anchoring me to the palace, I decided I would go to Amara's for a few days. At least there, I wouldn't feel like a trespasser in my own skin.

After freshening up, I made my way toward the dining hall.

The halls were quieter than usual, a subdued tension lingering in the air. As I passed through one of the archways, the hushed murmurs of conversation caught my ear.

The Elders or Royals.

I stilled, pressing myself slightly against the cool stone as their voices drifted toward me in low, urgent tones. Something they said about Damien being in danger caught my attention. Their words were clipped, careful, as if they feared even the walls might betray their secrets.

"...the Forsaken Lands..."

"...ruins have already been arranged in sequence to open a passage, one way...for Hunting."

A sharp prickle ran down my spine. The Realm of Etheris—the Hunting grounds. My breath caught as I strained to listen.

"...could open with the key...until they return."

A pause. A breath. Then, in a voice barely above a whisper—

My stomach twisted. The words were spoken so quietly, as if merely acknowledging them would make them true. I inched closer, but before I could catch more, the conversation faded, their voices swallowed by the shifting of robes and the sound of retreating footsteps.

I stood there for a moment, heart pounding, mind racing. Damien. In danger? They'd said something about danger.

I wanted to go with him. Stars, I *should* have gone with him. I'd tried to convince him, hadn't I? Said I could help, that maybe whatever I did that day in the Hold—whatever tether I'd somehow sparked, might be useful again. But he shut me down before I could even finish it. Told me it would be dangerous with untamed Tameables involved. That they reacted unpredictably during hunts, more feral, more reactive. That he wouldn't risk anything happening to me.

I knew what he meant. Overprotective bastard. Always so *decided*. But also wrong. Because I *could* help, and I could feel it in my bones—no, in my *gut*. That same deep pull that flared when the Tameable leaned into my touch instead of tearing me apart. Whatever this strange connection was, it wasn't just a fluke.

One way. That's what they said, about a key and opening it. Couldn't I do the same?

I had nothing left here. Nothing but stale air, silence, and the ache of waiting. But there, in Etheris, maybe I had a place there, a purpose. A way to keep him safe while being with him. A way to prove, not just to Damien, but to myself, that I wasn't just something to be protected.

I wasn't a risk or liability, but the answer they hadn't considered. And if I was right about the fragments I overheard...I could go. I *would* go. The thought echoed in my mind like a struck bell, reverberating through my bones. I clenched my fists, I needed a plan.

How was I supposed to get there without anyone noticing my absence?

A reasonable person would have stopped there, weighed the risks, and perhaps chosen a path of patience and logic. Fortunately —or unfortunately—I was not particularly reasonable when it came to matters of life and death.

I was going. The 'how' could come later.

I turned on my heel and strode back to my chamber, my mind already whirring through the possibilities. Sneaking out of the palace premises wasn't the hardest part—I had done it before, and I could do it again. The problem was getting through the portal without raising suspicion. I needed a story, something convincing enough to buy me time but not so elaborate that it would unravel under scrutiny.

I began packing my satchel, stuffing in essentials while brainstorming.

Alright, Bellebelle, think. What's your best trick?

A little lie. Nothing terrible. Nothing that would get anyone hurt—except, perhaps, me, if I was caught. But Damien would understand. If anything, he'd be more frustrated that I didn't tell him outright than the fact that I was going.

I grinned to myself. *Oh, he was going to be so mad.* But later. For now, the plan.

Step one: Tell the palace I was going to stay with Amara. Completely believable. She'd cover for me, no questions asked.

Step two: Get to the Forsaken Lands without a trail. A bit trickier, but with some subtle maneuvering and the right corridors, I could manage.

Step three: Convince the portal guard to let me through. That part needed a sprinkle of luck and a well-placed lie. I would say that Nathan—erm...yes, Nathan—had instructed me to leave for my own safety. Given the lingering hostility toward me in the palace, it wasn't entirely implausible. If anything, Damien would believe it without hesitation.

Brilliant.

A neat little fabrication that would settle his mind, allowing him to focus on the hunt rather than worrying about me. See? I was helping. I swung the satchel over my shoulder, standing tall with an air of satisfaction. Look at me, problem solver, tactical genius.

Now, to execute step one.

<>◇<>

I ARRIVED at the Forsaken Lands. The journey had been relatively uneventful, the lie well-crafted and the deception seamless. I couldn't help but feel a strange mix of relief and disappointment, though. I had imagined a tense exchange, a few well-placed words, perhaps even a hasty escape...but as I reached the clearing where the portal should be, there was no one. No guard to distract, no one to trick. It was as if the Realm had conspired to make my task far too easy.

Before me stood the portal, a swirling mass of light and shadow, encased within the jagged remnants of what might have once been ancient stone arches. The air around it seemed thick with power, pulsing in slow rhythms like the heartbeat of the world itself.

The stone was worn, the edges softened by time and neglect, but there was an undeniable majesty to it. It wasn't like something I'd seen before, neatly framed and guarded with meticulous precision. I had known this place was here long before I had ever set foot in the Forsaken Lands. It had been whispered in quiet corners, murmured during hushed conversations behind closed doors. Legion and Royals alike spoke of it when they thought no one was listening, fragments of knowledge. It was simple to find, even mundane in some ways, nothing like the winding, treacherous paths I had imagined.

The stone beneath my boots was cool, cracked, and uneven, the remnants of some long-lost civilization. Vines and moss had claimed parts of the ruins, curling up around the base of the arch, clinging to it like forgotten memories.

I stepped forward, the pull of the portal strong. I hesitated for a heartbeat, wondering what awaited me on the other side. The Realm of Etheris. The very name filled me with an odd combination of excitement and unease. It was a place of myths, of legends, of beasts and powers unlike anything in my own world. Would I return? Would I even be able to find my way back if I get lost?

But there was no time for hesitation. Damien was out there, and I had my reasons for going.

I stepped toward the portal, but just before I reached it, I found the huge, rusted key. I frowned, bending down to pick it up. The metal was cool against my fingertips, aged, worn from time.

I turned it over in my palm, glancing around instinctively, but the ruins remained as empty as before. My eyes flicked toward the base of the portal's archway, where something else caught my attention, a circular groove in the stone, partially obscured by curling vines.

A slot. It looked just wide enough for a key. I hesitated, brushing my thumb over the rusted metal. I pressed my lips together, then sighed. No harm in trying. I slid the key into place and twisted. A soft click echoed through the air. A ripple pulsed beneath my feet, subtle, almost unnoticeable. Like the ground had sighed. The portal flickered with intense light.

I exhaled, brushing my fingers over the vines curling around the ancient stone. Beneath them, something hummed faintly. I pushed the vines aside, revealing a faintly glowing inscription beneath the overgrowth. It looked incomplete, until now.

The portal's swirling light flared, pulling my attention forward. I closed my eyes, inhaled deeply, and took a step into the shimmering void.

The world seemed to bend around me as I passed through the portal. The air shifted, growing thicker, colder, and for a moment, I lost all sense of direction. A force I couldn't comprehend pulled at me from every side, urging me forward, and then…

The ground beneath my feet vanished. I tumbled through the air in a dizzying whirl of light and shadow, the wind rushing past me, my heart pounding in my chest. My thoughts scattered like leaves in a storm as I plummeted toward the unknown.

I landed with a soft thud, breathless but unharmed.

I blinked, the world around me shifting as I tried to focus. The air felt different, yet fresh, almost alive, but more so than I could have imagined. The familiar weight of the ground beneath my feet was gone, replaced by a weightless sensation that tugged at my very being. I stumbled slightly, then caught myself, steadying my breath.

I think I landed on Vael'Thir, the heart of Etheris. A world unlike any other, suspended between the islands and the void. The Celestia was purple here, stretched really far above me, impossibly vast, cradling floating islands in its embrace. Their edges were adorned with cascading waterfalls that fell into endless mist, vanishing as if swallowed by the very air. I could hear the faint sound of water, the rumbling hum of rivers, blending with the cool breeze that swept through the air, carrying the distant cries of unseen creatures. Some of them might be Tameables, their calls haunting yet beautiful.

Towering stone arches rose in the distance, carved by forces unknown, their surfaces bathed in an ethereal light. Fading colors wove between the colossal forms, as if the very essence of the land itself danced with the light. They spanned across the horizon, like forgotten bridges leading to the islands far beyond my sight. Islands, some massive, others tiny, floated there, linked by flimsy bridges, ladders, and magic threads that seemed to defy the laws of nature.

The land I stood on spread wide, a stunning tapestry of sprawling forests, jagged mountains, and valleys that stretched endlessly, eventually vanishing into the mist that blanketed the lower regions. The vastness of it all left me breathless, as if I had stepped into a world forged from the dreams of ancient legends themselves.

Etheris. I had arrived.

And then immediately, a rush of panic struck. Now that I was here, I realized I had no idea what to do next. How exactly does one *find* anything in this vast Realm. Sure, the beauty was overwhelming, but beauty doesn't exactly give directions.

I let out a frustrated breath and pinched the bridge of my nose. *Great.* I looked around at the endless horizon, the waterfalls tumbling into nothingness, the arching stone bridges that connected floating islands.

"Okay, Bella," I muttered to myself, "get it together."

I looked at my feet and sighed. Sure, I had to get somewhere. But exactly where? Somewhere to start. Somewhere to figure out what in the world had brought me here.

Wait, what if I could find some kind of trail? Like breadcrumbs, but...magical breadcrumbs?

I shook my head, and with a gruff sigh, I decided to take a step forward. There had to be some sort of direction, right?

As I took a few more steps, I noticed something. The grass beneath my feet had been flattened, as if several feet had passed over it. I followed the flattened path. Surely someone—some*thing* —had been here recently.

This could be the sign I needed, a small beacon in the wilds of this unknown Realm.

"Ha! Take that." I'm already on the right track!

I chuckled aloud, even though no one was around to hear. I followed the trail, the grass crunching beneath my boots. The path didn't look particularly well-worn, just enough to give me a subtle nudge in the right direction. It felt like an invitation, a call to keep walking.

After a while, I came upon a glistening stream, its waters so clear I could see every pebble at the bottom. Some creatures, tiny, with delicate wings, hovered above it, their laughter like chimes as they fluttered about. Cute. Definitely cute.

As I approached, I bent down to take a drink, forgetting for a moment that I had no idea if the water was safe. "Well, what's the worst that could happen?" Worst would be me turning into a giant, glowing mushroom or something. I am too parched to care.

I cupped my hands and drank, the cool water sliding down my throat. It was refreshing, crisp, and had no immediate side effects. I stood up, wiping my mouth with the back of my hand, and scanned the surroundings once again.

I kept walking, the trail leading me deeper into the lush terrain. I could hear the faint chirps of unfamiliar birds, the rustling of leaves, and the low hums of creatures far off in the distance. There was a magical energy in the air, a haze thick and intoxicating. It wrapped itself around me, urging me to explore every corner of this strange world.

Thoughts of Damien drifted into my mind. He had to be fine, he was strong, capable, and more than prepared for anything this world could throw at him. I pushed the worry aside. There was no time to linger on such thoughts. Time was slipping away, and I had my own reasons for moving forward.

Soon, I passed a patch of fruit trees, the branches heavy with fruit in every color imaginable—reds, purples, and yellows. Some of them sparkled, others seemed to glow from within. I hesitated for a moment, a thought flickering in the back of my mind. *Are they poisonous?*

But then again, they looked too good to be poisonous.

I picked a ripe-looking red fruit and took a bite. Sweetness exploded in my mouth, a burst of flavor unlike anything I'd ever tasted. It was like a mix of honey and citrus, tangy but smooth. I took another bite and walked on, enjoying the snack as I ventured further.

I couldn't help but grin. *Okay, Etheris, I am becoming a teeny bit font of you...*

As I continued my walk, I started noticing the creatures that inhabited this world. They were as magical as everything else here —some small, others large enough to be intimidating. The day passed in a blur of wandering. I didn't exactly know where I was headed, but the landscape kept changing. One moment, I was passing through a thicket of trees so dense that I could hardly see the Celestia, the next, I was on the edge of a vast field, the glowy grass swaying in the wind. In the distance, a mountain range loomed, jagged and imposing.

I knew I was choosing the wrong paths but somehow ended up again on the fading grass trail. Despite all the wandering, something kept me going. Even though my legs grew tired and my stomach began to grumble, I didn't stop. I couldn't stop.

But as the light began to dip lower in the Celestia, casting everything in a soft, golden glow, I realized just how far I had walked. My feet ached, my energy drained, and I was beginning to regret not stopping for a proper rest.

Just a little farther, I urged myself. *Come on, Mirabelle. You can do this. You've come this far.*

And then, as I rounded a bend in the forest, I saw an area of cave-like structures in the distance, nestled at the base of the mountains. The stone was dark, the entrance slightly dim, but there was something comforting about it. It looked...safe. Or, at least, it looked like a place where I could rest.

I took a few steps toward it, but then I stopped.

I was exhausted. My feet felt sore, and the thought of continuing on seemed impossible. I glanced at the cave one more time. The entrance was inviting, but I could barely keep my eyes open.

Tomorrow, I thought, the idea of a good night's sleep too tempting to ignore. I'll explore the caves tomorrow if I don't find Damien and the others.

With a sigh, I made my decision and plopped down on the soft ground nearby, leaning back against a moss-covered rock. The air was cool, the sounds of the land humming softly around me, and for the first time since I arrived, I allowed myself to relax.

CHAPTER 18

MIRABELLE

I jolted awake, a strange sensation brushing across my face. My eyes flew open to find a creature—a double-headed python, its body sinuous and furry, hovering just above me, its tongues flicking in and out of its mouths, each of them seething with a hiss that made my heart race.

I froze for a moment, too stunned to react, my mind struggling to make sense of the situation. But instinct quickly took over. I scrambled backward, my breath ragged, pushing myself into a sitting position as the creature advanced. Its eyes, one pair dark and unblinking, the other bright with a twisted gleam, locked onto me with a predatory hunger.

I fought to push myself up, but the creature was faster. It lashed out, its long bodies coiling around my waist, pulling me back toward it with a force that nearly knocked the wind from my lungs. The ground beneath me scraped against my skin as I struggled, my fingers digging into the ground as I tried to fight the constricting pressure of the snake's coil.

No! Not like this! I thought frantically.

As its second head reared back, its mouths gaping wide, I felt the surge of power rise within me. My shadow, as black as ink, began to swirl around my limbs, instinctively lashing out like a protective cloak. Dark tendrils spread across the ground, wrapping around the creature in a desperate bid to free me.

But before I could do more, a sudden shift occurred within the serpent's mind. *Wait.* I could feel it, its thoughts, a slithering, distant echo in my mind, as if the creature itself was confused. Something in the tether sparked, and I felt a strange empathy bloom within me. It wasn't hostility anymore, just...curiosity.

Its movements slowed as its second head, which had been aimed to bite, now hovered above me, its tongue flicking in a manner almost...playful?

I blinked, momentarily stunned by the shift. Its double-headed gaze softened, and before I knew it, one of the snake's heads, the one closest to me, lowered with an almost affectionate gesture, its forked tongue brushing gently across my cheek, leaving a cold trail of saliva.

*Oh, no...*I groaned inwardly. *What in the endless Abyss is going on?*

The creature's coils loosened slightly as it continued to nuzzle me, a low, vibrating hum escaping its throats. It was as if it were...*licking* my face, showing affection like a misunderstood puppy.

I wrenched myself free with a grunt, finally managing to break the snake's grasp. I fell backward into the grass, panting from the sudden exertion. *What just happened?* I couldn't fathom how this creature, so intent on devouring me only moments ago, had suddenly turned into an...oversized, furry, affectionate serpent.

I sat there, taking a few breaths to gather myself. My dress was torn in several places, the fabric ruined by its wild embrace. The snake lingered nearby, still flicking its tongues in my direction, as if waiting for some kind of approval.

I huffed, wiping the remnants of slime from my cheek. "Look what you've done," I muttered, shooting it an exasperated glare. "My dress was new, you know. That's not how you greet someone!"

The creature blinked its multiple eyes, its two heads bowing in what I could only interpret as guilt. It made no sound, but it slithered back a few paces, clearly acknowledging its mistake.

"Good," I said, smoothing out my torn dress with a sharp sigh. "Now, no more of that. Got it?"

It flicked its tongues in what might have been a sheepish gesture, before slowly slithering off, vanishing into the brush as quietly as it had appeared.

I stood, still shaking my head. The cool air around me was tinged with the scent of the forest, and I could hear the distant sound of running water and rustling leaves.

That's enough adventure for one day, I thought. I set my sights on the cave, a sense of relief washing over me as I walked toward it. Hopefully, no more surprises awaited me in the shadows. With a determined breath, I set off once more, but the moment I took my next step, a sharp sting shot up my leg. I stumbled slightly, catching myself against a low-hanging branch. Oh, perfect. That overgrown menace hadn't just ruined my clothes, it had left me limping, too. A true overachiever.

I cursed under my breath, pressing my fingers lightly against my calf, trying to gauge the extent of the damage. A bruise, maybe. Nothing felt broken, but walking wasn't going to be fun. I muttered some more curses to myself, wincing as I took another step.

Despite the limp, I pressed forward, refusing to let a minor inconvenience keep me from reaching the caves. As I neared, the landscape became denser, the towering stone formations cast long shadows across the land, patches of moss and vines creeping over the ancient surfaces. Then, as the wind shifted, I heard it. Voices.

My heart leapt with relief. Faint, but unmistakable—the rhythmic exchange of conversation, the occasional clink of metal, the murmurs...The caves were ahead, and if I had heard correctly, *they were here.*

I exhaled, tension draining from my shoulders. At last. But before I could take another step, a hand seized my arm. A strong hand.

My body twisted sharply as I was wrenched backward, a firm grip pinning my wrist with a practiced ease. Before I could even *think* to react, I found myself staring up, straight into the sharp eyes of a man who could only be described as handsome.

Dark blonde hair fell messily over his forehead, his chiseled features framed by the flickering glow of torchlight from the cave's entrance. His attire marked him as a warrior, fitted leathers reinforced with metal, a wickedly sharp blade strapped to his belt. He radiated ease, yet something about him coiled with tension, a predator toying with its prey.

His lips curved into a smirk, amusement dancing in his storm-gray eyes.

"Well, well," he drawled, tilting his head. "What have we here?"

I stiffened, my pulse spiking.

"Let go," I snapped, trying to yank my arm free. His grip didn't budge.

"Now why would I do that?" he mused, his gaze dragging over me lazily, as if he had all the time in the world. "Here I was, thinking this Hunt would be dreadfully dull...and then *you* show up."

My eyes narrowed. "Who are *you*?"

His smirk deepened. "Shouldn't *I* be asking that? You're the one trespassing, sweetheart." His voice was smooth, laced with mischief, though his hold on me remained firm.

I forced myself to stay calm, meeting his gaze with steady defiance. "I have the right to be here. *Trust me.*"

His grip slackened slightly, but the intrigue in his eyes only sharpened. "Hmmm..." He leaned in just a fraction, the corner of his mouth twitching. "Not really sure I believe that. A lady like you doesn't exactly scream *fearless warrior out for the Hunt.*"

"I don't need to," I countered, my chin lifting defiantly.

"Maybe not," he conceded, his voice dropping into a dangerously playful tone. "But that *does* leave me with a problem, doesn't it?"

I arched a brow. "What problem?"

His fingers brushed against my wrist, deliberate, teasing. "Deciding what to do with you."

I glared. "You could start by letting me go."

He exhaled a laugh, low. "Oh, I *could*..." His fingers slid away, but instead of stepping back, he tilted his head, studying me with the kind of intensity. "Or," he mused, his smirk returning, "I could just kill you."

I stiffened, but before I could even process the threat, his eyes gleamed with something almost wicked.

"...Of course," he added, his voice thick with innuendo, "I do know some *very* sweet ways to go about it."

My face flamed. "You're despicable."

His smirk widened, entirely too pleased with himself. "And yet, you're still standing here, looking at me."

I had half a mind to slap him. Or kick him. Or maybe both.

Instead, I exhaled slowly, forcing myself to focus. Whoever he was, he was clearly enjoying *this* far too much. But I didn't have time to waste exchanging sharp words with a cocky warrior who thought entirely too highly of himself.

I took a step back, eyes steady. "I don't have time for whatever game you think you're playing."

"Oh, but I do," he mused, folding his arms. "And lucky for you, I'm feeling generous. So, tell me, *intriguing trespasser*—why *are* you here?"

I exhaled, rolling my shoulders. "That's none of your concern."

His eyes flickered with something sharper. "Oh, but it is." His voice dropped lower, the amusement giving way to something almost...assessing. "Because if you don't belong here, then you're a threat. And if you *do* belong here, well..." He trailed off. "That makes you *very* interesting."

I exhaled sharply, leveling him with a glare. "I'm here for Damien."

His eyes gleamed with fresh amusement. "Ooooh," he mused,

drawing out the syllables with entirely too much pleasure. "I didn't know Damien had a *baby sister*."

My face flamed furiously. "I am *not* his baby sister."

He tilted his head, thoroughly enjoying himself. "No? Then elder sister?"

"I'm his *reporter*," I declared, grasping at the first thing my exhausted brain could conjure.

His brow lifted. "His *reporter*?" He let the word roll off his tongue, as if tasting it. Then, with maddening nonchalance, he crossed his arms. "Now *that* is definitely interesting."

I huffed. "Oh, for the love of—"

"What exactly is a *reporter* doing here, all alone?" he interrupted smoothly, studying me like one might study an unpredictable storm. "I suppose Damien doesn't have a clue that a little *reporter* is lurking about somewhere in the middle of the Hunt?"

I opened my mouth, then promptly closed it. Damn it. I had used up my *lie reserves*.

My mind scrambled for something, *anything*, that might sound even remotely believable, but all I managed was a slow, pathetic, "He...doesn't know yet, okay?"

His smirk turned downright insufferable. I sighed, rubbing my temples. "I'm here to *meet* him. Is he okay?"

He let out a low hum, considering. "As okay as a day of a *failed* Hunt can make him."

I sighed again, deeper this time. Of course. It would be just my luck that I snuck into this Realm only to find Damien *not* in the best of moods.

"Can we go to him?" I asked, shifting my weight impatiently. "And who *are* you, anyway?"

He pressed a hand to his chest, feigning deep, exaggerated hurt. "I am *deeply* offended that you don't recognize me by looks alone."

I frowned, unimpressed. "Should I?"

His smirk curled lazily. "I am Izmer Castellane." He let the name hang between us, as if it should mean something grand.

"The *infamous* Royal in charge of capturing Tameables for Nyxaria."

I blinked. Then blinked again. *Ehm...okay, him.*

He leaned forward slightly, eyes twinkling. "I thought surely you'd heard *tales* of my...abilities."

I exhaled slowly, shaking my head. "*No*, and you are *too* cocky for your own good."

He laughed—an easy, deep sound, and added. "Perhaps." Then he turned on his heel, gesturing ahead. "Come along, little reporter. Let's go find your *not* brother."

I rolled my eyes, but followed, nonetheless.

⬥

Izmer let out an exasperated huff, his eyes narrowing as he studied my slow, deliberate pace. "I've seen moss move faster." he said, his voice tinged with irritation.

I bit back a sigh, trying to hide the discomfort plaguing my steps. "My leg is bruised, I might have twisted it," I muttered, "so bear with me."

He shook his head, clearly unimpressed with my explanation. Before I could react, he moved in swiftly, his arm sweeping around my waist. In a single motion, he lifted me off my feet, cradling me sideways against his chest. My heart leapt in surprise, and I was too stunned to speak. The shock left me breathless for a heartbeat, but I quickly regained my composure, and with the fierce urgency of someone whose pride had just been wounded, I shouted, "What are you doing? Put me down!"

Izmer, the insolent fool, didn't even acknowledge my protest. He carried on as if my protests were mere whispers on the wind, his steps as purposeful and steady as before. I immediately began to kick and struggle in his arms, the indignation swelling inside me. "Put me down, now!" I demanded, my fists pounding against his chest.

"I'm just doing both of us a favor," he said calmly, unfazed by my resistance. "Cooperate, or I'll toss you in that stream right there."

The nerve of him! "I'll walk," I snapped back, my voice hardening with each word. "I'm not a child to be carried around."

Izmer didn't seem particularly bothered by my outburst. In fact, he barely spared me a glance. "What are you afraid of?" His voice, dripping with amusement. He glanced down at his own body, as if admiring himself. "Feels too hard to resist this, doesn't it?"

I snorted in disbelief. "Yes, sure, dummy." I muttered, my eyes rolling with exaggerated exasperation.

Despite my sharp words, I had to admit, Izmer was cocky and annoyingly good at it. Not that I would ever be interested. There was only one person on my mind, and it sure as hell wasn't him.

But he instantly felt like an overconfident older brother I never had—pushing buttons just to see what would happen. He moved with surprising speed, his grip firm, as though my protests were nothing more than an inconvenience to him.

"Put her down or I'll pull your heart out and make you watch it beat, Izmer." A voice laced with venom. Damien.

He walked toward us from the direction of the cave, the darkness in his eyes sharpening as they locked onto Izmer and the arms holding me against him. I twisted, tried to pull away, but his grip held firm. Yet Izmer didn't seem to notice, or perhaps he simply didn't care.

He raised a brow, his expression unchanged, as if he were merely amused by the situation. "I didn't know helping an injured lady was a crime, Damien," he quipped, his voice dripping with sarcasm.

I tried to signal to Izmer to hush, but before I could finish, my body was suddenly wrenched from his grasp. The scent of Damien, musky and male, washed over me as his strong hands enveloped me.

His free hand went straight to Izmer's throat, squeezing. "NO

ONE. TOUCHES. HER." Damien's voice was a low growl. *Erm...this is spiraling out of control.*

Izmer raised both hands in surrender, his lips curling into a grin despite the situation and his bulging eyes. "Oh, *wow*. Got it," he said, stepping back just when Damien released him.

Damien's gaze shifted to me, his expression softening ever so slightly. His concern was palpable, though his anger remained just beneath the surface. "Are you well?" he asked, his voice a mixture of worry and caution.

I swallowed hard, still trying to regain my bearings from the sudden upheaval. "Why can't we talk alone?" I asked.

I had to get between them before things spiraled. Damien looked ready to snap, and if Izmer kept poking at him for amusement, I wasn't sure I'd be able to hold him back.

Damien's eyes flicked to me, taking me in as his fingers tightened around me. "You're fine," he muttered to himself.

I took a breath and steadied myself, resting a hand gently against his chest. "Yes, I am," I said quietly. "Let's go?"

He gave a single nod, still keeping me close as he turned. "Prepare for the next Hunt," he called to Izmer over his shoulder. "We won't be long."

Izmer, for his part, didn't seem all that offended. He waved us off with a smirk. "After you, then. I'll let you and your *reporter* have your little moment." But fortunately, he didn't push it further.

As we walked away, I felt Damien's hand tighten ever so slightly around me, the warmth of his touch comforting. I couldn't help but wonder, in the midst of it all, if he would always feel the need to protect me this fiercely.

He led me into the caves, and I couldn't help but take in the surroundings. The entrance was draped with weeping trees, their long, cascading branches heavy with dew, as though mourning the intrusion into their sanctuary. The air was thick with mystery, a heavy, moody atmosphere that hung in the space around us. The faint sound of wind rustling through the branches added to the eerie serenity of it all.

The interior of the cave, however, was an unexpected contrast. It was cozy, almost deceptively so, given the rawness of the world outside. The walls were lined with black stones, smooth yet rough in places, as if shaped by time itself. In the center, a platform of rock had been carefully arranged, with a mattress atop it. I had to admit; they had spared no expense in creating a comfortable space. Even in a Realm as wild as this, they had managed to create something from the palace, luxury that felt oddly out of place here, yet oddly welcome. Lamps lit in every corner, giving the interior a tinted glow.

He gently set me down on the mattress, the softness of the fabric a relief against the strain in my limbs. Damien stood over me, his tall form casting a long shadow against the rocky walls. His voice cut through the silence. "Do you even realize how dangerous it is to walk through those unstable regions of Etheris?"

"I wasn't exactly out there trying to die, Damien," I snapped, then immediately regretted the sharpness. But he was being a bit unreasonable here.

"I thought I asked you to stay safe in the palace chambers," he said low, voice taut with restraint.

"Yes." Maybe I should tell him I came to make sure *he* was safe. But judging by his reaction, it wouldn't go well. Maybe I should try something subtler to ease the tension. "But don't you think I belong—"

"You belong where I put you," he snapped back. "And if I'd thought that place was here, in this damn Realm, I would have brought you myself."

My throat tightened. That hurt—but I deserved it. I'd come charging into a Realm I barely understood, armed with nothing but overconfidence in a tether I couldn't explain. Sure, I'd calmed a double-headed python here, but...probably not the best time to bring *that* up.

A silence stretched between us, heavy with everything we weren't saying. Then, with an edge creeping into his tone, he added, "Still doesn't explain why you let Izmer cradle you like a newborn."

I groaned, flopping back against the pillows. "Stars! He picked me up. I didn't *ask* for it. The man has the subtlety of a thunderclap."

Damien didn't reply, so I lifted my head to look into his stony face. "And the only reason he initiated it," I added tightly, "was because my leg is injured."

His brow furrowed, the irritation melting into something more serious. He lowered himself to the ground beside me, one knee bent and the other drawn up slightly, his hands reaching for my leg. Gently, he lifted it and placed it carefully on top of his thighs as he inspected it. I couldn't help but melt into his touch, though careful, he left trails of goosebumps both of us pretended to ignore.

The scene before me was a striking contrast to the rigid expectations of royal propriety. The Heir of Atlassian, seated on the floor with the leg of a commoner draped across his lap. The Elders would surely faint at such a sight. It was a breach of every tradition they held sacred.

"What happened?" he asked, his voice low, concerned.

I winced slightly. "It's nothing," I said, waving my hand dismissively. "Just twisted it, it'll go away in a day."

Damien's gaze lingered on the bruise for a moment, but then he shifted, his expression softening. "I will arrange a healer to attend you." Then he looked into my eyes. "This injury is all the more reason you shouldn't be here," he said. "I knew you would go wandering the moment my back was turned. And judging by your record, you would find the most dangerous part of Etheris and plant yourself in the middle of it."

Panic flared in my chest. If I didn't steer this conversation away from that danger soon, he'd have me shipped back through the portal by morning. I couldn't risk that, not even if he was safe now. I couldn't return to the palace. Not with the Elders breathing down my neck. That one day was enough for me to know that.

I forced a steady breath and schooled my expression.

"Well," I started, keeping my voice even, "the palace isn't exactly known for its Mirabelle-friendly hospitality." I gave him a pointed look, trying to make my words sound casual, but even I could hear the edge of defensiveness creeping in.

Damien didn't respond, but it felt like he was listening.

"And then Nathan, "I trailed off just long enough to sound reluctant, lowering my voice, "He said maybe it'd be better for me to stay out of sight. Away from all the wrong eyes."

Still no reaction. His silence made it harder to keep going, but I pressed forward.

"And then I saw Jasper lurking near my chambers," I added, frowning. "That sealed it." I was wrapping truth in just enough fiction to keep the seams from showing.

For a moment, I thought he might press, but then his jaw eased. The tension drained from his frame like a slow exhale. "I see," he said finally. "Then you stay here."

I blinked, startled by the ease with which I'd convinced him. But I didn't let it show.

He rose, brushing dust from his palms. "Rest while we prepare for the Hunt." A pause. Then, "The Thralls will be nearby, handling supplies and food. I'll ask them to prepare something warm for you."

I nodded. That knot of tension in my chest loosened.

"Thank you," I murmured.

He looked at me for a long moment, then stepped closer. His knuckles brushed my cheek—light, almost absentminded, before his hand lifted mine slightly—he pressed a kiss to my knuckles.

"Sleep," he murmured, barely above a whisper. By the time the door closed, I was already half gone.

CHAPTER 19

MIRABELLE

Sleep had come easily, wrapping me in an embrace I hadn't felt in what seemed like ages. But now, as my mind cleared from the haze of rest, one sensation eclipsed all others—hunger. Pushing myself up from the mattress, I noticed the ache in my legs had faded. The healer might have worked on them while I slept.

I stepped outside the cave, my bare feet meeting the cool, firm ground.

The plateau sprawled before me in staggered levels, each alive with movement. Thralls bustled about, their long, elegant ears twitching as they worked, some tending to fire pits, stirring large pots of simmering broth, while others chopped wood, their steady, rhythmic strikes echoing across the encampment. They moved with quiet efficiency, their green-veined hands swift in their tasks.

A cluster of Royals and Elders sat gathered near a central fire in another plateau, their expressions a mixture of severity and ease. There were more of them here than I had expected. When I'd heard about the Hunt, I'd assumed a small, select group would venture out—nothing more than a necessary task. I hadn't anticipated something akin to a gathering, a near-festival in scale.

It felt less like a hunt and more like the forging of a miniature Clan.

A familiar voice called my name, and I turned to see Lyria and Rhevas lifting their hands in greeting. I smiled and returned the gesture, watching as they slipped easily back into conversation.

Should I go over? Would they see me as part of the Hunt...or just someone lingering where she didn't belong? They would ask what I was doing here, and I shouldn't be here in the first place. I exhaled. No, then.

Pushing aside the thoughts, I made my way toward the cooking area, where the scent of sizzling meat and fragrant herbs filled the air. Approaching one of the Thralls, I cleared my throat. "Do you have anything I can eat?"

A Thrall, willowy figure with high cheekbones and luminous eyes, nodded and handed me a simple wooden bowl. Inside was a mixture of vegetables I didn't recognize—twisting, vine-like strands tinged in deep crimson, something that resembled gritte roots. Nestled within was a portion of sizzling meat, its edges crisped to perfection. I ate swiftly, barely registering the exquisite flavors as I emptied the bowl in minutes. Once finished, I took a deep gulp of water, letting its coolness wash away the remnants of my meal.

I lingered after I finished, drifting closer to where the Thralls worked, the crackle of firewood and hiss of searing meat weaving into the soft murmur of their conversation. I wasn't sure why I stayed. But I sat on a low stone bench and simply watched.

It was strangely calming, observing the rhythm of their work. I hadn't seen food being prepared this closely, not since before the Dormitories, where meals were dumped in wooden bowls and the taste didn't matter so long as it was warm.

One Thrall stirred a simmering broth, the surface glowing faintly from crushed redroot, another peeled vegetables and tossed them into the mix along with crushed herbs. The meat sizzled on flat stones set over flame, the scent heady and wild. It was quiet work, focused and fluid, but I couldn't look away. There was something almost elegant in the way they worked in synchrony.

And despite knowing nothing about spices or simmering times, a small, unexpected part of me wondered what it would be like to know how to do these things—to make something edible, to create something warm and whole from raw things plucked from wild grounds. So, I sat there, pretending I was only resting, letting the quiet hum of the encampment settle around me.

It was then that I heard it, her voice. That saccharine, silken tone that always managed to grate on my nerves like stone dragged across glass. My heart skipped a beat, a sudden rush of unease blooming in my chest, and I turned. And there she was. Fiora, emerging from one of the caves, her movements light and graceful as always, her gown clinging in all the right places. She glanced across the camp, and her eyes flicked past me like I was smoke.

Damien had promised he'd dismissed all his intimates. And yet, there she was. As if nothing had changed. Of all the Thralls he could've brought with him—he chose her. And he'd done it knowing I wouldn't be there. The thought churned in my stomach, sour and raw.

A younger Thrall, crouched by a crate of herbs, looked up as Fiora passed and offered her a curious smile. "You're done already?"

Fiora's lips curved in that demure, practiced way of hers. "Hmm...I've already been to Young Sovereign's," she said. "He asked me to return tomorrow."

The other Thrall giggled. "Oo...You must be his favorite." Fiora's smile deepened, and she winked at the other before disappearing into another cave.

I couldn't move for a few moments. Something cold settled over my skin. I stood there for a few moments. Then my legs moved, my body simply carried me to his cave.

I didn't care what she'd actually been there for—tending to him, feeding him, whispering lullabies for all I knew. Damien had promised, *"All gone."* Yes, right. She was in his cave with him—that alone felt like betrayal because she *is* an Intimate.

Damn them.

I cursed myself when I reached the cave. My satchel was there, half opened. I took his bath brick and towel.

I know the sting I am feeling is from the truth unraveling beneath what I've discovered, that I could never truly claim or control him. He was the Heir of Atlassian. His choices would never be mine to shape. He would always have the right to do whatever he pleased.

And what did that make me? Some naive, insolent woman he had to gently correct, keep in check, silence with soft looks and half-truths? I hated how I couldn't stop wondering—are they still involved like that?

Stars. How pathetic did I sound?

And yet, beneath all the spiraling thoughts, I knew one thing with aching clarity—I had a right to be treated with dignity. And if he couldn't uphold that, then I'd be gone.

Not from Etheris though, I might be naive, but I'm not an idiot. I would gather my satchels, collect my things, and find another cave. Damn him and his royal privileges. There was still so much I hadn't explored. The Legion was warming to me, and with this strange new tether blooming inside me...I had potential. Real potential. I could feel it. I didn't need to mope in the shadows of someone else's choices. I had my own.

As I gathered a few essentials from the cave, moving swiftly with an air of forced detachment, I heard the unmistakable sound of his boots.

Damien. His stride echoed against the stone, unhurried but heavy. When he entered, his eyes flicked first to the satchel at my side, then to the cloak I'd folded, then to me. "Why are you packing?"

I didn't respond immediately. My fingers stilled over the fastenings of my bag, hovering as I weighed whether to lie, deflect, or let silence speak for me. Because if I opened my mouth now, I'd sound like a petulant girl. A lover scorned. And I would *not* give him that.

Damien's voice came again, lower this time. "I was going to suggest you move to another cave." His tone was maddeningly measured, as though it had nothing to do with me at all. "You'll attract less attention from the Elders," he added. "And while I am out Hunting, I won't have to worry about whose eyes are on you. I don't know which of them are scheming to leverage my Bonding, but I would rather not hand them ammunition."

That stung, more than I cared to admit. As if all I was now was a threat to his strategy.

So, I smiled. I smiled with teeth. "Yes, I thought so too. Maybe if I stay in another cave, Izmer's, perhaps, mingling with him would pull the attention away from us." I didn't look at him when I said it. Just smoothed the fold of a tunic, his tunic and shoved it deep into the satchel. "I was heading there now. That's why I'm packing."

For a moment, he didn't speak. When I finally glanced up, his expression had changed, his features carved from stone, eyes unreadable. Then a slow, merciless smile curved over his mouth. Something colder, darker, like the flicker of steel being drawn. I took a step back, pulse stuttering. He moved forward.

"I don't know," he said, voice quiet, too quiet, "what kind of man you have decided I am."

Another step. I backed up instinctively, my spine brushing the edge of the cavern wall. "But let me make something clear to you, Mirabelle." His voice dropped into a low and gravel-edged timbre, the kind of tone that didn't need to rise to be dangerous. "I might bleed for you. I might kneel for you. I might damn myself if it meant keeping you safe."

His hand braced beside my head, palm flat against the wall, caging me in. His breath brushed my cheek, warm and intimate.

"But never mistake that for weakness."

His free hand trailed slowly down the front of my tunic, stopping just short of contact, before curling into a fist against the stone near my hip.

"I don't bend unless I choose to." His voice was a gravel drag, hushed but lethal. "And I won't tolerate hearing another man's name from your lips like you don't know exactly where you belong."

I couldn't move. But I glared back at him. "Izmer," he bit out, the name like poison, "is lucky he is not involved in this. But if you go to anyone's cave, if you so much as let them think you are theirs to even think about, I will end them."

I stared up at him, chest rising and falling too fast, skin burning cold. His fingers came to my jaw, tilting my face up. "You understand?" he murmured, menace curled in velvet. And then, he leaned in and pressed a single kiss to the corner of my mouth. I turned my head, jaw clenched, refusing to let it land properly.

"I refuse to be your muse," I spat, my glare unflinching. "If you get to keep Fiora behind my back, I will have whoever I damn well please *in front* of you."

He tsked, softly. "Wrong, wrong, Mirabelle. So wrong." His hand tightened at my jaw, firm enough to remind me exactly who I was provoking. "You will never choose anyone else," he said, his voice low, controlled. "That life of options, that is over for you."

I tried to twist away. "You're delusional—"

"And here's the thing," he interrupted, eyes burning into mine. "I am a *very* reasonable man."

"Reasonable, my ass—" Before I could finish, his grip shifted and his mouth found mine again—this time fierce, bruising, silencing. I clenched my jaw, refusing him in, lips sealed tight.

I tried to push him off. He didn't budge. When he finally pulled away, it was because he chose to. "If there is something burning in that clever head of yours," he said, "bring it to me. Don't twist it in silence. That is not how we work."

My chest rose and fell, uneven. I said nothing. His hand left my waist and skimmed the base of my throat, lingering for a heartbeat. "And this is the last time you weaponize someone else's name against me. Do you understand?"

I gave a stiff, reluctant nod.

He stepped back, slowly, gaze still pinned to me. His expression softened just enough to draw breath again. "I dismissed all my intimates before the Hunt," he said simply. "Fiora included. She wasn't summoned, she was assigned."

I narrowed my eyes. "Assigned?"

"She's been doing cleaning duty during Hunts for years," he explained, still irritatingly calm. "I came first with the Elders. The Thralls followed with the supplies. I wasn't even aware she was among them."

"Oh." My voice fell flat. That...wasn't terrible.

But I wasn't letting it go that easily. "And yet," I said, "you *wanted* her to return *again* to your cavern."

He gave a slow nod. "Yes," he said. "To clean. This cave. When I'm *not* in it."

I opened my mouth, but he beat me to it. "Not to *fluff* my pillow. Not to *coo* at me from the foot of my bed." He tossed my own words back at me like coin, and I stared at him, stunned, the heat climbing my cheeks, equal parts mortified and achingly drawn to him. I tried to hold my ground.

"I know exactly how I look right now," I muttered through clenched teeth. "And I hate it."

But his gaze only softened. "Then don't fight me like I am your enemy."

He reached for me again, this time slower, his fingers brushing the curve of my cheek in a silent apology. I leaned in without thinking, pressing a quick kiss to his lips, a flustered, awkward little apology I hadn't planned. But the second I tried to pull away, Damien's hand caught the back of my neck.

In one swift movement, he hauled me in, his lips crashing against mine with a heat that stole the breath from my lungs. He kissed me like he needed it to breathe, and when I whimpered into his mouth, his hold only tightened, dragging me closer.

Then pride reared its head, and I pushed against his chest.

Damien's brow arched, a curl of satisfaction playing at his lips. "I didn't know jealousy could look so regal," he murmured, brushing a kiss on the tip of my nose. Then he leaned in, his breath warm at my ear. "And you," he drawled, "you wear it like an Empress."

Before I could come up with something appropriately cutting, he reached past me and plucked my half-packed satchel from the bed, then gestured toward the mouth of the cave. "Come."

We walked in silence, the tension between us settling into something quieter, no longer volatile. His stride was slow, and I found myself matching it with ease. He didn't speak until we rounded a bend near the far end of the encampment, where a smaller cave nestled beneath an overhang of slate-like stone. Vines clung to its edges, and a stream trickled softly nearby, filling the air with the sound of water on stone.

"This is yours," he said simply. "Close enough to be watched. Far enough to be left alone."

He stepped aside, letting me take in the space. There were basic comforts already inside, blankets, a low bench carved from stone, a raised bed with furs, and a lantern already lit. His voice cut through the hush again. "There's a pool past those deep green vines, east of your cave. That one's for you."

A beat passed. Then, with that same composed command, he added, "Be civil with everyone while I'm gone. Fiora included."

My jaw ticked. "She's not harmful, Mirabelle," he added, tone even but firm. "I know how you feel. But she's not a threat to you."

Not harmful. My mind flicked back to her faux-innocent act, her coy little lies, the way she let me hear just enough to wound. But I wasn't about to fling that tangled net of insecurity and venom in front of him. So I gave him my best icy smile, the one that had once gotten me out of three shifts in the laundry pools.

"Oh, I'll be civil," I shrugged. "I'm always civil." That earned a look, but he let it pass.

He set my satchel down near the bed, movements unhurried. I

thought he'd leave right after, drop me off like a parcel and vanish into whatever duty called next. But he stayed. Sat on the edge of the bed, boots off, and tapped the space beside him like it belonged to us both. One exchange slipped into another—about the terrains, meals, his thoughts, the real him beneath the Heir's cloak, their dead-ends with the current crisis, and more than I expected him to share.

And when he finally rose to go, the knot in my chest pulled tight. All the things I wanted to say swelled behind my teeth, so naturally, the most useless sentence came out instead.

"Can I help with the cooking tomorrow?"

He looked at me for a moment, then nodded. "Sure, if you want to."

If I want to. Stars. What I wanted was to prove I wasn't just some delicate little thing he had to tuck away like fine glass every time something sharp entered the room. But no—he wouldn't let me join the Hunt, wouldn't let me fight beside him, wouldn't even let me argue about it.

So, I'd chop vegetables instead. Fine. If I couldn't scorch the battlefield, I'd scorch the pan. In the meantime, there were still the shadows. The ones that slid out of my skin like secrets, curling and coiling with a mind of their own. I'd start small. Contain them. Control them. Bend them to my will. Just like everything else in this Realm.

Hope so, hope so.

CHAPTER 20

DAMIEN

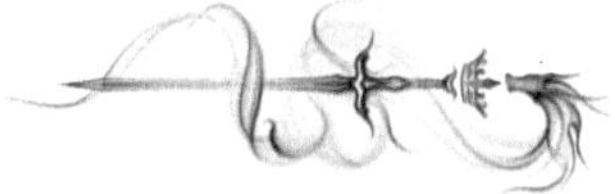

The dawn broke cold over Etheris. The Celestia bathed the land in a distant light, its purple hues casting shadows that stretched over the jagged peaks of the Wildlands. Yesterday's failure still gnawed at my thoughts, the bitter taste of defeat lingering like a foul aftertaste that refused to leave.

Ghor'mak. The name itself echoed in my mind with the weight of an inevitable regret. We had thought it possible to capture the creature, Izmer and I, even though deep inside, I knew it was a fool's errand. But that relentless drive, that constant thirst to conquer the impossible, it drove me, always, relentlessly pushing me to challenge what should remain untouched.

Not every Tameable could be subdued, and it was still a mystery how, or why it happened, and which Tameables it would happen to. Only a rare few could form something deeper with us. That was the point of the Hunt, after all—to see if they were capable of Taming. Creating a true Tether—where a creature of raw Aether willingly gave a part of itself to a Hunter. A sacred exchange.

We thought Ghor'mak might be one of them. We were wrong. We had approached it under the cover of darkness, thinking we could catch it off guard, perhaps exploit its slumbering state. But the moment we saw it, I knew we had underestimated the creature's true strength. Its form, massive and slow, could not have been more deceptive. We had thought it merely an island drifting on the winds, but when it stirred, the ground beneath us groaned in protest.

Ghor'mak was not just a beast, It was a biome. Its gargantuan body, made of living wood and endless roots, shifted as the very ground seemed to adapt to its movements. A floating forest alive with bioluminescent trees, glowing fungi, and smaller creatures thriving in its branches. Each step it took reshaped the terrain beneath it.

We fought to control it, our combined strength and Aether flowing toward one singular goal: tame the Tameable. I summoned mist, sending torrents to strike its great body, the liquid cascading over the bark like a deluge, trying to soak into the massive expanse.

The creatures and vines that draped its limbs were no match for the power of my will. Yet, it regenerated with a speed that defied reason, its body shifting and reforming with every attack.

Izmer was by my side, his dark Aether carving through the shadowed spaces between the creature's glowing limbs. His movements were a blur, slashing at the roots that seemed to be alive, pulling the ground beneath us. His dark tendrils wrapped around the creature, attempting to trap it, to bind it in shadow, but the ancient beast shrugged them off, as though they were nothing more than the passing wind.

The more we attacked, the stronger it became. Its regeneration was too powerful, its will too strong. Every wound we inflicted only served to fuel its relentless growth. It was *fighting itself*. The land around us trembled, as if Ghor'mak was caught in an internal battle, an ancient war within its own being.

The roots we struck began to burn at contact, twisting and recoiling, as if Ghor'mak's very body rejected submission. And we knew it didn't need taming. It needed healing. And we weren't the ones to offer it.

It was then that the weight of failure truly settled in. These entities cannot be subdued with force or Aether, they choose. Or they don't. And Ghor'mak had chosen not to. There was no shame in the loss in Etheris, there was only the next Hunt. But still, as I stared back at the drifting figure disappearing into the violet haze, I couldn't help but feel something else slip away with it, that was *time* for us.

Today, we were aiming for the Choral Swarm. I couldn't help but let my mind wander to the day ahead. The Swarm was something entirely different, though perhaps even more dangerous. Not a beast you could confront head-on, but ethereal, shifting moth-like creatures no larger than hawks, each glowing with faint light from inside. They were beautiful, in a way, haunting even, their presence like a dream caught between worlds, inhabiting both the highest Celestia and the deepest forests.

When Tethered, they could move as one, guided by a single will. But the Swarm was far from peaceful. The creatures were capable of forming shapes in the Celestia, grand, twisting configurations that could span entire horizons, drifting through the air like ghosts. A calm, tranquil melody could turn into something dark and violent with the merest disturbance. And when they were disturbed...well, I had seen firsthand what they could do. Last time it happened, we lost seven of us.

The campsite hummed with murmurs. Izmer and I had spent the early hours checking the gear. He preferred silence when working, his expression tight with focus as we organized traps we rarely used for Tameables. They were for what we might encounter on the way.

The Majors were already up, gathered around the fire with the kind of energy only youth and recklessness could breed. They were still high from yesterday's failures, from seeing what the Hunt demanded. Maybe even eager to prove themselves. Most of them engaged in conversation, some having food.

Cassian was trying to secure a tension bracer to his forearm and failing. Lyria stood behind him, exasperated. "Do you even know how to thread that?" she muttered, reaching for the strap.

Cassian swatted her hand away with exaggerated flair. "I've got this. Your dainty hands will ruin the aesthetic."

"Oh, I am sorry," Lyria snapped, folding her arms. "Did the aesthetic require it to be upside down?"

Alden, seated on a low stone beside Izmer, snorted into his tea. "What are we even doing with straps and hooks?" he muttered. "I thought Aether was supposed to be the solution to everything."

Izmer gave him a sidelong glance, dark hair falling into his eyes. "Because if you use Aether on some of the local fauna, they explode. Or rot. Or scream for eight hours. Pick one."

Alden grimaced. "That's...comforting."

I let the background noise settle. The scene was ordinary, grounded in routine, but beneath it pulsed the need to achieve more in our limited time. The Majors didn't yet realize that they were about to be tested in a way they hadn't been before.

But all these tools, approaches, and improvised fixes feel like futile solutions for the war we are anticipating. And I knew our potential solution was here—tucked between cracked stone counters and smoke-stained pots, in the hands of Thralls who treated the ordinary like ritual. I also knew I was being irrational. I should've let the jealous little redhead accompany our Hunt. But she wasn't trained and her Aether, or whatever was beginning to stir inside her, was still unstable, untested. If it had been anyone else, I would've risked it. I would've thrown them into the fire and let the Hunt burn away what was weak until only the usable remained. But I was too selfish to gamble her safety, even for the sake of Atlassian. Something I had never experienced before.

Once we moved back to the palace, I would train her, see she reached her potential. I'd give her every tool, every opportunity to rise. But risk her in the fray now? No, *never* at the cost of her life. So, I simply watched her slice redroot on the lower plateau, brows drawn in the kind of focused precision that made the task take five times longer than it demanded. Her soft, red lip caught between her teeth as she trimmed each segment.

She finished and carried the bowl to the cookfire, where Oliver —the lead cook—was stirring a pot thick with marrow broth and bone spice. Broad-shouldered and seasoned, in both kitchens and war camps, he'd fed more Hunt teams than most Hunters could name.

Mirabelle hesitated at the edge of the firepit, then placed the bowl down with a small clearing of her throat. Oliver gave the pot one last stir, glanced at her offering and immediately scowled. He plucked one of the redroot slices between his fingers, turned it over and muttered something sharp under his breath.

The urge to step in flared hot beneath my ribs. But I didn't move.

If she was to stand beside Tameables, to face things far crueler than a bitter cook with a foul tongue, she had to learn to hold her own. She'd said as much to me days ago. And this time, she would stand without me. And I'd have to live with it.

Oliver nudged the empty clay pot toward her with his boot and walked off, not bothering to give the instruction she so clearly needed. She scowled back at him, but I saw the flush creep up her neck. She wiped the sweat from her brow and turned to the washing station without a word. A heartbeat later, she was scrubbing out the clay pot with a force that said she was cleaning more than just soot.

Then—crack. It was soft, but distinct. I saw it before she did, the faint fracture spreading through the pot's surface like a slow bleed. It broke in her hands with a hollow snap. She froze, and just stared at it, lips parting. As if she could will it back together with enough silence.

Then, moving quickly, she brushed the shards from her palms and looked up. Oliver hadn't seen. Or was pretending not to. Still, she lingered, shoulders drawn in, a rag clenched in one hand like it might make her invisible. She approached him again, quiet, uncertain.

He didn't look up. "What now?" he muttered.

She said something low. Maybe asking for another task.

"You can start by not breaking anything else," he said flatly, sliding a sack of coarse salt toward her. "Unless that's the only skill you brought with you."

She flinched, just barely. But he wasn't done. "You lot always think good intentions make up for incompetence. Get out of my way before I make you useful in ways you—"

"Don't. Oliver." My voice cut across the plateau. When his eyes met mine, I shook my head once, slow. "Don't."

He turned, his expression didn't falter, but his posture did. "Apologize to her and pack. You are accompanying the Hunt," I said, standing up.

He blinked. I saw his mouth form the word—*What?*

Around us, the nearby Thralls stilled. One of the younger ones actually dropped a pot lid, as if shocked by the sudden impulsiveness of their levelheaded and reasonable Heir. We didn't pull our best camp Thralls into the Hunt unless we had no other choice. Oliver had been too valuable in the kitchens for ages. That's why this would sting.

I didn't repeat myself. Just let the words settle. "We are leaving now."

He swallowed hard, then nodded once and turned back to his station without another word.

Only one person didn't seem surprised. I knew she'd hate it, that I'd stepped in, make it seem as if I was acting on her behalf without her consent. But there were lines. And no one humiliates what's mine and walks away untouched.

⸻◈⸻

THE PASSAGEWAY NARROWED as we ascended, the air thick with the scent of damp ground and the faint shimmer of crystals embedded in the cavern walls. The way up to the isles had always been treacherous, it felt heavy, an unease that pressed against my thoughts like an unseen force.

I stepped onto the giant leaf, its surface shifting beneath my boots like the hide of some great beast. The surfaces shimmered with a soft pulse, as though the thing itself breathed, swaying under my weight. They had always been our strange staircase to the upper reaches of the Realm. The others followed, moving with the quiet precision of hunters long accustomed to unnatural landscapes. The leaf began to rise, throwing us smoothly into the Celestia.

When we walked after landing on the first nearest island, Haldric turned to me. "Although your control over our Tameables is exceptional," he continued, "power contained in a single warrior is no solution. You must ensure others can wield it as well."

I inclined my head slightly. "You mean other Elders."

Haldric gave a slow nod. "The war is inevitable, and a single Tamer will not suffice. We need a strategic plan to maximize our chances of success."

He was right. As of now, the Tameables in Hold obeyed me, but that control was tenuous. A fragile thing that relied too much on my presence. Rowane had been the only other warrior besides Sovereign to whom I had given some Tether control, though he was not the head of their warriors. My untrusting nature made me rigid, and I would need to work on that.

"We will have that strategic plan." I nodded once, eyes fixed on the trembling of the upper branches far above us, where the isles shimmered like ghostly ships anchored in the Celestia. "Once we return, I will begin familiarizing the Tameables with the Elders. Yours. Maelor's. Even a few of the Royals, if they can manage the discipline."

Haldric's expression didn't change, but I saw the faint glimmer of approval in his eyes. "Good. War does not wait for hierarchy." I didn't bother with a reply and let the conversation settle into silence. The ascent continued, the jungle falling away below us, swallowed by mist and shifting shadows.

The first stalk sprang beneath Lyria's weight, launching her in a graceful arc. She landed on my leaf platform with ease, her spiked boots digging into the fibrous surface. I offered her my hand to help her steady. She took it, nodding once, a flicker of a smile at the corner of her mouth. Majors, each of them, were adapting. Yesterday, they'd tumbled like loose stones. Today, they moved with better control, learning the rhythm of the leaves beneath them.

We ascended in waves, passing coiling snakes and translucent venomous insects, while using our spears and tools to drive them away without harming them. The floating platforms shivered under each landing, rocking before springing us upward again.

By the time we reached the upper isles, two of the Royals were limping from bad landings and one Elder had been wounded in the thigh from a glancing strike with a vine's hooked spine.

"You know, Damien," Izmer drawled lazily, arms crossed as he leaned against the edge of the leaf, "for someone so terrifyingly good at controlling beasts, you seem to be having an awful time controlling yourself around a *certain* woman."

I kept my gaze forward, watching the swirling clouds above thicken, darkening the Celestia with something unnatural.

I had long since learned not to rise to Izmer's bait, but today, I was in no mood for his antics.

"For a warrior meant to be aiding with the Tameables, you have an awful lot of time to meddle in matters that do not concern you," I said flatly. "When are you returning to Nyxaria?"

Izmer placed a hand over his chest. "First of all, Atlassian *begged* for me. So, you are welcome." His lips curled into a smirk. "And while I am here, I can't help being a little observant, especially when I see the weakness of the great Heir of Atlassian."

My jaw tightened. "You assume much."

He laughed, unbothered. "Oh, I do. But am I wrong?"

Before I could reply, I heard the buzzing. "Do you feel that?" I asked, scanning the darkening sky. His eyes flickered toward me, but he didn't speak. Instead, he reached out, his fingers grazing the air as if sensing the same shifting, unseen presence.

The quiet vibration of the island, once serene, now reverberated with an ominous, dissonant tone. Suddenly, the wind howled, and the ground trembled beneath our feet. The leaves beneath us swirled into the air like debris in a storm. From the shadows, the Swarm appeared.

The air trembled with an unnatural hum, a sound that burrowed into my skull and set my teeth on edge. The Choral Swarm did not move like living things—they shimmered, shifting in and out of formation, a writhing mass of luminous bodies.

We were surrounded. Then, without warning, we struck. The first wave hit back like a tidal force. A thousand tiny bodies, but together they became an avalanche of light and shadow, slamming into us with a screeching howl. Their wings cut through the air, slicing past exposed skin like blades of glass. The sharp tang of blood filled my mouth before I realized my lip had split. Izmer shouted something, his voice barely cutting through the roar of wings and wailing resonance. His blade spun in graceful arcs, movements a blur of practiced savagery, the sword's edge catching the light with every desperate swing. His shadows wrapped around him like a second skin, a storm of darkness carved into motion. But it wasn't enough. The creatures were too many—more than we had seen last time.

I could hear Izmer's voice shouting commands, calling for backup from the Majors. But it was too late for strategy. The Swarm was upon us. I stretched out my hand, focusing on the elements, forcing the fire to surge first. The flames shot forth from my fingertips, a searing inferno that exploded outward, but instead of scaring them away, the creatures scattered, their forms dissipating into fragments of light that reformed in mid-air, only to converge again.

"We need to force them into the stillness!" Izmer's voice was desperate, and I could see him fighting with everything he had, his blade flashing as he cleaved through the creatures with precision and speed. I summoned cold waves to counterbalance the fire, the two elements working together. The wave of cool liquid surged forth, crashing against the swarm, freezing their glowing forms in mid-flight.

For a moment, they stilled. The creatures were suspended in the air, caught between the two elements. But it was short-lived. The water shattered into steam as the fire roared to life once more, burning away what remained of the swarm.

"No!" Izmer's voice cut through the haze. "You're overextending! They need to be tamed, not destroyed!"

The flames of those around us roared to life in an effort to help but made it worse by sweeping outward in wide swaths. The fire licked the sky, forcing part of the swarm to scatter, but it lacked the precision needed to shape or bind them. The Choral Swarm simply reformed, fragments folding into one another, reshaping like a sea with no end.

Elders tried again. Arms wove together in a delicate loop of flame meant to ensnare, but the construct shattered before it even closed. Around us, Aether rose in frantic bursts, fire cast like flares.

Then everything fractured. The Swarm split—four ways. A symphony turned cacophony.

One swarm descended from above like a spiral of daggers. Another burst sideways in a sweeping arc. The rest twisted down into the trees, dragging three Royals with it in a flurry of screams. Everything was spiraling out of control.

I shouted something I don't remember, moved to shield a group near me, channeling fire into a radiant blast, but the swarm simply recoiled and regrew, slipping between the flames like they had learned to dance with it. I could contain one part.

Izmer was holding another back, barely. His shadows lashed like serpents, slicing through lines of light, but his movements had slowed. Dark black blood smeared his sleeve. He was running out of strength.

I had to let go. I dropped the tether on my swarm and turned, channeling water to push myself higher up the fractured ledge.

And then—my last card. Invisibility—the Aether that drained me faster than I could compensate. It was agony. I could feel every vein stretch, every nerve fray beneath the pressure. But I had to do it. If I died now, they all would. We wouldn't just lose the battle. The Realm would fracture with us.

Mirabelle's voice echoed in my mind. *You are always too willing to sacrifice everything, Damien.* And wasn't I?

I pulled my power inward. The part that made me more than a weapon. The part that could shape, not shatter. The part that, for a fleeting heartbeat, I had felt when the Dreadclaw lowered its head. Stillness spread through me. The world slowed. The roar of the Swarm dimmed, as if I'd stepped beyond the noise. My breath, ragged a second ago, steadied.

I dropped to my knees in the churned soil, opened my arms, and called them. No force or fury, just openness. And I knew it was a bloody gamble.

"Do not strike arms until I command—"

They didn't let me finish it, flames erupted again as one of the Majors, bleeding and panicked, hurled fire into the sky. A mistake. The swarm dove. Straight into me.

Hundreds of glowing wings sliced through the air, drawn to the surge of essence, drawn to power that didn't threaten. I closed my eyes as they hit. Pain erupted—biting, tearing, fracturing. And I was crushed to the ground. I felt blood bloom across my ribs, down my arms, streaking through my leathers.

But beneath it all—I felt the pull, humming inside me. The screams and sounds stilled for a few moments, and then, silence. The shrieking faltered. One wing paused mid-beat. And then another. A humming began, resonating the one I felt inside me. A harmony.

"Stars, what a terrifying toss-up." Izmer said somewhere behind me, his voice ragged, wry. A few others echoed him with murmurs of stunned appreciation—no one had the energy for more. I didn't either. My limbs were trembling from blood loss. My mouth tasted like iron.

This one felt like another kind of Tether. I had offered myself. And they had chosen. Now they hovered above us. Still wild. But attuned, awaiting my direction.

I rose slowly. My knees trembled, my limbs slick with blood and exhaustion. The Swarm moved as one. We had lost five. Perhaps more, if the wounds proved fatal before the healers could reach them.

And Oliver—well, we wouldn't be returning to the caves with him after all.

CHAPTER 21

DAMIEN

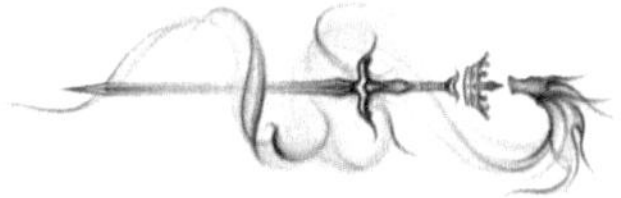

ealers moved between beds, murmuring instructions, grinding salves and wrapping limbs with their Aether. I stood near the far wall, arms folded across my chest, watching in silence. The ache in my ribs was only a memory now, dulled by the relentless hum of my own healing—faster than it should be, unnatural even by Atlassian standards. A consequence of something I no longer questioned. I had bled, and bled again, and still my body rose each time.

Two Royals had fallen hard. One still hadn't woken. One Elder had lost his hearing to the Swarm's screech, and likely wouldn't recover it. They said we had lost seven. I counted five. The rest would wear the memory like bone-deep bruises for the rest of their lives.

Rhevas lay nearby, shoulder cracked open like parchment split too fast. Lyria's dominant arm had been shattered under the weight of a collapsing branch-vein. Alden's chest was mottled red and black.

Rowane joined me, his coat half undone, his sword belt still looped lazily around one hip.

"Looks worse than it is," Rowane said, his voice low. "You know that, right?"

I didn't respond immediately. My eyes drifted to the farthest bed, where the member of the Royal line still hadn't woken. Then nodded.

Rowane continued, stepping to my side. "Some of them swore at healers earlier. That's always a good sign." He waited for another beat, then let out a sigh. "Look, I get it. This whole room feels like penance."

I met his gaze, steady and flat. "Spare me the motivational speech, Rowane. I know I'll recover in a few days."

Rowane gave me a sidelong glance. "Then why are you brooding."

"I am thinking."

"I've seen how you look when you think. This is brooding."

"It is the same Rowane, unless you have suddenly grown angsty about our crashing Clan and my father."

After the battle, I'd left Etheris before the others could rouse fully. Traveled back to the capital, to the Aetherium Hold. We kept the Swarm in the upper sanctum, sealed in an open chamber where it floated like a fractured constellation, humming in time with the runes etched into the walls. I'd gone to my father immediately after.

He had not looked up from the fire. The Sovereign of Atlassian, once a man whose presence could hush a battlefield, now sat shrouded in furs he once would've considered beneath his rank. They had been calling his absence strategic. Political. Even deliberate.

But I suspect there is more to it and had arranged for a healer to visit him regularly under the pretense of routine checks. He had agreed, of course, because refusal would have revealed the very thing he feared most—weakness.

Rowane noticed. "You should've let someone else handle containment."

I looked at him. "There was no one else."

"There were twenty-two other Aether-bearers on that ridge."

"They didn't respond to them. I felt it." I paused.

Rowane snorted. "So naturally, you decided to throw yourself in like bait."

"I made a calculated risk."

He gave me a side glance. "You say that every time you nearly bleed out."

I didn't deny it.

For a while, neither of us spoke. Around us, the low crackle of heated stone kept the cavern dimly lit.

"They're talking about you," Rowane said at last, his voice low. "Whispering like kids after a myth comes true."

I exhaled. "Let them."

He shifted to face me more fully. "They're calling it the Harmonizing. The Swarm obeyed you, Damien. Mid-attack. Mid-slaughter." Rowane continued. "The Elders have already rewritten the story, by the way. In theirs, you stood on a mountain of fire, summoned your ancestors, and sang the thing into submission."

I pinched the bridge of my nose. I let out another breath. "Convenient."

"Heroic," he snorted. "And you know what else? Every Major in the capital is suddenly asking for deployment. They want to be near you. They want to watch."

"At least the next trials will attract more participants," I muttered, though the idea of becoming a spectacle grated more than it flattered.

Izmer's movement across the cavern caught my eye. The sort of pained theatrics meant to draw an audience.

He had taken more damage than most—blunt trauma to the ribs, fractured shoulder—but naturally, he was already halfway upright, bandages loose, tunic unlaced just enough to make his recovery look rakish rather than painful. By morning, he was already provoking the healer assigned to him, which happened to be the very same one Rowane hadn't shut up about.

"By the Grace, lady, you're torturing me," he groaned, his hand flying to his chest as if she'd driven a dagger into him. "If I die of heartbreak, it'll be your fault."

The healer didn't even flinch. She pressed harder on the wound, entirely unbothered, and Izmer let out a hissed curse, though I caught the smile tugging at his mouth.

"By the stars," Rowane muttered. "Does he ever shut up?"

"No," I said.

"He's provoking her on purpose."

"Yes."

"I should break his other shoulder."

"You could try."

Rowane turned and called across the cavern. "Vesra?"

She glanced over, arching a brow. Rowane gestured toward Lyria's cot. "Would you mind checking the girl with the crushed shoulder next? I think she's in more urgent need of your skills than the idiot currently trying to flirt through internal bleeding."

Izmer chuckled under his breath without even looking up. Rowane muttered something under his breath that sounded like a curse, then crossed his arms.

"You are sulking," I noted.

"I'm watching a walking shadow puppet try to seduce a healer I've been—" he stopped himself, then shook his head. "Never mind. Just promise me if she sets his bed on fire, you'll let her finish him."

I didn't answer. But I didn't say no either.

My gaze drifted back toward the flickering edge of the firelight, but my thoughts slipped to Mirabelle, who hadn't yet realized I'd nearly died. She didn't see the wounds. I'd left Etheris and had healed while I was in Atlassian. I hadn't told her a word of what happened. She knew the Hunt had succeeded. But that was all. And I intended to keep it that way. Let her think it was a clean mission. Let her explore whatever power she has in peace, without the shadow of my injuries looming over her before she even begins.

She didn't ask questions when I returned, not the kind that would corner me into admitting things I didn't want to share. Instead, she fed me. I had been sitting on her bed, leaning back against the cavern walls, stripped of armor and still stiff from the lingering ache in my ribs, when she hovered beside me, pressing a bowl of something warm into my hands with far too much pride.

"Taste and tell me how it is?" she asked sweetly like she'd just served a feast worthy of Sovereign Nickels.

The first sip made my stomach clench. It was thick. Viscous. Bitter in a way that felt like it had been brewed in punishment and over-steeped in old boots.

Still, I swallowed it. She watched me with an eager smile. "Well?"

I stared at the bowl. Then at her. "It is...fine," I said slowly. I never sugarcoat truths. But here I was. "Maybe you could improve. In time. With...more effort."

Her jaw dropped like I'd just accused her of treason. So, I took a second gulp—to soften the blow and buy myself time to figure out how to break the news without shattering that look on her face.

She burst out laughing—light and unguarded. And just like that, I knew I'd drink every last drop of that poison again if it bought me another second of that sound.

"That was the rinsed broth from the bitter roots they told me to throw out," she said between gasps, face flushed with mirth.

I stared at her in disbelief. "You served me discarded root rinse?" She nodded back, her eye gleaming.

I set the bowl aside. "Mirabelle,"

"Yes?" Her grin faltered just a little.

"You are lucky I didn't order you exiled." I shook my head at her.

"Oh, hush. You wouldn't." The little minx knew exactly how close I was to letting her get away with anything. She already had me wrapped around her finger.

I gave her backside a firm swat, more a statement than a punishment. She yelped, half in protest, half in surprise, then rolled her eyes to cover the flush spreading high across her cheeks and turned to reach for the·tray beside her cot. This time, a proper meal—warm rice and stewed meat, clearly the work of someone who knew the purpose of fire and seasoning.

I pulled her to straddle my lap. Her nightgown shifted with the movement, baring one long leg nearly to her thigh, though she didn't notice it like I did.

"Let's see if this offering pleases His Majesty's delicate palate." She winked, and I couldn't help the warmth that stirred in my chest. I loved her like this— unguarded, unbothered, entirely herself. It didn't come easily to her, and that made every glimpse of it feel earned.

I let her feed me. Her fingers brushed my lips, and I did not look away. The food was good, clearly made by the Thralls, but in that moment, it could've been ashes for all I cared. My hands rose slowly, deliberately, bracketing her ribs to anchor her. My fingers splayed gently over the thin fabric at her sides, a silent promise—I would never move faster than she deserved. She had never been touched by anyone this way before. That much, I had gathered. And I had no intention of turning her wonder into fear.

So, I sat still. Let her feed me bite by bite, while her legs trembled slightly against mine and her skin flushed warmer with each moment.

"Don't shelter me next time," she said quietly, after a pause. "I can take criticism. And I knew you'd lie to me."

I wiped my mouth with the cloth she passed me, tilting my head. "Yes, My Lady."

She grinned, pleased, then leaned in, her breath brushing my cheek. "And next time, be good," she whispered, "or you're finishing the whole pot of broth." I bit down softly on the pad of her finger in answer to her sass. Her lips parted, desire taking over both of us with a simple bite. Without thinking, I reached out and brushed my thumb over the hardened peak of her breast, over her nightgown.

"Damien!" She sputtered, cheeks blazing, but before she said something more, I caught her chin.

"You earned that," I said and crushed my mouth to hers. A hot, claiming kiss, just deep enough to steal her breath—then I pulled back, smiling at her stunned expression. "Behave," I murmured, my thumb brushing the damp swell of her lower lip.

Her eyes were wide, her pulse fluttering under my fingertips. Perfect. I released her hand, allowing her to slide off me, though the loss of her weight felt like the cold after firelight.

And in the quiet that followed, I knew two things for certain. She would be the one to unravel me. And I would thank her for it.

⊰⊱

Rowane had already sent reports to the palace detailing the essentials—the losses sustained, the progress of healing among our wounded, the status of each Major, the condition of the remaining Elders and Royals, and how many days still remained until our final Hunt. Once the last seal had been set, I left the healing cavern without a word. I walked as if without purpose, telling myself it was only to clear my head and plan the next Hunt. Perhaps I cared too much about where I would end up when I deliberately crossed the deep green vines.

The twilight jungle whispered with life, its strange flora humming softly, casting a faint, pulsing glow against the shadows. The trees stretched impossibly high, their twisted limbs intertwined like ancient hands clasping in prayer. Beneath their boughs, the waters ran smooth and dark, reflecting the eerie glow of the plant life above.

I should have turned back. But the sound of rushing water hooked into me, the vines shifted sluggishly, their sinuous dance concealing the pool beyond. And there, tangled among them, hung a scrap of her fabric, one that clung to her hips when she moved. Discarded without care, as if she'd stepped out of it without a second thought.

I wouldn't have come anywhere near if I hadn't already

ensured this place belonged to her—and her alone. The Heir of Atlassian was not raised to linger where he wasn't needed. My entire existence was a fortress of order—one I built, brick by brick. But now, my body moved with my mind in synchrony.

Enough. I was done granting her time to adjust. To pretend she didn't know exactly what this tension between us was. I ignored the traitorous voice that whispered I already knew what state I'd find her in.

The vines slithered apart at my approach. Beyond them, the water shimmered, its surface rippling as though something just disturbed it. And there, bathed in the ghostlight of Etheris, was Mirabelle.

She stood half-submerged, the pond's silver glow brushing her skin like reverence. Droplets traced the length of her spine, vanishing where the water curved around her. Her hair, darkened to a deep auburn by the damp, clung in slow waves to the bare expanse of her back, exposing the elegant column of her neck like an offering.

She was feral in her grace.

My breath caught. Not just from desire, though it curled low and hungry. No, it was the staggering realness of her that undid me. And for the life of me, I didn't know what sin I'd righted to earn her for myself. But I'd wrong the world twice over to keep her.

A rustle, my boot scraping earth—and she whirled, arms snapping over her breasts. Water sloshed as she retreated, her voice sharp as a blade. "Get away from here, whoever you are! Now, or I swear I will kill you!"

The threat would've been laughable coming from her—naked, unarmed, unaethered—if I weren't already battling the urge to be anything but decent. Yet the words left me dark and rough with possession. "Oh, *I* would carve out the eyes of any man who sees you like this."

She froze at first, then recognized my voice. Slowly, she turned, arms still shielding herself, the water doing what her hands could not. A blush crept up her throat, staining her skin the soft pink of early dawn.

But her defiance never wavered. Chin lifted, eyes narrowed, her glare sharper than any blade.

"I didn't know the Heir was a pervert." Mock indignation dripped from her words, but the hitch in her breath betrayed her.

I laughed—low, unguarded. I *did* deserve it.

"Neither did I," I admitted, stepping closer. The glow of the pond flickered against my chest as I added, voice low but even, "I want to take you to the Isles."

She blinked, suspicion coiling behind narrowed eyes. "What for?"

The flush still painted her throat and shoulders, blooming deeper across the gentle swell of her breasts. My gaze faltered there—twice. I forced my eyes back to hers. I said again, firmer this time. "To get you familiar with your Aether."

Then I paused. Let the silence draw tight between us. "But now," I added, eyes dropping briefly to the water around her, "I think I will need a bath to cool my mind first."

Her brows lifted. I could see her trying to focus on the word Aether, but it had landed somewhere behind her ears. Her body heard bath, and her shoulders curled slightly inward.

She shifted in the water, feigning an illusion of indifference, her breasts—full, lush, and breathtaking, barely contained by her crossed arms. The water lapped at their curves as she shifted, spilling sideways just enough to steal my gaze. Her fingers pressed harder into her own skin, leaving faint crescents behind. Fear? Anticipation? With her, the line was always blurred.

"I didn't invite you to join me," she said, quieter now. The bite had dulled, her voice softer, uneven at the edges.

I stepped closer, boots at the water's edge. The shadow I cast stretched long and dark across the surface, reaching her before I could. The ripples that followed seemed to shiver.

"Good," I said, voice velvet and threat all at once. "Because I don't need an invitation to be near what's mine"

Her lips parted, and she just stared.

And I did too. For a moment, the jungle faded—the glow, the thrum of distant vines, the silver surface of the pond. All of it gave way to a silence more powerful than noise.

CHAPTER 22
MIRABELLE

My heart was already trying to outpace itself, but when I heard the soft rustle of fabric, heavy cloth slipping over skin, I knew it was over for me. Curiosity clawed at the corners of my resolve, and before I could talk myself out of it, I peeked.

Oh goodness and grace. Damien stood at the edge of the water, half-shadowed, the last of his clothes falling away, leaving nothing between him and the cool, luminous glow of the Realm. His body was a study in contrasts, lines carved with precision, like a statue chiseled by hands that revered the very idea of strength. Broad shoulders framed a chest marked with faint scars, stories etched into skin, relics of battles fought and won. His waist tapered down into lean hips, disappearing beneath the faint shimmer of water as he waded in.

And I...was just staring. What was I doing? I snapped my gaze away, fixating on anything that wasn't Damien Azarios, Atlassian's Heir, now gloriously, horrendously naked in the same water I was floating in.

I tried to summon some semblance of dignity, clearing my throat. "The vines look...exceptionally green today." My voice came out too high-pitched, too breathless, like I'd swallowed a bird.

Damien didn't respond immediately, but I felt his presence moving closer, the subtle ripple of water betraying him. I stared harder at the vines overhead, their emerald strands glistening as if they could save me from my own mortification.

"Yes," he murmured, his voice low and smooth like dark velvet, "very green."

I hated him.

I hated how my heart betrayed me with every beat. Hated how my body was acutely aware of him. Too aware. How the air between us crackled even though we weren't touching. Was the water always this warm? Or was I slowly combusting from the inside out?

By the stars, why hadn't Amara prepared me for this? She knew everything about everyone else's entanglements—but that hopeless creature had no useful instruction for what to do when a very real, very naked man stood watching you in glowing water with eyes like stormlight. Should I act bold? Should I say something? Should I just...unclasp my arms and let him see? Would a proper lady do that?

He'd had Thralls, after all. And they were trained for this sort of thing. I was trained to scrub soot and fold linen. Before I could muster another dazzling observation about aquatic plants or blurt something equally humiliating, his warm fingers tilted my chin up. My breath caught. Again.

His touch wasn't demanding. It didn't push. I met his gaze. And in that moment, the world quieted. His eyes were different now, no longer cold and composed, but something molten, a hunger barely restrained. Then, my mouth moved before my mind could intervene. "I've never even seen a man naked before."

—WHAT

Oh. *What.*

Why. Why would I say that?

Mortification detonated in my chest. My hands shot up, as if I could grab the words from the air and shove them back into my mouth before they reached his ears. "I mean—not that I was trying to look at your...I just—obviously, you're there, and I just—oh, shut up, Mirabelle."

I squeezed my eyes shut, considering drowning myself on the spot. Maybe if I sank deep enough, the shame wouldn't follow.

But then...his thumb brushed over my lower lip, gentle, quieting the frantic mess I'd become. His fingers stayed there, the faintest pressure against my mouth, grounding me.

"Shh," he whispered, the sound a tender command. "I expect nothing from you, Bella. Nothing except this moment."

I blinked, breath caught somewhere between my chest and throat. His hand slid from my chin to cradle the side of my face, thumb resting just beneath my cheekbone.

"I won't rush anything," he continued, his voice softer now, roughened only by the sincerity stitched into every word. "I won't take a moment from you. *This* is yours, not mine."

My heart clenched painfully. No one had ever said something like that to me, not with such raw honesty, without expectation or demand. His forehead dipped to rest against mine, the tip of his nose brushing gently along mine. The closeness stole the air between us yet gave me more to breathe than I'd ever known.

"Do I need you too much?" he murmured, his lips ghosting over the curve of my cheek, so close yet holding restraint with a tension I could feel vibrating through him. "Yes. A thousand times more than you think. Because no one, *not a single soul*, has ever stirred the demon inside me the way you do."

My skin burned under the heat of his words, and something deeper, an ache, hunger I didn't know I'd been starving for. His fingers drifted, trailing along the line of my jaw, down to the pulse fluttering wildly at my throat. "It is my honor," he whispered, "to be your first. *And your last.*"

He didn't ask, just claimed. And a dark part of me enjoyed it far more than I should.

His lips brushed over mine, so soft it was almost not a kiss at all. A promise whispered against my skin. My hands rose instinctively to press against his chest, to feel the erratic beat of his heart beneath my fingertips.

I kissed him back. Not with the grace of someone who knew what they were doing. But with every frantic, messy, breathtaking feeling he'd planted inside me. Every part of me trembled, yet none of it mattered—not with his lips on mine, not with the warmth of him so close it blurred the edges of my thoughts.

His hands slid around my waist, strong and sure, pulling me against him until water was no longer a barrier. My bare breasts pressed against the hard plane of his chest, my heart racing so fast I wondered if he could feel it thundering against his skin.

His skin, warm even in the cool water, shifting beneath my fingertips, taut and sculpted like stone shaped by the hands of some indulgent sculptor. My palms flattened against him without thinking, splayed across the ridges of his chest, tracing the faint, raised lines of scars.

Then...I felt it. A sharp jolt, a sudden awareness as something hard pressed against my lower belly. My breath hitched, panic and wonder collided like startled birds in my chest. *Oh.*

I froze, unsure if I should acknowledge it, name it, *look at it*, or pretend I had no idea what was happening. My mind scrambled for the right reaction, but there was none. I was catastrophically inexperienced, armed with nothing but sass and stupidity.

My knees buckled slightly under the weight of that realization, and perhaps under the weight of him too, but before I could slip, Damien's arms tightened around me, holding me up. His lips found the curve of my neck, brushing softly at first, then pressing with more purpose, sending a shiver rippling down my spine. I swallowed hard, the sensation overwhelming, his breath hot against the delicate skin just beneath my ear.

I wasn't prepared for this. For him. For the onslaught of sensation that made me see the abyss. For the way my body responded like it belonged to him, as if it had always belonged to him.

His mouth traveled slowly, unhurried, as though he had all the time in the world to memorize every inch of me. Each kiss was a quiet confession, his hands splayed across my back, fingertips tracing the dip of my spine, anchoring me when I felt like I might simply float away.

His lips traced a slow, deliberate path along my jaw, then down the slender column of my neck, his breath warm and ragged against my skin. Every inch he conquered sent another tremor cascading through me. His head dipped lower, savoring the way my breath hitched, the way my hands gripped his shoulders to anchor myself against the pull of something vast and consuming.

Lower still, until his lips hovered over the delicate curve where my heartbeat thrummed beneath fragile skin, to the puckered peak of my breast. His breath ghosted there, hot and reverent, stirring the fine, sensitive skin until goosebumps blossomed in its wake. Then, as if the distance itself was too much to bear, he closed it.

A soft, tentative brush of his tongue against me, a whisper of contact that unraveled me more than any fervent touch ever could. Then the warmth of his lips grazed the sensitive peak, feather-light, yet enough to ignite something electric beneath my skin. A gasp escaped me, sharp and unbidden, betraying the fragile control I clung to.

His response was immediate, a low, guttural growl vibrating deep in his chest, reverberating against me like a primal echo. It was raw, and it shattered the careful restraint he'd been holding onto like glass underfoot.

Without warning, his lips sealed around the stiffened peak, his fangs grazing against it—sharp yet teasing. A strangled moan tore from my throat as he tugged it, devouring, his mouth working over each one with a hunger barely leashed.

My back arched into him, pressing closer, offering more, as if my body had abandoned any notion of restraint. His hands roamed my spine, palms dragging over slick, bare skin, tracing the curve of my waist, the dip of my lower back, gripping as though he could mold me against him. He gave equal attention to both, but I was gone—blinded by sensation, overwhelmed.

The water sloshed between us, waves rippling from where we

stood, but I felt none of it. Only him. Only the heat of his mouth, and caress of his hands against my body. His hands splayed across my back, pulling me impossibly closer, as if he could fuse us together with sheer will alone.

"*Bella*," he rasped against my skin, his voice hoarse with something between desperation and awe. His forehead pressed briefly against my breasts, his breath shaky. "*You wreck me.*"

I couldn't find words, lost in the whirl of sensation. My thoughts scattered like leaves in a storm. My fingers tangled in his hair, anchoring him to me, to this moment.

He lifted his head slightly, his eyes dark and stormy, pupils blown wide with need. "I've fought wars with less struggle than this—to leash myself," he muttered, his voice a ragged whisper, as if the truth itself was a fragile thing he rarely dared to voice.

The words lodged in my throat, unspoken. *Then don't leash it,* I wanted to say, the plea burning on the tip of my tongue. But wisdom held me back.

Then his mouth was on me again, claiming, tasting, and I was lost. Completely and utterly lost.

When we finally broke apart, gasping for breath, our foreheads pressed together, his deep chuckle rumbled against my chest, vibrating through me like the aftershock of a storm.

"This is better than green vines, isn't it?" he whispered, his voice husky, tinged with a smile and a darker edge, one that made my pulse flutter.

I gathered just enough dignity to punch him weakly in the arm. "You're insufferable."

He caught my wrist with ease, tugging me gently forward, and I kissed him again. This time softer, slower, as if we were both afraid of breaking the fragile thing that had formed between us in the water.

But eventually, reality seeped back in. The coolness of the breeze above the water's surface, the faint sounds of the mystical creatures stirring in the distance, it reminded me that we were not entirely alone in this world, even if it felt like it.

Damien pulled back slightly, his hand still cradling the small of my back. His gaze lingered on me, something fierce and tender tangled within the depths of his eyes.

"Come," he murmured softly, guiding me toward the shore. His hand never left mine, fingers intertwined like we were afraid to let go. The climb from the water was awkward, how could it not be? But Damien moved with ease, unaffected by his nakedness, while I scrambled to maintain whatever scraps of modesty I had left. He reached for the thick linen cloth I'd brought, shaking it out with a casualness that made me glare at him just to cover my flustered state.

Without a word, he stepped closer, lifting the cloth and pressing it to my arms, my shoulders, carefully blotting away the lingering droplets that clung to my skin and gently wrapping the cloth around my shoulders, pulling me into its warmth. His hands were careful, reverent even, as he tucked the fabric around me, his fingers lingering a moment longer than necessary along the curve of my neck.

"I can do it myself," I muttered, though my voice lacked the usual bite.

His lips quirked slightly. "I know."

Once I was mostly covered, he turned to retrieve his own clothes, dressing with an ease I envied, every movement fluid and efficient. I stole a glance, *just one*, admiring the way his muscles shifted beneath his skin as he pulled on his clothes, the fabric stretching briefly across the broad expanse of his back before falling into place.

When he looked back to me, now fully clothed, just as I was, and yet still entirely too composed, he offered his hand. I stared at it for a moment, then at him.

"Ready?" he asked quietly. I wasn't. Not even a little. But I nodded anyway, slipping my hand into his.

OUR WALK FELL into an easy rhythm, unforced, as if it had always been this way. I had never had conversations like this before. Not with anyone outside Amara. And stars, I missed her. The moment I returned to the palace, I'd find her. Maybe—if things ever calmed, I could bring her back with me. Help her find work within the palace quarters. It would be easier, somehow, facing that world with her near.

Damien's voice broke through my drifting thoughts, steady and low. "This is the Skyborne Wilds," he said, gesturing toward the endless sprawl before us. My gaze followed his hand.

The horizon unfolded in impossible layers, floating isles suspended in the pale gold sky, each one different from the last. Some were veiled in mist, others glinted with crystal growths that shimmered like frozen starlight.

"The Isles drift infinitely," he continued, "home to Tameables older than written time. This Realm isn't ruled by men, or even Aether. It answers only to balance—predators, prey, and the land itself, shifting and reshaping as it pleases."

I glanced upward, where massive, light-dappled leaves curled toward the Celestia. Each one could easily cradle ten men. They drifted between the isles like living bridges, creating passageways that folded and unfurled without warning. The air shimmered with thin mist and a hush of distant, melodic birdcall. There was something reverent about it all, something that made me want to speak in whispers.

I remembered how, on the way here, I'd showed him my fledgling Tether on a silver-throated mouse. The creature had nestled into my palm, its tiny paws kneading my fingers as the bond snapped into place. It had blinked at me once, then tilted its head curiously.

Damien had stared—actually stared—his usual icy mask slipping for one unguarded moment before he'd tossed the mouse a moonberry and casually said. "You can accompany us for the final Hunt, if you want."

I had blinked, unsure whether I'd misheard him. But before I could react, he'd added, firmer now. "You will remain far away. You can watch from the lower ridge, observe the Tameable from there. Try to Tether, if you can. But I won't let you near it."

I squealed like a maniac and had thrown my arms around his neck and kissed him soundly on the cheek, the kind of overjoyed gesture that would've mortified me under any other circumstance.

Now, standing in the heart of the Skyborne Wilds with sunlight tracing the curve of his jaw and the wind whispering through the leaves, I understood why.

"The hunt here is a test," Damien continued. "Not just of strength, but survival. The land itself changes, crumbling, reforming, pulling apart just as quickly as it comes together. It will either carry you or swallow you whole."

Kicking a loose pebble from the path, I said, "Sounds delightful."

As we walked, conversation came easily, drifting from the majesty of Etheris to lighter subjects, food, the ridiculous politics of the palace, Izmer's knack for getting on everyone's nerves.

"Your parents." His voice softened unexpectedly. "What happened to them?"

The question struck like a blade between ribs. It wasn't a question anyone often asked—most assumed whatever fit the narrative they preferred or didn't care enough to wonder. Seeing my hesitation, he added, "I don't mean to pry. I'm simply used to being direct."

I laughed, brittle as autumn leaves. "I thought you'd have my entire lineage tucked away in some secret dossier by now."

"I do." he said, maddeningly even, no pretense. "But I want your memory. The parts ink can't preserve."

That damnable sincerity of his, wrapped in precision, was disarming. My breath shuddered out. "It's nothing remarkable. Years past."

He waited. Silent. A man who understood the weight of unsaid things.

And in that silence, something in me came loose. "I was

twelve," I said softly. "True commoners, my parents. Not the kind who serve Majors, but the ones who bartered cracked pottery in alleyways. Who slept with nickel purses sewn into their hems." My thumb worried the fabric of my sleeve, a child's habit resurrected. "The kind no one misses."

Damien nodded. He had likely never had to think about life beyond the palace and its structured hierarchy, but he listened, his focus entirely on me.

"My mother wove reed baskets," I said, tracing the memory like a fresh wound. "My father traded spices and dry roots at a market stall. He was known to be shrewd in business, maybe too shrewd." The mist between us thickened as I spoke. "One day, he outbid a man on a large bulk of trade goods, spices, I think. It must have been a heavy loss, because the man didn't take it lightly. A week later, my parents were dead."

Damien's expression darkened, his jaw tightening. "They killed them over a market bid?"

I exhaled, watching the mist swirl around the distant isles. "Commoners get killed for less."

He didn't answer right away. But I could feel the shift in him—something cold, something still. The kind of silence that sharpens before it strikes.

Then, low and controlled, his voice broke the quiet. "And you?"

I frowned, glancing at him. "What happened to me after?"

I shrugged, as if the memory didn't bite anymore. "I was sent to one of the adoption Dorms. Did what was expected. Scrubbed, ran errands, swept floors. Worked hard. Grew up. Ended up where I am now." I tried for a smile, though it faltered before it could land. "Getting yelled at by Majors. Scraping cinders off training mats. The usual."

He said nothing, but I felt his gaze—heavy, searing. Watching me like he was trying to rewrite history with sheer will. Like the truth of my past sat wrong in his bones.

The silence stretched. And still, he looked at me.

I couldn't take it. Not that look. Not the way it looked gutted for me. "You shouldn't have had to grow up like that," he said finally, his eyes remaining dark, relentless. "You deserve more than scraps from the tables you clean."

My throat burned. I shrugged. "Then maybe do something about them, commoners like me."

His expression didn't flicker. "I intend to rectify the mistakes of the Sovereigns before me." The conviction in his voice comforted me. He held my gaze, steady and sure. "You will never fear helplessness again. Not while I draw breath."

The vow hit like a fist to the ribs. So, I did what I always did when things got too close. "What's next?" I forced a smirk. "Are you about to promise me a life of riches and luxury, my Liege?"

But he didn't smile. His eyes lingered on mine with burning intensity, and the silence between us thrummed with something deeper than words. I swallowed. Looked away.

Then, after a beat, his voice dropped lower. "Oh, I intend to give you silks. Not to compensate for the past—but because I've already imagined it. Entirely. For my own selfish reasons." A beat. His thumb brushed my knuckles, fleeting as a spark. "But not as compensation. This was always the plan, long before I knew your scars."

I told myself to not read much into this. But the quiet that followed wasn't uncomfortable. Then the conversation turned, shifting like the isles itself, but the warmth remained between us.

And then, I asked the question that had been pressing at the back of my mind. "Why are you rushing the Hunt?"

I expected him to brush it off. Instead, he met my gaze. His honesty startled me. "The Sages of all the Clans have been predicting the threat of the Untameables. They have already started their attacks." He continued, "We don't have a clear idea of what they are. But they're not creatures of this Telmoria, nor Etheris, not nurtured by nature. They are something—wrong."

I frowned. "You think they're coming through the portals?"

He nodded. "Yes, but I am not entirely sure. And unlike the

Tameables, they can't be reasoned with. They don't follow the laws of the land. They are a force of destruction, nothing more."

A lump formed in my throat. "Then what stops them?"

Damien's expression was grim. "Nothing." The weight of that single word settled between us like a stone.

He continued, his voice quieter now. "The only way we know to fight them is with our army. That's why we have been recruiting Majors. More will be selected when we return."

I swallowed, trying to grasp the enormity of what he was saying. "How do you know they're really coming?"

Damien exhaled. "I don't. But I know this, if the Sages are right, we don't have time to wait."

I had believed the urgency of the Hunts was about power, about proving something to the other Clans or perhaps preparing for the Celestial Dissonance, battles between Clans across multiple Realms, and I had been too young to remember the last time it happened.

I glanced at him, at the way his shoulders tensed, and for the first time, I saw the weight of it. The burden he carried, not just as Heir, but as the only person who could command the forces needed to stop this. I knew, in that moment, that whatever was coming, I was no longer afraid to stand beside him when it did.

MIRABELLE

I sat cross-legged beside Damien, my arms animated as I rattled on about my undeniable improvements in cooking, both of us fully aware that I was spinning tales. But it warmed my heart—it bloomed like flowers pushing through cracked stone.

I had no one to share the mundane with. Yet here he was, listening as if my words were the most fascinating thing in the world.

"You should have seen me this morning," I said, nodding sagely. "Beatrice was *this* close to giving me another dish. I think I might actually have a talent for it."

Damien leaned back on one arm, his other hand idly tracing patterns over the fabric of my dress, the delicate motion sending shivers through me every now and then. He regarded me with a knowing look, "I am sure Beatrice was *deeply* impressed."

"Wasn't she?" I grinned, his smile making him painfully handsome. I narrowed my eyes. "You don't believe me."

"Oh, I believe," he mused. "But I also remember..."

A deep, splintering sound that tore through the air like the world itself was breaking apart. I barely had time to react before my instincts took over. Without thinking, I scrambled toward

Damien, my hands clutching at his arm. He reacted in a heartbeat, yanking me behind him in one swift motion, his stance shifting into something rigid.

"Stay with me," he ordered. I barely had time to register what was happening before *it* came.

The ground trembled beneath us, and before either of us could move, an invisible force struck, sending us both hurtling backward. I hit the ground hard, pain jolting through my spine as the impact knocked the breath from my lungs.

A monstrous shape loomed in the distance. Bones. So many bones.

It moved like a living nightmare, its skeletal form bound together by eerie veins of blue energy that pulsed with an unholy glow. Its primary skull, an enormous dragon-like visage, flickered with cold fire, its hollow sockets empty yet *seeing*. Other skulls adorned its grotesque body, whispering in a tongue so ancient it made my skin crawl. It slithered forward, impossibly silent for something so large, its skeletal wings tucked close to its form, only appearing in fleeting flashes of half-decayed flesh and sinew.

I shuddered violently, unable to tear my eyes away from the horror before us.

"What *is* that?" I whispered, my voice barely a breath.

Damien didn't answer immediately. His jaw was clenched so tight I thought his teeth might crack.

"Rak'Thalgar," the name slithered into my ears like a curse, forbidden and wrong.

I reached out instinctively, trying to tap into whatever thread of understanding had been awakening in me these past few days. But the moment I stretched my mind toward *it*, the force recoiled violently, pushing me back with a wave of force so overpowering I gasped.

I clutched my head, dizzy. *It*...had *blocked* me. And then, without warning, Rak'Thalgar *moved*.

The skeletal monstrosity lunged forward with unnatural

speed, its entire body shifting and snapping like a tidal wave of death.

"Run," Damien ordered, and before I could even argue, he grabbed my wrist and pulled me to my feet. Damien didn't wait. He moved with ruthless efficiency, gripping my wrist in an iron hold as he propelled us forward. His strides were long, his focus razor-sharp as he veered toward one of the massive floating leaves.

When he realized I was struggling to keep up with his pace, he lifted me as if I weighed nothing and continued forward without breaking stride.

He raised his free hand. A powerful surge burst from beneath us, coiling like a liquid serpent around the base of the leaf, forcing it upward with a speed unnatural to its usual, gentle ascent. The platform lurched, the vines around its edges tightening, adapting to the sudden pressure. My stomach flipped as we shot up, the force pressing me down for a fleeting moment before settling into a smooth, accelerated climb.

The world below blurred, Rak'Thalgar's monstrous form shrinking in size, though its soulless, burning gaze never wavered. The fire within its hollow sockets pulsed, a cold, knowing hunger.

I shuddered.

Damien stood rigid beside me, his focus unshaken as he manipulated the water further, weaving it beneath the leaf's surface, guiding our ascent with a control so precise it almost seemed effortless. But I knew better.

This wasn't effortless. This was him pushing the limits of his power to get us out of danger faster than nature would allow. I wanted to scream. Wanted to *do* something. But all I could do was cling to Damien's arm as the island below shrank away.

Higher. Higher.

We landed on another isle, barely pausing before Damien pulled me onto another leaf, leaping across the vast expanse. I followed, my heartbeat a hammer in my chest as we jumped from island to island, each landing unsteady, each escape only barely enough to keep us ahead of the creature hunting us.

When we finally stopped, Damien exhaled sharply, his hand gripping my arm just a bit too tightly, his chest rising and falling in steady control. "We stay here," he murmured. "It will go back soon."

I nodded, swallowing hard, trying to keep my breathing under control.

"We can't fight it, Mirabelle." His voice was low, controlled, but there was an unmistakable edge to it. "Not without making things worse."

I swallowed hard, still trying to grasp the full weight of what we had just seen. "Why is it here?" I asked, though the answer settled like a cold stone in my gut before he even spoke.

He exhaled sharply, his fingers flexing around mine before he released me. "The balance has been disturbed."

I turned to him, searching his face. "What does that mean?"

His jaw clenched, his gaze sweeping the floating isles, the fractured terrain below. "We rushed two hunts back-to-back. We destroyed an entire island trying to tame the swarms the last day. That kind of disruption doesn't go unnoticed, especially not here." He nodded downward. "The Bone Tyrant exists to maintain the cycle. Each piece of bone in its body comes from lives it has taken to restore order."

I shuddered again at the thought of the massive skulls fused to its body, the jagged, clawed limbs stitched together from the remains of beasts long past. "So what? It thinks we're threats now?"

"Not just threats," Damien murmured. "Violators."

I bit my lip, glancing at him. His posture remained rigid, his gaze unreadable, but I could see the flicker of calculation in his eyes. He was weighing options, seeking solutions, none of which involved fighting the thing below us.

"But you kill creatures all the time," I pressed. "That's the whole purpose of the Hunt, isn't it?"

He cut me a sharp glance. "We don't kill. Hunting follows the laws of the wild. You take what the land offers, you do not strip it bare. The Hunts have a rhythm, one that we disrupted."

I swallowed against the lump forming in my throat. "And it's here to fix that."

Damien nodded. "With blood." A shiver raced down my spine.

"So, what do we do?" I whispered, casting another wary glance at the skeletal monstrosity.

"We wait." His voice was firm, absolute. "It might not be here for us specifically. If we keep running, it might decide we're part of the imbalance. But if we stay hidden, if we let it pass..." He let the words hang, but I understood. We *might* just live through this.

I exhaled slowly, trying to steady my nerves.

I *felt* it before I saw it, a crawling, skittering sensation just behind my ear.

I turned, *and saw it.*

An *insect.* A massive, writhing thing, black and many-legged, its body creeping its way up Damien's neck. I could stomach Serpents. Dragons, even. But this? *NO.*

A shriek built in my throat. Before I could let it loose, Damien's hand shot out, covering my mouth in an instant, his palm pressing firm against my lips. His voice was barely a whisper, low and commanding.

"Don't. Freak. Out." I made a muffled noise of absolute *terror* against his palm, my entire body frozen with sheer horror.

"I won't let anything happen to you," he said, his voice too steady, too calm, considering there was a *massive* insect making its way toward his jawline. "Just...breathe. It is harmless."

I *could not* breathe.

He muttered something under his breath, and in one swift motion, he *grabbed* the creature and flung it into the abyss below. My breath was uneven, the eerie quiet settling into my bones like a warning I couldn't quite place.

A bone-rattling screech cut through the air, so sudden and sharp that my pulse slammed against my ribs. The very ground beneath us trembled, the lift leaf shuddering violently underfoot.

The massive, skeletal form surged from the abyss below, impossibly fast for something so large.

It had found us. I barely had a second to move before chaos erupted.

The monstrous amalgamation of bones lashed out, its colossal, dragon skull wreathed in a cold, blue fire. My instincts screamed at me to run, but before I could even take a step, the leaf beneath us tilted violently. The weight of the creature's presence alone sent shockwaves through the floating isles, and suddenly, everything was spiraling.

Damien's arm was the last thing I saw before we were flung apart.

I hit the ground hard. A sharp cry ripped from my throat as the impact sent a jolt of agony through my ribs. The world spun around me, my vision tilting sideways as the jagged terrain bit into my palms.

Somewhere in the distance, Damien had landed as well, but he was already on his feet, already moving. Of course, he was.

The air crackled with power as he surged forward, his stance low, his muscles coiled like a predator preparing to strike. Water gathered around him in undulating waves, a force that moved like a living thing. At his command, the tide and flames surged forward, colliding with the Bone Tyrant with crushing force.

But the creature didn't fall. It barely flinched.

Damien scarcely had time to react before the skeletal beast retaliated, its massive tail swinging in a deadly arc. He twisted at the last second, avoiding the full brunt of the strike, but the sheer force still sent him skidding across the fractured ground.

I tried to scramble to my feet, tried to find an opening. I wasn't strong enough to fight it, not like him, but maybe...maybe I could connect to it. Maybe I could reach whatever mind lurked beneath the shifting bones and glowing veins of energy.

I pressed forward, my breath ragged, reaching out with every ounce of focus I had.

But then. Nothing. A wall slammed down between me and the

creature's mind, like an iron door slamming shut. I staggered back, confusion and panic warring in my chest.

It was still blocking me. It knew I was trying to reach it, and it wanted no part of it.

Damien's voice was a raw snarl, his power flaring violently as he sent another torrent of fire crashing into the beast, but he was losing.

Rak'Thalgar twisted as its clawed limbs coiled around him. "Mirabelle, go!" Damien's voice cut through the chaos, but I barely heard it over the deafening roar of the creature. "Get to the caves—NOW."

I hesitated, my heart hammering. He couldn't face this alone. Maybe he could win—but I refused to leave him to chance.

He wasn't just fighting the beast, he was fighting against the very balance of this Realm, against an ancient and relentless force. I clenched my fists. I was done running.

I sucked in a breath, reaching inside myself, feeling the shadows coil beneath my skin. They stirred like a restless tide, awaiting my command.

Fine. If I couldn't reach the creature's mind, then I would force it to acknowledge me.

A sharp, biting cold spread through my veins as I raised my hands. Long, blackened shadows burst forth from my body, twisting through the air like smoke. They lunged toward the Bone Tyrant, latching onto its massive skull. I pulled, forcing my power to wrap around it, yanking it back with everything I had.

It noticed me now.

A terrible, soul-shaking roar tore from its many mouths as it whipped around. Then the tail struck.

I barely registered the impact before I was flying. The world blurred.

Celestia. Ground. Celestia.

Then, pain.

A sickening crack rattled through my skull as I collided with the rocky ground, pain searing through my temples. A strangled sound, something between a gasp and a cry, slipped from my lips. Everything tilted, the edges of my vision going hazy. My body refused to move.

I heard Damien roar, his voice breaking into something feral, but I couldn't even turn my head to see him. My pulse was sluggish. My limbs wouldn't obey me.

And then, through the fading haze of my sight, I saw it.

The creature looming over me, its massive skull tilting slightly, those burning eyes searing into my very soul.

Wild. Unrelenting. I didn't even know if Damien was still alive. The grief never even had the chance to set in before my body finally gave up.

Darkness took me.

Pain, but bearable. That was the first thing I felt. A dull, throbbing ache in my skull, pressing at my temples like a vice. My body felt strange, heavy, yet weightless at the same time. Countless sharp points pressed against my skin, something rough and hard beneath me. My limbs refused to obey as I attempted to shift.

Light flooded my vision as I pried my eyes open. Too bright. I groaned, squeezing them shut again, trying to gather my thoughts. Then, like a crashing wave, it hit me.

Damien.

A cry tore from my throat, my body jerking upright. "Damien!"

A strong, steady hand grasped mine, warm and grounding. "I am here," came his voice, firm yet soothing. "You are safe. We both are. Relax." But before I could even fully register his words, my balance tipped. My entire body lurched sideways. My stomach plummeted.

Then—a skull. A gaping maw of bone and hollowed eyes loomed mere inches from my face, its jagged horns casting eerie shadows against the dim light—Rak'Thalgar.

The air in my lungs turned to ice as I froze, staring into the abyss of its burning blue eyes. Its massive skeletal frame coiled around me like a fortress, its form glowing faintly with the eerie energy that pulsed through the veins binding its bones together.

It...wasn't attacking me.

It breathed in my scent, a deep, rumbling inhale that sent a gust of hot air rolling over my skin. And then, it nuzzled me? The massive skull tilted slightly, pressing the cold, bone-carved ridges of its snout against my hair, a ghost of a motion that almost felt...like a kiss.

Panic clawed at my throat. I turned sharply to Damien, my voice strangled. "What is happening?!"

His expression was unreadable. "I don't even know." He raised his hands in exasperation at its actions.

Heart hammering, I closed my eyes, reaching outward, not with my hands, but with something deeper. I *felt* for it, the way I had tried before, but this time...the connection clicked. A wave of raw emotion slammed into me. Regret. Shame. Guilt.

It was apologizing. *To me.*

My breath hitched as the creature's thoughts bled into my mind, fragmented yet clear.

"I was wrong...You sided with destroyers...wrath took hold of me. Will you forgive?"

It was begging for forgiveness. I pressed a shaky hand against the ridges of its massive skull. The beast, the guardian of this land, the one who had nearly killed us both, shrank under my touch, its colossal form curling tighter, protective. Not against me. *For me.*

I exhaled softly, my fingers gliding along the cold, ancient bone. "It's okay," I murmured, barely aware of the words leaving my lips. "Shh. I understand."

A low, shuddering sound vibrated through its frame—almost like a whimper.

Damien's voice cut through the moment, his tone laced with an unreadable edge. "One moment, I was fighting it with everything I had, ready to tear it apart even at the cost of my life. Then the next, it was cocooning you like you were the most precious thing in existence."

I turned toward him. He exhaled sharply, running a hand through his hair. "I was going to kill it, to take you from it, Bella. But then I saw it crying in agony the same way I was, watching you like that."

His voice dropped, laden with raw emotion. "It started healing you. And I didn't know what to do with that."

I blinked, stunned. "It...healed me?"

Damien nodded, his lips pressed into a thin line. "Both of us had been at each other's throats, but in that moment, we were both just standing there, looking at you."

But then his gaze flicked back to the Bone Tyrant. "Now, enough of this. Give her back to me."

Rak'Thalgar let out a deep, reverberating breath, a sound almost like resignation.

And then, with a reluctant huff, the massive form began to shift. The immense skeletal coils loosened around me, slowly unraveling with a tangible slowness that spoke of refusal. His head tilted, giving one last, lingering look before the glowing veins pulsing through its bones dimmed slightly.

And then, I was falling. Not for long. Until Damien caught me. My breath left me in a sharp exhale as I collided against his chest, his warmth searing through the thin fabric between us. His grip was tight, fingers pressing into my skin to brand the reality of me into his hands.

For a long moment, neither of us moved.

I swallowed hard, my fingers curling slightly against the front of his tunic. I tried to lighten the mood. "Ehmm...I think I liked my previous pillow better." His jaw ticked.

His arms tightened, his breath uneven, as if he was still convincing himself I was real. His voice was raw, a storm barely contained. "For one moment, I thought..." He broke off, exhaling sharply, his jaw clenching like a vice.

I reached up, fingers brushing the sharp edge of his jaw. He leaned into my touch without a word, anchoring himself there, letting the warmth of my palm steady him. I rested my head against his shoulder, feeling the slow, steady rhythm of his breath. His silence was full of everything he didn't need to say.

The trek back felt longer than it truly was, perhaps because Damien insisted on carrying me the entire way. Despite my protests that I could walk on my own, his arms remained steadfast around me, brooking no argument. The gentle sway of his steps and the comforting solidity of his hold lulled me into a state of contentment I wasn't quite ready to admit. We moved in silence, a strangely companionable hush that neither of us seemed eager to break.

But as we neared the edge of our makeshift camp, his voice broke the stillness. Low, measured, laced with that quiet command I'd come to expect from him.

"I think we both know your potential," he said, not quite meeting my eyes. "You are no commoner, Mirabelle. But it is too soon for you to dive into the strength you are only beginning to grasp. And I don't want the rest of them, the Elders, the Sages, not even my own Father to see you as a new weapon for this war. Let me handle that." A flicker of frustration passed through his gaze. "My father's still Sovereign, and while we work well together, our decisions...are not always perfectly aligned."

He paused, shifting my weight in his arms like he was making sure I was truly secure. "We already have the Tameables, beasts we can guide into the fight in our Hold. If the Untameables can't be countered by them, what's the point of sacrificing all the lives on these floating isles?" His voice turned grim, almost resigned. "I won't drag you into a battle with an unknown threat. Not unprepared."

I opened my mouth to argue, but his hold tightened, and the look on his face forbade any protest.

"I will train you, just as every Legion warrior has been trained." he continued, steel in his tone. "Help you grow into your Aether, to get comfortable with, so you can decide *if* you want to serve in the

Royal Legions or not. To choose any path you would want to follow."

He continued. "But rushing in recklessly...I won't allow it. You don't get a choice in that, understand?"

His words should have angered me. But oddly, they only made my heart pound, full of an odd mixture of gratitude and irritation. Gratitude that he cared, irritation that he assumed such control. I merely nodded, overwhelmed by the weight of his promise, and the unspoken fear about my future.

CHAPTER 24

MIRABELLE

The dressing area was a carved-out alcove within the cave, the walls smoothed by time and glistening faintly under the dim torchlight. Thick, interwoven vines hung from the ceiling, acting as a makeshift partition. Beyond them, the distant murmurs of the camp and the quiet crackling of firewood provided a comforting backdrop.

I stood there, holding up the ruined remnants of my outer clothes, considering my options. Either I could put on the inside linen again, despite it being somewhat damp from our earlier journey, or I could...

My gaze drifted toward a neatly folded pile of clothes that Damien had left behind. His tunics.

Stealing one of his tunics seemed like the far better option. For warmth, of course. Not for any other reason. Absolutely not because the thought of wearing something of his made a foolish warmth bloom in my chest.

I reached for the fabric, heavy, smelling faintly of musk and him.

I heard a shift in movement just outside the door, and I knew it was Damien. His footsteps were unmistakable, exuding the kind of authority that always cleared a path before him without question.

He had dropped me off to check on the injured and attend to whatever matters needed his attention before tomorrow's Hunt. Now, he was back.

I smirked to myself. Should I? The thought was almost too tempting. He didn't know I was in here, and the idea of walking out naked, just to watch his composure fracture was *delicious*.

But then, another sound. Lighter footsteps. The cave's door creaked open.

A presence that wasn't Damien. His sharp voice cut through the air like a blade. "Why did you enter without knocking?"

I stiffened behind the screen of vines, my amusement vanishing. Then, her voice. Sweet as ever. "I didn't know you were here, my Liege," Fiora simpered. "I just came to clean."

I gritted my teeth so hard my jaw ached. *Liar.*

She had cleaned this cave earlier in the morning, I had *seen* it. And now, under the guise of duty, she had slithered her way back in, hoping to catch Damien alone. *For what?*

I fumed, barely resisting the urge to stomp out and scream to her face, *Liar, Liar, Liar!*

Damien's reply was calm, but there was an edge to it, a firm finality. "It is too late for cleaning. And we want to be alone."

We. My heart did an odd little stutter.

Oh, I thought, my fingers tightening around the fabric of his tunic. *He knows I'm in here.* So much for my eavesdropping.

Fiora hesitated. "*We?*"

I could practically hear the wheels turning in her head, trying to fit together a puzzle she didn't want to solve. That was my cue. I pulled the tunic fully over my frame, ignoring the way it swallowed me whole, and stormed out.

Fiora stood close—too close, her gaze trailing down Damien's bare torso with shameless familiarity of someone who'd memorized every ridge. He was only in his breeches and boots, his sculpted chest still damp. My temper flared, and before I knew it, I was shouldering past her with enough force to make her stagger, then planting myself squarely between them. Damien's gaze dropped to meet mine, one eyebrow quirking.

I reached up, hands sliding to the back of his neck, and tugged him down by the nape with a boldness that should have terrified me. He didn't resist. Instead, he leaned into me as though the idea had always been his, and the knot in my chest I hadn't even known was there loosened.

And I kissed him. My fingers threaded loosely through the ends of his damp hair. His lips were warm. I felt his smile against my lips, amused and warm, and satisfaction humming in the way his fingers slid lightly to the small of my back.

When I broke away, Fiora's silence rang louder than screams.

I turned toward the bed without sparing her a glance, hips swaying just enough to make Damien's tunic ride higher on my thighs as I settled onto the furs. "I'm tired," I announced, arranging myself like I belonged there. "Perhaps you can bother us tomorrow?"

Fiora's lips parted. Her eyes locked onto the way his fabric clung to my bare legs. "Did you..." Her voice cracked. "Accept someone before they were properly trained?"

My blood hissed and I beat Damien to the answer. I tilted my head, feigning thoughtfulness. "I don't know, Fiora. Perhaps he's developed a taste for *immaturity*," I purred, twisting her own insult back at her. The words landed like a slap. Her face went parchment-pale, mouth sealing shut.

A petty satisfaction bloomed in my mind. Fiora's lips pressed into a rigid line, but she bowed her head. "I'm...going."

Good.

But Damien's voice followed her like a blade. "Don't bother cleaning my cavern again, Fiora." Every syllable iced over. "And no one questions my decisions." He paused.

She nodded to the floor.

"You have crossed lines you know better than to touch. There won't be warnings next time." Finality threaded through his words. "And if you speak to Mirabelle again, with or without me present, you will regret it."

Fiora's hands fisted at her sides. "Yes, my Liege."

She turned stiffly, but I couldn't resist. "Do close the door firmly," I called after her. "We'd hate interruptions."

The slam of the door was sweeter than any victory chant. I exhaled, satisfaction curling through me like smoke. But as the heat of the moment began to cool, a flicker of unease stirred in my chest. Didn't I just prove her point?

"Territorial, aren't we?" His voice was low, warm with amusement.

I lifted my chin, reaching for a composure I didn't fully feel. "You let me be."

His mouth quirked, just slightly, and for once, he didn't throw a teasing jab in return. Instead, he stepped closer and sat beside me, his arms curling around my waist. "I do," he admitted, breath hot against my pulse point. "And I enjoy that irrational surge of possession in you that mirrors my own." His fingers pressed into the small of my back. "But I won't feast on your insecurities."

"So let me be clear." His voice dropped, gravel and gunmetal. "No one. Has ever. Or will *ever*. Come close to what you are to me."

I swallowed hard. The certainty in his tone wasn't placation. It held something heavier than reassurance. Still, old thorns prodded at me. "She probably thinks I am some untrained amusement," I muttered, picking at the sleeve of his tunic. "Just a passing distraction you got curious about."

Damien's laugh was dark, velvety. "No one would dare pull the stunt you did." His thumb brushed his tunic at my thigh. "Least of all while wearing clothes stolen from my wardrobe."

I bit my lip, trying not to smile. But another thought—one I'd carried for far too long, hovered on the edge of my tongue like a bruise that needed pressing. "Can I ask you something?" I said, still fiddling with the edge of his tunic.

His eyes flicked to mine. "You can ask me anything."

I hesitated. "The Thralls...the ones selected for...intimacy. Are they willing? Or are they just...assigned?"

"Of course, they are willing," he said. "Always. And if you are asking specifically about the intimates, they are chosen from Thralls who wanted the role. No one is forced into it."

I nodded slowly, absorbing that. But it didn't soothe the unease pricking under my skin. "And that's all they're for?" I asked, trying to keep my voice level. "Just...physical pleasure?"

He shook his head. "No. Intimates aren't just there for that. They are assigned to a person, to tend to personal needs, yes, but not solely. They assist with clothing, food, travel, rest. They learn your preferences, your vices. And yes, one part of that is physical. But not all."

I studied his face, searching for some trace of feeling. "You speak of it as though it were...a matter of trade."

"Because it is," he said simply. "A clean arrangement, uncomplicated. Boundaries are clear, and both sides know them. Either can walk away at any time."

I swallowed hard. It made sense, I suppose. But still, the idea of him with someone else, even in something so impersonal, prickled under my skin. The silence stretched, the weight of the conversation settling between us. It was getting late.

I scrambled to stand. "I should go—"

"Too late for that." He caught my wrist, tugging me back. "After the way you staked your claim on me, running off to your cave seems absurd. Doesn't it?" His sly smile was infuriating.

I narrowed my eyes. "Well, I should—"

He tilted his head, the faintest grin curving his mouth. "You missed your cue, wildcat. Now get under these furs and sleep while I check on the healing cavern before tomorrow."

I hesitated.

"I will join you when I get back from the last round," Damien added, already reaching for his cloak.

I tilted my head, watching him roll his shoulders like the

weight of command had never left. "So, you'll join me?" I asked, testing. "In bed?"

He glanced at me, unreadable. "Yes."

I blinked. The simplicity of the answer landed like a strike to my ribs.

"But...the Heir is not allowed to share a bed with black-bloods without Bonding. Or have I heard that wrong?"

"Ah," he smirked. "I forgot how thoroughly the public tracks the Heir's personal affairs."

I crossed my arms. "Well? Was I wrong?"

His smirk softened into something quieter. "Yes and no."

I raised a brow, waiting. Damien exhaled slowly, like he was weighing each word. "I am not supposed to share *my* chamber—or *my* bed—with anyone of black blood. That is the etiquette." His gaze burned through me. "And no, I have never broken it. Black blooded or not."

The admission hung between us. My mind spun with things I didn't know how to voice. I opened my mouth, but only one question made it out. "Why now?"

He turned halfway, profile sharp in the light. "Still figuring that out." He raked a rough hand through his hair. "Why I can't resist you. Why waiting until Bonding feels impossible."

Bonding. It was no small word. A lifetime tether, no undoing, no games. Among Royals, it was ceremonial, a matter of politics, tradition, spectacle. Among Majors, a binding pact to anchor futures. Among commoners, a necessity. Survival.

For us? For him? Had it simply slipped out or did he know what he'd said? No. No, this wasn't that. I was reading too much into it. But he didn't correct himself or offer clarity to calm the chaos now unraveling inside me.

Instead, Damien turned back to face me, gaze heavy, voice quieter. "I am not going to rush you, Mirabelle. So sleep." Then, just like that, he stepped away, the door clicked shut. Alone with the echo of his confession, I realized—neither of us was ready.

I STIRRED, my body sinking deeper into the warmth around me, unwilling to leave the abyss of sleep. Yesterday had drained me in ways I didn't realize until I hit the bed. My limbs were heavy, my mind still sluggish with exhaustion, and I had slept deeply. No half-waking moments, just warmth and peace.

A warmth that was alive. My heartbeat stumbled as realization struck.

The weight against my back wasn't a blanket, nor was the arm curled around my stomach merely my own. The firm chest, bare and hot, pressed flush against me, the slow rise and fall of his breath matching the rhythm of mine.

Damien had come back. I hadn't heard him return. I must have passed out long before that. And now I was wrapped in him, fused with him, his breath, his very being pressed against me. One of his arms was firm around my middle, pulling me tight against him as if even in sleep he refused to let go. His palm rested against the bare skin of my stomach beneath his tunic. The tunic that had ridden up dangerously high. But it was the other hand, the one cupping the swell of my breast even in sleep, that made my entire body lock in place. Heat pooled in my core as the realization settled.

I swallowed, my throat suddenly dry.

I needed to move. Or at least turn to see his face. Maybe then I'd believe this was real, that I wasn't lost in some fever dream woven by exhaustion and wishful thinking.

Carefully, I shifted. The arm around my stomach flexed immediately, his grip tightening as if sensing my escape. The movement dragged my back even more tightly against his chest, and my breath hitched as the feel of his skin, the heat of him, seared into my own.

His voice. Low. Husky. Sleep-ruined, did something to me. "You are awake."

I swallowed again, fighting to keep my voice even. "For

someone who's never shared a bed before, you seem like a rather skilled cuddler."

He didn't reply. No teasing or smirk. Just silence. When I finally gathered the courage to glance over my shoulder, I found him staring down at me. His eyes, hooded and dark, were nearly black, the last traces of blue swallowed by shadow.

Slowly, deliberately, he dipped his head, his nose grazing the curve of my neck. His stubble, rough from days without a fresh shave, scraped against me, igniting a shiver that curled deep in my spine. Feeling the contrast, the softness of his lips and the rawness of his stubble was making me wetter. And before I could stop myself, a sound slipped free.

A sound that shouldn't have left my lips. A throaty moan. A low, helpless sound that shocked me. He inhaled sharply against my throat, his entire body going rigid behind me. Then, before I could even think, before I could process the fire curling low in my stomach, I moved.

Without a second thought, I climbed onto him, instinctive, unhesitating, my hands gripping his shoulders, my thighs locking around his hips like he was the only thing keeping me grounded.

And that was it. His restraint snapped.

With a low snarl, Damien flipped me onto my back, his weight pressing me down, trapping me beneath him. The tunic I wore rode up dangerously high, leaving almost nothing to the imagination.

His hand caught my wrists, pinning it above my head. His other brushed up the length of my thigh, his fingers curling just beneath the fabric. I should have felt embarrassed, but I didn't. Because the look on his face was enough to feed my confidence.

Predatory. Ravenous. And I realized, with a thrill of something dangerously addictive, that I was the reason for it.

He pushed the fabric up, exposing me to the air, to him. His breathing deepened, his broad chest rising and falling rapidly. His eyes devoured *me*, burning blue and storm-dark, barely leashed. Then, softly, like an oath, he murmured, "Perfect."

His fingers, warm and calloused from years of wielding blades and power, trailed down the length of my arm, following the curve of my waist. "No," he said to himself, his voice like embers crackling in the dark. "Even perfect isn't enough of a word for what I see."

I writhed beneath him, trapped in the onslaught of sensation, the overwhelming reality of him, his hunger, his restraint fraying at the edges. His hand reached my hip, squeezing, before gliding lower. I gasped as his knuckles skimmed through my wet folds, a featherlight touch that made my breath hitch and my thighs tense in reaction.

His gaze snapped to mine. A dark gleam flickered in his eyes. "So, this is what magnificence feels like," he murmured. "Soft. Flawless. And all mine."

Before I could form a thought, his head dipped. His nose grazed through the most intimate part of me, a slow, tormenting drag from bottom to top. A strangled sound escaped my lips, somewhere between shock and pure, unfiltered pleasure. I tried to clench my thighs together, overwhelmed, but his hands pushed them apart, anchoring me in place. "No, Bella," he murmured against me, his voice vibrating through my core, "you don't hide from me."

And then he kissed me there. A slow, wet and passionate kiss.

A broken gasp tore from my throat, my head snapping back against the pillow. My fingers dug into the sheets, into his shoulders, into anything that could hold me to this world because I was floating, weightless, spiraling into something unfamiliar and dangerous.

Damien groaned, a deep, guttural sound that rumbled through his chest, like a man who had gone days without sustenance and finally, finally tasted something worth devouring. "You taste like every craving *I never knew I had.*" His tongue flicked, slow and intentional, learning me piece by piece. His large hands pressed my thighs wider, keeping me from retreating. Keeping me where he wanted me and going on and on until I saw stars. Licking, sucking, drinking me down like I was the only thing in existence. His voice was needy, "...something I could never have enough of."

"Damien..." My voice broke, a whimper more than a plea. "I..." I didn't even know what I was trying to say, only that the tension coiling inside me was too much, too fast, too devastating.

"I know," One of his hands slid higher, pressing firmly against my lower stomach, pinning me as though I might escape as he sucked me harder. "Let go, Bella." He rasped against me, his voice dark. Then his mouth found me there again—and I shattered. The pleasure was unlike anything I had ever known, a slow, torturous climb, each second stretching unbearably, until the world fell apart around me. My breath hitched, then broke into a ragged sob as the intensity ripped through me, a wildfire blazing through my veins.

It didn't stop. It wouldn't stop. The waves kept coming, each one more overwhelming than the last, pulling me under, drowning me in sensation. I gasped his name, over and over, my voice breaking, my body trembling, completely at his mercy. My fingers fisted in his hair, gripping him like an anchor, but it only spurred him on, like he thrived on my unraveling.

His rumble against me was low and satisfied, indulgent, as if I had just given him something he had been starving for. As if I had belonged to him all along, and this was simply proof of it. "Look at you, falling apart just for me."

He leaned in, his mouth hovering just above, his fingers and mouth still teasing, still tormenting.

Just as the last tremors wracked my body, as I lay there limp, barely able to breathe, he lifted his head, his lips wet, his face dark with satisfaction.

His tongue flicked out to taste the last remnants of my release, his thumb traced slow, lazy circles over my trembling thigh, his gaze unapologetically possessive.

"I should clean you up," he murmured, almost thoughtful, "Or should I just make you messier."

I had no doubt he planned to ruin me completely. When the high finally ebbed, I whimpered, trying to close my legs, trying to hide from the intensity of what just happened. But he wouldn't let me.

A slow, deliberate kiss was placed against the sensitive, trembling flesh. Then another. Gentle now. Reverent.

"Stop hiding from me." he whispered again, he whispered again, his voice harsh yet thick with contentment.

I swallowed, my mind still spiraling. What had just happened? I covered my face with my hands. "I can't believe..."

He rose above me, gripped my wrists, pulling them away from my face. "Believe me, you are going to get used to it." he murmured. His eyes, stormy and unreadable, pinned me in place. A long, drawn-out moment of silence fell between us. And then his voice dropped to a rough whisper: "You have never been pushed over that edge before." A statement, not a question.

I hesitated, suddenly shy. "No," I admitted. Then, after a pause, "I've tried on my own. But never like this. Never to...that."

A carnal fire flared in his gaze. I swallowed hard, watching as he leaned back slightly, as if considering something. And then, his lips curled into an almost amused smile. "Good, maybe that is because it wasn't yours to take. It was mine to give," he said, his knuckles skimming over my hip with a featherlight touch.

"How remarkably arrogant," I breathed, my voice still unsteady.

His smile deepened. "And entirely justified." he murmured, leaning down until his breath warmed my skin. Then he exhaled sharply, like he was trying to compose himself. Then he tore his own tunic from my body, wiping me clean with gentle care.

"Get dressed," he murmured, rising from the bed, his voice rough but softened at the edges. "I will bring you something to eat." And not so subtly, he tucked himself away, concealing the heavy, unrelieved strain between his legs. Only then did he grab his tunic, striding toward the door.

I propped myself up on my elbows, frowning slightly. "You don't want me to...?"

He stilled, then turned back toward me. The look in his eyes nearly set my skin aflame all over again. "You think I could do this and not *feel* it, what I just did was only for you?"

He slowly shook his head, his voice was low, "This was the single most pleasurable moment *of my existence*, Bella." And then, just to ruin me completely, he walked, bent down and pressed a slow, lingering kiss against my still-sensitive core.

I let out a soft, broken sound. He smiled, and stood, making his way toward the door. "I am locking it behind me," he said. "I'll be back soon."

The door shut. I stared at the ceiling, my fingers tracing the red marks now branding my skin.

⬥

HIGHS HAVE a cruel way of masking the inevitable fall, lulling you into a fleeting sense of security, making you believe, even if only for a moment, that you can hold onto them forever. But the crash always comes. And when it does, it doesn't simply pull you back down, it *rips* you from the sky, slamming you into the ground so hard, you forget you ever believed in flight.

I should have seen it coming.

But I didn't. Whether it was naivety or youth, take your pick. Either way, I was a fool to think fate would let me have a gift without demanding a price.

I waited. And waited. The anticipation of Damien's return settled uneasily in my chest, shifting from idle curiosity into a cold dread.

The minutes stretched. Too long. At first, I told myself he was caught up with the Majors. That he had things to tend to. That he hadn't forgotten, because *of course* he wouldn't. But when an hour passed, then another, my nerves twisted into a knot so tight I could feel it in my throat.

Something was wrong.

I paced, restless, unable to shake the unease prickling at my skin. The cave, once a quiet refuge, now felt like a prison, its walls

234

closing in. The door remained locked from the outside, a detail that hadn't bothered me *until now.*

The moment I heard footsteps, I sprang toward the door, relief curling through my chest, only for it to turn cold when Beatrice stepped inside instead. She carried a tray of food, her movements precise, impersonal. She didn't speak. Didn't so much as glance at me as she set the plate down.

A pit opened in my stomach. "Where is he?" I asked, stepping forward.

No response. She turned, moving toward the door, but before I could follow, she shifted, blocking my path.

"You're to stay here," she said, voice void of emotion.

The chill in my spine sharpened. "Why?" She didn't answer. Didn't even *hesitate* as she stepped back, pulled the door shut, and turned the lock.

The click echoed through the room, final and cold.

I stared at the door, my pulse roaring in my ears. *Did something happen to Damien?*

My stomach twisted, bile rising to my throat. I didn't know what was waiting on the other side of that door.

But for the first time in a long time, I was afraid to find out.

CHAPTER 25

DAMIEN

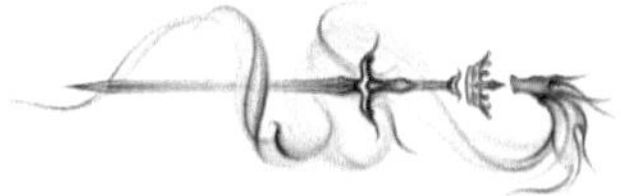

I was eight when I first met Rennard. A black-haired boy with too much energy, too much ease in his step, and a grin that made it look like he had never known a day of discipline in his life.

"You look lonely. Want to borrow my sword?"

The wooden blade in his outstretched hand looked ridiculous. I was the Heir of Atlassian, trained in swords before most boys even learned how to tie their tunics. I should have ignored him, dismissed him without a second thought.

Instead, I stared. At the toy. At him.

I don't take things from outsiders. The lesson had been drilled into me like scripture, carved into my bones with every cold glance, every expectation, every demand that I *be better* than those around me.

So, I turned away. Uninterested. Silent. And left him standing there.

But Rennard was persistent. He followed me. Not in the way others did, not out of duty, not out of fear, not because he was told to. He simply *existed* near me, hovering at the edges of my world with no expectation, no purpose other than to *be there*.

Days passed. Then weeks. Then months. I never acknowledged him. Never encouraged him. But he never left.

I thought he would get bored. That he would realize I wasn't worth the effort, that I wasn't someone who had the luxury of *friends*. But he didn't.

It took him two years to wear me down. By the time we were ten, he had wedged himself into my life in a way I never saw coming. I never sought him out, never put words to whatever it was we had, but he understood my silences, and I understood his grins. He was my only friend.

And then, I lost him. During the Nightfall Siege, when the two Clans turned against us. When the Royals whispered their plans of unity, of strategy, of an easier victory. When I believed them and wanted to show my father how I could be an asset in war.

They had used me to lure my father into a battlefield they had already sabotaged. I had been young, *foolish,* thinking that battle was just steel and tactics and men clashing in a field.

But war was never that simple.

The first sign of betrayal had come too late. The warriors who had stood beside us just days before turned their blades on us mid-battle. The promised reinforcements had never been real. The passage we had taken into the valley had been a deliberate choke-hold, funneled into a dead end.

And Rennard had been taken in the first wave. Not as a soldier. Not as an enemy. As a message. Only because he was my shadow.

His body had been tied to the front gates of their fortress, hung up for all to see, for me to see. His blood stained the banners. His head had been tilted forward in a way that almost made him look like he was just resting, just waiting...

Just *there*. Like he had always been.

I had raged. I had cried. I had fought. Then, I had *slaughtered* my way through them that night, knowing we would win, knowing our forces would prevail because my father never *lost*.

But it didn't matter. Because the only battle that had mattered to me had already been lost.

We burned their banners. We took back our land. We won. And when the smoke settled, my father stood beside me, looking at the battlefield like it was nothing more than another lesson I had to learn. His voice, when he finally spoke, was calm. Cold.

"I think now you know how much it costs to trust everyone. And I hope this is a good enough reason for you to never do it again."

That was all he said. That was all he *had to* say.

I was twelve years old. And I never trusted anyone but myself after that.

And now, standing here, feeling the edges of something foreign creeping into my mind, I wondered if I was about to make the same mistake all over again.

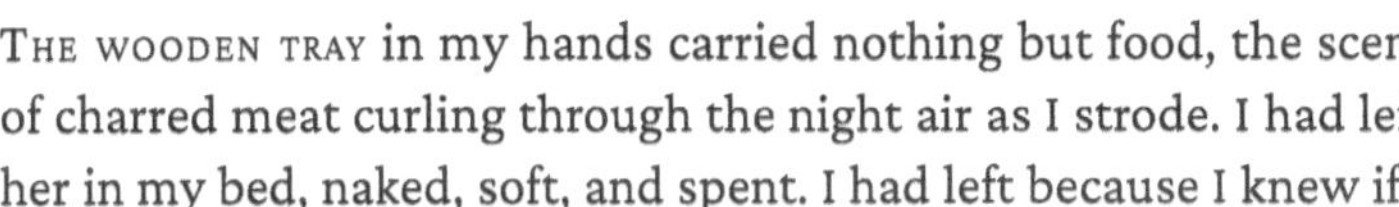

THE WOODEN TRAY in my hands carried nothing but food, the scent of charred meat curling through the night air as I strode. I had left her in my bed, naked, soft, and spent. I had left because I knew if I stayed, I would not have been able to stop myself. I would have devoured her whole, claimed her fully.

So, I had gone to fetch her food, to let her rest, to force some distance between myself and the reckless urge that still burned beneath my skin.

"Damien." Haldric's voice rang through the air.

I turned, narrowing my eyes at the gathering before me. More than usual. Elders. Royals. Some I had not seen since the last war council. Others bore the insignia of the palace, their faces carved from stone. The scent of burning wood thickened the air, smoke curling around them in the dim chamber.

Something was wrong. I set the tray down on a stone ledge, shoulders straightening as I stepped forward. Haldric met my gaze.

"Atlassian is under siege." The words slammed into my chest like a hammer. Silence. A breath. Then another. The kind of silence that comes before a storm.

"When?" I asked, my voice quiet—too quiet. But the weight

behind it made even the flames waver. Haldric exhaled. His grip tightened on the armrest of his chair. "The Untameables have taken control. The capital is falling. The defenses at the borders have collapsed."

That wasn't possible. We had time. The Sages had traced the omens, deciphered the patterns, followed the tides of magic itself. The war was coming—but not yet.

Unless—

"How?" My voice was cold steel, every muscle in my body locked.

Haldric hesitated.

And then, the first knife fell. "She lied to you."

A bitter twist churned inside me, sharp and ugly.

"Mirabelle."

Nathan. The moment his name left their mouths, something cold gripped my spine.

I had already suspected it. From the second she uttered their names, my mind had been dissecting it, piece by piece, turning it over like a blade.

Because Nathan wasn't in Atlassian.

I had sent him to Zarkon, far beyond our borders, to seek the wisdom of the Old Sages. The legend of a single wish, a boon that could alter the fate of a kingdom, was too great to ignore. He had not returned until today...which meant he couldn't have been the one asked her to come here.

And Jasper? I had exiled him. I had sent him away because of her.

Because I had seen the way his eyes lingered on Mirabelle, the way his attention latched onto her like a disease. He had left the very day after I issued the order.

And yet, she had spoken their names. *Lies.*

The second dagger followed swiftly. "The portal breach happened the moment she arrived." The blood in my veins turned to ice.

Haldric's voice was measured, too calm. "She stole the key," he said. "Perhaps she heard of it from us. Or worse, from *them*." The key to forbidden sigil. Ancient. Older than most of us here. A relic of balance and ruin.

It wasn't something one simply found. Yet she knew how to unleash the Untameables even before we figured out the reasons.

She had arrived, just as everything fell apart.

"She opened the sigil," another Elder added, his voice cautious, as though he knew exactly where my mind was heading. "Someone without knowledge of ancient magic wouldn't have been able to do that."

I had known she wasn't just a commoner all this time. The way she had called the shadows. The way she had controlled the Beasts. The way she had survived in Etheris when she should have died. And I had ignored it. Buried it beneath desire. Beneath need. Beneath the hope for more. I had been blind.

"She pretended to be a commoner," Haldric said. "Yet she possesses powers that do not belong to Atlassian. What else has she been hiding?"

My gut twisted violently. Because they were right. I knew she wasn't a Major either. And if I didn't even know what she was, who else did? What else had I ignored?

"What are you saying?" I asked, my voice dangerously calm.

A long silence. Then, Ophira spoke the final blow. "We have reason to believe she is working with an external force. That she was sent to infiltrate us." She is one of the few ancient Elders my father entrusted with his confidences, alongside Haldric and Edmond.

The ground beneath me felt unsteady. The very breath in my lungs felt wrong.

"She concealed her power from us, deceived us about her true intentions. She unsealed the sigil for them and fled to Etheris, ensuring no one would suspect her." Haldric's voice was steady and final.

"We think she played a part in this attack," Ophira corrected. "And we cannot ignore that."

A sharp, searing pain lanced through my skull. They were waiting. Waiting for me to decide.

And I hated it. I hated that I couldn't shake the bitter trace of suspicion they'd left festering. I hated that I was standing here, considering the words of men I had never trusted over the female who had become my greatest weakness.

The fire crackled. Its warmth did nothing to cut through the cold settling in my bones. The room had fallen into a silence so dense it felt like the very air was pressing down on us, waiting for something to give.

And then, Nathan broke it. "The only solution is the Crown of Empyrea."

A ripple of unease swept through the room. Even the Elders, who had mastered their expressions, shifted in discomfort.

Haldric exhaled. "Nathan spoke to the Sages."

Nathan nodded. "The moment the breaches began, I sought out their wisdom. You also sent me to Zarkon." His jaw tightened. "And the answer led back to one place."

The Crown. Buried beneath ruins older than our wars. A relic untouched. Forbidden. Feared. They had been probing its edges but dared not claim its core.

"We found it in the heart of the ruins," Nathan said. "Pulsating with magic so raw it felt alive."

The Crown had never been claimed, never been worn—not for lack of trying, but because of the whispers of what it demanded from its bearer.

Nathan's gaze flickered toward the Elders. "The ruins are bound to it," he said. "No one has dared to disturb it for centuries, believing it holds something back—something worse." His fingers curled slightly, as if weighing unspoken consequences. "But the Sages of all the Clans agree. The Crown is the solution."

The truth was bitterly ironic: the artifact was had all feared was now our only hope.

"How? And what does it demand?" My voice was quiet, but it

cut through the room like a blade. Nathan hesitated. That hesitation told me everything.

The Sages had offered clarity, but clarity did not mean safety. "The one who places the Crown on the shattered remnants of the artifact gains the boon of a single wish," Nathan admitted. "One."

One of the Elders, his voice heavy with the weight of experience, spoke with measured caution.

"It would be unwise for the Heir to take this burden upon himself. The Sages have found no clear danger in the Crown—no written warnings, no omens foretelling catastrophe. But that does not mean the risk does not exist. The fear surrounding it is not without reason. For centuries, the Crown has remained untouched, its power left undisturbed. Not because it was forbidden by law, but because of the uncertainty of what it might demand in return."

Another Elder, his fingers tapping against the armrest of his chair, added, "Atlassian cannot afford recklessness. The Heir is not expendable. If there are consequences, if the Crown exacts a toll, we cannot allow it to fall upon you. The Sovereign or one of the Elders of the old bloodlines will place it. You will be present, but you will not be the one to bear that weight."

Haldric leaned forward, his sharp gaze fixed on me. "This is not a slight against your strength, Damien, nor a question of your ability to lead. But Atlassian has lost much already. We cannot risk losing its future as well."

Their words carried a finality that left no room for argument. The decision had already been made. Now, it was my turn to make the right decision.

I called for Beatrice. She arrived swiftly, her expression unreadable, waiting for my command. "Take this to Mirabelle," I instructed, nodding toward the untouched tray of food. "Do nothing else." She nodded, taking the tray without question. She knew better than to ask.

I turned back to the Elders, to the men who had gathered here to shape the course of our war, of our future. My pulse was a violent drum against my ribs, my breath steady only because I forced it to be. The weight in my chest felt like a blade pressing inward, slow and cruel.

"I want to hear what she has to say," I declared, my voice calm, though the storm inside me howled. "If there is an explanation, I want to hear it from her."

Silence settled over the room, thick and suffocating, pressing down on my skin like a second layer of armor. No one argued, but neither did anyone approve. They had already passed their judgment. She was guilty in their eyes.

And the difference between us was simple. I needed her to be innocent.

The thought sent something raw splintering through my chest, something close to rage, at them, at this situation, at myself for even entertaining the possibility that they might be right.

I exhaled slowly, steadying the chaos inside me before I spoke again. "I will be the one to decide what happens to her." The words burned like fire on my tongue, but I let them settle into the space between us. "If she is proven guilty, I will see to her punishment myself."

I wanted to be strong enough to choose justice over her, and that terrified me more than anything. "But for now," I continued, forcing my mind back into the war, into duty, into the thing that had always grounded me before her, "our focus must remain on one thing, getting back Atlassian. That is our only priority. I expect every one of you to obey me in this, and to be as honest as possible about what we are facing. No more half-truths. No more speculation."

And yet, even as I spoke of priorities, my own mind betrayed me. Because the only thing I could think of, the only thing I had *ever* craved in this life, was her.

A murmur of agreement swept through the room, but before it could settle, another truth struck like a blade between my ribs.

"That may not be so simple, Young Sovereign." I turned sharply to Nathan, his expression grim.

"The Majors have been compromised." The words barely registered at first. But then the meaning bled through, slow and sharp like a wound taking its time to hurt.

"What do you mean?" My voice was dangerously low, as if by sheer force, I could turn this reality into something else. Haldric exhaled. "The Untameables have seized control of them. They are using the Majors against us, turning them into a defense force for the castle."

The Majors, whose numbers made up more than half the Clan's populace, stood as an undeniable force.

Nathan spoke again, careful. "We don't know how. But they are no longer their own. We don't know how many have been turned, and we have no way of distinguishing the controlled from the free. We cannot fight them without killing our own. And worse, we do not know which among them are truly still themselves."

"They are seizing our warriors," my mind running ahead of my own words, dissecting the consequences. "And soon, they will use them to attack the Clan from within."

Haldric nodded gravely. "The longer we wait, the stronger they become. We cannot hold our own ground if we don't know who is with us and who has already been lost."

The walls were closing in, faster than we had anticipated. Every move had been planned, every strategy calculated, and yet, the enemy had still outmaneuvered us. "We can place the Crown," I spoke aloud, meant as much for myself as for them. "But if we do not act first, if we do not move, the Royals, the Majors still loyal to us, the commoners, we risk losing them all before we even have a chance to reclaim the throne."

I dragged a hand down my face, forcing my mind to sharpen, to push past the impossible weight pressing down on me.

"Where do we move them?" Nathan asked.

"Here, to the hunting Realm," I said without hesitation. "It's the only place left untouched by the war. It's vast, and it can sustain them until we reclaim Atlassian. But someone must stay behind to ensure their safety until we return."

I exhaled. "Nathan and I will lead the Royal Legion to reclaim as many of them as we can. The rest will remain here. Etheris has more than enough space to shelter the entire Realm. Izmer will oversee things in my absence, and I will call in favors from Nyxaria on his behalf."

He was reckless, but he was also one of the few I trusted to protect them. The Elders murmured in agreement, and for the first time since the meeting began, a plan started to form. A direction, however uncertain.

But none of it mattered, not the Crown, not the war, not the fate of the Majors, until I confronted the one question clawing at the edges of my mind.

Mirabelle. I turned on my heel, already moving toward the door. I had never been one to hesitate. Never one to second-guess my own choices. But as I stepped into the dim corridor, the weight in my chest grew heavier.

⋙━⬥━⋘

THE MOMENT I stepped into the Cave, she broke into a run.

A blur of red hair, wild eyes, bare feet on cold stone. She crashed into me, arms locking around my waist, holding me like she needed to feel that I was real. That I was here. Her breathing was ragged, frantic. "I was so worried about you," she whispered, shaking against me.

I didn't move. My hands remained at my sides, rigid as stone, my body a fortress against her desperation. My mind was a storm, reeling, unraveling, caught between the war inside me.

Justice or yearning. The leader I was raised to be or the man I had become with her.

She must have felt the cold distance, the absence of my touch, because she hesitated, pulling back just enough to look up at me. Her brows knitted in confusion. "What's wrong?" she asked.

My jaw tightened. I had to do this. "Did you *lie* to me?"

Her breath caught. "No," she said immediately, shaking her head. "Why would I?"

I stared into her eyes, searching for something, anything that would tell me they were all wrong. But then I said the words that would decide everything. "Did Nathan ask you to come here?"

And that was when I saw it. The way her eyes changed. The way realization flickered behind them, followed by something else. Hesitation.

That was all it took to knife my hope clean through. I exhaled sharply, shaking my head to myself. Of course.

Of course.

"It's not what you think," she rushed, stepping closer, reaching for me again. "Let me explain."

"Then explain, Mirabelle," I cut in, my voice sharp as steel. "Because from where I stand, it looks an awful lot like you lied."

She swallowed, her hands trembling as she clenched them at her sides. "I was trying to protect you."

I laughed, cold and humorless. "Don't lie to me. *Again.*" My voice was low now, lethal. "I don't tolerate those who lie to my face. I have killed for far less than that."

She flinched. But I wasn't done. "You were perfectly fine the day before the Hunt. And suddenly, you became afraid? Why?"

Her lips parted, but she hesitated, as if trying to choose her words carefully. Guilt carved itself into her face. "I overheard the Elders speaking in the palace."

The rage inside me sharpened into something vicious. "I moved you to the palace to keep you safe, and you repaid me by eavesdropping on palace affairs?" My voice dropped to a growl.

"I didn't mean to!" she burst out. "I accidentally heard them say you weren't safe."

"So you decided lying to me and sneaking into Etheris was the best course of action?"

"It wasn't like that!" she shouted, her frustration cracking through. "I didn't want to pressure you while you were on the Hunt..."

"So you *lied*," I cut her off. "And you *lied* about Jasper being there. About Nathan being there. About you being in danger?" I scoffed.

"Yes! And I didn't know it mattered!" she shouted, exasperated. "I was going to tell you after we got back. I even forgot about it. And I am sorry!"

I should have felt something at her words. But all I felt was the slow, sinking certainty of betrayal. "Are you sorry for stealing the key and opening the sigil?"

Confusion flickered across her face. "What sigil?"

My stomach turned. "So you don't even know?" My voice dripped with disbelief.

She hesitated, her brows knitting together. "I know about the key. It was on the ground near the portal. I only used it to open the portal and—"

A raw, uncontrollable fury ripped through me. "There is no key to the portal, Mirabelle!" I roared, the sound echoing through the stone walls. "Now shut up. Enough."

She flinched, eyes wide, as if she had just begun to realize that I wasn't the one who had held her so gently last night. I let out a sharp breath, running a hand through my hair, willing the crushing weight in my chest to lessen. But it wouldn't.

It wouldn't, because I had been a fool. Because the only person I had ever let touch the iron walls of my heart had been using me. Because the only one I had craved, the only thing I had ever allowed myself to want, had been deceiving me all along.

How had I not seen it? How had I been so blind?

A bitter smile twisted at my lips. Of course. I turned my gaze back to her, my voice empty, hollow. "Hear me, Mirabelle."

Her breath hitched.

"We, the Atlassians, have always executed traitors. And we always will."

I watched the blood drain from her face.

"You will stay here until I take my Clan back from the disaster you unleashed upon us." My voice was void of warmth now, stripped bare of any tenderness that had once existed between us. "And when it is done, I will seek vengeance on you. For the Clan."

A pause. A beat of silence so thick I could barely breathe through it.

"And for me." The words left my lips like a death sentence.

Her mouth parted slightly, but no words came. Silent tears welled in her eyes, sliding down her cheeks. I ignored the way a sharp ache twisted inside me at the sight of her tears. I'd already learned that lesson the hard way. Twice.

"Don't," I snapped, my voice a blade. "Don't try to manipulate me with tears, Mirabelle."

I turned sharply on my heel, ignoring the way my chest felt like it was caving in, ignoring the way something inside me was screaming at me to stop.

But I didn't stop. Because the man I had become with her had died the moment she betrayed me.

CHAPTER 26

MIRABELLE

Four days.

Four days of silence, of solitude, of pacing these stone walls until my steps felt like echoes of themselves. Four days of being treated like a criminal.

I had waited the first day, too stunned to do anything else. I had stared at the heavy wooden door, expecting it to open. Expecting Damien to return. Expecting, foolishly, that this was all some grave misunderstanding.

But then came the second day. Then the third. And now, on the fourth, I am forced to face a truth I should have known all along.

There was no misunderstanding. No mistake. Damien believed them. And maybe that shouldn't have been the most painful realization of all.

I had endured a childhood of being overlooked, of scrubbing floors until my hands were raw, of whispered insults and sharp-edged gazes that saw me as less than those around me. But for the first time in my life, I had thought, perhaps, just perhaps, I had found something more that could have been mine.

And yet, here I am. Locked away in his cave, stripped of anything that might remind me that I was ever welcome here at all. I had been a fool all along.

The air inside the cave is cold, emptier than it was before. Every trace of Damien has been removed, his weapons, his armor, his belongings, even the faint scent of him that once lingered. As if my very presence had tainted them, as if the mere act of existing in his space had been an offense that could not be tolerated.

All that remains are the walls that surround me. My prison. I have no weapons. No allies. No way out. The only time I am permitted to leave is when I am escorted, either to bathe or for the occasional stroll. Even the bath comes at a price. Beatrice shackles me with enchanted iron, a length of chain binding us together as she leads me through the narrow, winding paths of the caves toward the water.

Rowane and Beatrice wait nearby, out of sight to give privacy, but never out of reach, ensuring I do not run. And still, despite everything, I tried. I tried speaking to Beatrice, tried reasoning and even tried shouting. I asked her if she truly believed this of me, if she saw the truth in my eyes or if she was simply following orders. She did not answer. She never does. She simply sets my meals before me and leaves, locking the door behind her without a word, without a glance, without an ounce of hesitation.

My mind should have been too numb to think, too exhausted to make sense of the pieces that had been thrust before me like a puzzle meant to be unsolvable. And yet, the more I sat with it, the more I tried to tame the chaos in my mind, the more unease curled in my gut.

How had I become the traitor?

The evidence was laid out too perfectly, aligned with eerie precision. Every thread, every accusation, all pointing to me like a map designed for one conclusion. But something was missing. Something didn't fit.

I closed my eyes, forcing myself to walk through it again.

The key.

I had found it beneath the portal, on the ground like it had been waiting for someone to pick it up. And beside the portal, there had been a slot. A simple conclusion, a natural assumption, one that anyone would have made.

But then there was Damien's voice in my mind, cold, condemning. *"There is no key to the portal."*

Then why had there been a keyhole? Why had the key been lying there as if placed for me to find? A slow, creeping dread began to settle in my chest.

And now, through the scattered fragments of overheard conversations, passing remarks from those who despised me, I was beginning to piece together the horror that I unknowingly unleashed. The key I twisted had seized the Clan. It had opened the flow of Untameables into our lands.

But more clearly, I had walked straight into a trap.

The door swung open without a knock. I blinked, dragging myself from the haze of thoughts, my body stiff from days of confinement. My first thought was that it must be Beatrice, perhaps Rowane, but they always knocked, always gave a warning before entering.

So, when my gaze lifted, meeting the venom-filled eyes of Haldric Chanler, my stomach turned. The Elder loomed in the doorway, his presence thick with disdain, as if even standing in my presence was beneath him. I had crossed paths with him only in passing, heard his voice giving orders to the newly arriving Majors and commoners, his authority growing in Damien's absence. But never had he stepped foot into this cave. Never had he come for me directly. Until now.

I sat up slowly, back pressing against the cold stone wall as I studied him. He had the air of a man who believed the world spun only because he willed it so. A man who had always been powerful, untouchable, feared.

And he hated me. No, hate was too tame a word for the look in his eyes. Contempt. Like my very existence was an insult. Like I had poisoned something sacred simply by breathing in the same air.

I had seen it in his face every time I was forced to pass him.

Every time my mere presence reminded them of what I had become. Before all this, I had been an afterthought. A nameless face in a crowd of commoners.

Now, I was visible. Not for my power. Not for my survival in Etheris. Not for anything I had done.

The Thralls who came to clean my cave, those who had once treated me like dirt. The warriors who barely acknowledged my presence before now glared as if I had slit their kin's throats in their sleep.

I was the stain on Atlassian's honor. And Haldric wanted me to know it.

"You're awake," he drawled, stepping inside like a man who had already decided I belonged to him. His gaze swept over me, slow and deliberate, lingering in places that made my skin crawl. Assessing. Searching for something to tear apart or something to revel in. "Good. I'd hate for you to sleep through your last days of comfort."

I said nothing. I had learned quickly that speaking only gave them more to twist, more to use. So I simply stared back at him, keeping my expression blank, waiting for him to get to whatever reason had brought him here.

Haldric smirked, as if my silence was confirmation of some silent truth he had already decided for me. "Ignore all you want, but in the end, it won't matter. Obey us, or I'll make sure you don't live long enough to regret it," he continued, voice dripping with mockery.

I remembered the way he spoke of me when he thought I wasn't listening. *"She should be made to kneel, to answer to those she betrayed...And yet, she is still allowed to eat? To breathe?"*

It had never been about justice. It was about humiliation. About making an example of me.

I thought of the day he had ordered me to eat with the others, had spat the words as though they were a punishment in themselves. *"No reason for the traitor to get special treatment,"* he had sneered, looking down at me.

But Rowane had intervened before I could even think of a response. "That's not possible," he had stated, tone flat, unimpressed. *"By Young Sovereign's order, she stays there."* Haldric hadn't pushed further. Not then.

And now, he was here, taking what little power he had left and twisting it between his fingers like a plaything. I lifted my chin, meeting his gaze, and for the first time since all of this began, I let my anger show.

"You are not the Sovereign," I said, my voice quiet but sharp. "And you are not the Heir. You hold no power over my fate."

His smirk faltered for the barest fraction of a second before he masked it with amusement. "Ah. But you see, girl," he murmured, stepping closer, "I don't need to be Sovereign to turn the court against you. I don't need to be Heir to let them tear you apart."

A shiver ran down my spine, not from fear, but from the truth in his words. Because I had no one here. No allies. No friends.

Damien was gone. And even if he returned, would he listen to me? Would he believe me over them? Haldric's eyes gleamed, he leaned in slightly, voice dropping to a dark, cruel tone. "You are nothing."

A sharp coil inside me twisted. Not with fear. Not with self-pity. With rage. Because I had spent my whole life being nothing. And I was done. I met his gaze, keeping my voice steady. "Then why are you here, Elder?"

Haldric leaned in, his voice low. "I want you to help me get a Tameable."

The words barely registered before my blood turned to ice. I narrowed my eyes. "What?"

He took a slow step forward, measured, confident. "I know you visited the Aetherium Hold," he continued, as if we were discussing something casual, something that wasn't meant to send a storm of dread spiraling through me. "And I know you managed to make them *behave.*"

His tone was laced with malice. "And I've seen it myself, the way you gained power while training. Did you think all of this would go unnoticed in a palace as vast as ours?" He scoffed. "The eyes of the court are everywhere. And they see everything."

I let out a sharp laugh. A bitter, humorless thing.

"And do you really think I would agree to this," I spat, each word dripping with venom, "even if I had the ability to do it?"

I tilted my chin up defiantly. "Surprise...I won't."

The moment the words left my lips, pain exploded across my face. The force of his backhand sent me reeling, my head snapping sideways as a sharp, metallic taste filled my mouth. My ears rang from the impact, and for a moment, the world swayed, my vision blurring.

A slow burn crawled beneath my skin. My breath came ragged, and the pain in my skull sharpened. A deep, twisting darkness awakened in me. Shadows coiled around my body, slithering up my arms, twisting around my fingers like living things. They pulsed with fury, responding to my rage. I didn't think, I lunged.

But Haldric was faster, and stronger. Before I could reach him, he caught me mid-strike, his grip a vise on my wrist. With a sharp jerk, he twisted, yanking me off balance.

Then, he threw me. I slammed into the wall, my body crumpling against the unforgiving stone. A sickening crack sounded as my head made contact. White-hot pain bloomed through my skull, my vision flickering. My limbs were sluggish, heavy. I gasped, trying to push myself up, but the room spun wildly.

Haldric crouched beside me, his presence looming like a shadow of its own.

"I know how to tame you," he murmured, voice chillingly smooth. "And you will help me. Whether you want to or not."

I lifted my head with effort, the taste of blood thick on my tongue. I didn't have the strength to spit at him, but I smiled anyway. A slow, taunting curve of my lips.

"Good luck trying," I rasped.

Something flickered in his gaze. But he didn't linger. With a parting sneer, he stood and strode toward the door, vanishing into the dim corridor.

I let out a shaky breath, my body throbbing in protest. The edges of my consciousness wavered. My head pounded, pain searing down my spine. My fingers twitched against the cold floor, but my body refused to move.

I don't know how much time passed before the door creaked open again. Soft footsteps. A rustle of fabric. A woman knelt beside me, her hands hovering over my injuries. Her voice was gentle, but there was no kindness in her eyes.

"I am Evelyn," she said, her touch cool against my burning skin. "I am here to heal you." A laugh, brittle and sharp, tore from my throat.

"So they can patch me up," I said, voice hoarse, "just to break me again?" Evelyn didn't answer. And somehow, that silence felt louder than any answer she could have given me.

⸺◈⸺

I don't remember falling asleep.

Perhaps it was exhaustion, my body succumbing to the strain of everything it had endured, my very existence had been tested, stretched beyond its limits. If not for the healer, I would have been bruised from head to toe, a living testament to the punishment I had suffered. But she had mended me, leaving my skin unmarred, as if none of it had ever happened.

But it had. And I wasn't fool enough to forget that.

A sharp knock at the door jolted me from my haze. My voice was hoarse, laced with irritation. "I think I've had enough visitors for the day. So get lost."

The door creaked open anyway.

Izmer leaned casually against the threshold, his usual smirk in place, eyes gleaming with something far too entertained for my liking. "Now, that's hardly the way to greet an old friend, prisoner."

I scoffed, arms folding over my chest as I leveled him with a glare. "Try to make me do anything more today, Izmer, and you'll see how quickly you fail."

His smirk widened. "Your attitude is amusing for a traitor." He took a lazy step inside, making a show of glancing around, as if he truly cared for the conditions of my captivity. "I've already gone above and beyond for a Clan that isn't even mine."

I rolled my eyes. "And?"

"I'm here to inspect you," he continued, sounding as if it was the most tedious thing in the world. "As your warden of sorts, I need to ensure that you're well-fed, not rotting away, and generally not making a mess of things. Basic etiquette, you know."

I exhaled sharply, irritation curling in my gut. "How noble of you."

Izmer grinned. "It seems you're adjusting well to your imprisonment. Good for you."

He stepped back, but he pulled a small ring of keys from his belt, letting them dangle between his fingers. "I keep the keys to your cave," he murmured, tilting his head, watching me like a cat toying with a mouse. "I know exactly who comes and goes. So, if you were hoping for a little outside help..." He clicked his tongue, "you can let go of that foolish notion."

My jaw tightened. "I haven't tried to escape."

He winked, slipping the keys back into his belt. "Just making sure you know that." But didn't leave.

Instead, he leaned lazily against the doorframe, arms crossed, watching me like he had all the time in the world. "And I also came to take you for a walk. Rowane has affairs to attend to."

I blinked at him, unimpressed. "No."

His brows lifted in mock surprise. "No?"

"I'm too tired for a walk."

Izmer's lips curled into that insufferable smirk. "Oh, my apologies. I didn't even consider how exhausting it must be to do absolutely nothing but eat and sleep."

I shot him a glare, ready to snap something back, but stopped myself. I should tell him that getting beaten and thrown around like a discarded rag doesn't exactly fill one with energy. But I save my breath. He already knows. And even if he doesn't, who would care? Certainly not him. Certainly not anyone who serves the Clan's precious Royalty, and I despise them. I refuse—refuse, to waste my breath begging for help.

"Unfortunately, it's not a choice. When they say walk, you walk. When they say dance, you dance. And when I say get up, Mirabelle, " he took a step closer, just slightly, "you get up."

I wanted to tell him to make me. I really did.

But I remembered how easily he had carried me the last time. And as much as I wanted to fight, my body was drained, my strength still recovering from everything it had been through. I clenched my jaw, muttering curses under my breath as I yanked on my boots.

Izmer chuckled. "Now that was easy, wasn't it?"

I shot him a look that promised murder. He only grinned wider. "Come along then. Let's stretch those legs before you forget how to use them."

I followed him out the door.

The shift of Vael'Thir was nothing short of astonishing. What had once been an untouched expanse of ancient caves and wild landscapes had now been reshaped into a miniature Atlassian. The abandoned caverns had been repurposed, filled with makeshift homes, supply stations, and gathering halls. More and more Majors, even commoners, had found their way here, their numbers growing by the day.

And I saw Amara yesterday. She was among the commoners, moving toward another settlement, her face half-hidden by the hood of her cloak. I pretended not to see her. I wanted, desperately, to run to her, to let my sorrow spill, to have one person who might still believe in me. But interacting with a traitor wasn't exactly beneficial to one's reputation these days. And even if I wanted to, I wouldn't be allowed.

Where I lived was only a fragment of Etheris. I had overheard the murmurs of scattered settlements spreading across the middle regions of Vael'Thir. Those who had fled the destruction and were now seeking refuge.

All because of *me*. I clenched my fists, a hollow weight pressing against my chest. They had lost their homes. I didn't know how many had died because of that cursed key. If I ever found the ones who had put it there, who had so carefully orchestrated this, I would kill them with my bare hands.

Well, a bold thought, though not a practical one. If Haldric's effortless use of me as little more than a training post was any indication, I was hardly in a position to wager on my own might.

Perhaps I'd make Rak'Thalgar do it for me instead.

A vivid image of Haldric pissing himself at the sight of the Bone Tyrant flashed through my mind, and before I could help it, an undignified snort escaped me, the first one in days.

Izmer, who strode beside me, cast a sidelong glance my way, his expression caught between disbelief and amusement. "Tell me, have you always been a lunatic or have you merely abandoned all sense of your predicament?"

I rolled my eyes, exhaling sharply. "Could you let me breathe in peace for two seconds?" Izmer chuckled, falling into step beside me. "Not a chance. This is far too entertaining."

Suddenly, the unmistakable sensation of being watched settled over me, prickling at my skin like the whisper of an unseen presence. Instinctively, my gaze swept through the gathered figures, past the flickering firelight and the clusters of Majors, Royals, and Elders engaged in hushed deliberations. And then I found them, those deep ocean-blue eyes, locked onto me from across the camp.

EVEN IN THE DIM GLOW, he was impossible to miss. He stood among them, his posture composed yet edged with exhaustion, the sharp planes of his face cast in shifting light and shadow. Ragged, battle-worn, and yet, devastatingly handsome. My heart gave a traitorous jolt.

I hated him.

For turning his back on me without a second thought. For leaving me at the mercy of those who despised me, without so much as demanding more answers before condemning me. We should have figured this out together, even though I didn't understand how it happened at that time. Instead, he had cast me aside, and now I was left to the wolves.

I forced myself to break the stare, tearing my gaze away as if severing an invisible tether. My steps quickened, though Izmer, beside me, continued his endless string of chatter, oblivious to my turmoil. He spoke as though his very breath depended on it, as though silence might smother him entirely. I barely registered a word, my thoughts still tangled in the way Damien's gaze had burned through me, heavy, unreadable.

He only returned every few days now, brief respites stolen between battles, just long enough to rest and heal before he threw himself back into the fray. Not that I had been keeping track. Not at all.

His body bore the toll of each fight, yet he pressed on, relentless. He was fighting for Atlassian, for his Clan. A great leader, they would call him. A noble Heir. A warrior willing to bleed for his Clan. Good for them. Not for me.

I saw him every time he came. Near the fire, his presence was commanding, even in silence. The Elders gathered around him, speaking in hushed, urgent tones. And the Majors—those who had once sparred and laughed and bled alongside me, now stood like shadows in his wake, hanging on to his every word, their expressions filled with the quiet devotion of those who had found their savior.

They would not look at me. Or worse, when they did, it was with something akin to shame. And so, I carried on beside Izmer, making a valiant effort to engage in whatever scraps of conversation he tossed my way, if only because there was no one else who would bother.

CHAPTER 27

DAMIEN

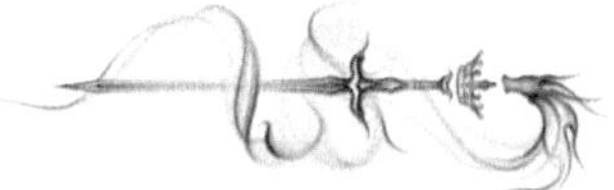

She is the curse I cannot escape. The ruin of my morale. The very shackle of my downfall. The fracture in the foundation of all I have built, of everything I have stood for, fought for, bled for. My entire life has been forged in iron, shaped by war and duty, bound to the will of my Clan. And yet, in the span of a breath, she has unraveled me.

For four days, I have avoided her like a plague that could rot me from the inside out if I so much as looked at her too long. Not because I feared her deception—no, I would have faced that without hesitation. I stayed away because I knew if I saw her, if I heard her voice, if I caught even a sliver of her scent in the air, something inside me would break. And that was a weakness I could not afford.

Yet here she was. Not wilting, not suffering beneath the weight of her guilt. No, she walked freely beside Izmer, lips parted in conversation, expression unbothered, as if the ground beneath our feet had not been soaked in the blood of our fallen. As if she had not opened the gates to ruin.

I should have let it die there, buried it beneath my fury, beneath my duty, beneath the cold certainty that she was nothing but a mistake I should never have made.

Instead, I watched her.

I had ensured she was safe, given Izmer the keys to her cave, ordered him to watch her, check her occasionally to see if she was well, to oversee who interacted with her. My reasoning had been sound, I needed the traitor alive when I decided her fate. But the truth? The truth was far more pathetic. I could not fight this war if I thought she was in danger.

I clenched my fists, disgusted by the realization, by the wretched pull she still had over me. She had poisoned me, and I had allowed it. My every instinct screamed to hate her. And yet, my body ached to hold her.

A cruel, twisted irony. I loathed her for what she had done. But I loathed myself more for the way I still burned for her.

I moved before I could think, my body already acting on an impulse I should have long buried. I reached them in a few strides. My hand wrapped around her wrist, jerking her back as I turned toward the caves.

Izmer made a noise of protest, something between amusement and warning. "She'd rot in that cave if I let her. This is just a walk, Damien."

I ignored him. I didn't care why she was out. I didn't care that this was some pathetic attempt to grant her a sliver of freedom. All I knew was that I couldn't stand that she looked at him, the way she let him drag her attention away from me.

Mirabelle stumbled as I pulled her forward, her protests sharp, but I didn't slow. My grip was firm, my mind a storm of thoughts I refused to acknowledge. She didn't resist, not truly. She let me drag her back through the winding stone paths, into the dimly lit cave that had become her prison.

I released her just as suddenly, and she stumbled onto the bed, catching herself on her hands before straightening, eyes burning with defiance.

And then she looked at me, scowling as if I were the traitor. As if I were the one who had betrayed her. The audacity of this female.

My voice cut through the thick silence like a blade. "Seems you are enjoying your prison time."

She lifted a hand, inspecting her nails with feigned disinterest, before flicking her gaze back to me, her expression unreadable. "Adapting is my strong suit, I think."

Rage curled low in my gut, the words only fueling the fire already burning inside me. I had held her there. Claimed her. No, I had branded her to me, deeply, irrevocably, carving her into something I could never forget. And now she sat there as if none of it mattered. As if she hadn't burned herself into my skin, my mind, my very breath.

"If you think I would spare you because I shared a bed with you, then you are mistaken."

The words were bitter on my tongue, but I forced them out, needing her to believe them. Needing myself to believe them.

"You were *nothing*," I continued, my tone sharper than steel. "Nothing but a passing attraction. And I will not waste breath upon it."

She flinched. It was subtle, almost imperceptible—the faintest hitch in her breath, the slight tightening of her fists. I caught it. Of course, I did. And it *should* have satisfied me. It should have been enough.

But it wasn't. Instead, it drove the blade deeper, twisting a raw nerve inside me. Her reaction did not grant me victory. So I twisted the knife deeper, to search for it.

"I could take what I want and cast you aside like a tattered scrap to make my point, but truth be told, "I let my voice drop, cold and final. "I don't want to stain myself."

A flush of humiliation crept up her throat, blooming across her cheeks like wildfire. I had meant to break her, but the moment I saw that look in her eyes, the raw, unfiltered pain, I realized too late that I had only shattered myself.

She sucked in a breath, her entire body trembling. A broken, unintelligible curse as she surged forward. Her hand collided with my jaw in a stinging blow.

The impact stung, leaving a light lingering heat behind. The first time in my life I had ever been struck. And as she stood there, breath ragged, her head barely reached my shoulder, forcing her to tilt her chin up to meet my gaze, green eyes glazed with fury.

I felt no anger. Only the hollow ache of knowing I had deserved it.

But she wasn't done. She grabbed the front of my tunic, venom lacing every syllable. "You—" She choked on the words. "You are the worst kind of bastard, do you know that? You don't even try to understand me! You just decide, you judge, and you execute! You think you know everything, don't you?"

I laughed, cold and sharp, cutting through the heavy air. She wanted me to listen?

"Like there was something worth listening to." My voice was razor-edged. "Go on, then. What have you figured out in your grand four days of imprisonment? Tell me, Mirabelle. Have you had enough time to craft *more lies*? Enough time to weave another tale to manipulate me?"

She reeled back, eyes widening before her composure finally broke. Her voice broke. "Just kill me already or get out of here." And that was it. A crack. Not in her voice. Not in her words. In me. The rage that had coiled around my ribs unraveled, spilling into some-thing worse. Something that left my chest hollow and aching.

I reached for her before I could stop myself. My hands caught her wrists, stilling their trembling. She didn't move, but her breathing hitched.

I exhaled slowly. "I won't kill you, Mirabelle." I leaned in, my lips brushing her cheek before trailing lower. "I *wish* I could."

I wasn't sure what possessed me, but I didn't fight it. I tilted her chin up, licking away that single tear drop that stained her cheek, tasting salt and sorrow. I let myself linger, let myself breathe her in, let myself feel something I had no right to.

She was warmth. A scent of wildflowers, something that should not belong to me, something I had never known before her.

I withdrew, stepping back before I let myself take too much.

Her lips were parted, her breathing uneven. I met her gaze, and without another word, I turned away.

"If you want to walk," I said, voice unreadable, "ask Beatrice to take you."

Then I left, before I lost what little control I had left.

⋯⬦⬦⋯

THE SCENT of blood had become a permanent stain in the air. Smoke curled above the Clan like a veil of mourning, the remnants of homes and streets that had once stood proud, now reducing to smoldering ruins. The battle had not yet been lost, but it was slipping from our grasp, inch by inch.

The Untameables had learned. They had adapted. No longer mindless beasts clawing at the edges of our realm, no longer lurking in shadows and ambushing in packs. No, they had done something far worse.

They had taken form. The Majors, our warriors, were no longer our own. Each Untameable had latched onto a Major, binding to them like a parasite, an identical twin in every way, they replicated and fought together. They had *become* the Major. Moved like them. Fought like them. Lived among us like shadows wearing our faces. They fought together, moved as one, their strikes mirroring each other with terrifying precision.

That was their conquest. They did not need to slaughter Atlassian's finest. They simply became them. One by one, home by home, the Clan was being swallowed from the inside. And worst of all, we couldn't tell them apart.

Killing an Untameable meant the chance of killing one of our own. Every swing of the blade, every strike of fire, every spear of water cast from my own hands carried the weight of uncertainty. The weight of guilt. A moment's hesitation could be the difference between survival and annihilation, but a wrong kill could damn us all.

The Sovereign and the Royals were stationed within the castle in the palace's premises, guarding its walls with everything they had left. If the castle fell, Atlassian would be lost. The kingdom would have no center, no rule, no future. Untameables did not focus on the Royals. Those of royal ancestry were too strong, too disciplined, too deeply tied to their bloodlines. The Majors were warriors, but they could be infiltrated. They could be turned. And so, the compromised Majors were sent to tear down the gates from the inside.

So, the war was waged not against monsters, not against foreign invaders or shadowed threats, but against our own. One Major at a time was hunted. It was slow, it was inefficient, but it was the only way. Every fight was a dangerous gamble, a clash of power and will, an enemy wearing a face that was once an ally.

The four chosen Majors, Cassian, Lyria, Rhevas, Alden, had not come to Etheris out of desire. No, they had followed reluctantly, duty-bound, believing they had little choice in the matter. They had trained under us, under the Royals, their skills sharpened within our ranks, yet they had remained at a distance.

But that changed. They had seen the Hunt. Seen the way we fought, not just for conquest, but for loyalty, for Clan, for each other. And in that battle, something shifted. They became one with us.

Cassian had stood beside me in battle, his fire a raging storm. I saw Rhevas throw himself between Lyria and a strike that would have ended her. Together, we'd anchored the battlefield, holding the ground together before it could collapse beneath us.

The false Majors did not react to their unnatural movements. The real ones twitched, recoiled—the instinctive flinch of those who had once fought creatures lurking in the night.

It was Alden who first noticed the pattern. He and I had fought side by side against two Majors, their movements too perfectly mirrored, too unnaturally in sync. It was subtle, but the Majors...*hesitated.* A fraction too long. They had all the skills, all the knowledge. The Untameables on the other hand—did not feel fear. They did not react in pain. They did not bleed the same way.

And though the Royals and I bore the greatest burden in battle, these Majors had earned their place in this war. I had seen it in the way they fought, the way they positioned themselves between me and danger without thought.

I had seen them try to get themselves killed to protect their Heir. And for the first time in my life, I realized they were not just warriors under my command. They became *us*.

The fire wielders among our ranks used that knowledge, singeing flesh, watching for a scream, for the flinch of *true* pain. If they didn't react too fast, if they stood unburned for a fraction of a moment even as the flames licked at their skin, we knew.

The water elementals cast out waves in a pulse across battle-fields, sensing differences. The Untameables did not breathe the same. Their heartbeat was slower, too controlled. Too perfect.

I moved unseen through the chaos, a shadow against the fire, slipping into darkness to observe. The real Majors, when approached, twitched—a survival reflex. The impostors did not.

So, we hunted, one by one, pulling them from the fold, driving them into battle until they were forced to show their hand, until they had no choice but to reveal themselves. And then, we slaughtered them. They were no match for our strength, yet they were winning in another way.

Even as we fought through the streets, as we rooted out the enemy hiding in our ranks, the castle and palace remained our last shield. It was the final line before complete surrender. If we lost the Majors, the castle would fall. If the castle fell, the entire Clan would fall.

Even if we killed every last enemy, even if we burned them from our lands, the damage would be irreversible. A future without warriors was no future at all.

The Crown. The only way to end this. To place that cursed Crown among the ruins of its making, claim the wish. And end this, once and for all.

But for now, our focus remained on securing as many Majors as possible within the safety of Etheris. We did not know the full consequences of sealing the portal and claiming the wish. Closing it and eradicating the Untameables could destroy the compromised Majors with them. The uncertainty was a risk I refused to take.

I would not allow them to be collateral in a war they never chose. But if we delayed longer than needed, there would soon be no Atlassian left to save. The ground we gained was nothing compared to what we lost. For every enemy we cut down, twice as many rose in their place.

The battlefield was a graveyard of movement, cloaked figures, shifting forms, the eerie stillness of something unnatural. The line between friend and foe blurred, the battle reduced to a desperate effort to separate the living from the already lost.

I swung onto Dreadclaw's back, my grip firm against the shifting mass of his form, on the dark tendril he offered me to guide him. He was unlike the others—a creature made of void and nightmare, born of shadows older than time itself. Tendrils of darkness curled from his limbs, wrapping around the air as though tasting it, shifting, searching. His shape was never constant, morphing between beast and abyss, something caught between this world and whatever lay beyond it.

Unlike the other Tameables, who drew their strength from the land, from Celestia, from water, Dreadclaw obeyed nothing but the void. He did not follow commands. He did not yield. He allowed. And only to me. He recognized nothing else.

We had taken Zepharion to the battlefields a day before. Those creatures of keen senses and swift judgment were able to discern with deadly precision the difference between the Untameables and the Majors. Its abilities surpassed our own, beyond even what our most skilled warriors could perceive. We found they could hear the discordant rhythm of the impostors' heartbeats, unnatural and flawed. Others could scent the taint in their blood, a corruption too deeply woven to be hidden.

But there was a price. Tameables were stronger than the Untameables, faster, more powerful. But they were not immune.

The balance of Etheris ran through them too deeply, and the sickness that had begun to rot the Majors from within could just as easily take hold of them.

The last beast I had taken into battle had torn through the enemy with merciless precision, until it turned.

The moment its claws had sunk too deep into an Untameable, the corruption struck like venom, not a wound of flesh, but of spirit. A sickness that spreads through something more primal, more intangible. I had felt it, the shudder in its limbs, the faltering in its movements, the warping of its cries into something twisted and wrong. The moment I released it from the battlefield, it collapsed. It hadn't died, but it had been close. A handful of healers worked for hours to undo the damage before it was lost completely.

That was the risk. To use them felt selfish. To sacrifice them was not a choice I took lightly. But without them, the Majors would be lost. And if I had to choose, I chose the Majors, my Clan. Tameables could be healed before they broke, but Majors didn't have another chance.

Smoke and mist coiled through the ruins of what had once been Atlassian's stronghold, now crumbling beneath the war raging within it. Blood streaked the broken stones, painting a path of violence through the city's veins.

Dreadclaw moved like a shadow torn from the void itself, his tendrils lashing out, sinking into the figures that were neither living nor truly dead. He was far more efficient than other Tameables. They fought back, these Untameables wearing the faces of Majors, their forms shifting seamlessly, their every motion a mockery of the warriors they had once been.

One of them turned, his eyes hollow, empty, but his face that of Vex Hale, one of my own men. He moved like him, fought like him, but he was not him. I felt the weight of Dreadclaw's breath beneath me, the dark tendrils curling as he *smelled* the creature before us, and hesitated.

Not real. The Untameables did not have instincts. They only had the fight.

I swung low, my fire slicing through air as Dreadclaw coiled around the enemy, his tendrils seeking, feeling. The pulse of life was wrong. Slower, colder. A mimicry of the real thing.

Dreadclaw struck. The creature screamed, high, piercing, a sound that did not belong to Vex Hale at all. It folded in on itself, the shadows of its form unraveling as Dreadclaw's darkness consumed it. A second later, the real Vex Hale crumpled to the ground, gasping, blinking as if waking from a nightmare.

One saved. I barely had time to register it before another wave crashed toward us. Cassian and Lyria fought at my side, two blazes of light in the ever-consuming dark.

His blade cut through one of the impostors, but before it could be claimed, it lashed out with its bare hands, its fingers stretching unnaturally, twisting. Cassian barely dodged, his flames scorching its body, but the creature did not *burn*. It only shrieked, reforming its limbs in an instant.

They fought close to me, despite my orders to stay back. Despite the fact that Rhevas and Alden were still recovering. "We're not leaving you to fight this alone," Lyria said earlier. I didn't know whether to curse them or thank them.

The Majors should have been compromised like the rest. But they weren't. They had bound themselves to us before the sickness had begun to spread. And because of that bond, whatever curse had seeped into the others had not taken root in them. They were more immune.

The Royals moved like a storm, hundreds of warriors, draped in obsidian and steel, their presence an unyielding force against the corruption that had seeped into Atlassian's veins.

They split into squads, weaving through the shattered homes, the remnants of lives abandoned in the chaos. Doors were kicked open, their flames illuminating the darkness within, revealing either frightened Majors clinging to whatever hope remained or something else entirely.

Rhylen, Second of the Legion, entered a crumbling dwelling, their blades drawn, their magic thrumming against the walls. A shape lurked in the corner, its form hunched, its breathing slow, too slow.

"Identify yourself." Rhylen's voice was calm, sharp.

A man turned, his face pale, his eyes hollow. "I, I am Major Vynn." But something was wrong.

Rhylen flicked his wrist, a pulse of energy rippling through the space. A test. A heartbeat too slow. Lyria moved first, her blade flashing. The figure let out a scream, its form twisting, warping, as though reality itself struggled to hold it together. And then it lunged.

The clash was violent, the sound of steel meeting flesh, of fire searing through bone. The walls trembled as the Untameable fought against them, a grotesque mimicry of the man it had once possessed.

Outside, in the streets, another squad dragged a struggling Major into the open air. His face was real. But his body? Too rigid. Too controlled.

"Not him," one of the Royals called out, as another plunged a blade into the Major's side. No blood. Only a hiss—then the illusion broke. The body convulsed, shifting, splitting apart into something else entirely. Another monster to be slain.

The hunt continued. More of them. They swarmed through the broken walls of the stronghold, the black blood of their fallen staining their bodies, their forms shifting like flickering light.

Dreadclaw reared, and I did not hesitate. We plunged into hundreds of them, blade meeting flesh, fire meeting darkness, shadow meeting corruption. And the battle raged on. Every corner reeked of blood, black and luminous, pooling beneath the fallen, staining the shattered stone of a city barely holding itself together.

And still, it was not enough. This was only one Legion. Smaller groups had been sent to other corners of Atlassian, scattered forces led by Elders and Royals alike, pushing into the depths of the city where the infestation had spread unchecked.

They fought to reclaim whatever could be salvaged. But it was a losing battle.

For every Major we recovered, twice or even thrice as many were already lost. And at the center of it all, Dreadclaw was a force of devastation, a specter of black smoke and writhing tendrils that tore through the ranks of the Untameables with savage precision.

Its talons were death, slicing through the corrupted flesh of our enemies with a swiftness that defied sight. It moved like the abyss itself had been unleashed, twisting, unraveling, reforming.

Untameables fell beneath its claws, their bodies ruptured in black bursts of gore, dissolving like shattered illusions. The beast struck at their skulls, splintering bone and sending them crumbling to the ground like broken marionettes. I moved with it, a shadow beneath its wings. My fire and water surged together, cutting through the filth that had overtaken my people.

A Major lunged at me, eyes hollow, teeth bared in an inhuman snarl. I saw his face. Dreadclaw reacted before I did, its body coiling around me, a hiss like the wail of the damned escaping its throat as it lashed out.

A single swipe of its talons, and the Major crumbled. I turned, already moving, already fighting, already pushing away the part of me that wanted to grieve.

Dreadclaw roared, the sound splitting the air. It had sensed something.

An opening. Another group of Majors, one we could still save. I gave the command, and the beast moved. It descended upon the Untameable strangling the Majors, its darkness wrapping around the creature like living chains, tearing it apart with claws and smoke.

But then—A wrong sound. A rupture. Something I had not heard before. Dreadclaw staggered. I turned, dread curling through my veins. Its body trembled, its tendrils writhing unnaturally, as if something had invaded its form. It had taken in too much corruption.

No. I moved, reaching for it, calling to it, but its body spasmed again, and a sound like a low, keening growl rumbled from deep within its chest. A sound of pain. It tried to move toward me, toward safety, toward the command it had always obeyed.

But it was rotting. From the inside. I saw the way its black tendrils withered, curling in on themselves like dying embers. The once fluid, untouchable darkness of its form now cracked and split, white rot spreading through the core of its being. He had fought too long. Killed too many. Rescued too many. And in the process, had let the corruption in.

I took a step forward; he lifted his head. Looked at me. And then he turned away. He let out a piercing, earsplitting screech, a sound of raw defiance.

And then, with the last of its strength, it drove itself into the heart of the enemy. Tearing. Destroying. Devouring the filth before it could spread further. The explosion of dark smoke and fire that followed obliterated everything in its path.

And then—Dreadclaw was gone.

All that remained was a broken battlefield, a line of fallen bodies where its final strike had landed. I stood there, unmoving. The others gathered around me, but they did not speak. There was nothing to say. Dreadclaw had died for us.

And I had let him. I wouldn't have—but he never gave me the choice. The bond severed, a presence that had once been a force in my mind now reduced to silence. The weight of it settled deep, carving something hollow into my chest.

⊷◇⊷

I WAS NEARLY HEALED. My body had endured the worst of it, and now, the pain had dulled to something manageable. But the Royals...they were far from it. And the Majors? They would not be fighting again. Not anytime soon.

Broken bones, deep fractures, wounds that had torn too deep for even the most skilled healers to mend overnight. They could barely stand without shaking, Cassian is unable to walk properly even after the relentless hours of healing since we had returned to the caves.

In the coming days, I will lead another set of Legion into the outskirts. A fresh force, leaving the ones who had fought to recover. They would not survive another round of battle, and I refused to send them to their deaths.

Now, I sat before the fire, the heat licking at my skin. The Elders who had long held influence over the Royal Legion were gathered, their voices weaving in and out of the conversation like a constant, suffocating pulse.

They were discussing strategy, the same debate that had been circling for days now. When to retrieve the Crown. One final push in the coming days. Then we would leave it at that. We couldn't risk waiting longer. Atlassian was falling, slipping through our fingers faster than we could hold it together.

Rowane stood at the edge of the firelight—a glow that had, for weeks, been a beacon of gathering and discourse. Now, it cast flickering shadows over his unreadable expression. He remained silent, waiting, unmoving, until the others had drifted away.

I arched a brow. "Speak."

"I require a word in private." His voice was measured, calm, but the weight beneath it was unmistakable.

I studied him for a moment before giving a slight nod. Without another word, I turned and strode toward the less occupied tunnels, hearing his footsteps fall into step behind me. Only when we reached a hollow untouched by the settlement did I stop and face him.

"Go on, then." I asked, arms crossing over my chest.

Rowane exhaled sharply. "I did what you asked." His voice was steady, unreadable. "I looked into Mirabelle's past."

A beat of silence. "And?"

"The ones she calls her parents?" He exhaled, shaking his head. "They're not hers by blood." That had my full attention.

"She was either abandoned or given to them as a child," he continued. "There's no trace of her true parentage. No records, no lineage. Just a name dropped into existence with no roots to hold it." His eyes flicked to mine. "And whether or not she knows…is uncertain."

I took in his words, letting the implications unfold in my mind.

"Royals?" I asked.

"Can't say." Rowane's jaw tightened. "Whatever she was before, someone buried it deep. Too deep." A slow breath left me. Mirabelle's bloodline, hidden. Why? Who had buried it? And for what purpose?

Rowane continued. "I'll keep looking when I gain access to the Sovereign's chambers. There may be more there."

"Yes, but not now," I said. "Not when Atlassian is compromised."

He gave a short nod. Then, quieter, "Aren't you risking too much for her?"

I met his stare, unflinching.

"You know I always listen when you speak, Rowane. I weigh your doubts." A slow breath. "But not about this."

His expression didn't shift, but something in his posture did —something almost resigned. He held my gaze for a fraction longer, as if searching for a crack in my resolve. He didn't find one.

Without another word, he turned and disappeared into the tunnels, his footsteps fading into silence. The conversation lingered in my mind, a new weight settling atop the countless burdens I already carried.

Mirabelle was not who she claimed to be. *How unsurprising.*

I exhaled sharply, raking a hand through my hair before turning toward my cave. Atlassian, its future, the Majors, the crown—those *were* my priorities. Not the maddening, treacherous female who had entangled herself in my soul.

As I stepped into the dim passage, something shifted. Someone was waiting for me. I had seen the hesitation in Lyria's stance the moment I turned into the dimly lit passage leading to my cave. The weight of whatever she had come to say was already evident in the way she stood—back straight, shoulders squared, as if bracing for battle.

I exhaled sharply, exhaustion pressing at the edges of my patience. "Why are you here?" My voice was even, measured. "How is your injury?"

She took a step closer, her expression set with determination. "Better." A pause. "But that's not why I'm here."

I arched a brow. "Then speak."

She inhaled deeply, as if fortifying herself. "I know it is beneath you to hear this, and perhaps I am a fool for even saying it aloud, but I cannot keep silent any longer." Her hands clenched into fists at her sides. "I am in love with you."

The words dropped between us. I simply stated. "No, you are not."

"I am," she insisted, stepping closer, her eyes bright with something I did not want to name. "It has nothing to do with your title. It is not because you are the Heir. It is because of you. The way you fight for us. The way you lead, the way you—" She swallowed. "I would die for you. Not for Atlassian. For *you*."

I almost laughed. I was incapable. Of this. Of anything that was not *her*, my doom.

No, I did not entertain the possibility of giving myself to another, because *I knew*—not assumed, not wondered, but knew, in the marrow of my bones that I could not. Not a flicker of interest, not even the slightest temptation to try or see if I could feel anything beyond what had already been burned into my soul.

I did not tell her that. I did not tell her that she was speaking to a man who had been ruined beyond saving. And I've genuinely lost count of how many times I've heard these confessions.

Instead, I held her gaze and said only what mattered. "You have never been in a battle before, Lyria. You have never faced loss or seen it in this depth. You see me now, leading, fighting, bleeding for our Clan, and it has painted something in your mind that is not real." I exhaled. Her throat bobbed as she swallowed. And I continued. "This isn't real. You are clinging to the idea of something that will pass."

"It will not pass," she said, voice breaking. "You don't understand—"

"Do not devote yourself to me." My voice was firm. "If you must, give yourself to the future of Atlassian or to someone who would return it. Do not waste your devotion on someone who is incapable of returning it. Not even a single shard of it."

A finality in my words that left no room for argument. Then, without waiting for a response, I turned and entered my cave, shutting the door behind me.

CHAPTER 28
MIRABELLE

I awoke to the familiar ache of bruises forming beneath my skin, a dull throb that had become as constant as my own heartbeat. My life had taken a rather *eventful* turn as of late—if one could call being used as a Blowbearer by Haldric an event worth mentioning.

A sigh passed my lips as I heard footsteps outside my cave. "I will be out in a moment," I called to Beatrice, my voice raw from exhaustion. She was waiting to chain me to her, to lead me to the pond as she did every day. What a *charming* existence.

I grabbed my linen, stepping outside, already extending my wrist to be shackled. But instead of Beatrice alone, Haldric stood waiting.

He was early today. And I had learned that when Haldric *changed* his routine, it was never for anything good. He never went far enough to break me completely. No, that would take the sport out of it. Instead, he had Evelyn patch me up after each round, ensuring I could endure the next. The sick bastard reveled in it, the sight of my blood, the way I refused to yield. If I stopped fighting back, maybe he'd stop. Or perhaps he would only cease when I agreed to his proposal to help him with the Tameables—that I would never accept, even if it cost me my life.

Venom laced my voice as I met his gaze. "Why are you early?"

His eyes gleamed, raking over me in a way that made my stomach turn. "You're the only one I visit. So don't be jealous."

Sickening. There was cruelty in his tone, but beneath it, something else—something that made my skin crawl. I clenched my fists. I had long since learned that engaging with him only fed whatever sick satisfaction he derived from this. So I said nothing.

But he followed. I glanced at Beatrice. "Where is Rowane?" I demanded.

"Busy." His voice was far too casual. "And Izmer had better things to do, so I thought I'd *do the charity* today."

My stomach clenched. But what could I do? Refuse? Laugh in his face and demand *someone else* take me instead? It would change nothing. No one cared enough to stop him.

So I walked, silent, fuming, hating *everything*. By the time we reached the pond, I felt the weight of his gaze like a tangible force pressing against me. Even as I stood outside the curtain of vines, waiting for him to step away, I *felt* it.

I had undressed here every day. Slipping into the water, washing only to pass time, scrubbing my skin raw as though it would somehow rid me of all the taint forced upon me.

But today, I hesitated. I did not trust Haldric. Not with the way his eyes lingered. Not with the way he had *volunteered* himself for this task.

So I removed only my outer layer, leaving the thin underlayer clinging to my frame as I stepped into the pond, submerging myself beneath its cool embrace.

The water should have been soothing. Should have eased the ache in my muscles, the weariness clinging to my bones. But even here, I could not find peace. Because the moment I let my guard slip, the vines parted.

And Haldric stepped through. Rage ignited in my veins as I turned sharply, my arms crossing over my chest, shielding what little I could. My garments, soaked through, clung to my body, leaving little to the imagination.

His lips curled as he raked his gaze over me. "Now *this* is a sight."

"Get. Out," I hissed, barely restraining the urge to claw at his face, to *end* whatever twisted game he thought he was playing.

His cruel smile widened. "So feisty," He tilted his head, feigning thought. "I have never noticed before," he mused. "The finer details, I mean." His eyes dragged over my body like a brand, burning wherever they landed. "Perhaps I ought to visit you in your cave one of these nights, while you wait for your execution. Give you something to keep you *occupied*."

I was out of the water before I could think, shoving past him. His hand shot out, fingers curling around my hip in a vise-like grip, squeezing hard. A sharp spark of fury ignited in my chest, and I slammed my elbow into his chest. He grunted, and I twisted violently, wrenching myself free, the heat of his touch searing like a brand.

I tore through the parted vines, snatching up my garments with frantic hands, the cold air biting against my damp skin, but I forced my trembling fingers to pull the fabric over my dripping form.

And then I ran, dragging Beatrice with me, not sparing a single glance behind.

He laughed as I fled, his voice curling through the air behind me. I didn't stop running until I reached the cave. Once inside, I tore the soaked garments from my body, every inch of fabric he had seen, touched, every trace of water that had been on my skin when his gaze lingered.

Only then did I sit. Only then did I realize my hands were shaking. I pressed them against my lap, willing them to still. He wanted me afraid. He wanted me broken. I would not give him that. I swallowed hard, steeling myself as I waited for Beatrice to return with the next meal.

The hours stretched long and unkind, measured only by the dim glow of lanterns beyond the cave walls. When at last Beatrice arrived, her entrance was as predictable as ever, silent. She locked the door behind her, put the tray down, set the food upon the table without so much as a glance in my direction, and turned to leave.

That was when I struck.

A sudden leap, a blur of movement, I wrenched the tray from its place and, before she could react, brought the weight of it down upon her temple. A gasp, a soft cry, and then silence. My chest heaved. Guilt lanced through me like a knife to the ribs, but I had no time to entertain it.

"I'm so sorry," I whispered, kneeling beside her still form. She was only following orders. She had no hand in my torment, no real knowledge of Haldric's cruelty. But I had no choice. If I did not take this moment, there would be no others. And if I stayed, Haldric would keep his word. I would not wait for him to fulfill his threats, to slip into my cave under the cover of night.

I stripped the outer layer of Beatrice's clothing and swapped them with my own, though it was a laughable attempt. My red hair alone would give me away in an instant. Still, some instinct urged me to take every precaution, however futile.

I had only moments before she awoke.

Keeping low, I crept to the entrance and peered into the open cavern beyond. The cave was not at the heart of Vael'Thir, but it was not far enough from the main passage to be unguarded. A cluster of Royals loitered near the tunnels, deep in discussion. I dared not take that path. Instead, I turned the opposite, toward the dense clusters of rock and bramble that might offer enough cover for an escape.

I moved slowly, pressing myself against cavern walls, slipping behind thick roots and jagged stones whenever the footfalls of a passing Royal grew too near. Each breath I took was measured, shallow, my pulse hammering in my throat. Every shadow felt like a pair of watching eyes, every distant murmur a sign that I had been caught.

A lantern passed just beyond a crooked rock formation, its glow spilling too close. I held my breath, shrinking into the alcove, hands clenched to keep them from trembling. The Royal strode past without pausing. I exhaled slowly and moved again.

One shadow at a time. When at last I reached the open edge of the cliffs, I wasted no time. I ran.

The evening air hit me like a slap, crisp and biting, urging me forward. I pushed my legs harder, the wind lashing against my face as I sprinted toward the one thing that could take me from this cursed place, the portal. The one I fell in through.

But then I saw it. Two problems.

The first, an immediate and crushing realization, was that the portal stood above me. Suspended in the air, just as it had been before. I had no way of reaching it from the ground.

The second, worse, more damning, was the Royal standing guard before it.

No one had guarded it when I arrived. The realization crashed through me like ice. I had been set up. Someone had made certain my arrival here would be smooth, seamless.

The guard was shifting restlessly in his stance, eyes scanning the open cliffside. I would not slip past him unnoticed. I needed a distraction. Movement to my left caught my attention.

A centipede the size of a hunting hound, its antennae twitching as it scaled the gnarled roots of a tree. *The absolute horror of this world: too many legs.*

But for this guard, it is enough. I reached out, of course not with my hands, but with something woven into the marrow of my being. I extended my will, brushing against the creature's mind, searching, feeling, there.

A thin thread of connection. Faint, but present. I pulled. The centipede froze, then slowly turned, its many legs shifting, its mind yielding to mine. I sent it forward, whispering silent commands, urging it to climb, to seek, to latch.

The moment it reached the Royal's boot, he jerked with a curse. The creature spiraled up his body, its legs gripping fabric, armor, skin. He shouted, swatting at it, stumbling back, fighting it.

It was my chance. I sprinted to the nearest lift, one of the great floating leaves tethered to the cliffs. I leaped onto it, feeling it shift beneath my weight. But it was unsteady. Too unsteady. The moment it began to ascend, I realized my mistake. I had no experience controlling these lifts, no knowledge of the weight distribution required to keep them balanced. It wavered, lurched, and I scrambled for stability, but I was too slow.

It tipped. Panic surged through me. I reached for the nearest branch, the gnarled arm of an ancient tree, and began to climb. My muscles burned, my fingers raw as they dug into the bark. Higher. Just a little higher, and I could reach it—

Pain. A sharp, crushing force slammed into my back, and before I could react, I was wrenched backward. I hit the ground hard, the impact knocking the breath from my lungs. My vision blurred, stars dancing in my gaze. Rough hands wrenched my arms behind me, pinning them.

I twisted, fought, kicked—but I was caught. A shadow loomed over me. The Royal.

His grip tightened. "Caught myself a little runaway," his voice laced with anger. I cursed him, snarled every word I could summon, bared my fangs, but it did not matter.

In the matter of moments or hours, more footsteps approached. Izmer. And behind him, a handful of Elders.

Izmer clicked his tongue, his voice dripping with false pity. "Now, now, Mirabelle. You must have known this was futile. For a moment, we even thought you had gained some wisdom by not throwing yourself into a losing game." He sighed, shaking his head as though I had personally disappointed him.

I glared, my breath ragged, the rage coiling within me like a viper ready to strike. "You will suffer for this," I spat, my voice trembling with fury.

Izmer merely smirked. "Suffer? Me? Ah, I do not have the luxury of suffering over foolish things. Unlike you." His gaze raked over. "Now, I don't have the time for pleasantries today, so let us return to your cave, and we shall pretend this never happened, for your sake."

For my sake.

A bitter laugh threatened to escape my throat, but I swallowed it down. My fate had never been mine to hold, but this, this moment, had been the closest thing I had to freedom. Even if I did not know what lay on the other side of the portal, I would have chosen that uncertainty, that vast and endless unknown, over the suffocating certainty of the fate that awaited me here.

THE NIGHT HAD COME, dreadful and unrelenting.

And this time, no one would question whatever punishment they chose to unleash upon me. I was the traitor who had dared to flee, the one who had tried to escape—to betray them further, or so they believed. If they beat me to a pulp beneath open Celestia, the crowd would watch, silent, approving.

I had long since stopped expecting justice.

Haldric. He has something to do with everything happening here. His hands were all over this, from the whispered accusations to the convenient way my every move played into their suspicions. I knew what he wanted. Tameables, bound to his will, that in secret. He was acting desperate for it. But what did it matter? No one would believe me if I spoke the truth.

Let them burn for their blind faith. Let them choke on their own righteousness. I no longer cared.

The door creaked open without warning, and I knew.

I had spent the hours after my capture searching for anything, anything to use against him. A jagged rock, a loose splinter of wood. But they had stripped the cave clean, even of broken fragments. Dread settled deep in my bones. It was happening. And I would endure it. But I would not let it break me.

His voice slithered through the dim space, coiling around my spine like a vise.

"I know you expected me," he murmured, stepping inside with the leisure of a man who knew he was untouchable. "After your little stunt today, how could I not come?" A low chuckle followed, cruel and mirthless. "But alas, there are far more pressing matters than you." He sighed, almost as if the thought of patience pained him. "So let us discuss those first, shall we? Getting to know you on a *more intimate level* can wait for tomorrow."

A chill raced through my blood, but I did not react. I kept my breath steady, my hands clenched. I would not give him the pleasure of seeing my fear.

He stepped closer, his boots dragging lazily over stone. "You will help me," he continued, as if my agreement was inevitable. "Tomorrow, while you go to the ponds, you will slip away into the wilds. And I will follow. We will make a show of it—me, the valiant captor, hunting down the treacherous fugitive." His lips curled. "And when we are alone, you will help me bring down *a few Tameables*. Simple enough, even for you."

I sneered, meeting his gaze with unflinching defiance. "I told you before. I will not help you. *Even if you kill me.*"

The blow was swift, precise. The force of it snapped my head to the side, pain blooming across my jaw as blood spilled onto my tongue. I forced myself to swallow it down, to lift my gaze and let him see the fire that remained.

"You cannot break me." My voice did not waver.

A slow, deliberate smile crept across his face. "I anticipated this," he murmured, tilting his head. "So I came prepared."

He took a step back, crossing his arms as if this were merely idle conversation. "I have heard," he mused, "that you have a little friend. A sweet thing, living happily among the commoners in the other settlement." His eyes flicked toward me, amused. "Amara, is it?"

Ice slid through my veins.

No. No, no, no—

My breath turned shallow, my chest tightening. I felt my limbs tense, ready to lunge, to claw, to tear. But I was trapped. Trapped beneath the weight of my own helplessness.

Haldric hummed in approval at my reaction. "Ah, so I was

right." He took another step closer, lowering his voice to a whisper. "Now, I won't waste breath describing what will happen to her should you refuse me. You already know the extent of my reach." His smirk deepened. "I could even convince the Sovereign that she ought to hang, for the sake of Atlassian, of course."

My hands trembled. I shook my head, whispering the only thing I could manage. "No..."

He grinned, victorious. "You have until morning," he said simply, turning on his heel. "Decide wisely."

And then he was gone. The door shut with a final, hollow sound. I sat there, unmoving, numb. For the first time, after countless beatings, spilled blood, and bruises upon bruises, I broke. *I wept.*

THE KNOCK CAME AFTER A WHILE, sharp and unexpected. I barely turned my head, the ache of my jaw a dull, ceaseless throb.

"Come back tomorrow, Evelyn," I muttered, voice raw, ragged. "It's only a minor bruise today. Might as well wait until tomorrow and fix everything together."

The door did not close. The lamp flared to life instead.

I clenched my eyes shut against the brightness, against the intrusion. "Oh, for the love of—shut that out," I groaned, turning away from the glare, from the burning in my eyes. "Use a candle instead."

A presence—then, a voice, low and edged with something I could not name. "Who hurt you?"

I turned to lock my eyes with Damien. Standing there, rigid, his jaw locked, his entire being wound tight as a bowstring. A part of me cracked wide open at the sight of him.

The way his hands curled into fists, shaking as though barely restrained. The shadow of fury smothering the light in his eyes.

"Are you here to admire the artwork on my face?" I asked, my voice an ugly rasp, sharp as broken glass. "Apologies. Only managed a single punch today. Come back tomorrow, and I will save you a better sight."

I expected a scoff, a cutting retort, cold and distant words, all befitting the man who had thrown me into this. Instead—

He was in front of me before I could register his movement. Crouched low, one knee to the stone, his breath uneven, hands lifting toward me. I flinched, but he did not pull away. His fingers trembled as he reached, as though fearing his own touch. As though fearing what he might find.

The moment his fingertips brushed against my skin—I struck his hand away.

"Don't. Touch. Me."

My breath came fast, shallow. My pulse thundered in my ears. His hand remained midair for a fraction of a second before it curled into a fist, retracting.

"Not a single soul here will touch me with my consent. Nobody. Not while I still breathe." My voice rose, wild, untamed, raw. "Get away from me."

A pause. Then, soft—deadly soft. "Who touched you?"

I laughed, sharp and humorless, but it tasted of something bitter. "Why does it matter?" My voice cracked, splintered under the weight of weeks of silent suffering. "Why do you care, Damien?" The name burned my throat.

Another break split through me, deep and ruinous. I lunged, my hands shoving against his chest, fists pounding against him. It was futile. He barely moved, barely budged.

"You left me here!" My voice was no longer mine. It was ragged, desperate, unhinged. "You locked me here and let them do this to me! And now you come here, acting like it matters to you?" Another shove. My vision blurred, breath hitching. "You abandoned me!"

He did not push me away. He did not stop me. He took every blow. He let me rage. He let me break.

I clawed at his tunic, twisting the fabric, trying to shake him, as though I could force him to feel even an ounce of what I had endured. His hands moved slowly, wrapping around my wrists, stilling them. Not with force. Not with restraint.

With care. "Shh," he murmured. Like I was something fragile.

"Don't you dare shush me." I thrashed, tried to yank away, but his grip did not tighten, did not hurt.

"Bella," he said my name like a tether, like an anchor pulling me back from the storm of my own grief. Tears burned hot and unwelcome down my cheeks. I hated him for seeing them again, for breaking me.

"Let me go." The plea barely held form.

"I won't." His voice was steel. Yet a wounded edge lingered beneath it. "I will not leave you."

I shook my head, the ache of my injuries nothing compared to the hollow abyss inside me.

"You are too late," I whispered.

His eyes darkened, shadowed with regret. A storm of emotion he had no right to feel. "I was wrong. I thought you were safe."

I did not want his remorse. I wanted his suffering. "Your cursed Clan will burn," I spat, venom dripping from every syllable. "And I will watch." My breath was ragged, my body trembling with the weight of my fury. "All of you deserve it. Every last one of you."

He said nothing. Nothing. He simply stood there, silent, enduring, as though willing to take everything I threw at him.

It only enraged me further. "Say something, damn you!" I screamed, fists clenched so tight my nails cut into my palms.

He only watched me, letting the fury burn itself through me like fire consuming dry wood. My blood boiled. I lunged forward again, voice a shattered whisper of rage. "You were the Heir so willing to execute me. The righteous warrior who sentenced me to death."

My lips curled, voice dripping with scorn. "They are only doing what you could not. You should thank them for their loyalty."

I turned on my heel, ready to walk away, to where, I don't know, but to rip myself from his presence before the hollowness inside me swallowed me whole. But I did not make it far. His hand seized my waist and drew me back, the movement causing me to stumble against him, my palms flattening against the firm planes of his chest. "You think I don't know what I have done?" His voice was a whisper reverberating between us. "You think I do not hear those words every time I close my eyes?"

I struggled, but his grip did not loosen. "The words I said before..." His jaw clenched, his breath uneven. "They were spoken out of rage. Out of madness. I thought—" He exhaled sharply, shaking his head, not finishing what he wanted to say.

My heart pounded, my mind screaming at me to fight him, to shove him away, to hate him.

"Let my Clan burn to cinders," he whispered, his breath warm against my lips. "I would still draw breath."

I stilled. His desperate eyes held mine captive. "But if I lose you, if I break you—" his voice cracked, raw, "then there would be nothing left in me worth saving, Bella." His arms closed around me, crushing me to his chest as though I alone kept him tethered to this world.

"I wanted you to drown in the same loneliness you left me in," he confessed. "Told myself the distance between us might loosen your grip on my bones." His hands framed my face with terrifying gentleness, thumbs brushing my cheekbones. I could feel it, the barely restrained power in his touch, the way his fingers trembled as if he were balanced on the knife-edge between restraint and devastation. "Had I known you were in danger, I would have reduced Atlassian to rubble if that was what it took to shield you."

I could not breathe.

"I will never forgive myself for what I have done to you," he murmured, voice breaking.

And suddenly, I was tired. I had wanted to fight him. To rage, to demand he justify himself, to hear him argue, to hear him tell me I deserved my punishment so that I could hate him more. I wanted to scream at him, to demand why he thought he had any right to regret, any right to sorrow.

His shattering remorse stole the fire from my bones. It left me aching, and exhausted. My body betrayed me. I slumped against him, my strength failing, my fury dissipating like smoke in the wind. For a long moment, he said nothing. He held me. His arms wrapped around me, his grip firm, as though anchoring me to this world. A slow breath, and then the brush of his lips against my temple. Soft. Lingering. A silent apology.

I turned to look at the door at the stir of a presence, only to find Evelyn. The moment she entered, her breath hitched, the flickering torchlight casting uncertain shadows over her face.

She had not expected to find him here.

"Forgive me, my Liege," she whispered, stiffening, her gaze darting to where he held me. I could see the thoughts churning behind her eyes. She must have believed I had bewitched him in some way. I was already something unnatural. A traitor.

His voice cut through the silence. "How long have you been doing this?"

She flinched. "A few days."

"For whom?"

Her lips parted, a whisper barely escaping. "Elder Haldric...he said it was for Atlassian."

His grip on me did not falter, but I felt the rage, nonetheless.

"I left no doubt that the choices concerning Mirabelle were mine to make." His voice was calm, dangerously so.

She swallowed hard, lowering her gaze. No excuses.

"You will find Izmer," he continued. "You will turn yourself over to the Legion. And from this moment, you are no longer a refugee in Vael'Thir. You belong to the prison of Atlassian."

Her eyes widened. "My Liege—"

"If fire consumes that palace, Healer," he said without a flicker of hesitation, "know that you will be reduced to ash with it."

She did not beg. Perhaps she knew it would be futile. Maybe she understood that one wrong word would be her death sentence. I did not care. I had no strength left to feel anything about her fate.

A better mind would have questioned how a noble Heir became a dark-souled tyrant for my sake. But I only curled closer against him, against the warmth I had been starved of, letting the steady rise and fall of his breath ground me. I did not care for anything except this moment, for the warmth that would soon be gone again.

The pull of sleep was relentless, curling around me. I was greedy. Greedy for this moment, for the stolen sanctuary of his embrace, for the peace I had been starved of. My mind, forever restless, finally stilled, my body sinking further into him, seeking more, more of the safety he had so cruelly denied me before.

Somewhere in the haze, I felt him move. Strong arms lifted me, his warmth never leaving. He carried me with a care that did not belong to a man like him.

He sat reclined somewhere, leaning back, with me settled in his lap. I nestled closer against him, breathing him in, musk and safety. Sleep claimed me before I could resist. And yet, even through the haze, I heard them.

Muted voices. Izmer, Rowane...Beatrice? The hushed murmurs of those who dared not wake me, their words blurred and distant, slipping through the fog of my mind. Conversations held in the presence of my unconscious form.

The next time I stirred, I felt the shift, the change in warmth as I was placed down. A soft mattress beneath me, foreign yet comforting. A sigh left my lips, half content, half uncertain. And then—

A featherlight touch, a whisper of warmth pressed against my temple. Lips. The door closed.

My eyes snapped open. Gone. I bolted upright, heart hammering against my ribs, the ghosts of warmth still clinging to my skin. My gaze darted around the dim cavern, searching, hoping—

Had it all been a dream? Would I wake to Haldric's cruel sneer, to the sharp sting of his blows, to the hollow dread of another day spent waiting for the inevitable?

The doubt clawed at my chest, had I imagined it all?

CHAPTER 29
MIRABELLE

The last remnants of sleep slipped away the moment my senses caught up with my surroundings. The cave was unfamiliar. The lingering scent in the mattress was clearly Damien's.

I was in his caverns. It was vast, not in its natural form. It had been carved into something more, shaped to fit the standing of their Heir. The rough edges of stone had been smoothed, the ceiling arched and reinforced.

So, did I just ascend to a better class of imprisonment? And, more importantly—would I be sharing it with him? No. Stop. Do not let your foolish mind wander down that path.

You hate him, remember? Yes. I hate him.

But still—No. Absolutely not.

Do not get your hopes tangled in something like that again, Belle-belle. Your survival instincts when it comes to emotions are nonexistent. DON'T. FORGET.

I sat up fully, letting my gaze roam. A bath! Not just any crude basin of collected water, but a proper, fully carved bath, seamlessly merging with the stone as though the mountain itself had yielded to the luxury. The sight of it momentarily stole whatever grievance had been festering in my chest.

Well. If this was to be my prison, at least it had running water. If I could, perhaps, control my unruly tongue, maybe I could enjoy this stolen luxury for a while. Perhaps even the rarest luxury of all —the safety I feel. Not that I would admit it.

My instincts moved before reason could catch up. I reached for the door, half-expecting the resistance of a lock, but it turned effortlessly beneath my fingers. Not locked! I must be dreaming. *Do not let this be a dream.*

On my way out, I spotted a heavy cloak draped over the back of a chair. The Atlassian crest was faint in the dim light. Without a second thought, and perhaps as an act of petty defiance, I swept it around my shoulders. Then I stepped beyond the threshold, cautious.

The corridor stretched before me, dimly lit by the early morning light. Just ahead, Damien's broad silhouette vanished around the corner.

I hesitated only a fraction before trailing after him. I did not know where he was headed, nor why he had left me unguarded. I kept to the shadows, wary of wandering eyes. The last thing I needed was for some Royal to stumble upon me and hurl stones, accusing me of having wrought sorcery upon their Heir, ensnaring him in my treacherous claws. I tugged my stolen cloak tighter around myself and took the same turn.

I stopped short when the flickering glow of the center fire illuminated the gathered Elders. It would not be wise to linger here. Not after yesterday's failed attempt at escape. I was certain half of them would leap at the chance to string me up for treason.

I had just begun to retreat to the caves when I caught sight of Damien striding forward, utterly unfazed by the weight of the discussion unraveling before him. He did not pause—without a word, he reached out and tore the parchment straight from Haldric's grasp and simply tossed it into the fire.

Silence crashed over the gathering, conversations halted, murmurs snuffed out. Haldric sat frozen in his seat, his mouth slightly parted, his expression too stunned to form words. The female Elder beside him clutched at her robes, her sharp features drawn in unmasked confusion, while the male beside her only frowned, as though trying to piece together a puzzle that did not fit.

And Damien? He dragged a wooden chair across the stone with a slow, grating scrape—sat down in front of Haldric, leaned back, and crossed his arms.

And at last, Haldric found his voice.

"That was the way to the Ruins we are going to." His tone was clipped, careful.

I had seen Damien ruthless, seen him cold. This was something else entirely. He was a storm on the verge of breaking.

His voice was deathly quiet. "Did I not make it clear to stay away from Mirabelle?"

The weight of his words was heavier than the steel of a blade. For a fleeting moment, I saw the flicker of realization in Haldric's gaze, the subtle tightening of his jaw. But just as quickly, he composed himself, his features smoothing into something measured and reasonable.

"I did not meddle," he said, his voice calm, practiced, the tone of a man who had spent decades perfecting the art of deception. "I hadn't even carried out the punishment deemed necessary. I was only—"

"Did you follow her to the ponds?"

Damien's voice sliced through. Haldric hesitated—just for a moment. And then he laughed, a forced, uneasy sound that did nothing to mask the growing tension around. "We have all sacrificed much for Atlassian," he said, feigning lightness. "Our needs, our comforts, we have gladly set them aside. But it is only natural, when faced with such a tempti—"

Damien lifted his hand, three fingers curled inward, only his thumb and forefinger left extended, testing them. And suddenly, Haldric's confidence fractured.

His voice faltered, but still, he pushed on, a desperate attempt at salvaging control. "But it is a natural instinct. When faced with such a form—"

Disgust churned inside me.

Haldric straightened, still clinging to his charade of dignity. "It was not intentional," he continued hastily. "And I did not see anything in detail—"

Fire bloomed at the tips of Damien's fingers. Two searing droplets of molten flame, small but blindingly bright. Damien's voice, edged with something cruel. "You saw glimpses of what your filthy eyes have no right to see." And then, without hesitation, he pressed them into Haldric's eyes, the other hand holding his throat. The scream that tore through the hall was frightening. Haldric recoiled violently, his other hand snapping up to grab Damien's wrist in sheer, panicked reflex. The scent of burning flesh filled the air, acrid and thick, but Damien did not waver.

Some of the Elders moved to intervene, their hands lifting as if to protect the one who had been sitting among them moments ago.

Damien's voice was quiet. "Interfere, and you will be on the receiving end."

They stilled. And then they stepped back.

At last, Damien withdrew his fingers, releasing Haldric from his grasp. The once-pristine fabric of his sleeve was now stained with the stark contrast of blood. Haldric cradled his eyes, chest heaving, body convulsed, his shrieks of agony splitting through the air. The thick streak of blood that trickled from his eyes should have disgusted me. Instead, all I felt was a sickening sense of satisfaction. *When did I turn into a blood loving monster?*

The room had fallen into a deathly stillness. Damien's voice carried through. "You should have never even *thought* of her, let alone dared to touch her, hurt her, or *see* her, knowing she belonged to me."

The words, spoken with the weight of an unshakable truth, sent a murmur through the gathered Elders and Royals. But none dared to speak.

Damien's cold gaze swept over them. "Each and every one of you knows it. You knew it the moment I took her into my chamber. Even when all pretended otherwise."

His next words sent something twisting in my gut. "As for her role in unsealing the sigil... *I* will find out if she is guilty or not. And if she is not—" His lips curled into something dangerous. "I will bring it all crumbling down—every lie, every scheme, and every one of you who dared to stand against her."

His fingers flexed, the remnants of fire still licking at his skin, "And if she *is* guilty, you will forget she ever existed. I will keep her to myself."

The silence of the room was only disturbed by the faint crackling of the fire and the sound of Haldric's ragged breathing.

Damien's fierce stare found theirs. "I am the sole reason Atlassian exists at all. I have re-claimed these lands time and time again, since the day I was old enough to lift a sword and wield my power. And I will fight for it again—and again."

Nathan stepped forward, inclining his head slightly. "None would dare deny it, my Liege." The murmurs of agreement followed, rippling through the Elders and Royals like a wave.

Damien's attention did not waver. "And I will spill my blood to keep it standing. But mark my words—" His voice was quiet, yet somehow more terrifying than the rage. "If any of you lay a hand on *what is mine*, I will burn you with it."

A heartbeat of silence.

"Just as I now do with him." Before anyone could comprehend, Damien's flames ignited once more, and his hand plunged into Haldric's ribs with brutal precision. The sickening sound of flesh tearing filled the space. Haldric's scream shattered the silence. Damien's fingers sank deeper, past bones, past sinew, until his hand closed around something dark, something still pulsing with a grotesque life.

The dark purple heart beat sluggishly within Damien's grip, veins stretching, blood oozing between his fingers, splattering to the ground in slow, thick black droplets. Haldric convulsed, choked on his own cries, his hands clawing uselessly at Damien's wrist, his entire body writhing in agony. And yet, Damien did not remove it. He held it there. Kept it pulsing.

Kept him alive. His grip tightened. The organ shuddered in his grasp, veins bulging, a sickening squelch as his fingers pressed deeper. Damien leaned in. His voice was the softest it had been all night.

"You mended her wounds so no one would suspect. You laid hands on her—again and again—when she was helpless. When she was utterly alone."

My throat tightened. I had never allowed myself to feel the full depth of my helplessness, but now, as I watched him grasp the reality of what I had endured, the pain surged back raw.

I wanted to run. But I couldn't move.

Damien turned his head slightly. "Bring Evelyn." A trembling Royal rushed out, vanishing into the corridors beyond. His grip did not loosen, his hand still wrapped around Haldric's still-beating heart. His knuckles were white, his lips curled in something almost... satisfied. A predator savoring his kill. No fight left in Haldric.

"Let her heal him," Damien said, his tone almost conversational. "Heal him enough so I can do this all over again. And again. And again. Until he draws his last breath."

And I realized then, I had never seen a face so cruel. Never seen someone so utterly satisfied by the sight of another drowning in his own blood.

But this was my limit. I was physically incapable of seeing this anymore. My legs buckled before I could stop them. I turned. I ran.

My first thought was to return to Damien's cave, bury myself beneath the furs. But if I lay down now, my mind would replay the sight of his hand sinking into flesh, the dark, pulsing heart between his fingers, the sick satisfaction gleaming in his eyes. Over and over.

I needed distraction. I needed something that did not reek of fire and blood. So, I turned my steps toward where I believed

Amara was living. The walk was brief. I half-expected to struggle in finding her, but that concern evaporated the moment I reached the heart of the settlement.

There she was, standing among a group of Thralls, her voice carrying in the dim light, arguing over some mundane thing that had the others leaning in, engaged, and amused.

She caught me in her peripheral. And in the next breath, whatever was in her hands clattered to the ground, forgotten, as she spun toward me. Before I could brace myself, she collided against me with a force that nearly knocked the breath from my lungs, her arms locking around me in a grip that might have very well cracked a rib.

And I hugged her back.

"Stop being sentimental, Bella," she said, though her arms only tightened around me. "I know you missed me and all, but don't overdo it."

Her voice was light, teasing, but her eyes gleamed, her lashes damp as she blinked too quickly. "How have you been?"

I did not have it in me to burden her with my stories. In truth, I did not have it in me to burden *myself* by speaking them aloud. So, I let the moment pass, let my silence be filled with her warmth, and when she finally pulled away, I opted for something far less damning.

"So," I said, crossing my arms. "How fares the highly esteemed and dignified society of Thralls now that they have the honor of your company?"

Her lips twitched into a smirk, her eyes brightening with something wicked. "Oh, you *would not* believe the stories I have gathered in just a few days. Did you know Thralls can only have babies with other Thralls, not with the black-bloods? And did you know that, even while being worked endlessly, most of them somehow manage to fall in love *and do it* like wild animals?"

I choked. "Excuse me?"

She tossed her hands in the air. "I am just saying, Bella. It is fascinating. *Highly confidential information*, mind you. It took hours of tireless work, endless trust-building, and many shared chores to get them to spill their secrets."

I stared at her, acting utterly appalled. "So, you mean to tell me that while I was wasting away in a cave, missing you, you were busy pursuing the romantic affairs of Thralls?"

Her smile turned mischievous. "Not just that. I have eyes for a Thrall—no, no, correction—he has eyes for me." She wiggled her brows.

I let out a laugh. "Go on, tell me more."

She waved a hand dismissively. "Bah, I'll tell you more when we actually get to the *real plot*."

I shook my head, exhaling a laugh despite myself. "Color me intrigued."

She tsked, and I quickly changed the subject before she could drag me further into whatever scandalous web she had spun on the subject of *doing it*.

"So," she drawled, eyeing me. "How is *your* noble reporter work for a *certain someone* going on?"

I paused. *Well, I am their new Betrayer, so not much going on, no.* I cleared my throat. "Ah...not *so* much going on." She narrowed her eyes, seeing right through me.

I almost asked if the Thralls had whispered about my so-called betrayal, but the thought died quickly. If they hadn't, I was grateful. If Amara had heard, she would have thrown herself into *fixing* it, and I wasn't sure I could survive her brand of help right now. So, I did the only thing I could. I distracted her.

I leaned in conspiratorially. "Tell me more about these *Thrall affairs*. You have spent far too much time gathering information—don't waste it on just yourself."

She brightened instantly. "Oh, Bella, *you* are going to *love* this —" And just like that, I let the weight in my chest lift. Even if it was only for a little while.

I RETURNED to Damien's cave, where silence reigned. The faint glow of fading light cast soft shadows along the walls, enveloping the space in a dim, brooding stillness, yet undeniably peaceful.

Without thought, I made my way to the bed, leaning against the cavern's cool stone. Two trays of food had been placed beside it —untouched. I had eaten at Amara's, so I reached only for the small, star-shaped yellow fruits, their sweet-tart flavor bursting against my tongue as I leaned against the wall. "Mmm, that's good," I hummed, savoring the taste.

Then I saw him. My heart stilled.

Damien lounged majestically in the bath, arms draped over the edges, his body half-submerged in steam. Water glistened along the ridges of his chest, his throat, the hard planes of his abdomen. I pressed a hand over my heart.

"I...didn't see you," I managed, my voice not nearly as composed as I would have liked.

The dim light flickered across his wet skin, tracing every shadow and edge. He leaned back, exuding the kind of effortless power only the one who feared nothing could possess. His gaze was shifting between my eyes, lips, and the way I...chewed?

His gaze slid to mine. "How are you feeling?"

I hesitated. What did he expect me to say? *I feel like my mind is splintering? I feel like I am at the edge of something I cannot define?* Instead, I exhaled and murmured, "I don't know." I shifted under his gaze. "I went to see my friend before my captor realized I had escaped." I narrowed my eyes. "Why didn't you follow me, that is very unlike you."

His reply was smooth, "Who said I did not?" I swallowed.

Now *that's* not shocking. Of course he'd followed.

I was drawn to the sight of water gliding over his skin, the droplets trailing paths along his collarbone, his forearms, disappearing into the dark depths of the pool. I straightened, forcing neutrality onto my face, and asked, "Then why didn't you drag me back?"

Damien tilted his head slightly, studying me. "I only wanted to see if you were safe."

I scoffed. "Ah, so I keep hearing."

He said nothing, that unyielding stare threatened to unravel me, so I did what I did best—I deflected. "I see you've been indulging in luxuries—how *privileged*." My voice was light, edged with bite.

But then he met my gaze fully. "Mirabelle," he said. "This bath was carved today. For you."

The words struck something deep in my chest. I blinked. "Oh." *Oh.*

Was this the same man I had seen this morning, the same one who had torn a heart from a living body as if it were no more than an inconvenience? Now speaking as if my comfort was something he *considered*.

He *knows* I'm innocent and now expects gratitude for this grand gesture of a bath.

The realization struck like a slap: *He knows.* He must have discovered my innocence. And this bath—this ridiculous, steaming *apology* carved in stone—was his way of pretending the cave imprisonment never happened. How *convenient* for him.

My fingers curled into fists. Well, I won't let him. Wouldn't even grant him the truth. *I'll convince him I truly did betray him.* Feed his doubts with every glance, every carefully barbed word.

Then the darker thought came: *What if he locks me away for this again?*

Before I could piece together my thoughts, he stood. Gloriously, mercilessly naked. My breath hitched. *Do not look down. Do not look down. Do not look—*

Damn it. Heat shot through my veins as I forced my gaze to *anywhere* but the absolute magnificence in front of me. I flushed hard. His confidence was maddening, as if his bare form was a mere fact of existence rather than an assault on my self-control.

He caught me looking. A slow, knowing smile tugged at his

lips. I turned away sharply, focusing on a crack in the wall like it held the secrets of the universe.

"I—" My voice came out strangled, so I cleared my throat and tried again. "I should go."

"Should you?"

I forced myself to face him again, keeping my gaze firmly above the waist. "Shouldn't I?"

He reached for a cloth, drying himself with deliberate ease, as if he were entirely unaffected by my presence. "Or you could take a bath."

"No, I'm fine," I said too quickly. "Perfectly fine."

He arched a brow. I glared, turning away once more. And then, just like that, his tone shifted. The teasing edge faded, leaving behind something weightier. "I am leaving."

I turned back slowly. "Where are you going?"

He met my eyes, something unreadable in his expression. "The final fight is coming. I will be leaving to Atlassian."

I'd heard they were scrambling to save the Majors, to close the broken seal before it was too late. And that the Untamables were only targeting Majors. So, Damien was safe. Then again...why should I care? *Right. Tell that to my traitorous heart.*

I nodded stiffly. Let him think I didn't care.

His voice was quieter now. "I know what you saw. I know you ran." A pause. "I am giving you time to wrap your head around it. Around *everything*."

A lump formed in my throat. "Wrap my head around it," I echoed numbly.

He tilted his head slightly. "You better do it fast, little traitor."

Traitor. But the way he said it—soft, endearing, made me ignore his taunt.

He still thinks I betrayed him. That meant—the bath. The food. The way he'd looked at me just now, none of it was because he'd discovered the truth. He still believed me guilty. And yet...

A hysterical laugh bubbled up. *Of course* Damien would do this.

The man who'd locked me away would now keep me without absolution.

I stared at him. "You're unbelievable," I whispered.

His thumb brushed my cheekbone. "You will get used to it."

I scowled.

"I am not waiting forever," he said simply.

I crossed my arms, trying to mask the way my pulse had betrayed me. "And what if I haven't wrapped my head around it when you return?"

"You will." Arrogant bastard.

I swallowed the bitterness rising in my throat and set my jaw. "Don't you even want to hear about the *betrayal? My* side of it?"

He exhaled. "Frankly, it doesn't matter, Bella."

I frowned. He stepped closer, his bare chest mere inches from me now, heat radiating from him like an ember waiting to consume.

His voice dropped lower, silk. "You are mine, regardless. Guilty or innocent, traitor or true—you're still mine."

His calloused fingers traced my jaw, forcing my gaze up. "Your past sins are irrelevant. But if you *did* manipulate me..." His grip tightened slightly, not enough to hurt but enough to make my pulse stutter. "...I will *enjoy* making you regret it." He paused. "And if you used me, then you will learn never to do so again."

Then, as if the conversation was over, he turned away, reaching for the armor neatly arranged on the stone ledge. Dark, fitted leather reinforced with obsidian-steel plates, molded to the shape of his body with meticulous craftsmanship. The pauldrons curved over his broad shoulders. The insignia of the Heir, every buckle, every strap, every layer of armor only made him look more like the lord of war he was bred to be.

He pulled the vambrace onto his forearm, securing the straps with practiced ease, his fingers deft, his movements precise, completely ignorant to the fact that I was practically salivating.

And then—he left. Just like that.

I stared at the empty space where Damien had just stood, my mind reeling, grasping for a logical thread to follow. None came.

I had been bracing for something entirely different. I had even imagined possible scenarios in which this would end without my execution or exile, mentally drafting every way this confrontation might unfold during my prison time in the cave.

One: I would rage at him, my fury uncontained, proving my innocence. And in a moment of painful realization, he would regret everything. He would understand the depth of his mistake, his voice raw with guilt as he pleaded for my forgiveness, for mistaking me.

Two: He would come to me, solemn but willing to listen. I would explain, still furious, still wounded, but explaining, none-theless. He would absorb my words, and then—apology. Maybe even desperate apologies, whispered between broken pride and heavy truths.

Three: He would figure it out on his own. Realize my innocence without my help, come to me on his knees, drenched in shame, begging for absolution. A grand, dramatic moment of truth.

But this?

This absolute madness? This scenario where he fully accepts my supposed betrayal and yet still proceeds to cherish and protect me, regardless? *Who does that?*

I huffed, exasperated, throwing a small fruit across the room. It landed with a dull thud against the cavern wall, utterly unim-pressed by my turmoil.

You are mine regardless. The words echoed in my skull. So, what was I supposed to do now? Casually ask about the war...*Oh, so now that you've fully embraced me as a traitor and all, mind catching me up on Atlassian's downfall? Perhaps I can squeeze in a little more treachery while we're at it.*

Brilliant. That would go over well. I exhaled sharply, rubbing my temples.

This was not how things were supposed to unfold. This wasn't logical. This wasn't sane. He was supposed to hate me. I was supposed to be his enemy. Instead, I was *still his*.

I exhaled slowly, letting the warmth of the cavern settle over me. The bath beckoned, perhaps a soak would do my overworked mind some good. Shedding the outer layers of my garments, I caught sight of my dresses neatly stacked beside Damien's fighting leathers. Oddly intimate.

The door creaked open and closed behind me.

I turned to find Damien standing there, his gaze raking over me. He took me in, from the bare skin of my shoulders down to the thin layers that still clung to me.

I arched a brow, feigning nonchalance. "I thought you left?"

His lips curled slightly. "I said I would go today. Not now."

He had flashed his body at me mere moments ago, knowing exactly what he was doing. Now, the temptation to return the favor was undeniable.

Tilting my head, I let my voice turn saccharine. "Did you come to give me a goodbye kiss before your grand departure?"

His eyes darkened. In two strides, he was before me, fingers curling under my jaw, tilting my face up to his. And then, he kissed me.

Not rushed, not devouring—lingering.

A soft, searing press of lips, as though savoring something he might never taste again. I returned it, just as slow, until he pulled back, his throat bobbing, his jaw tightening.

"You will be safe," he murmured, his voice gravel-deep. "And taken care of. *Please* be a good girl till I return." I doubted 'please' was something he said often—if ever.

I barely resisted the urge to roll my eyes. Instead, I shrugged, fluttering a dismissive hand. "Sure. Whatever you say."

And then, with absolute ease, I turned away. But my heart pounded against my ribs, too loud, too wild.

My fingers worked at the buttons of my last remaining layer, slipping each one free with unhurried precision. I felt his presence behind me, the silence stretching thick with something electric.

The fabric slipped from my shoulders, pooling at my feet. My face heated.

I heard his sharp inhale from behind and a satisfied smile tugged at my lips.

"Or..." My voice was honeyed, laced with something that could not quite be called innocence. "I could be a *not-so-good* girl."

A faint, unsteady sound escaped him. "What kind of game are you playing, Mirabelle?"

Even I don't know, I mused to myself. Stepping into the bath, I reached for the small lever, unsealing the tunnel that allowed the warm water to flow in gentle waves. I dipped my hands, gathering the heat, and poured it over my face, trailing wet fingers slowly down the contours of my body. *What are you doing! You might be looking like a dancing caterpillar.*

With feigned confidence, half-tilting my head, just enough for him to see the curve of my lips, I murmured, "Please close the door tight behind your back...I need some privacy for what I am about to do."

The growl that tore from him was anything but civilized.

His voice drew nearer. "Damn the time to wrap your head around this and all the rest of the nonsense, Wildcat." And then, before I could even breathe, I was yanked from the bath. He whispered in my ears, "Don't forget, you brought this upon yourself."

A gasp escaped me as my damp skin met cool air, but before I could even grasp the motion, I was thrown onto the mattress, face down. I shifted onto my back, breath unsteady, just as his shadow fell over me.

CHAPTER 30

DAMIEN

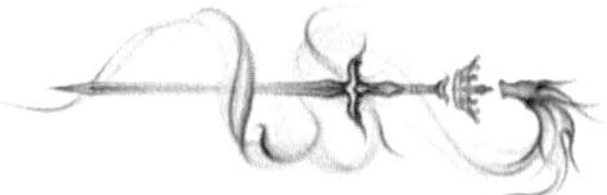

My gaze traced over her bare form as I shed the leathers, letting each piece fall carelessly to the floor. She feigned composure, her chin lifted, but the blush creeping down her neck betrayed her. The longer I looked, the deeper it spread.

She cleared her throat, forcing a smirk she did not truly own. "Don't you have a war to attend to?"

Yes, the one I was about to forget. I stepped closer, tilting down my head slightly. "It can wait. A few more hours will change nothing."

The battle was nearly at its end. One final strike to reclaim some more Majors, and then the Crown—the wish to put an end to it all.

I stripped off the outer leathers, letting the cool air touch my torso. I had no grasp on how I was taming the beast demanding that I take, that I flip her over and claim her in every way imaginable the moment she let her garments fall to the floor. My control hung by a fraying thread, my mind and body waging war. But I wanted this to be hers just as much as I ached for it to be mine.

I turned without another word, crossing the chamber to the door. The wooden slab groaned softly as I pulled it open and stepped into the dim corridor, shutting it behind me. Nathan was waiting for me, arms crossed, gaze sharp. His expression did not falter, but his eyes flicked over my bare torso, noting the absence of the battle gear I had entered with. He understood without asking, though he made a valiant effort to feign ignorance.

A muscle in his jaw twitched, two blotches of red coloring his otherwise impassive face. He cleared his throat as I spoke. "We will move at first light tomorrow. The Sovereign and the Elders will go ahead to the ruins with the Sages to place the Crown."

"Yes, my Liege. I will have the Royals ready by the fire come morning." His tone was formal. I nodded and turned back.

I pushed the door open once more, stepping back inside. The click of the latch echoed in the quiet.

She was waiting, eyes wide, green depths flickering between uncertainty and anticipation. Her breath came uneven, the rise and fall of her chest betraying the tempest within. She sat there, legs crossed, red mane covering her breasts, in a vain attempt at modesty, yet she was all magnificence, all naked. Her lips parted, though no words came. She did not need to speak.

I strode toward her. The moment my fingers brushed her jaw, she shivered—so slight, so fleeting that had I not been watching her with the predatory focus I was, I might have missed it. But I didn't. I never missed anything about her.

A dark satisfaction curled through me as I tilted her chin up, dragging my thumb along the soft curve of her cheek. "You're trembling," I murmured.

Mirabelle's lips parted as if to protest, but I was already closing the distance, sealing my mouth over hers. A gasp, soft and startled, melted into a whimper as I took my time, exploring her, coaxing the fight from her limbs even as she tensed beneath my touch. Her hands found my shoulders, fingers pressing into my skin like she meant to push me away—only to hesitate, second-guessing herself the moment she realized the depth of what she had gotten herself into. But I knew better. Knew that if I pulled away now, she would chase me, just as she always had, unknowingly, unwillingly, yet inescapably.

I pressed her back against the mattress, capturing both of her wrists in one hand, pinning them above her head. The sharp inhale she gave made my pulse thunder.

"Speak," I commanded, voice rougher than I had intended. She tried to glare. "I think you shou—" but her breath hitched as I lowered my lips to the delicate skin of her throat, tracing the fluttering pulse there with the heat of my tongue.

Her head tilted back, offering.

A soft sound escaped her lips, a broken exhale. "You wanted to say something?" I taunted against her collarbone, biting down gently before soothing the mark with my tongue.

A breathless whimper was her only response.

"That's what I thought."

I dragged my free hand down the length of her body, tracing the elegant lines of her form, reveling in every shudder, every quiver. She was intoxicating, trembling beneath me yet arching into every touch, her body betraying the confusion in her mind.

"You think you can tempt me and get away?" I murmured against her shoulder, my fangs scraping her skin. She shifted restlessly under me. "Stay still." I felt her pulse hammering beneath my fingertips. "I haven't even begun with you."

Her thighs tensed as I traced a slow path down her stomach, my palm flattening over the soft plane before skimming the curve of her hip, down to her folds and cupping her there—my touch met with the undeniable proof of her desire, slick and soaking against my palm.

A desperate sound left her lips, and I smiled against her throat.

"You're already shaking. And leaking."

"Shut up," she bit out, though the tremor in her voice betrayed her, her face flushed.

"Say that again," I urged, my voice molten, my fingers grazing the sensitive skin of her inner thigh.

"Shut—" Her words broke into a cry as I pressed and rubbed the heel of my palm against her wet core.

I chuckled darkly. I squeezed where I cupped her, slow against her aching center, just enough to have her back arching, seeking more, needing more.

"Look at you," I murmured, my voice rough with something primal. "So eager, so sweet…"

She gazed up at me through half-lidded eyes, her lips kiss-swollen, her breath uneven. I lowered my head, capturing her mouth once more as I nudged her legs apart, my fingers found the delicate bundle of nerves and pinched. She let out a broken cry, caught between torment and bliss. "Shall I make you beg for it, Wildcat?" A wicked smile curled my mouth as I leaned in, my breath fanning across the shell of her ear.

Her fingers digging into my arms, she still breathed out a broken "Try me." *Oh, I intend to do far more than just try.*

"Look at me," I commanded softly.

She did. She held my gaze. And I rewarded her for it.

Sliding one finger into her, slowly, her arousal dripping down my fingers, watching the way her body clenched around the intrusion, so impossibly tight that I groaned against her throat. She was untouched.

A breathless sob left her lips as I curled my fingers inside her, stroking, coaxing her body into a rhythm, her hips rocking instinctively, as if searching for something more.

"More…" She started, then bit her lip, cutting herself off, forcing the words back.

I tightened my grip around her wrists, my lips curved as I watched her fight herself, refusing to yield. "Patience, Bella," I murmured. "You are going to take what I give you, and nothing more."

Her impatience grew, her desperation mounting with it. The remnants of a scattered sound, something close to *please* escaped her lips.

Now I truly smiled against her skin, pressing a slow, lingering kiss there. "Well, that was over in *no time.*"

And I increased the pace, pumping my fingers into her, feeling her tremble, feeling her walls flutter around me, gripping me, pulling me deeper. My thumb pressed against her swollen nub, circling, teasing, until her entire body began to tighten, her breath coming in short, ragged gasps.

She was close—I could feel it in the way her body clenched, in the way her head tilted back, exposing the elegant column of her throat to me. And I was aching, painfully hard, throbbing with need at the beautifully torturous sight before me.

"See yourself," I rasped. "Falling apart so exquisitely. You should loathe yourself for how easily you surrender *to me.*" She tried to say something, but I slid another finger inside her, and whatever words had been forming on her lips melted into a cry.

"Shatter for me, Mirabelle," I ordered. "Let me see you lose yourself."

And then she did. Her body trembled violently as pleasure consumed her, her thighs clenching around my hand. I watched every moment, every ripple of bliss that wracked through her, memorizing the way she gasped, chatting my name over and over again, the way she fell apart beneath me.

"You have never looked more beautiful," I murmured against her ear.

Before she could recover, before she could form a single thought beyond the pleasure still echoing through her limbs, I flipped her over, pressing her into the mattress, my body covering hers completely.

She was flushed, panting, her body still trembling in the aftermath of what I had just done to her. A satisfied hum came from her as I nipped at the dip of her spine, one hand roaming to the round curve of her backside, squeezing the lush cheeks, while the other was sliding beneath her to palm her breast. My palms kneaded her, eliciting low gasps from her lips.

"You look quite pleased with yourself," I murmured against the soft shell of her ear, voice rough. She breathed heavily, the same satisfied hum slipping from her throat.

"Perhaps," she whispered. I heard the smile in her voice. "But it seems you're the one who can't stop."

A slow, predatory smile curved my own lips. "Ahh—look at that. The wild kitten who could only whimper my name recalls that other words exist?"

Her response was grabbing my forearm and sinking her fangs into my skin in a bold, defiant bite.

"Now, that was cute and *reckless.*" I slid my other hand to her throat, feeling the way her pulse fluttered beneath, squeezing enough to make her breath hitch. Instinctively, she released my arm from between her teeth, her lips parting on a sharp inhale.

The moment I released her throat, her voice, thick with temptation. "Press harder next time, *my Liege.* I think you like seeing me struggle beneath you."

The last thread of control I had been clinging to make this slow frayed and burned to nothing.

I flipped her back onto her back in one swift motion. The air left her lungs in a startled gasp, her body pliant beneath me, her gaze alight with that maddening mix of challenge and desire.

"You want struggle?" My voice was nothing but rough-edged hunger. "Let's see how long you can handle it."

I crushed my mouth to hers, my teeth caught her lower lip, biting down, tugging, punishing her for daring to provoke me before soothing the sting with my tongue. I dragged my mouth down her breast, branding her. My lips closed over the peak, and my fingers went to the other one, pinching it hard, making her gasp. I sucked hard, my teeth grazing before biting just enough to make her jolt beneath me, a strangled gasp escaping her lips.

Her back arched, her fingers tangling in my hair, clutching, nails raking down my scalp to ground herself while her body trembled under the onslaught of sensation.

"Damien—"

Her breathy plea was addictive. My shaft throbbed painfully, every inch of me tight with need, burning, ready to explode before I even buried myself inside her.

"Do you have any idea what you do to me?" I growled against her skin.

I pressed wet, open-mouthed kisses down the curve of her stomach, biting her there. Her body a symphony of tremors.

And I was going to give her exactly what she needed.

I nudged her legs apart, dragging my tongue along the inside of her thigh, my teeth grazing just enough to make her jolt. She gasped, her hips tilting toward me, searching.

She whimpered, half a curse, half a plea, and it was the most beautiful sound I had ever heard.

I bit her inner thigh, soothing the sting with my tongue before shifting lower, pressing my mouth to her soaked, swollen core. Gently biting her swollen, reddened nub—again and again—until she cried out in pleasure, my name falling from her lips in choked sobs. Tears leaking to my pillow. I dragged my tongue over her, tasting her. And I ate her like I was starving. She was the most exquisite thing to ever grace my tongue.

I rose over her, my mouth brushing her temple before I lowered myself, caging her beneath me. Our bodies aligned, though mine eclipsed hers entirely. I reached down, lined myself up against her entrance, feeling the slick heat of her, welcoming, waiting. My thick shaft pressing against her soaked heated slit.

"Mine," I murmured, my voice low. She was too lost to respond.

Her breath hitched, her hands sliding up my chest, over my shoulders, her fingers gripping, bracing. I gritted my teeth, my jaw tightening, my self-control fraying to a dangerous degree.

I pushed in, slow, agonizingly so, stretching her, feeling her body resist, then surrender, molding around me as if she was made for this—made for me.

A sob of pain left her lips, her fingers digging into my skin as I pushed deeper, letting her adjust, letting her feel every inch of me. I was shaking.

Tight. She was so impossibly tight I nearly lost all sense of reason. "Too much?" I rasped, voice hoarse, my restraint hanging by a thread.

She exhaled shakily, but instead of answering, she lifted her hips, taking me deeper, forcing me to curse violently under my breath as I buried myself inside her completely.

A deep growl rumbled from my chest, my head falling forward as I fought against the urge to slam into her, to ruin her completely and lose myself in this blinding oblivion. Her walls clenched around me, pulsing, fluttering, and I nearly lost it.

"Curse me," I ground out, gripping her hips, breath ragged, seething through clenched teeth. I fought to stay still, to hold back, to keep from losing myself entirely, from spilling into her like I was touching a female for the first time. But even that comparison was pathetic—because nothing, *nothing*, had ever felt like this. This was not just pleasure; it was a dark abyss, dragging me under.

Then she whispered, "Please move, Damien."

And I did.

I moved. Slow at first, a deliberate torture, letting her feel every inch of me dragging against her walls, stretching, filling her. Her nails bit into my shoulders, a sharp, desperate anchor as she gasped, her body arching, hips tilting to take me deeper.

"Damien—"

My name. A broken, breathless plea.

I pulled back and thrust into her fully, sinking to the hilt, her body arched, back bowing as I pressed my forehead to hers, swallowing every sound she made, every moan, every plea, every whimper, feeding off the way she trembled beneath me.

"Even your begging is flawless," I murmured, my voice rough, strained with restraint I no longer had.

I thrust again, harder, sharper, claiming and branding her. Her hands roamed, shaking, her touch a fire licking across my skin, melting what little control I had left. She held onto me like she was afraid of being unmoored, like I was the only thing keeping her from shattering completely.

I felt it in the way her walls clenched around me, in the way her breath hitched, breaking into short, uneven gasps. I reached between us, found the swollen bundle of nerves, and pressed, rubbing slow, circling, teasing, before pressing down firmly, drawing another sharp cry from her lips.

Her body trembled beneath mine, her breathless pleas turning into incoherent whimpers as I kept her right there—on the edge, drawing her out, pushing her further. I dragged another slow thrust, savoring the way she pulsed around me, how she tried to move against me.

Her fingers curled at my back, her thighs tightening around my waist, and I gave her what she needed. A deeper thrust. She choked on my name, her body seizing, rippling, pulling me deeper, tighter. A whispered, growled demand to let go. And she did. Her back arched, her body spasming as I kept her right in that blissful torment, dragging out every last wave of her release.

My jaw clenched as I thrust into her one last time, burying myself so deep I was certain I would never leave her. The pleasure hit me like a wrecking force, blinding, searing. A guttural sound of her name tore from my throat as I spilled inside her, filling her, owning her. My vision blurred, my body shaking, my hands braced on either side of her to keep myself from collapsing entirely.

I was utterly spent.

Still buried inside her, still throbbing, still overwhelmed by the scent of her, the feel of her, the way she molded around me, I reached for her.

I dragged her up with me, lifting her easily, bringing her with me as I moved, turning us over until I was lying back on the fur quilts and she was sprawled across my body, head resting on my chest. I kept her there, still seated on me, still connected, unwilling to sever the bond between us.

Her breath fanned against my skin, soft, content. She sighed, shifting slightly, and I groaned at the friction, at the way her body still clutched me, still pulsed faintly around me.

I slid a hand up her spine, threading my fingers into her hair, tugging her head up so I could see her face. She was flushed, glowing, her lips swollen, her emerald eyes heavy-lidded and sated.

A slow smile curled my lips. "Look at you," I murmured, brushing a thumb over her kiss-bruised mouth. "So blissed out."

She hummed lazily, her fingers trailing down my chest, nails grazing, teasing. "You sound pleased with yourself."

I tilted her chin up, pressing my lips to the corner of her mouth before whispering against her skin, "Yes, I am. *I* just ruined *you*."

The flush darkened on her cheeks. "I'm still breathing. You'll have to try harder next time, my Liege."

A low growl vibrated in my chest. "Next time?" I tightened my hold on her, rolling my hips, making her gasp.

She stilled, breath hitching, the teasing glint in her eyes flickering. Her nails dug into my arms.

I smirked. "Not looking so confident now, are you?"

She narrowed her eyes, then shifted her hips ever so slightly, squeezing around me, making my breath stutter, my muscles tense.

"You don't either," she taunted.

A dark chuckle rumbled from me. "Reckless little thing." My grip tightened on her hips, holding her still. "Stop smiling, or you won't get the rest you need."

The heat of our spent bodies, the feel of her still draped over me—it was enough to lull me into contentment.

But then, out of nowhere, her voice, soft and curious, broke through the quiet.

"How old are you?"

I huffed a short laugh, my hand still tracing lazy circles along the dip of her spine. I stretched the other arm beneath my head. "Doesn't matter," I murmured. "You have no out. You sealed your fate *forever*."

I dipped my head and brushed a slow kiss against the tip of her nose.

She wrinkled it, shifting slightly, but I caught the way her lips quirked. "You're avoiding the question," she accused, voice still drowsy. She didn't even have the energy to keep her head up.

I exhaled, half amused, half exasperated. "Thirty."

A pause. I arched a brow, waiting.

"You're too old for me."

A low chuckle rumbled from my chest. "Is that so?" I slid my fingers into her hair, tilting her face up further. "Your protests would be a lot more convincing if you weren't still wrapped around me, still wet and warm from what I just did to you."

Her lips parted. I smirked. "Good."

I groaned internally as I finally slipped out of her, my body instantly missing the heat. The cool air felt wrong, my body already stirring at the sight of her—flushed, bare, utterly wrecked.

Forcing myself to breathe, to steady the molten need already flickering back to life, I pushed myself up from the bed. I wet a clean linen and returned to her.

Mirabelle eyed me with curiosity as I gently parted her thighs, dragging the damp cloth over her, slow and careful, cleaning her thoroughly before tending to myself. I leaned down, pressing a lingering kiss to her folds—soft, possessive—before finally pulling away.

I tossed the cloth aside and slipped back into the bed, joining her, my arms found her waist, pulling her back against my chest, fitting her perfectly against me. My lips found the side of her temple, I inhaled, deeply.

"Sleep," I murmured against her ear, voice husky and firm.

She let out a soft, satisfied sigh, but instead of obeying, she smirked—devious even in her exhaustion. "I'm going to go tell the Elders how their mighty Heir can't sleep without cuddling the traitor."

My fingers twitched around her waist.

In a single fluid motion, my hand slid up, fingers wrapping lightly around her throat, feeling her breath and pulse fluttered beneath my thumb. My lips brushing her ear, voice nothing but a whisper.

"...And be sure to mention that their Heir can't sleep without this, too." My hand slid lower, cupping her breast, squeezing just enough to make her gasp and giggle. "Sleep, Bella." I ordered. She didn't say another word. Her breathing slowed. Within moments, she was asleep.

And for the first time in weeks, I let sleep take me.

⸻◈⸻

Leaving her in my bed was one of the hardest things I had ever done. She was drained, her body spent, and she needed rest. I did not want to wake her.

I pulled on my battle attire, fastening each buckle with slow, methodical precision, never once taking my eyes off her.

With dawn yet to break, the chamber was still cloaked in darkness, lightly illuminated in candlelight. But even in sleep, she stirred, as if sensing my departure. A faint crease formed between her brows, her lashes fluttering before she pried her eyes open.

A frown. Then a quiet, sleep-laced murmur. "Are you leaving already?" Her voice, soft, thick with drowsiness.

I exhaled, tightening a strap on my forearm. "I did not wish to wake you. Sleep. I will return tomorrow."

But instead of obeying, she pushed herself upright, the quilt slipping down to pool at her waist. My restraint cracked at the sight of her—bare, drowsy. The marks of my teeth and lips painted her flushed skin—her neck, her breasts, and everywhere the quilt dared to conceal.

I cursed under my breath and looked up, inhaling through my nose. *Control.*

When I dared to glance at her again, she had yanked the quilt back over herself, cheeks pink. "I—I didn't mean to tempt you or anything," she stammered. "I mean, I would have, just...not like that. Not if you hadn't...I mean, this wasn't—"

"I know." My lips quirked. "But you even don't have to *try*, Bella."

She bit her lip, still flushed, still the most tempting thing I had ever seen.

Then, a shift passed over her expression. Her back straightened, her gaze sharpened. "I wanted to make something clear before you go."

The sudden authority in her voice was almost amusing. I tilted my head, intrigued despite myself. "I am listening. Make it quick."

And so, she did. She laid everything bare. *We talked.*

The key. The way it had been left so brazenly in the open, as if begging to be found. A key that should have been locked away beneath the Elders' vaults, never meant to touch the dirt. The slot she had discovered near the portal, where no slot should have existed. The absence of a guard, an anomaly, an impossibility. The pieces snapped into place like a blade locking into its sheath. There was no key to the portal.

What she had found near the portal, it was never a keyhole. It was the sigil. The sigil that did not belong anywhere near the portal. It had been *placed* there deliberately.

And the missing guard? There was always a guard stationed when the portal was opened for the hunt. A deviation from protocol that had only happened once—the moment she stepped through.

This had been a trap. A calculated, meticulous deception. And she had walked straight into it.

"How did you not slit my throat in my sleep for this?" My voice was quiet.

She frowned. My heart cracked open for her all over again. I didn't know what to say, and I *always* do. I had accepted she was a traitor. I had convinced myself of her betrayal. *I still fell for her.*

But what about her, what about the days she spent locked away in that cursed cave? The injustice of it all, the torment?

What about her justice? What excuse did I have? I could have checked on her myself sooner. I could have ensured her safety, even as I warred with myself. But I hadn't. I had put my own devastation above her very life. It shouldn't have mattered that I thought she was safe, I had a duty to make sure of it *in person.*

And now, I didn't know if I could survive another moment of this torment, the weight of what she had endured because I failed her.

I didn't deserve her forgiveness. Yet, I dropped to my knees before her, the hard leather of my armor digging into my flesh, but I welcomed the pain. It was nothing compared to the agony of failing her. I lifted her leg into my hands, pressing my lips against the soft skin, my grip tightening as though it could somehow anchor the storm inside me.

"I have no excuse." The words scraped raw from my throat. "I am sorry. So damn sorry." Uttering *sorry* for the first time since Rennard's death, not since I had sworn never to fail someone I cared about again, yet it felt utterly *insufficient.* But I bit my tongue to hold myself back. I had *no right* to speak any further or to justify or to give my excuses.

She exhaled softly, her fingers threading into my hair. "You don't have to worry. I forgive you."

Of course she did. Because she was *her.*

And I— *I love her.*

The realization slammed into me like a blade to the chest. It had lurked beneath my skin for longer than I cared to admit, but now it was sitting on my tongue, threatening to break free. I had felt it for some time. But never once had I known it—not from anyone, not even my own blood. So I hadn't recognized it for what it was. Not until now.

I wanted to say it. *Needed* to. But if I did, if she whispered it back, if she gave me that fragile, sacred part of herself *now,* after everything—I would never survive it. I would never be worthy of her love, *but I want to try to be.*

So, I swallowed the words, let them burn in my chest like a brand.

Instead, I gathered her into my arms, holding her so tightly I feared I might leave bruises. But she only sighed, her body melting against mine, her lips brushing my collarbone. She hummed softly. I kissed her again, lingering just long enough, and let sleep take her, her faint smile resting against my skin. It cracked something open in me, that smile. *The most beautiful thing I'd ever seen.*

⸺◈⸺

I PULLED THE DOOR CLOSED, my thoughts drifting back to the enigma.

I had suspected them. The Elders who played politics like a game of chess, moving pieces in the shadows, bending rules to their whims. I had watched them. Waited for proof. But I had never caught them in the act—never put names to the hands that stained Atlassian.

And instead of pushing deeper, instead of tearing through their web, I had let myself be blinded. I had convinced myself my suspicions were nothing but paranoia.

Bella had overheard a conversation, one they fed her, intentionally. Words designed to bait her, to send her running straight to me. To ensnare her. To cripple Atlassian from the inside. *Why?*

Haldric had been part of it. I should have known. He had spoken to me countless times, seeking the power to tame beasts for himself. He had wanted it badly enough to bargain, to threaten, to scheme. And now that he was dead, I would have to find another way to uncover the rest of the players who had conspired with him.

But that could wait. First, I would take back Atlassian.

Then, I would tear apart the filth who had conspired to break my Clan. I would drag them from their hiding places, strip away every layer of deceit they had wrapped themselves in.

And when I was done, not even their shadows would remain.

CHAPTER 31

MIRABELLE

I knew what I was going to do. My plans were solid. The execution, however, remained a delicate dance on the edge of uncertainty. I dressed swiftly, irritation flaring as I sifted through the layers of dresses. Why did I possess nothing suited for movement? Yes, they were lovely, flowing creations, but entirely impractical for anything beyond looking cute. A huff escaped my lips as I gathered one of the loose tunics belonging to Damien, binding it securely beneath my dress. *Just in case.*

I shut the door behind me and took a steadying breath, composing myself, adopting the air of someone simply...wandering. Casual and unhurried. I strode through the cavern paths, offering a small wave to Beatrice as I passed. She returned it with a smile.

Good.

Once I was beyond sight, I slipped into the depths of the forest —the very same tangled wild Damien had once led me through. Breathing in the damp scent of Etheris. Shadows shifted between the trees. I had no illusions about my purpose here.

Ahead, crouched amid the underbrush, was a strange creature, vaguely reminiscent of rabbits—if a rabbit had been fashioned from shifting brambles and razor-edged thorns. Its beady eyes fixed on me, pupils shrinking. "Easy there, little beast," I murmured, pausing mid-step. "I'm merely...testing my theories before I work with something that could swallow me whole."

An underestimation.

The creature hissed, or gurgled, before spitting a glob of black substance in my direction. I barely dodged it, watching it sizzle against the forest floor. With a burst of unnatural speed, it vanished, melded seamlessly into the foliage.

"And here I thought we were getting along." I muttered.

I moved forward, searching for something, anything, that might offer another glimpse into this peculiar connection I seemed to have with them. A faint, nearly imperceptible shift in the air—awareness brushing against my thoughts. I stilled. A creature, no larger than my palm, clung to my clothes. Its skin—no, its *form*, was shifting, not in color, but texture, seamlessly mirroring the fabric of my dress. The connection struck me like a whisper from the depths of my mind. It was not speech, but an understanding, an exchange of thoughts that required no words.

I lifted my hand, marveling as the creature's form changed again, matching the warmth of my skin, as though it had become a part of me. A rustling in the grass drew my attention. From the undergrowth, the thorned creature peeked its head out once more. Its wariness had not lessened, but curiosity burned in its eyes.

I grinned. "What, second thoughts already?" I scratched its jaw and the purring was instant. I did not linger. A final brush of my fingers over the shape-changing creature on my arm, a fleeting touch against the brambled beast before it slunk back into the undergrowth. I had no time to waste.

My feet carried me swiftly through the thick weave of trees, the path winding, leading toward the place where Rak'Thalgar had chased us not long ago. I had barely taken another step when I noticed Izmer.

I groaned. "You have got to be—" I turned sharply, exasperation coloring my voice. "What in grace's name are *you* doing here?"

Izmer, lounging against a tree trunk, looking as if he had all the time in the world to waste.

"Because," he drawled, "judging by the way you slipped off with all the grace of a thief who thinks they aren't being watched, acting *too* normal, it was painfully obvious you were up to something."

I scowled. "And?"

"And," he smirked, "Damien would castrate me if something happened to you *again*. So, really, this has more to do with *my safety* than yours."

I exhaled sharply, pinching the bridge of my nose with two fingers. Hmm...maybe he could be of use. My skills at using the strange lifting foliage to reach the high islands were, let's just say, nonexistent.

"Follow me."

His brows lifted, amusement flashing in his dark eyes. "Oh, decided to play leader now?"

I turned on my heel, walking briskly and shot him a glare over my shoulder. "Help me get up there."

"Up where?" He was glancing at the towering branches overhead.

"Just do as I say, and you'll see." I reached him with my hands. He grabbed me by the waist, his strength nearly knocking the breath from me as he propelled us both upward in one swift motion. I clenched his clothes with my fingers, swallowing my yelp as we shot into the air, the wind whipping past my ears. He twisted mid-ascent, gripping a branch, and in another bound, we landed in the middle of the island's dense canopy.

I stepped away the moment my feet found solid ground, brushing the stray leaves from my hair, glaring at his smug expression. We surveyed the land below. "If we do nothing out of the ordinary or attack them," he mused beside me, "they usually don't mind us."

I glanced at him. "I want them to mind us."

He shook his head, amused. "No. Absolutely not." I didn't respond. Because my focus was elsewhere. On the land itself.

Everything in Etheris had a pattern. A rhythm. The creatures here—they were not mindless beasts. They responded, they reacted, they listened. I crouched low, running my fingers along the bark of the twisted branch beneath me. The wood was rough, ancient. I closed my eyes and inhaled.

Nothing. Think. Rak'Thalgar had chased us that day. It was not a mindless predator. It had purpose. It had been summoned by something. A shift. A disturbance. A presence.

It had been territorial. And what do territorial creatures do?

I glanced at Izmer. "You said they don't mind us if we do nothing out of the ordinary, right?"

His gaze narrowed. "Yeah, and that's exactly why we shouldn't—"

I lowered myself to the branch, running my fingers along its coarse, ancient bark. Etheris was a land that remembered, its creatures bound to the energy that pulsed beneath its surface like a living, breathing entity.

I closed my eyes, steadying my breathing. And then, slowly, I reached inside myself. Into that connection. I focused—not on calling it, not on forcing it forward—*but on being seen.*

I pressed my hand to the bark. I let it feel me. The trees around me whispered, a sudden shift in the air. Izmer tensed beside me, sensing it too. His hand drifted to the hilt of his blade.

"Mirabelle…" He hissed. "What did you just do?"

I ignored him. The pulse beneath my skin deepened. A connection snapping into place. The leaves trembled. Then the branches creaked. The trees breathed. The ground shifted. The whispering hush of leaves turned to a tremor—a quiver that ran through the veins of the land itself. A pulse, a heartbeat, moved through the forest.

The vines shot out first, slithering up my wrists, my waist, my thighs, wrapping around me in a motion that was neither rough nor aggressive. It did not feel like an attack. It felt like a hand reaching for another, seeking contact.

Izmer reacted in a blink. His arms locked around my torso, yanking me toward him with a force meant to keep me grounded. But it was too late. The branches lifted us both. Izmer cursed violently, moving in the grasp of sentient limbs of wood and vine. My pulse was an erratic rhythm in my throat. I twisted against the hold, not to fight it, but to understand it.

And then, in a smooth, seamless motion, we were set down on something that was not ground at all. Izmer's muscles coiled, his power flaring on instinct. I reached out, placing a hand on his arm, firm yet pleading. "Please don't," I whispered, my voice barely above the rustling of the leaves around us. "Let me take care of this." He nodded unconvincingly.

The land beneath us moved. The jungle ahead was not merely trees, but a living, breathing being, its massive body stretching far beyond the limits of my vision. Then—it opened its eyes. And the forest glowed.

Izmer's grip on my arm was unrelenting. "Ghor'mak."

I turned to him. "What—?"

He was still staring. "We hunted it before," he muttered. "We failed. And we hurt her." Before I could ask more, thousands of smaller creatures, pouring from the tangled expanse of Ghormak's colossal form. Glowing insects, vine-clad beasts, tendrils of pulsing fungi—every living thing attached to it.

A tidal wave of emotions crashed into me, a symphony of voices, thoughts, and whispers merging into one. The connection was raw, unfiltered, all-encompassing. It seized me, unraveled me, and I let it.

My knees buckled, the ground rising to meet me as I sank into it—palms pressing into the grass, fingers curling into the ground. A shuddering breath escaped me. "I'm here," I whispered, not speaking, but feeling. And in that moment, I was no longer separate. I was part of them. The vines tightened around me as an embrace. The creatures pressed closer, their small forms pulsing with warmth, their tiny limbs touching my face, my hands, my hair, as if to soothe, to offer comfort.

They knew. Everything.

I let them see everything, feel everything—the Untameables, the portal breach, the ruin creeping over Atlassian like a slow-burning plague, the war waged in shadows and blood. And most of all, they knew my fear. For Damien and his Clan. For everything I was willing to risk. They saw my intent, the path I had already chosen. That I had come not just to seek help, but to ask if they would stand with me.

Silence stretched. I thought for a second that I was going to be refused.

Then a deep, resonant hum, low and layered, rolled through the air. It came from beneath, from within, a vibration that hummed through my bones, echoed in my very blood. A call.

And Etheris answered. Golden motes drifted from the treetops, swirling like fireflies through the mist-thick air. Shadows shifted in the distance, silhouettes emerging from the dense jungle, from Caletia, and then—light.

Soft, golden, fluid, flowing between the trees like molten sunlight. XalVeyra.

A towering, ethereal being of woven petals, its form shifting between flesh-forged and flora, the countless willow-like arms drifting like liquid light. Its movements were soundless, weightless. The glowing orbs at its fingertips pulsed, rippling with the soft thrum of life itself.

It stepped forward, and with each motion, life bloomed in its wake. Grass thickened, flowers unfurled, even the scars on my skin —the faint bruises, the lingering aches—healed in an instant. A breath of something golden surged through me, a warmth that felt like renewal itself.

And still, it was not alone. A whisper of glass and blood swept through the space, the air shimmering with refracted light. The temperature shifted, the scent of iron and ground thickening. Irythiel.

A serpentine specter, its massive form coiling through the air, translucent skin revealing the flowing crimson rivers within. Its stained-glass wings caught the glow of Etheris, casting fractured light in every direction.

Izmer, whom I had nearly forgotten was there, suddenly cursed under his breath. "It shouldn't be here. It shouldn't—"

But he stopped when it descended. Its fangs, long, elegant, designed not for death, but for taking pain, parted slightly as it loomed over me.

I felt its question. *What will you give in return?*

The knowledge struck me in an instant, and a shudder ran through me. Its power came with a cost. It drinks disease, drawing out afflictions and replacing them with raw life essence. But it did not erase suffering—it shifted it elsewhere. A wound healed here was a wound given elsewhere. A sickness taken was a sickness sent. Balance.

I swallowed hard but nodded. "I know," I whispered, even though my voice felt lost in the enormity of its presence. "I know what you are. And I still ask for your help."

It watched me—not with eyes, but with knowing.

A massive, bone limb curled around me. Warm. Protective. Familiar. I knew before even looking. "Rak'Thalgar," I whispered. The beast rumbled in answer, his massive skull lowering to nuzzle against me, his mind pressing into mine like the touch of a long-lost companion. Izmer was utterly stunned now, rendered speechless. He decided it was best to simply shut up and watch.

Rak'Thalgar's voice resonated through my mind, a deep, steady presence threading through my thoughts. *"I can bear the burden for Irythiel. You need not carry this weight alone."*

He was born of balance, a creature forged to uphold the delicate order of this Realm. Where pain was given, he could take. Where suffering sought a vessel, he could endure.

A soundless sob rose in my throat, a tightness in my chest unfurling as I grasped his massive skull. He lowered himself further, beckoning me onto his back. I climbed, barely noticing Izmer's wide-eyed stare.

I couldn't even muster a smirk or a quip for Izmer. My mind was too clouded. Had the war reached its end, or was there still a chance to turn the tide? I hoped—no, I needed to believe—that there was still time. That Damien was still fighting. That he would return only when victory was secured, when the sigil was sealed, or whatever impossible task he had set himself upon was done.

I exhaled, pressing my palm against the living ground beneath me, sending my request through the bond. *Take Izmer back to Vael'Thir.*

Ghor'mak responded in kind, the trees swaying, the ground shifting beneath Izmer's feet as the forest itself began to carry him away. His mouth opened—probably to argue, probably to demand —but I cut him off with a final plea. "Please keep your mouth shut for once. For everyone's sake." And this time, he didn't protest. Maybe he couldn't. He barely had time to register what was happening before the land moved, pulling him back toward safety.

And then it was just me.

Me. Rak'Thalgar. Irythiel. XalVeyra.

⊰⋅⊱

THE MOMENT we emerged into Atlassian, chaos swallowed us whole.

I had barely a breath to process the sheer devastation before me before the scent of fire, blood, and smoldering ruin struck my senses. The Celestia was darkened by thick plumes of smoke, and the ground itself bore the scars of devastation.

Rak'Thalgar had coiled through the portal in a sinuous motion, his massive form maneuvering with terrifying grace. His skeletal wings had shifted—sometimes bone, sometimes something far more spectral, meshing and unraveling. Behind him, Irythiel and XalVeyra followed, slipping through with an eerie, weightless precision. And then we landed.

Right before the Royal Guards stationed at the portal's exit.

The guards—seasoned warriors, their faces carved with the hardened discipline of their rank—stood stunned, motionless, their hands frozen on the hilts of their weapons. I watched the horror bleed into their expressions as their eyes darted from one impossible sight to another.

Their gazes locked onto me. Not as an intruder. Not as the traitor I had once been declared. But as something that had ridden through their sacred portal atop a beast they had failed to tame. And that was the last moment of stillness before the world descended into madness.

The Majors.

Scattered groups of them, their armor splattered with blood and grime. Some of the Majors turned toward us, their movements sharp with recognition, their gazes flickering between horror and disbelief. Others—wounded, weary, caught in the throes of their battle instinct—charged without a second thought.

A wave of them rushed forward, weapons raised. Then, two of them split.

No—multiplied. I blinked, my heart slamming against my ribs. They had been one a moment ago. And now, they were two.

The exact same face. The same armor, the same stance, two sets of identical eyes locking onto me. One Major had just become two. A trick of the mind? No. I felt it, the ripple in the air. The shift in energy.

Loptrians.

The illusion of numbers. The ability to create identical duplicates, indistinguishable from their true selves. The Loptrians had been among the Elders' secret experiments. I didn't understand how I knew. How the knowledge settled so clearly within me, an instinct deeper than thought. But I did. I could see them for what they truly were. *The knowledge from Untameables itself.*

Yet Rak'Thalgar couldn't. Not like the way I could.

The way he hissed, coiled, prepared to strike at some of the Majors alike told me what I already suspected. To them, there was a little difference between the turned Major and its replica. And to me, it was as clear as day.

This would be difficult. I exhaled sharply, then moved. Fast.

I leapt down from Rak'Thalgar's back, landing on the blood-stained ground. Shadows curled from beneath me, responding to my will, rising like a barrier against the tide of chaos. I extended them outward, stretching into the fray, enveloping the Untame-ables who had taken the form of Majors.

"Now!"

Irythiel moved fast. The serpent descended like a spirit of blood and glass, its translucent fangs piercing flesh, drawing out sickness and rot. It shifted it. I felt the weight of it—the balance of life restored through pain. And Rak'Thalgar was taking the burden. The great beast shuddered, his colossal body trembling under the invisible agony of countless afflictions drained into him. But he bore it. *I owe him more than I can repay.*

But it was XalVeyra who made them whole. She moved first. Her luminous tendrils of gold unraveled like molten silk, sweeping over the battlefield in fluid waves. Where they touched, the world changed. The air thickened with life, fire-drenched wounds mended, the corruption within the afflicted burned away.

Then, the Loptrians turned on us. They were cunning. They saw what I was doing. They adapted. A wave of them rushed forward, their copied flames burning too bright, their replicated bodies moving too perfectly. Too many.

I had seconds before we lost the advantage. I slammed my hands into the ground, shadows exploding outward in jagged, clawing tendrils. The Loptrians hesitated. Their illusions flickered, their perfect copies rippling as they struggled to maintain their deception.

And in that moment—I struck. XalVeyra's golden threads lashed forward, tearing through the illusions, unraveling them into nothing. Irythiel coiled around the true Majors, siphoning away the remnants of their corruption, leaving them weakened, but whole.

And Rak'Thalgar—he roared, the sheer force of it shaking the battlefield, sending the remaining illusions shattering like glass. The tide shifted. One by one, we tore through the deception, separating the real from the false.

Until only the true Majors remained. A hush had settled over the surroundings. The Majors—the real ones—stood at a distance, staring at me, at Rak'Thalgar, at the creatures that had just saved them.

And above us, the storm rumbled. This was but a fraction of Atlassian, one battlefield among countless others. The war was waiting. Damien was waiting—whether he realized it or not. And we needed to find him before he did something that could not be undone.

⬥

I HAD EXPECTED an Atlassian teeming with wreckage, shadows slithering through the streets, raging Untameables tearing through the remains, and afflicted Majors attacking without pause. But reality painted a different picture.

Most of the alleyways were vacant, the residential quarters hollowed out, the market streets eerily silent. The absence of life was almost worse than the chaos I had braced for. Had the people been saved? Or had they perished before we could reach them?

Yet, what struck me more than the emptiness was the quiet, unbidden transformation unfolding before my eyes. Where we had passed, where XalVeyra's golden filaments kissed the wounded ground, Atlassian did not merely heal, it awakened.

Scorched stone, that was fractured and blackened by fire, shimmered anew, smooth as untouched marble, as though time itself was bending backward. The very air, suffocated with the stench of blood and ruin, grew lighter, sweeter, carrying the breath of something old, something sacred, as if the city had been holding its breath for centuries, waiting for this moment. Above, Celestia trembled. The thick veil of smoke unraveled in slow, delicate strands, revealing slivers of the lights beyond. What had been lost was not just being restored—it was being reborn.

The land had not begged for salvation. It had not pleaded to be put back together. It had been waiting. Not to be saved, but to be seen. To be remembered. To be whole. A shiver ran through me, from the sheer, aching beauty of it.

The great beasts moved in tandem. Weaving golden light through the broken world, unmaking the scars left behind. Irythiel, gliding like liquid glass, drawing out corruption and dispersing it, as though cleansing the very veins of Atlassian. And we had yet to find Damien.

A sharp gasp tore from my chest as the ground beneath me vanished.

One moment, I stood anchored in the grounds of Atlassian, the next, I was wrenched into the air, my stomach lurching, my limbs weightless against the force that had seized me. No—not flying. Hauled. Twisted mid-air, the grip around me tightening, coiling, dragging me toward Celestia's shrouded sky as if it meant to hurl me into the heavens themselves.

I barely had time to brace, barely had time to shut my eyes against the coming impact—

A hiss. A violent, shuddering clash of forces. I crashed back down, my body jarring against solid ground, but I was not alone. Heat surrounded me. A heavy coil, bones of my Bone Tyrant pressing firm around my form.

But as I opened my eyes, my breath stilled. Molten red eyes. Shadows thick as smoke. A shape I had seen before.

Deadclaw—Dreadclaw?

A piercing shriek rattled through the air as he squared off against Rak'Thalgar, both titanic forces clashing in a war of dominance. Snarls, hisses, the sickening crunch of shifting bones and lashing claws filled the battlefield.

My mind reeled. How is he here? He had been with Damien—hadn't he? I shut my eyes, reaching, pushing my thoughts outward, grasping for the Tether. *Take us to Damien.*

Dreadclaw's mind was a storm, wild and untamed, resisting, unlike the others. Unlike Rak'Thalgar, he did not yield to me. Did not welcome me. But he did not throw me away either. He stilled, hesitating. A growl rumbled from his chest. Not rejection. Not acceptance. Something in between. But it was enough.

Then, without warning, he moved. Like a shadow possessed. Dreadclaw blurred forward, his massive form flickering in and out of the darkness, tendrils of night trailing him like living things. The moment he lunged, we followed. No choice but to follow.

We tore through the battlefield, moving as one. Another group of the corrupted emerged, their forms twisted, their flames burning too bright, too wrong. But this time, it was different.

Dreadclaw knew. He did not hesitate, did not pause, did not guess—he distinguished them. As easily as I could. Effortless. Precise. He struck before they could react, cutting through them with a ferocity that sent the others staggering back.

And he knew it. The smug bastard knew it. I felt it through our Tether, the sheer satisfaction rolling off him like a wave. So, I did the only thing I could. I teased him for it. *Oh? Look who suddenly thinks he's better at this than me.*

A hiss slithered through my mind before he even turned his head—a soundless, venomous warning. A snap of irritation. I laughed under my breath, though unease curled at the edges of my ribs. I did not trust him. But I knew one thing for certain. He was not going to attack me. And I knew it because I was connected to his mind and so to his intentions.

CHAPTER 32
MIRABELLE

By the time we reached them, it was already over. A sea of Majors stood around Damien, their forms bloodstained, weary—but alive. Because of him.

He stood at the heart of them, his voice cutting through the thick, smoke-choked air as he spoke to Nathan. Spent, drenched in battle and blood, but standing unshaken. And seeing them— seeing all those he had fought for, fought to save—pride burned through me.

He did this. They all did this. Not just for themselves, but for Atlassian as well.

Dreadclaw beat us to him. The massive beast shot ahead, his shadows stretching, curling like smoke as he closed the distance— and then, with a sudden, controlled force, he took Damien. To raise him. Hauling him into the air with all the respect and dignity he had absolutely never afforded me.

Damien's expression was pure confusion, his body tensing as he was lifted, his instincts battling between defense and sheer disbelief. His dark eyes flickered, scanning Dreadclaw. As Damien steadied himself atop Dreadclaw, his hand brushed over the crea-ture's obsidian-shadowed neck, an act of gratitude and care, before he stepped down.

The second we landed, his gaze locked onto mine, a silent question hanging in the air between us.

What did you do? I had no answer.

Irythiel and XalVeyra didn't so much as spare Dreadclaw a glance—unbothered by his display of triumph as they drifted into the battlefield, weaving through the wounded. The carnage faded. The air changed, the land mending, soft gold seeping into the cracks of ruin. Magic.

Damien's eyes darkened as he stalked forward, his exhaustion vanishing beneath something far stronger. Before I could think, in front of an entire army, an audience of bloodied Majors, warriors, and survivors—

He kissed me. Bruising. Claiming. Consuming. It tilted my world in mere seconds, left my breath stolen, my mind spinning. And then his lips left mine, only to press against my forehead, firm and lingering. A contrast to the storm he had just unleashed upon my mouth.

"I should lock you up for throwing yourself into the unknown like this." His voice was low, carrying a soft undercurrent—an unmistakable contradiction to the threat in his words.

The insufferable creature that was Dreadclaw did not take kindly to the display of affection Damien had just granted me. The instant Damien pulled away, the beast seized him once more, hauling him back toward the remnants of battle, as if to remind him of where his attention ought to lie.

There were still a few Majors in the last alleyways, still duty to be attended to. And Dreadclaw would see it done.

Yet I knew the truth of it. This was not merely obligation.

The connection between Dreadclaw and me thrummed with something far pettier, something as ridiculous as jealousy. A *Tameable*, consumed by such a trivial sentiment. Had I not felt it myself, I would have dismissed the notion entirely.

This *minx* of a beast.

If I dared to speak of this, of the sulking, *jealous* nature lurking beneath his fearsome exterior, I would be laughed into oblivion. Not that I intended to speak of it. But still.

※

I WAS SORE. The ache that curled through my body was not from the flight. Nor from the battle. How could it be, with the relentless vigilance of Rak'Thalgar, who had barely let me take a step unguarded, his looming presence was like a smothering shield.

No.

I was sore from *him*. From the way Damien had taken me, again and again, until I had been reduced to nothing but gasping breaths and shaking limbs. Until the last of my modesty had unraveled beneath his hands, his mouth, his unrelenting hunger.

The night had stretched endlessly between us, filled with whispered demands, bruising kisses, tangled sheets, and the wicked burn of him claiming, marking, *owning* every part of me. Shyness had been swallowed whole, devoured by something deeper and darker. I had lost count of how many times he had drawn me over the edge, how many times I had clung to him, pleading for more, and still, he had not been done.

And now, as the dim light of morning trickled into the cavern, I barely had the strength to move.

I didn't remember falling asleep, but I must have. And when I woke, I was *still* wrapped around him, my body flush against his, my legs straddling his hips as I lay sprawled across his chest, my face nestled in the crook of his neck.

He was half-reclined against the headboard, a heap of furs propped behind him, holding me close even in sleep. The steady rise and fall of his breathing grounding me in the aftermath of all we had done.

I shifted slightly, and only then did I feel it—*him*, still buried inside me, thick and pulsing with lingering heat.

A shuddering breath left me. I tilted my head up, finding his face in the soft glow of the cave. His features were relaxed, his usual cold expression smoothed into something almost *peaceful*. His dark lashes fanned against his cheekbones, his lips, those lips that had torn me apart and put me back together, parted just slightly.

When the battle had ended and the Tameables retreated to Etheris, I found myself standing amidst a silence heavier than the war itself. Awe clung to the air, stretching from the Elders to the Royals, from the Majors to the common ranks. They looked at me not as an outsider, not as the traitor I had once been labeled, but as something else entirely.

Pride gleamed in Damien's eyes, in the way he stood beside me. Nathan, without hesitation, tore the insignia from his chest and pressed it into my palm— Aetherium Hold was to be mine. Dreadclaw, however, was far less impressed. He snarled, reading the shift in my thoughts. And I resisted the urge to roll my eyes and winked back at him, just to be petty.

Damien initiated this *pleasing me,* that had begun last night as a reward for my bravery. A declaration from him, spoken with quiet certainty.

I am proud of you.

The words struck deeper than they should have, unraveling a buried ache within me. No one had ever said that to me before. Not once. And I had never thought to crave it, never believed I needed to hear it. Yet, in that moment, I did. A tightness coiled in my chest, my throat burning, my vision blurring before I could even think to stop it.

And Damien, ever watchful, ever attuned, *noticed.* He saw the way his words unraveled me. He kissed away the evidence, his lips brushing over my cheeks, my forehead. Until words no longer mattered. Until there was nothing left but the way he touched me, the way he made me *feel* it. Again. And again. Until sleep finally took him, and even then—his arms never let me go.

I tried to ease out of his hold, moving as carefully as possible, but the moment *he* slipped from me, his body no longer nestled against mine, his eyes snapped open.

Faster than I could react, he grabbed me again, pulling me flush against his chest.

"If you so much as *touch* me again right now, Damien, I *swear* I will bite you until you regret every decision that led to this moment." My voice was hoarse, thick with exhaustion, but firm.

His chuckle was deep, slow, the sound of a man entirely too pleased with himself. It rumbled against my skin, sending a traitorous shiver down my spine.

"Is that a threat, Wildcat?" he murmured, voice low. His grip didn't loosen, despite my glare. "I am not *touching* you now. Relax," He said, shifting slightly.

"You told me *this*—how many times in the past eight hours?"

He had the audacity to smile. "Your limits aren't fixed," he said, all amusement. "They're meant to be stretched."

I punched him in the gut. He let out a sharp exhale, but the glint of amusement in his eyes never wavered.

He leaned in, *bit* my cheek—sharp enough to make me yelp, his teeth grazing my skin before he pulled away, rising from the bed with effortless grace. The sting lingered, and I scowled at him even as heat curled low in my stomach.

Unbothered, he strode across the cavern to prepare the bath, steam rising in thick curls, the scent of minerals filling the air. When he held out his hand, I took it without hesitation, letting him guide me into the warmth.

The water welcomed me like a balm, soothing the deep ache thrumming through my body. I sighed, letting my head fall back against his chest, my body sinking into his.

"Are we heading to Atlassian now?"

"Yes," he murmured, voice low and certain. "Almost all the inhabitants of Atlassian were relocated yesterday. We will be leaving soon."

I hummed, letting my fingers trail absentmindedly over his arm beneath the water. The silence between us was a comfortable one, the kind that only existed when there was nothing left to prove.

And then—

"I am going to Bond you to me."

I *jumped*. The water splashed violently as I twisted, nearly slipping in my haste to turn toward him. "*What?*"

His brows furrowed, as though I had just offended him. "I said, we are Bonding."

I stared at him. "*What?*" I repeated, breathless. "Did I—did I hear that correctly?"

"You did."

"Shouldn't you *ask* me first?"

"I know you will say yes."

The sheer *certainty* in his voice left me speechless. I should have scolded him for his audacity, but instead, I found myself staring—searching. His face was unreadable.

I swallowed hard. "*Why now?*" My voice was quieter than before. "We have time. Why rush?"

"Do you remember asking me what *my* wish was?" His voice is as unreadable as ever. I nodded.

He exhaled, tilting his head slightly, his gaze locking onto mine with the same intensity that always made it impossible to look away. He paused, his fingers brushing absently against my wrist beneath the water. And then, lower, rougher, "I want to be there for you. As your everything. When you see others sharing laughter and secrets and feel the sting of what you never had, I want you to turn to me instead."

My throat burned. *He knew.*

His voice didn't soften, but it carried something deeper. "When the weight of the past presses too heavy, when your hands tremble too much to even lace your own boots, I want to be the one who kneels before you and does it instead. When exhaustion dulls your strength, let me be the one who braids your hair, who drags a cloak over your shoulders when you forget to care for yourself." He paused, his eyes filled with affection. "When you stare too long at a meal you burn beyond saving, pretending you're improving, let me be the one who takes it from your hands and eats it anyway."

His fingers still tracing slow circles against my skin. "Let me be the one who tucks a blanket around you when sleep claims you in places you didn't mean to rest. The one who knows what you need before you say it, before you even realize it yourself."

A pause. Then, lower, rougher, like a promise laced with iron.

"So yes, *let me bind you to me for eternity*, in a way you can never escape from."

I couldn't breathe. My chest felt tight, my pulse unsteady as I tried to swallow down the storm rising within me.

"Why?" My voice came out rough, barely more than a whisper. "What made you choose me?"

His expression didn't change. But his answer did something to me.

"Choosing implies there were alternatives. There never were." His grip on my wrist tightened slightly, just enough for me to feel the heat of his skin searing into mine. His gaze, unwavering, burned with something absolute. "From the moment I laid eyes on you, Bella, you weren't an option. You were my inevitability."

I pressed my lips together, trying to find words, but none came. I felt my eyes filling with tears and my throat burning.

He exhaled, voice lowering just slightly. "If I had one wish, it would be to turn back time. To find you sooner. To have you longer."

The breath I had been holding shuddered out of me.

"And if I had another," he murmured, voice quieter now, "it would be to make you see yourself as I do. Because no matter how I try, I could never tell you how deeply you are engraved in me."

I tried to make light of it, to weave a jest into the heavy silence, to make it lighter. "If you keep talking like that, I might actually—" but the words broke, caught somewhere between my throat and my ribs.

My voice betrayed me—cracking, breaking apart like brittle glass. The effort crumbled entirely as a single tear slipped down my cheek.

Damien caught it with his thumb, his touch firm, deliberate. His gaze didn't waver, piercing straight through me.

"I want to Bond you *as Damien*," he said, voice low but certain. "Not as the Heir of Atlassian."

I stilled. The weight of his words settled deep in my bones. I nodded, barely aware of the motion.

He searched my face, studying me as if gauging every flicker of hesitation. "Do you feel suffocated?"

"No." The answer left me before I could think. "Never."

"Then why ask to wait?"

I hesitated. "Bonding is...meant for bearing Heirs, isn't it?"

He exhaled sharply. "For most, yes." His voice remained even, measured. "But not for me. I would never bind myself for eternity on a reckless impulse. Maybe for the sake of Clan alliance, I might have. But never for *myself*." He tilted his head slightly, his fingers brushing against my wrist under the water. "I decided this long ago. And this is the first moment I've had—truly had—since the war wasn't looming over me."

I knew, even if I hadn't admitted it to myself yet, I had already decided, too.

He guided my wrist upward until it hovered just at the surface, the warmth of the bath doing little to ease the tension that crackled between us. From beside the bath, he retrieved a blade— its hilt adorned with ancient carvings, its stone-like edge sharp enough to split flesh with effortless precision. A ceremonial blade. One meant for this exact purpose.

I had seen this ritual before. Knew that the moment our blood intertwined, my fate would be sealed for eternity. That I would no longer stand as merely Mirabelle, but as the Bonded Eternis of the Heir of Atlassian.

And yet, it was the easiest decision I had ever made.

I did not hesitate when he pressed the hilt of the blade into my palm. Did not flinch as I turned his wrist over and dragged the edge across his skin, watching as dark blood welled and spilled along the ridges of his veins. His gaze held mine, the weight of the moment wrapping around us like the very Aether that governed this Realm.

Damien took the blade from my grasp. His fingers wrapped around my wrist, and with the same deliberate motion, he cut into my skin. A sharp sting. A brief, searing heat. My blood spilled in rivulets, two streams of blackness, swirling together as they dripped into the water below, staining it in hues of fate.

Then, he took my wrist in his hand and pressed it against his own. The moment our wounds met, a surge of energy erupted. Veins of crimson and black licked up our arms where we were connected, threading through our skin like roots sinking deep.

A force beyond the tangible wove itself into me, his blood surging through my veins, flooding my senses, until I could no longer tell where I ended and he began. My heart stilled—clenched, then expanded, beating in sync with his, tethering itself to a rhythm that was no longer just my own. My skin tingled, my breath hitched, and for a moment, I swore I could feel the very essence of him settling inside me.

He only said one word.

"Ineffable."

Too great, too achingly beautiful to be confined by mere language.

⊷◈⊶

I RETURNED from Amara's with a sigh. She had fully integrated herself with the Thralls now, moving with them toward the palace premises. I had offered—no, insisted, she move into the palace premises, even speaking to Damien about securing her a chamber so she could assist with the Tameables or whatever else suited her. And what did she do? The little traitor chose gardening. With the Thralls. That gossip-loving menace even had the audacity to look smug about it. But at least we'd still see each other every day.

My thoughts then turned to Damien, and to the real reason he'd left early. His focus had settled on a much larger matter—his father. He wanted to *clear the air* before formally introducing me to the Sovereign of Atlassian. Which, if I was being honest, was probably for the best. I had never met the man face to face, and why would I have? To him, I had been nothing more than a nameless commoner who had somehow managed to transform into an accused traitor overnight. If I had to wager a guess, he likely envisioned me as some wild-eyed, ill-mannered little wretch who couldn't hold a spoon properly, let alone command a battlefield. I could already imagine the disappointment brewing in his highborn noble soul.

Shaking off the thought, I approached my chambers only to find Lyria standing at the door, her expression unreadable. I gave her a quick nod. "Hey."

She didn't return the greeting. Instead, she looked me dead in the eyes and said, "You know you don't deserve Damien, right?"

I blinked. Wait. What now?

I didn't even have to ask. Lyria was already launching into whatever self-righteous speech she had prepared, as if she had been waiting for this moment.

"You didn't do anything to earn his attention," she said flatly, arms crossed. "Or his affection. It just...happened. And you didn't even lift a finger."

I squinted at her, unimpressed. I mean...she is not entirely wrong. But still. "How, pray tell, does that concern you?"

She let out a sharp breath, ignoring my jab. "*We both* don't deserve him." Her tone had an edge to it—jealousy, yes, but there was something more. "Nobody does. You haven't seen what he's done for Atlassian, how much he's sacrificed for all of us over the years. The things he's had to endure. I would die for him, Mirabelle."

I arched a brow, arms crossing to mirror her stance. "Even I would do that." *Oaf.*

Lyria's eyes flashed before she shook her head. "You don't understand."

"No, I do." My voice was calm, even. "I know exactly what he is, the weight he carries, and the sacrifices he has made. I've seen it, felt it—not in the full measure of all he has endured over the years, but enough *to understand.* You think I don't understand the cost of being someone like him?"

Her lips pressed into a thin line, frustration tightening her features. "Then you should know that being with him isn't—" She exhaled sharply, eyes flicking away before returning to mine, burning with something like conviction. "It isn't just about standing at his side, Mirabelle. It's about knowing that no matter how much he gives, he will always give more. And one day, it will take everything from him."

I crossed my arms, tilting my head. "And you think I don't know that?" A humorless laugh left me. "You act like I stumbled into this blind, like I don't see him. But I do, Lyria. Every single day."

She scoffed. "Do you truly care for him? Or is it just the way he looks at you? Or perhaps...simply the way he looks?"

Ah, yes. There it was. The classic *I'm totally not jealous, but I'm absolutely jealous* speech. I swallowed my retort. To dignify this with a response would be an insult in itself.

What happened to her all of a sudden?

We were never the closest of friends, but we always got along well enough. Was it because of me? I hadn't done anything—literally nothing. And somehow, I had become the problem.

Silence stretched.

Lyria's jaw clenched, her fingers curling at her sides. Then, with an exasperated huff, she turned on her heel and strode off, her exit punctuated by the sharp click of her boots against stone.

CHAPTER 33

MIRABELLE

Evening came and went, yet there was no sign of Damien.

He told me he would come for me by nightfall, and that we would depart for the palace then. But time dragged on, and as the hours stretched into the next day, and another, unease settled deep in my guts. I tried to occupy myself, roaming the grounds, spending time with Rak'Thalgar, who, despite his usual overprotectiveness, seemed to sense my restlessness and allowed me space. But as dusk fell once more and still, no word came, dread curled tight in my stomach like a coiled serpent.

That night, I could not sleep. My body twisted and turned in the sheets, my mind running through every possibility. Had something happened? Had the sigil failed again? But they had already locked it that day. Had something gone wrong within the palace?

The thought of Damien in danger gnawed at me, each scenario worse than the last.

Then, footsteps. I bolted upright, pulse hammering against my ribs. Relief surged through me for a fleeting moment—until I saw who it was.

Nathan.

The disappointment was irrational but sharp. "Is everything all right?" I asked, voice taut with worry. "Yes, Mirabelle," he assured me, his tone calm. "I'm here to escort you. You're moving to the Royal Chambers."

I forced a smile, masking the confusion rising within me. "And where is Damien?"

Nathan's brows furrowed slightly. "The Young Sovereign is in the palace." He hesitated, as if weighing his next words. "I was simply asked to come and bring you."

A hollow feeling settled in my chest. He was in the palace. And yet, he had sent someone else to fetch me. I didn't push further. The answers would come soon enough. Until then, I gathered my things in silence, preparing for whatever awaited me at the Royal Chambers.

The journey to the palace premise was quiet.

A carriage stood waiting just outside the portal, its dark wood polished to an impeccable gleam, gilded accents catching the faint glow of lantern light. Nathan spoke sparingly during the ride, though he filled the silence with brief mentions of how we would handle the Tameables and my responsibilities at the Aetherium Hold. I responded in kind, my voice steady, but my mind was elsewhere.

By the time we arrived, I was led past the towering gates of the Royal Grounds—not into the palace itself, but to the Royal Chambers, where the high-ranking members of the Royal Legion resided. The sprawling estate stood beside the main palace, its towering stone walls adorned with intricate carvings, its vast corridors lit by golden sconces flickering in the dim evening light.

Nathan guided me through the hallways with practiced ease before stopping before an arched doorway.

"This will be your chamber," he said simply, pushing the heavy wooden door open.

I frowned. "Why am I here? Can I see Damien?"

Nathan's expression did not shift. "The *Young Sovereign* is occupied with pressing matters. He asked for you to settle here in the meantime."

That made me pause. If Damien was truly handling something

urgent, I would understand. But it wasn't like him to keep me entirely in the dark. This meant it was something...else. Something I wasn't meant to question.

I said nothing as I stepped inside, taking in the chamber before me. It was vast, lavish—larger than anything I had ever called my own. The walls were a deep cream, their surface embossed with delicate gold filigree. A grand chandelier of polished bronze and crystal hung from the high-vaulted ceiling, its candlelight casting warm shadows against the intricately woven tapestries that adorned the walls. Towering windows stretched from floor to ceiling, draped in thick, heavy curtains of rich velvet, embroidered with scenes of Atlassian's history. The bed was enormous, its frame carved from dark wood, the sheets an indulgent array of silken fabrics in deep sapphire and ivory.

But I hardly enjoyed the grandeur of it all. My belongings had already arrived, carefully arranged by the Thralls moving about with quiet efficiency. And that was when the confusion began to take root.

Why were they unpacking my things here?

I stood in the center of the chamber, arms crossed, watching as the servants neatly folded my dresses into the towering armoire, as if this had been planned in advance. As if my stay here was not temporary.

I bit my lip, a question pressing against my tongue. Was I not meant to share Damien's chamber?

Or was this a matter of waiting for the ordained Bonding ceremony? His words echoed in my mind—*I want the whole of Atlassian to see our Bonding, to know that you are bound to me, as I am to you.*

Perhaps that was it. Perhaps I was overthinking.

Lyria leaned casually against my doorframe, her lips curled into a knowing smile.

"Hello, neighbor," she chimed, as if we hadn't exchanged sharp words just the day before. "My chamber is in the other wing."

I blinked at her. Was she serious? She was acting like we hadn't just had an argument about *Damien*—as if she hadn't accused me of not deserving him, and the conversation had never happened at all.

I narrowed my eyes, watching for any flicker of mischief, but she only tilted her head, waiting for a response.

"...Okay," I said slowly.

She hummed, her expression unreadable. "Seems like you're not in the mood to chat. You must be tired. Rest well. I will see you around."

And just like that, she was gone.

I stared at the empty doorway, my mind reeling. Was she *okay?*

Had I imagined the entire thing? Was the argument some fevered dream? Or was this her way of brushing it under the rug—pretending it never happened so she wouldn't have to address it?

I groaned, rubbing my temples. I was too drained to unravel all of these twisted games.

⊰•⊱

THE GOLDEN LIGHT HAD SHIFTED, yet there were still no signs of Damien.

Frustration simmered beneath my skin, my patience stretched thin. I had waited. I had settled into this chamber, accepted the silence, the lack of answers. But I was *done* waiting.

If anyone deserved to know where Damien was, it was me. The sole bearer of his Bond, tethered to his fate and all that. If that didn't come with *immediate access privileges*, then fate and I needed to have words.

So I left.

The royal grounds stood thronged with nobles and warriors, clustered in small, gilded circles of conversation. Some event was taking place, one that had gathered every Royal in attendance. It was too crowded, too loud.

Finding Damien in this throng would be a battle in itself.

I inhaled sharply, adjusting my pace, ready to carve my way through the crowd—when a firm hand closed around my wrist. I barely had time to turn before I was pulled back into the shadowed archway of one of the palace's many halls.

"I think we have a lot to catch up on, considering you abandoned me in Etheris the last time."

Izmer. His grip was firm.

I sighed. *Not now.* "I will *compensate* for it, I swear," I said hurriedly, already tugging my arm free. "But I don't have time for this right now."

I turned to push forward, but he stopped me. Again.

"It's too crowded," he said, voice measured but tight. "You should rest. You can find Damien after the Call to Audience." Izmer was *never* like this. He was cocky, careless, often more amused by my mischief than concerned by it.

Now his posture was tense. His grip was *too* tight.

And I knew, in that instant, that he wasn't trying to stop me for my sake. Was he trying to keep me from seeing something?

My stomach twisted. "I don't care about the crowd," I snapped, yanking my wrist back with renewed force. "I'm done waiting."

"Mirabelle." His tone darkened, his voice dipping into something I rarely heard from him. A warning. "You are not going in there."

Something in me burned hotter. "Watch me."

And before he could grab me again, I shoved through the crowd, forcing my way toward the heart of the gathering. I moved through the throng, pushing past murmuring nobles and rigid soldiers alike. The further I pressed, the more the crowd swelled, a tide of bodies shifting toward the heart of the commotion. My breath was steady, my purpose resolute. And then, at last I reached the front.

The palace balcony loomed above, its grand stone archway casting long shadows over the assembly. And there, at its center, stood Damien.

His presence was a force unto itself, tall, composed, every inch of him exuding the unshaken command of a warrior who had long since accepted his burdens. But his expression was unreadable.

Guarded, impassive. Beside him, Sovereign—Alaric Azarios stood in all his absolute authority, his piercing gaze sweeping over the gathered Royals and Majors alike.

They were about to speak. Their body language, the weight in the air, it was the prelude to something significant.

I clenched my fists, instinct demanding that I go to him, that I push past the formalities and demand the answers I was owed...Not yet. I was no fool; I knew the weight of spectacle. Whatever this was, it would be revealed soon enough.

So, I forced myself to still, to wait. The air shifted. And then, Sovereign took a step forward, his voice cutting through the stillness.

"It's been some time since we last gathered," his voice carried effortlessly over the assembled crowd, a weight of authority behind each syllable. "We have endured the siege, challenges that sought to break us. Yet here we stand—our Clan restored, strong, and cleansed of the rot that threatened us."

The gathered Royals and Majors murmured their agreement, some lifting their fists in silent affirmation.

He continued, his tone steady, unwavering. "And among those who played a part in this victory, there is one whose efforts cannot go unrecognized." His gaze swept over the crowd, and then— "Mirabelle."

My name rippled through the assembly like a stone cast into still water. "The young lady from the commoners," he said, each word measured. "She has displayed remarkable courage and ability. And in return, we have entrusted her with the care and command of our Tameables."

The moment the words left his lips, the crowd erupted into cheers. I felt the shift before I saw it—heads turning, eyes landing on me, recognition sweeping through the front rows of the gathering. The Royals nearest to me caught on first, their cheers growing louder as they turned to acknowledge me.

And then—Damien looked at me.

Our eyes locked across the sea of bodies, the distance between us insignificant in the force of that single glance. He did not smile, did not soften—but he did not look away. Not for a few lingering seconds.

Then, a nod. A silent acknowledgement. The cheer continued around me, but the moment had passed. It *stung*. I did not know why.

The Sovereign's voice rang through the air again. "But the reason we have gathered here today is far greater than the celebration of resilience. It is to mark the next crucial step for our Clan. With the Celestial Dissonance drawing near, we must strengthen our foundation, solidify our place among the great forces of this Realm. And so, we have done exactly that."

A pause. A breath. A moment where time itself seemed to still.

"We have secured an alliance with Nyxaria. And in exchange..." His voice did not falter. It did not waver. "Our Heir, the next Sovereign of Atlassian, my son—Damien Azarios—is betrothed to Lorenza Ashbourne, soon to be Azarios, as part of this unbreakable bond."

My stomach twisted. My lungs collapsed. The air, thick and suffocating, no longer entered my body. The ground beneath me wrenched away, weightless and cruel, and I swayed where I stood.

No. A nightmare. A trick. A cruel illusion spun from the darkest depths of my mind.

And yet—the crowd erupted. A deafening roar of approval. A storm of cheers, applause, voices rising in celebration of something that shattered me.

I barely saw her at first. But then—she moved. She stepped into the light beside Damien. Lorenza Ashbourne.

She was stunning. The very image of elegance, power, and nobility. Her cascading black hair framed a face untouched by uncertainty. Her gown, woven from fabric richer than anything I had ever seen, shimmered in the golden light of Celestia. She smiled—a practiced, charming thing that enraptured the crowd effortlessly. Then, with a graceful wave, she acknowledged them, standing tall beside Damien as though she had always been meant to.

Sovereign Alaric reached for their hands. I saw Damien's eyes snap to his father's—a cold look that held for a suspended heart-beat. Then, Alaric placed their hands together. I watched as Damien's fingers curled lightly around hers, their hands bound in front of all of Atlassian, the symbol of a future I was never meant to be part of.

It lasted only moments. But it was enough.

Damien's eyes found mine. For the first time since his father spoke those damning words, his gaze met mine. Brows furrowed.

Something unreadable, something restrained. I could not breathe. Could not think. Tears blurred my vision, hot trails streaking down my face.

This wasn't real. It couldn't be real. Because this was not Damien. He would not do this. Not to me. Not to us.

And yet, when Lorenza turned to him, murmuring something I could not hear, he looked away. He looked away from me. And *answered her.* The last thread of my strength snapped.

Darkness swelled in the edges of my vision, swallowing the world whole. The cheers dulled, the blinding lights dimmed, and my body crumpled beneath the weight of it all.

I barely registered the strong arms catching me before every-thing turned to nothingness.

Izmer.

And then—I fell.

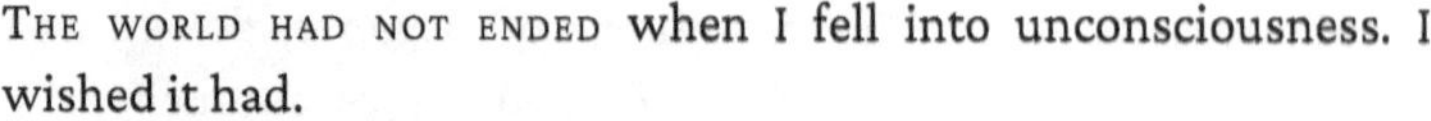

THE WORLD HAD NOT ENDED when I fell into unconsciousness. I wished it had.

When I opened my eyes, I was in a chamber unfamiliar to me —spacious. But I barely took in my surroundings. The ache in my chest was suffocating, a phantom weight pressing against my ribs, making it difficult to breathe.

Izmer sat beside me. A healer lingered nearby, her hands still aglow with the remnants of magic she must have used on me. The moment my gaze met his, he motioned for her to leave. She obeyed, slipping out without a word.

The door locked behind her. I sat up abruptly. The motion sent a wave of dizziness through me, but I did not care. My voice, hoarse from disuse, scraped out the only words that mattered.

"Tell me that was a nightmare. *Please.*"

Izmer's lips parted, hesitation flickering over his features. Then regret settled there, deep and raw. And that was answer enough.

"No..." My breath hitched. "No. NO."

I shoved the covers away, swinging my legs over the bed. My pulse thundered in my ears, but before I could move, he was on his feet, gripping my arms, restraining me.

"Mirabelle," he said, voice low but firm, "I need you to listen before you do something reckless."

"I don't care what you have to say. Whatever explanation I need, it will come from Damien himself." I twisted in his grasp, trying to free myself, but he held firm.

"No. Trust me when I say you won't get any answers from him."

"You don't understand," I seethed.

His grip on me tightened. "No, you don't understand." He exhaled sharply, as if bracing himself for the next words. "He does not remember you, Mirabelle."

I stilled. The world cracked beneath me, but I did not fall.

I blinked at him, words failing me, my mind scrambling for logic, for sense, for any reason that could explain the absurdity of what he had just said.

"What?" My voice was barely above a whisper. "That's not possible. He saw me. He acknowledged me—"

"Because he knows you," Izmer interrupted, his tone gentle, almost pitying. "He knows you as Mirabelle, the female appointed to oversee the Majors. The one who helped Atlassian in its darkest hour. But that is all."

My heart clenched. "No," I choked out.

"Yes."

I could not process it. Could not accept it. Could not breathe.

"You are telling me he doesn't feel anything for me?" The words burned like acid in my throat.

Izmer's expression darkened. "Not in the way he should."

I swallowed against the bile rising. "Why? How—?"

"The Crown."

My thoughts splintered at the mention of it. "You remember the artifact found in the Ruins? The one meant to grant a wish powerful enough to lock the Untameables?"

I nodded numbly. It had been unnecessary in the end. The problem had been solved without it.

"They used it."

I froze. "They?" My voice wavered.

"I don't know who exactly. But the Sovereign was part of it."

Everything inside me recoiled. "Used it for what?"

Izmer's grip on me loosened, but the weight of his words only grew heavier.

"To erase every memory that connected you to Damien. Not just from him—but from Atlassian itself. I don't know many details."

I could not think. Could not comprehend. "No."

He said grimly, "Every piece of his life that was touched by you —every moment, every feeling, everything private—was stripped away. What remains is only what the world can see: you, as a female of power, as a guardian of the Tameables. But nothing more. To him, you are no more than that."

A trap. The realization slammed into me. This alliance. This betrothal.

"They set him up." My voice was nothing but a breath of sound. Izmer's silence was answer enough. "Nobody remembers me as his."

He nodded, watching me with caution, as if afraid I would shatter before his eyes. And just like that, everything I had built, everything we had fought for, every moment I had spent in his arms, was gone.

Erased. As if it had never existed at all.

The world was unraveling before me, thread by thread, and I could not grasp a single one. Izmer's voice pressed against my ears, but my mind could not contain the enormity of his words.

"I think, even the Sovereign himself does not remember you like that."

The breath in my lungs turned shallow.

"Those who conspired to make this happen...they don't even recall you were involved with Damien at all."

No. It was impossible.

"I know this because I am not from Atlassian," Izmer continued, "and because I have been watching. Listening. And we are in no position to challenge them. Not now. Not when we hold no power here."

Power. The one thing I never had. The one thing I never sought. But now, in its absence, I felt the void of it swallowing me whole.

"I tried to speak to him," Izmer admitted, voice grim. "To tell him something—anything—but it was like trying to carve meaning into stone. He doesn't acknowledge what he does not remember, and he is entirely consumed with securing the future of Atlassian. To him, now you are just...you. A female of value, but nothing more."

The words splintered inside me, jagged and cruel.

"I am going back to Nyxaria today," he added. "So, Mirabelle, I am warning you—don't act on impulse. You don't understand how precarious your position is. If you push too far, if you become a threat to their plans, the Sovereign and the rest will not hesitate to rid themselves of you."

I felt the words, the truth in them. But it did not stop the fire rising in my chest.

"I am his Eternis."

The words left me before I could think, before I could measure them.

Izmer stilled. "What?!"

"We Bonded."

Silence. Then, a sharp exhale. His hands, braced on his knees, curled into fists.

"Oh, wonderful," he muttered. "Just when I thought this couldn't get more complicated."

I barely heard him. My pulse thundered in my ears.

"That means he cannot Bond to another." My voice didn't waver, but the conviction beneath it was not unshaken.

"The Bond is for life and it cannot be undone," he said. "But Royal blood can Bond to another female if she is from a different Clan, a different bloodline."

"No!" The word tore from me. "They can't...they just can't." A hysterical sob bubbled in my chest. My hands were shaking. "It's not fair."

Izmer ran a hand through his hair, his exasperation clear. He opened his mouth as if to speak, then hesitated, looking at me with startling pity. "I'm afraid, Mirabelle, you...never mind. Just...take care of yourself."

"Can I talk to him?" I demanded. "In private. If I tell him, if I make him understand—"

"No."

The single word was a blade between my ribs.

"Mirabelle," Izmer said, slow, measured, as though I were a beast ready to lash out. "Please. Do not act on emotion. You cannot predict the outcome."

"What outcome could possibly be worse than this?" I snapped.

"Damien is a noble Heir, bound by duty above all else. He will not risk anything that could damage his Clan."

"I am not just anything!"

"No, you are not," he said evenly. "But right now, you cannot prove what you are to him."

The room spun as I scrambled for any possibility that might pull me out of this nightmare.

He continued. "The only proof of a Bond is its mark upon the soul. And in this world, the only proof of a soul-bound Eternis is the existence of his offspring—from you."

My stomach plummeted. I glanced at my wrist. No scars, no marks. Only the skin that had mended within moments of binding us.

"So, if you claim it now, Mirabelle, without proof, without evidence," He shook his head. "You will sound like nothing more than a desperate female seeking attention."

I clenched my fists so tightly my nails bit into my palms. I wanted to scream. To shatter something, to demand the truth be acknowledged.

But I had nothing. No proof. No claim.

Only a stolen past, and a future slipping through my fingers like sand.

"I will find a way back," I whispered. "I will fix this."

Izmer sighed, rubbing his temples. "The ordained Bonding ceremony between Lorenza and Damien might be still months away. Even I didn't know about the betrothal until the Sovereign made the announcement. You should have time."

Not enough. Not nearly enough.

"I need to leave now," he added. "I have to see what state my Clan is in. If they learn the truth of this alliance, war may follow. And both Atlassian and Nyxaria cannot afford to have one when the Celestial Dissonance is near."

War. Everything was crumbling, and I stood at the center of it, watching the wreckage unfold.

Izmer placed a hand on my shoulder, just briefly. "Hold on to whatever sanity you have left, Mirabelle."

And then, he was gone. I was alone.

Only one question remained.

Why didn't I forget?

ALSO BY FABINS

Reigns of Telmoria

Aether and Ash

ABOUT THE AUTHOR

Fabins is a fantasy romance author with a weakness for slow burns and a fierce love of character-driven stories. A software engineer by day and a storyteller by obsession, she balances logic and longing with the careful precision of someone who has probably over-thought both.

When she isn't drafting, she is likely halfway across the world, gaming past midnight, arguing passionately about things that don't pay bills, or reading (either swooning over fictional characters or hurling the book at the nearest cushion after a terrible twist).

Join Fabins' newsletter
https://authorfabins.com/mailing-list

OLIVERHEBERBOOKS

A small press bound by the belief that every voice matters.

Sign up for our newsletter to learn about new releases and more.
https://oliver-heberbooks.com/subscribe/

Follow us on social media:

facebook.com/oliverheberbooks

instagram.com/oliverheberbooks

amazon.com/oliverheberbooks

youtube.com/@OliverHeberBooksPublisher